One
for the
Morning
Glory

One
for the
Morning
Glory

John Barnes

A Tom Doherty Associates Book
New York

ONE FOR THE MORNING GLORY

Copyright © 1996 by John Barnes

This book is printed on acid-free paper.

A Tor Book
Published by Tom Doherty Associates, Inc.
175 Fifth Avenue
New York, N.Y. 10010

Tor Books on the World-Wide Web:
http://www.tor.com

Tor® is a registered trademark of Tom Doherty Associates, Inc.

Library of Congress Cataloging-in-Publication Data

Barnes, John
    One for the morning glory / John Barnes.—1st ed.
       p.   cm.
    "A Tom Doherty Associates book."
    ISBN 0-312-86106-0 (acid-free paper)
    I. Title.
  PS3552.A677O5   1996
  813'.54—dc20   95-40884
                                                  CIP

First edition: April 1996

Printed in the United States of America

0 9 8 7 6 5 4 3 2 1

For Kara Dalkey

That they should be principal liars, I answer paradoxically, but truly, I think truly, that of all writers under the sun the poet is the least liar, and though he would, as a poet, can scarcely be a liar. The astronomer, with his cousin the geometrician, can hardly escape when they take upon them to measure the height of stars. How often, think you, do the physicians lie, when they aver things good for sicknesses, which afterwards send to Charon a great number of souls drowned in a potion before they come to his ferry? And no less of the rest which take upon them to affirm. Now, for the poet, he nothing affirmeth, and therefore never lieth. For as I take it to lie is to affirm that to be true which is false; so as the other artists, and especially the historian, affirming many things, can, in the cloudy knowledge of mankind, hardly escape from many lies.

—Sir Philip Sidney, *Defence of Poesy*

Most high and happy princess, we must tell you a tale of the Man in the Moon, which if it seem ridiculous for the method, or superfluous for the matter, or for the means incredible, for three faults we can make but one excuse: it is a tale of the Man in the Moon. It was forbidden in old time to dispute of chimera, because it was fiction; we hope in our times none will apply pastimes, because they are fancies. For there liveth none under the sun that knows what to make of the Man in the Moon. We present neither comedy, nor tragedy, nor story, nor anything, but that whosoever heareth may say this: "Why, here is a tale of the Man in the Moon."

—John Lyly, *Endymion*

7

Contents

I

The Morning Glory

I

A Difficult Day in the Kingdom

*I*t was an old saying in the Kingdom that "a child who tastes the Wine of the Gods too early is only half a person afterwards." Because the wise men of the Kingdom had taught from time immemorial that older sayings were truer, no one, as far as anyone knew, had ever given any of the Wine of the Gods to young children.

This was also a matter of expense. The Wine of the Gods was so costly that even the King himself could only have it on special occasions—half a glass, perhaps, shared with an unusually important ambassador, or a spoonful for persistent melancholy, or just a drop when duty demanded he get up despite a bad cold. Thus, even if adults had not cared about the saying, they were most likely to keep the Wine of the Gods—what they could get of it—for themselves.

It was not expensive due to its ingredients, which were common as dirt. Indeed, common dirt was one of them. The Wine of the Gods cost what it did because it required the combined efforts of an alchemist of at least twenty years' experience and of a witch of at least one hundred years in age. Merely to distill the scent of baking bread in fall, without getting any November into it, was beyond all but the most exacting skill, and that was the easy, first step that everyone started with. The last step—dropping in the common dirt just when the color of a cloudless sky at seven on a summer morning had been fully absorbed and the snowflakes from an untouched moonlit field were still floating on top—took many years to master. It was said that after one thousand attempts, a fine alchemist could get it right once by accident, and that after a thousand more, he got it right just barely more often than not. And if the ingredients had not been prepared by an exacting witch, his skill was still of no avail.

So there was no prospect that the Wine of the Gods would ever be plentiful or cheap, and thus no reason for anyone to test the saying that "a child who tastes the Wine of the Gods too early is only half a person afterwards." Even if anyone in the Kingdom had been cruel enough, the stuff was far too costly and well-guarded for any child to get hold of it.

What the saying meant might have been written down in the grim, dark-covered volume in the Royal Library, *Highly Unpleasant Things It Is Sometimes Necessary to Know,* or perhaps, if it were sufficiently horrible, in the dusty, locked tome titled *Things That Are Not Good to Know at All.* It was by no means a thing anyone would know off the top of his head.

But since the subject had came up in fairy tales, it was certain to happen sooner or later, and thus there remained no excuse at all for those responsible when Prince Amatus—sole heir to the throne, the Queen having died at his birth—just four days after his second birthday, contrived to gulp down a full glass of the Wine of the Gods.

There were four responsible parties, and when the event was informally announced by shouts of horror, none of them stood a chance of escape. King Boniface heard the shouts of horror, ran to the Royal Alchemical Laboratory, was apprised of the situation, and, being High, Low, and any other altitude of Justice which might be had in the Kingdom, conducted the trial and the sentencing then and there, to make sure that nei-

ther verdict nor sentence had any unseemly taint of cool delib-
eration.

"You," he said to the Prince's Personal Maid (an older
woman who seldom smiled and never because she was happy),
"you were, as usual, measuring dosages of cod liver oil,
smoothing sheets, and arranging toys into neatly orthogonal
positions, and not watching the Prince at all." He turned to
the Captain of the Guard and said, "You will cut off her head
now, please."

The Maid might have had something to say, but it was
drowned out in the wicked *skrang!* of the Captain's escree
coming out of its scabbard and the shriek of its slicing air.
Then her head was off, and the Captain, a tidy man, gave her
headless body a hard kick on the sternum, so that it dropped
backward out the window to the pavement below, making
much less mess in the laboratory than might have been expected. The Maid's head, lips still pursed in disapproval,
landed on the floor and sat squarely on the end of its neck,
staring at them. With a soft *snick* the blade was back in its
scabbard.

The second of the four, just as obviously responsible, was
the Royal Alchemist. "You," King Boniface said, and his tone
was now dark and thick with anger, "you, you were supposed
to be supervising the whole process of manufacturing the
Wine of the Gods. If you were an alchemist of perhaps barely
twenty-five years' standing, then I might understand why it
was that you were so lost in admiring your own skill—don't
try to deny it, I've watched you work—that you failed to attend to the essential administrative task of making sure that
no one stole the Wine of the Gods. Or if an extraordinarily
bold robber like Deacon Dick Thunder had somehow got
hold of a teaspoonful, then it might be regrettable but under-
standable. But in reality—" and now the King's brows knit
together in the middle, which would have given him a terrible
headache had he not already had one, and his voice rose to a

roar, which would have terrified the Royal Alchemist had he not already been frightened—"in reality, I say," the King roared, "I find that an alchemist of *fifty-seven* years' standing was so lost in admiration of his own legerdemain that he had a whole glassful stolen from him by a two-year-old child!"

He nodded to the Captain of the Guard, and once again a savage *skrang!* blended into the howl of split air, the thud of a severed neck, and the *snick!* of the blade returning to its scabbard.

The Captain's foot struck the Royal Alchemist's chest before any echo had time to reach their ears, and the body dropped to the pavement, landing exactly on top of that of the Prince's Personal Maid. The Royal Alchemist's head—a great mass of white hair and a wrinkled visage that had always seemed wise, but now (with beard and hair trimmed) merely looked pompous—thudded to the floor, balancing on the stump of its neck just to the right of the head of the Prince's Personal Maid.

The King, having discharged the relatively pleasant part of his duties, turned sadly toward the Royal Witch.

"Majesty," she said, "I see no way in which I can avoid a share in the blame. I was myself in the room. I should have felt some part of the magic turning over or going back as I worked it. I did not feel aught awry, and with a stray person—and one of Royal blood—in the room, aught should have been awry *in extremis*. I have failed in my craft, Majesty, and a witch must not do that."

King Boniface had always liked the Royal Witch. She was kind-hearted and laid curses that were easy to lift, and set quests that anyone could complete. She—along with gunpowder, the printing press, and perspective drawing—had almost removed the fear of magic from the Kingdom. Hard tasks and dark dooms were all but forgotten, and most people seemed to regard them as sheerest history, not worthy even of the attention normally given to myth or fairy tale.

But he had to concede that she was right, not just today, but in general; a part of her famous kindness was due only to her ineptitude. She had not been *able* to put a truly effective curse; or to set the precise quest that would bring the hero face to face with his deepest flaw; or to weave a doom with sufficient options, dilemmas, and double binds to be truly inexorable.

Still, Boniface hesitated, for he knew that the one who tolerates incompetence—as he had done—bears some of the guilt, and he felt now that though his fondness for her had not been foolish, to have kept her as Royal Witch because he was fond of her had been foolish indeed.

Even as he thought this, the Royal Witch turned to the Captain of the Guard and said, "Will it help if I stand next to the window, here?"

"A bit to the left, and half a step forward, if you don't mind," he muttered. "And if you could pin up your hair—"

She did so, carefully and a bit shyly. Though like most witches she was dreadful to look at, her neck—folded, warty, and reptilian—had not been seen in public before, and so embarrassed her more.

When she had finished, the Royal Witch stood carefully straight and tall, as a child does at a funeral. The Captain had already silently drawn his escree, and he rested the blade on his flat palm and asked, gently, looking straight into her eyes, "Is there anything you would like to say first?"

On the word "anything" he whipped the escree forward in an arc so flat and hard that he had severed her neck before she knew what was happening, and with a kick put her body out the window and down to the pavement. Her head flipped once, scattering pins as it flew, and landed to the right of the Royal Alchemist's.

Her face showed neither surprise nor fear, only a certain thoughtfulness, because she had been listening to the Captain, trying to foresee exactly how his question would end. She did not look as unpleasant as the other two, but she was as dead.

King Boniface, who had been starting to say that it was not the custom in the Kingdom to grant last words to condemned criminals, was startled to silence so that before the next thought in the sequence could come to mind, the Captain of the Guard was already saying, "What our gracious Sovereign is about to say next—and is finding it difficult to say due to his own deep mercy—is that I too bear a measure of the guilt. The final share of blame to be allocated today must fall to me." This was far wordier than anyone had ever before heard him to be, but since it was evident that he would die when he stopped speaking, no one much begrudged him a few extra words. "Now, it will have occurred to His Majesty, and per- haps to all of you as well, that there may be a problem in that a situation has arisen in which it would appear to be necessary for me to cut off my own head, at a minimum, and ideally speaking to place my head here, to drop my remaining, er, re- mains through this window, and to sheathe my escree. You may all consider how difficult this will be for one minute of complete silence, if you will. Certainly I would appreciate hav- ing that time in which to think."

The room fell dead silent except for one or two nasty *spat!*s from the gore dripping from the windowsill. The Cap- tain's shoulders sank into perfect relaxation; his breathing slowed; his gaze became clear and far away; and at last a smile formed on his lips.

Now he will say, "I have the answer," Boniface thought, *and that will be a relief. Because I don't.*

The *skrang!* of the escree leaving the scabbard was louder and more evil than for the Maid and the Alchemist combined, but the motion of the blade was even more silent and swift than it had been for the Royal Witch. Whirling behind him- self, the Captain of the Guard set the blade spinning in air so fast that it barely sank before he had completed his turn, flung his scabbard up into the high vaulting of the ceiling, and flipped up in a back somersault.

His body sailed out the window just as his head thudded to the floor beside that of the Royal Witch, and at that same instant the deflected, spinning escree flew up into the air and inserted itself into the descending scabbard, making a mournful, almost lonesome little *snick!* just as escree and scabbard dropped onto the stone floor where the Captain had stood.

"Truly," King Boniface said, "*that* was an escreesman." All applauded.

Taking two steps forward to better examine the row of heads, carefully not trailing any of his robes into the little puddles of blood here and there on the stone floor, the King contemplated the four of them for a moment. Finally he pointed at the Prince's Personal Maid. "Put her in the garbage to offend her neatness," he said.

Then to the Royal Alchemist: "Give him to an old herbwoman somewhere, for use in love potions and other trivia, to humble his pride."

To the Witch: "A decent burial."

And to the Captain of the Guard: "Full honors."

Vassals and lackeys—especially lackeys hoping to be promoted to vassal—rushed forward to carry out the royal orders.

Prime Minister Cedric tugged at Boniface's sleeve. He knew the King hated that, but it was often the only thing that would get his attention. "Majesty, we now have four critical vacancies to fill at Court."

"Advertise to fill them, then," Boniface said. He was a little impatient, partly because he had just had to deal with a difficult situation and mostly because he disliked several things about Cedric, not least his tendency to bring trivia to the King's attention rather than decently dealing with it himself. "Put word out through troubadours and travelers, wayfarers and wanderers, rogues, rovers, and road agents, vagabonds and vagrants, the usual sort of thing."

"But"— the Prime Minister sputtered nervously—"but but but until such time as the positions shall be filled—which is to say advertisements answered, inquirers interviewed, and final selections finally selected—until such time, which may be a matter of many months—who will do the needed offices?"

Having had to question the King's reply made Cedric so nervous that he forgot himself and did the very thing the King found most annoying—he jammed his beard into his mouth and chewed on it furiously. Realizing what he was doing, he furtively pulled it back out and wiped it on the black velvet collar of his scarlet silk gown. King Boniface found this just as disgusting.

The King, however, was an intelligent man, and valued Cedric's better qualities, including that the Prime Minister was an able administrator who often remembered important things. "I had not thought of that," Boniface said, smiling in a way he hoped was reassuring so as to keep the already-sodden beard out of the Prime Minister's mouth. "But I suppose—well, we shall not have any children of great lineage born for at least a little while, I think, and hence no curses will be required. Indeed, curses have been so mild that it is possible no one will notice." He remembered now, with some irritation, that the last three curses had been that the first time the child attempted to walk, he or she would fall down. "There is no one eligible to go questing who is not already on one, either, so we can live a few months without the Royal Witch." In fact, the Court's youngest courtier had only recently returned from borrowing a cup of sugar in distant Hektaria, in order to cure his lady's hiccups. The former Witch had been no better at quests than at curses.

"Moreover," the King said, realizing that they had in fact

gotten along just fine without much of a Royal Witch for some years, "I think we need not worry about the Royal Alchemist right away. Our old one tended to make large batches of everything and save all his leftovers, and I would wager we have more than a year's supply of everything we need. As for the office of the Captain of the Guard—"

Here a happy inspiration struck Boniface, the sort of thing that had made his reputation as a first-rate king. "Cedric, since we have no parliament, no elections, and only the crudest of states here, it has long seemed to me that the office of Prime Minister should be downgraded to part-time, and if I were to do that, you would be free to take the job of Captain of the Guard and General of All the Armies. You are quite a fair swordsman, and I can think of no hands better to put the task into than your own."

The Prime Minister was all but overcome, and his hand went to his beard, but he fought down the urge and said, "Yes, Majesty, I can do that for you." In fact his heart was leaping upward, for he had never wanted to be any sort of courtier, and had always longed for the soldier's life. "With proper time management, Majesty, the job of Prime Minister might be cut to no more than half a morning a week, if ceremonial duties were allocated to the Chancellor." The Chancellor was a cousin of Cedric's, whom he had always disliked.

"Done, then," the King said. "Naturally you will be expected to find a suitable permanent person for the post, but you will continue to draw full salary for both positions, and after you return to the job of Prime Minister perhaps we can discuss how such things ought to be handled in the future."

Privately Cedric resolved to do so good a job as Captain of the Guard as to be irreplaceable.

The feeling of having made that resolution gave him the courage to venture one more remark to the King. "And the job of Prince's Personal Maid? Who will perform that function, Majesty?"

"Well—ah—" The King thought for a long moment. The Prince's Personal Maid had to be someone of impeccable conduct, not because the Prince was expected to be so, but so that the Prince would know what it was. Historically the position was usually filled by an ugly princess with a great love for children and no dowry.

Unfortunately every princess within a full year's ride the King could think of was either attractive and therefore marriageable, or else was somebody's wicked stepsister and thus *extremely* unsuitable.

"Well," the King began again, delaying, and then again, "Well," until finally, not before the Prime Minister's beard had virtually disappeared into his madly chewing jaws, he said, "I suppose I could—uh, that is, I *shall*—tend the young fellow myself. Nothing to it, really, I should guess. Have to get a couple of our ladies to show me the, er, fundamentals, but after that I can't imagine the job will be one whit worse than slaying the Dragon of Bat Mountain—which I did as a prince—or any more complex than commanding the army at the Battle of Bell Tower Beach, just last summer."

The Prime Minister, who had raised several children, was frantic to say something to the effect that the job was a bit more complex and demanding than it appeared to be, but by now Cedric was gagged by his great thatch of spit-soggy whiskers, so by the time he had wrenched his jaws open and hauled out the sloppy mess of hair, the moment was past. He might have tried all the same, but just then someone finally looked at Prince Amatus and shrieked.

He was indeed, and obviously, half a person; everything to the left of center (if you took the bridge of his nose as the center) was quite gone. Yet it seemed to do him little harm. He was giggling and clapping his right hand against his nonexistent one. He seemed unaware that his left side was lacking, and was chortling happily, but no sound emerged from his mouth.

"Why can't we hear him, do you suppose?" King Boniface asked, after an extremely long awkward pause.

"Er—" The Prime Minister was now recovering rapidly, for it was only being shouted at by the King that he feared, and since that apparently was not going to happen, his competence and efficiency was reasserting itself. "It would seem to me, Majesty, that his chortling is being drowned out by the sound of his clapping, and since of course we cannot hear his clapping—"

"Because he is only doing it with one hand. I see. Well, what there is of him seems to be perfectly fine. You don't suppose he is merely half-invisible, in which case a good coat of paint might alleviate most of the problem?"

Cedric shook his head solemnly. "If that were the case, we should hear both hands clapping. And notice as well that his right eye is focusing, so his vision is binocular, yet we do not see his left retina, and if we can't see it, then it is stopping no light and I don't see how it can be seeing us." As he had been saying this, he had been slowly, gingerly, approaching the young Prince, and finally he scooped him up in his arms. The Prince giggled. As he carried him back to the King, Cedric added, "You see, Majesty, only half of him is here. I feel no ghostly arm or leg, and my hand passes directly through the space where half of him should be. The left side of him is not here."

"And—just out of curiosity—when you turn his left side toward me—" the King said.

"I can't, Majesty. He doesn't have one."

"Then, er, face me and turn his right side toward yourself. Now—dear me. I don't see anything."

"But of course." The Prime Minister, now thoroughly a soldier in charge, stood tall and straight, all vestiges of his former bureaucratic self gone except for a faintly malodorous dampness in his beard. "You are facing his left side, which is not there. And if you are looking at something which is not there, what would you expect to see?"

There was no way to argue with it. The King nodded. "Well, surely it is too much to hope that he will only be half as much trouble or need changing half as often. Have a couple of nurses come and show me what to do and how to do it. And do be quick about advertising—it is a nuisance to fill a vacancy, but I'm sure in a couple of weeks we will have suitable candidates with suitable references."

He scooped up Amatus—who did not seem to him to be half as heavy—had it been that long since he'd held the boy?—and strode out.

The moment the King was gone, Cedric, no longer at all constrained, was happily bellowing orders just as if he had always been the Captain of the Guard.

2

Suitable Applicants

*T*he King was right. Within two weeks, since the Kingdom was known to be a rich place, they had more than enough qualified applicants.

But still they had no Prince's Personal Maid, no Royal Alchemist, no Royal Witch, and no Captain of the Guard.

The problem in part was that the first priority was the Prince's Personal Maid. To Boniface, something seemed to be wrong with each applicant. Some of them seemed harsh, cold, and far too orderly; others indulgent, sentimental, and far too sloppy. Young ones were still children themselves and how could old ones be expected to understand a child? Fat ones lacked self-control and thin ones seemed stingy and austere—something there had already been too much of.

There were a half dozen who were thoroughly intermediate in every regard. The King found them intolerably bland and dismissed them faster than all the others.

Cedric, who watched all this closely, would have felt wry amusement, except that it is difficult to feel wry amusement while simultaneously being as joyous as a piranha in a goldfish pond.

The wry amusement had every reason to be there, nonetheless, for what had happened was that Boniface, a serious man who had never thought about anything other than being king even while still a young prince, had discovered a liking and a talent for fatherhood. He took Amatus everywhere, all the time, to tournaments and to the Leghorn Herders' Ball, hunting zwieback in the Isought Gap, sailing on Iron Lake, patrolling the deserts to the east with the army, to graduation at the University of the Kingdom, and to the launching of the mighty riverboat *KS Boniface*.

He carried the young Prince on his shoulder or in his arms; walked with him for short distances (but increasing—it was so interesting how they increased) holding his tiny hand; rode with Amatus in front of him on the saddle or clinging to his back.

They ate every meal together; laughed together; talked (especially as Amatus got better at it) about names of trees, proper grip on an escree, the importance of deploying omnibusmen where they could guard the culverts on a battlefield, habits of birds, tactics in fighting dragons, the Vulgarian tea ritual and the importance of not filling your cupola or tipping the sampan, and the special importance of saying "thank you" to commoners; more than anything, they got to know each other. As a child will, Amatus blossomed under the regimen, and as some rare and fortunate men do, so did Boniface.

So it was no surprise that for all his complaints of doing double duty, the King could not find anyone suitable to be the new Prince's Personal Maid, however many he interviewed.

Yet, as has been said, however wryly amusing this might have been for Cedric, it was drowned out by his own keen pleasure. It happened that the Kingdom had been at peace for some years prior to last summer's sudden invasion from Overhill. That war had come so quickly (they had barely had time to hear of Waldo's usurpation and the massacre of the rightful King's family before the attack was on its way) that it had been fought entirely with what was on hand in the western provinces, but since they had smashed Waldo's army at Bell Tower Beach, the risk of war was currently slight.

Now, the custom in the Kingdom was that the Captain of the Guard was also General of All the Armies, and since one job called for a brave and alert master swordsman, and the other for a capable and cunning administrator, only rarely were both jobs done well. During the long period of peacetime, the last Captain of the Guard, though a swordsman without peer, had neglected the army into a shocking state of disarray.

Fortunately Cedric was no more than a gifted amateur as a swordsman, and knew it in his heart of hearts; even more fortunately, he was in fact an adept administrator, as might have been guessed from his previous line of work. Shortly after taking the job of Captain of the Guard, he had begun probing, prodding, pressing, questioning, quantifying, quarreling, rationalizing, reordering, and finally roaring as he swiftly yanked the army back into decent condition.

Practically nothing had been as it should be: roads and fortifications were in ruins, soldiers and officers sunk in lazy complacency.

Orders went out to rebuild, strengthen, retrain, regroup.

Deacon Dick Thunder's band had raided all the way into the city itself, and on one occasion waylaid a captain with his company and robbed them of a number of objects of sentimental value (they had little else for the quartermasters had been embezzling their pay).

Expeditions were mounted, posts manned, watchfires lit. Culverts roared from fortress walls, volleys of omnibus and festoon fire swept the battle plains of the north, escrees clashed at a hundred dark crossroads, and shortly Thunder and his not quite so merry and certainly not so numerous men were again eking out a precarious existence along the Long

River Road in the far north, where they were permitted to remain because Cedric considered them an important part of
the natural balance.

One entire Royal Armory was found to contain nothing
but scraps of mildewed leather, brass buttons and buckles,
and great piles of rust. There was not a thing in it that might
explode, so Cedric did. Shortly the forges and powder mills
were going night and day and the smiths and armorers were
growing rich with new business, particularly since they need
hire no one to work the bellows—that job was done by officers formerly in charge of the rusted-out armory, somewhat
encumbered by manacles and leg irons.

In all this, Cedric was merrily in his element. He discovered inadequate drill and paunchy soldiers; they groaned at
the heavy training that followed, until they found it made
them far more successful with the sort of wenches one finds in
the taborets down by the river, and the kind of Vulgarian girl
who waits the tables and wipes up the spilled bilj in the little
sidewalk cafes they call stupors.

He sniffed out embezzlement and corruption, flogging
most offenders and putting the worst cases to death, for as he
pointed out, if he threw them into prison they would only
steal from other prisoners, who had it hard enough already.
Cedric was up early every morning, and slept the delightful
sleep of the completely fulfilled.

Naturally he tended to delegate the job of "standing use-
lessly about the palace wearing an escree and taking the blame
for every silly thing that goes wrong" (as he called it privately)
to his more reliable troopers.

Busy as he was, Cedric of course had no more time to interview candidates for Captain of the Guard than the King had
time to interview candidates for the Prince's Personal Maid,
and, given that he would revert to Prime Minister the moment
he hired one, it was easy enough for him to perceive that every
applicant was a mere metal-clanger without a brain in his

head, bound to neglect the army back into rust and sloth, and so his inclination also matched the King's. There was some truth in it, anyway, for he got few exceptional generals among his applicants—the fame of the former Captain of the Guard was such that great swordsmen all flocked to try to claim his old place, while great generals, doubting their swordsmanship, failed to apply.

Thus both places went unfilled, and since those were supposed to be the priorities, the applications for Royal Witch and Royal Alchemist never got looked at at all. None were even interviewed.

The shabby treatment caused many of them, witches especially, to grow fed up with the long wait, and on their way out of the Kingdom they tended to curse trees, roads, or bridges. Also, more than one alchemist, with malicious glee, poured drakeseed—the dreaded potion used to turn snakes and lizards into dragons—into ponds and ditches, producing all sorts of foul and noxious monsters.

Privately, Cedric was delighted, since it gave his soldiers so much more to do and provided much useful training, and of course the larger monsters also gave the King something to use for quests for knights-candidates.

A year and a day had gone by in just this fashion. The army was in better shape than it had been in many years. Boniface was becoming known as a "merry" king, and it was whispered that rather than going down in the chronicles as Boniface the Shrewd as had been expected, he might well end up in the histories as something like Boniface the Jolly. Cedric was pleasant and courtly at Court, rough and cheerful in the field, and clearly enjoying himself wherever he went. He had even stopped chewing his beard, and he and the King had become friends. And Amatus was thriving and much larger, or his remaining half was, anyway.

By that time applicants for the four openings had virtually ceased to arrive, for the same travelers via whom Cedric had advertised were also carriers of news, and no fools besides, and so word got around that the journey into the Kingdom was not worth undertaking. But since Cedric now set the watches on the castle, when a party of four people came into view from the west over the Bridge of a Thousand Faces, displaying the traditional green banner that indicated one or more of them were applicants, the horns sounded at once and the bells rang.

Now, it happened that there had been no applicants for at least a month, so naturally the arrival of new ones—which would hardly have been news ten months before—was greeted with some interest. Moreover, the King was in the castle that day—as always, with Amatus—and so was Cedric, spending the hour or so a week he spent being Prime Minister (usually just filling out some simple forms and sending memos back to various vassals who were trying to shirk hard decisions).

And since there had been no occasion for pomp in some time, Cedric's troopers made a parade out of conveying the four travelers into the castle.

The moment Prince Amatus heard all the pageantry and uproar, he was overcome with a desire to see the parade, so, since Boniface had no particular objection to at least pretending to do his royal duty, the King, the Prince, and the Prime Minister hurried to the throne room to await the procession.

All around them, those who had heard the bells and horns were forming into a genuine throng, hoping for a little excitement. Boniface's merriment and Cedric's efficiency had resulted in that most desirable of conditions, a Court so devoid of intrigue and crisis as to be dull.

King Boniface had barely gotten seated, with Cedric just behind him to his right, and the Court as a whole had just put on properly dignified expressions—except for Amatus, who had a broad half-grin at the prospect of a parade—when the first of the honor guard entered.

Four pikemen flanked a vassal who carried the Hand and Book banner of the Kingdom. Cedric noted with pleasure that they were precisely in step, carried themselves with a perfectly erect dignified carriage, and had boots, pikes, and triolets in perfect order; his pleasure deepened when King Boniface, under his stole, quietly punched him in the arm in congratulations.

The four pikemen were followed by four knights-candidates, young courtiers not yet sent on their first quests, spurs jingling and feathered caps swaying. As befit their rank, they wore an amazing array of colors, with loose folds of rich cloth protruding through the slashing of their triolets, and no two caps even remotely alike save for the long black feathers that denoted their rank.

And after the knights-candidates came the applicants.

It was at once obvious that more than one of them was applying. The first man the eye was drawn to was big, square-built, and full-bellied with dark wavy hair down to his shoulders, a trim spade-shaped beard, red skin that suggested much time outside or much time drinking or perhaps both, big twinkling green eyes, and an expression around his full red mouth of being about to burst into song or peals of laughter. He wore the brown knee-length triolet and wrapped leggings, heavy sandals, and mortarboard that in the Kingdom denoted a wandering scholar, and the retort and the small still hanging from the huge pack on his back identified him as an alchemist. Amatus made a little gurgle of pleasure and whispered "Nice man" to his father, and Boniface could hardly repress a smile himself.

The woman who followed the alchemist was obviously the rarest sort of witch. Her hair, rather than filthy and gray, was snow-white, fine, and clean, like that of a very young blonde child. Her eyes were as large as those of the alchemist, but they were lightless voids without discernible whites, irises, or pupils, as if night itself had puddled in the sockets. Her skin was covered with little soft scales like a garter snake's, the shade of pale, clear blue that sometimes reflects off a snow-field at dusk on a very cold day in January, and perfectly white fangs protruded from her thin pink mouth. Her cheekbones and the edge of her jaw shone through her blue skin as if her skull were trying to shed its wrapping. She wore the tradi-tional dress—black and long—but where other witches did their best to hide their sagging toad-bodies in yards of black sacking, this witch instead wore a long dress that clung to every inch of her, glittering in oily rainbows as she moved, revealing the voluptuous body of a young woman. A man who looked only at that body might have found her desirable.

Compared to the alchemist and the witch, the other two seemed nearly invisible, yet the eye stayed on them longer, as if there were more that needed to be seen. The girl, who could not have been much past sixteen, could have been a com-moner dressing up or a noble dressing down, for she wore a simple dress that had probably once been white linen, clean now but gray from many washings and dusty roads, and a woolen shawl in the same condition. She seemed neither par-ticularly slim nor at all heavy; her hair was the color of old walnut-stained wood, falling thick and straight to her waist, and if the girl had an aunt, she had undoubtedly been told by that aunt that it was her best feature. Her skin was pale and lightly freckled, her eyes sea gray, and she seemed to look around her as if she had never seen a Royal Court before, did not know what it was, and had no idea she should be im-pressed.

At first glance it seemed the man behind the girl must be a servant, for he wore a battered cloak of no particular color, one that might have blended into a field of hay in which he slept, or a muddy road on which he walked, with equal ease, and the clothing which peeked out its rents was of the same color. His face was hidden by a wide-brimmed hat; if one were to describe the cloak as grayish then one would say the hat was brownish.

Yet the eye stayed on him longest of all. At first you saw he was a giant, towering over everyone; then that the way he walked and moved was asymmetric. The clothing must hide severe deformities, though his motion gave the impression of great strength and agility. Then what was in the shadow under the hat came into focus, not a face but a thin gray mask of iron, spotted with white, brown, and red streaks.

At his side he must be wearing a whole belt full of weapons; for one moment the cloak opened, as if gratifying everyone's curiosity, to reveal an escree, a mace, and three pongees, all seemingly larger than most men would ever attempt to wield.

"There must be thirty pounds of iron on that man," Cedric breathed, "and he drags his foot and humps that shoulder oddly, yet I would wager on him in a footrace against any youth in the Kingdom. And that bulge in his cloak, I'd warrant, is made by two festoons and a double-bladed ax besides."

King Boniface nodded to Cedric. "This is a year and a day after the, er, unfortunate event, is it not?"

Cedric's breath caught a little. "Why, yes, Majesty, it is. And you are right. It's the sort of time that turns up in a fairy tale. I think perhaps we are about to see something remarkable."

Amatus commented loudly, pointing at the visitors, "Nice—scary—nice—scary."

Boniface, too late, covered his son's mouth and whispered for him to hush. There was a long silence, then the alchemist and the girl behind him burst into merry laughter, and the corner of the witch's mouth twitched a little, and Cedric fancied that perhaps there was a brief shaking of laughter under the cloak and hat of the strange man behind them . . . though if there was, Cedric would realize many years later, and write in his *Chronicle*, the best account we have of those days, that it was the only time he had seen the man laugh.

At this, the Court felt free to laugh too, a jolly sharing with the strangers, and even the guards seemed to be fighting grins—successfully, Cedric noted with pleasure—as they brought the four travelers to face the throne. As was proper, the alchemist, who carried the green applicant's banner, laid it at the King's feet.

Boniface smiled at them. "Clearly at least some of you are here to apply."

The alchemist bowed low. "Indeed, there are four of us, and we seek the four positions advertised. Suitable references are available, or demonstrations of our abilities may also be given."

"And your names?" Cedric inquired. His heart was sinking. *I surely would not want to fight that strange-looking fellow, and I do believe he would make a fine Captain of the Guard. I suppose I shall have to go back to filling out forms and enforcing protocol all the time, and the armories will probably all be rust again before next year is out.*

"I am called Golias, probably because it is my name," the alchemist said. "As you might guess, I am an alchemist of great ability, though thus far of little experience. I seek the post of Royal Alchemist, and may I add—"

The witch coughed.

Golias hastened on to explain, "My friend here is Mortis, who seeks the post of Royal Witch. She was, herself, once a queen, though that was long ago, and so knows the ways of a Court well and thoroughly. Stern and commanding, not often speaking, but with a mighty power that is as remarkable as it is—"

"Get on with it," the witch said. Her voice made a sharp, sibilant hiss that stopped the breath of everyone in the room.

Golias seemed to jump, but nodded and said, "My male comrade here, whose appearance might arouse comment, is under a curse that will not permit him to speak his own name or disclose the nature of his curse. Where he has been, he has often been called the Twisted Man. A fighter, bodyguard, swordsman—"

"A manslayer," the Twisted Man said. The voice came out of his mask like a breath of damp air from a cave, and it felt like the sound of a window breaking at midnight. "A fair hand at monsters and such as well. But no general. No man will gladly follow me, nor take orders from me. You would need a separate General of All the Armies, but still, I seek the post of Captain of the Guard."

King Boniface nodded soberly. He knew how much the job of General of All the Armies had come to mean to Cedric. He had thought that he might well wish to divide the functions of Captain of the Guard and General of All the Armies, thus giving Cedric the job he loved on a permanent basis and at the same time getting himself a proper bodyguard, for Cedric sometimes failed to post truly first-rate troopers to the job, preferring to keep them on duty at the barracks. Thus the Twisted Man was proposing what King Boniface himself had already been thinking, and impressing the King very much.

"And," Boniface said, preventing Golias from any longer introductions, "I presume the young lady would like to seek employment as the Prince's Personal Maid, and no doubt has splendid qualifications." He tried for just enough irony to amuse the Court without hurting the girl's feelings; as usual, since he was King, no one revealed enough feeling one way or another for him to judge what effect he was having. Really, it was irritating.

"Majesty," the girl said softly, and her voice was so melodic that everyone leaned forward just a little to hear it better, "my name is Psyche. I have no qualifications except that I know how to do things, I work hard, and I usually like children, though to tell you the truth it depends a great deal on the child, for you know they are not all alike."

This was the first time Boniface had heard any candidate admit that not all children were equally suited to her, and instantly he liked her for that.

Amatus nearly clinched it then by bouncing up and down and saying, "Nice lady. Is she going to stay?" and then Psyche *did* clinch it by grinning.

After all, a year and a day is an auspicious time in a fairy tale, the King said to himself. Still, he knew the rules, and sure as he was that these were the right ones, he said, "I am well-disposed to all of you. Would you be so good as to undertake a project each to demonstrate your skills?"

Golias nodded. "Indeed, Majesty, we had thought we might propose such projects to you. Mortis and I should like to undertake to manufacture the Wine of the Gods."

A gasp ran through the Court.

Boniface frowned. "I tell you now, I would not like you to fail through mischance, and if you are little experienced, so many things can go wrong that through no fault of your own—"

A gasp ran through the Court again.

"The gasping is getting quite distracting," Boniface said, crossly. "Nobody asked anybody not to mention the Wine of the Gods, to my knowledge. If you have all been trying not to, I wish you would give up in that effort. I broke my arm falling out of a chestnut tree as a child, and no one went to any special trouble to avoid mentioning chestnuts in my presence. Amatus can bear to hear it mentioned; indeed, I doubt that he remembers he ever *had* a left side."

"Right hand," Amatus said, holding it up. "No left hand."

No one quite knew how to react to this; when the King looked at Psyche, she had a little upward turn in her mouth, not a smile unless he wanted it to be. He smiled himself, and then it was. "No matter how well we know them, there's always more to know," Psyche said.

The King beamed at her.

"Are you sure," Cedric said, clearing his throat, "that you wish to engage in anything as difficult as manufacturing the Wine of the Gods? I think that we all want you to succeed."

Mortis answered. "We are not just suitable, but perfect. We will show you that; we would not want you at any time in the future to have the least doubt about us. I myself am powerful enough to retain this appearance despite being many generations of men old; I will not fail as the witch. And though Golias is young and untried, I know he will do it without failure or error, for it is a saying in the Kingdom, is it not, that a witch knows the worth of an alchemist?"

"As for me," the Twisted Man said, "just point out the biggest and most dreaded monster in the Kingdom, and I promise you I shall deliver its head or heads at dawn tomorrow, having slain it at night when such things are at their most powerful. Send along any soldier you wish as a witness."

"There is a quite unpleasant hydra in the Bitter River Swamp at the moment," Cedric said, "and I think that is as big as we've got. Trooper Roderick's family are from out that way and I'm sure he can guide you to it. You are of course familiar with all the procedures?"

The Twisted Man nodded. "Scorching the necks. Yes. For the basilisk a polished mirror, for the dragon a stout shield with copper on the out face and oak on the in, for the vampire a stake of rosewood, and for the hydra, the blazing torch. These are the sorts of things they teach in the first week in the Academy of Heroes—though I am no hero, and know only because I have listened at fires when they talked of their lore."

Boniface was delighted again, for if the Twisted Man was not a hero but knew some of their ways, it was likely that the fairy tale, if it were a fairy tale they were in, would reveal someone already introduced as a hero—perhaps Amatus.

"Done," the King said. "Bring me whatever heads you take off the hydra, and Trooper Roderick will confirm its death. Now, with that accomplished—"

"Majesty," Psyche said.

"What—oh, dear. You're right. We need to have you do something, though I'm sure the boy likes you . . ."

"Tell me a story," Amatus demanded, "and fix me bombazine pudding, and play a game with me."

"Please," Psyche said, firmly.

"Please," Amatus said.

Boniface beamed at her; she already seemed to be good at this. "Well, the task is suited to the duty—yes, by all means."

And so, with the tasks parceled out, there was a great blaring of trumpets and a recessional, which delighted Amatus. Golias and Mortis climbed the long stairs to the Royal Alchemical Laboratory, the Twisted Man and Roderick saddled up in the courtyard in front of the clerihew, and Psyche, leading a cheerfully babbling Amatus by the hand, had gone off to the boy's room to get him ready for dinner, some quiet evening amusements, and bed.

Without the boy to distract him, Boniface had a pleasant meal with Cedric and his other advisors, did more real royal business than he had in a year and a day, and went to bed cheerfully. *Not my doing, of course*, he thought, just before he drifted off, *but things are turning out splendidly, with the single exception of Amatus's condition, and after all that is no worse.*

3

Tasks Are Completed, Appointments Are Made, Warnings Are Heard, and Several Years Go By

When the King opened his eyes, the room was bright with sun, and Psyche had brought him a wonderful breakfast of eggs exactly soft enough, bread fresh from the oven, waffles with fluffy white sugar, and chilled foamy chocolate milk. She looked clean and fresh and consented to have a couple of slices of bread with strawberry jam while the King ate. Mostly, she told him about clever and interesting things Amatus had done and said the night before.

Boniface discovered that they both agreed that Amatus was one of the most remarkable and intelligent three-year-olds the world had ever seen, and that the loss of one half of the Prince, while deplorable, had in no way affected his essential extraordinary qualities. Indeed, Psyche had independently discovered many of those qualities in Amatus that Boniface had noticed himself.

The King liked talking to her. He wasn't sure how he knew, but he was aware that he had to hire all four of this group of applicants, or none at all, so even more than before he hoped that the other three would succeed.

As he was finishing his breakfast, and thinking of changing from his pajamas, Mortis and Golias came in. The alchemist carried a silver serving plate covered with a mirrored glass dome; he bowed low, extending the plate to King Boniface. Mortis whisked the dome off, and there was a small bottle unmistakably containing the Wine of the Gods.

The King lifted it reverently; there was a full glass. "It went without undue difficulty," Golias said.

King Boniface smiled. "I shall pour five thimble cups, and as soon as your comrade returns we will all drink in celebration of your successfully completing your tasks and of my hiring you."

There was a loud single knock. The King shouted "Come in" and the Twisted Man entered, bearing a dozen well-washed hydra heads in a huge net bag. Each might have fit on a large dog, except that they were blue-green and shaped a bit like a lizard's head, with eyes on short stalks and a single curved fang protruding from the center of each set of jaws.

"Splendid," the King said. "Let us drink to your employment—and to my having solved some administrative problems rather neatly, for, even admitting it to have been luck, it is a good thing in a King to be lucky."

And they all drank together and it was settled.

It might be best next to tell quickly of what happened in all the years as Amatus grew big enough to be ready to go adventuring, so as to reach the adventures *per se* as quickly as possible, except that two other things of importance happened on the day the four Companions were hired. When Cedric was quite old, he ordered that those two other things be copied into his *Chronicle*, for looking back he thought that they probably mattered a great deal, and we will not second-guess his judgment.

The first was that the King made the Twisted Man his Captain of the Guard, and Cedric General of All the Armies.

The other matter, though, was more complex. Cedric and the King were going over the Royal Survey—a part of Cedric's job as Prime Minister—looking at the map together and trying to decide whether a new settlement in the northeast should be named Bonifaceburg, Bonifaceville, or just Boniface, when there was a faint, tapping knock at the door. If it was ever possible to knock apologetically, this was that knock.

King Boniface detected that apologetic quality, and raised an eyebrow to his trusted advisor before saying "Come in." Cedric, hearing it too, sat extra straight and tall, for he had a feeling that he might need his dignity.

Three people one would not expect to see together came timidly through the door.

The first, Wyrna, was very old. In Boniface's father's time, she had supposedly murdered her husband, but he had been the notorious Great North Woods Ogre—that is to say, an obnoxious and ill-mannered provincial lord whose castle was near the Great North Woods and who had turned highwayman and cannibal, rather than a particularly great ogre. Since her supposed crime had been more in the nature of a public service, it had seemed inappropriate to hang her, so instead the old King had sentenced her to sweep out the castle, in exchange for room and board and a bit of pocket money, on her solemn promise not to murder anyone not equally deserving. After living with the ogre, everything else seemed so nice that she had become merry and pleasant, sort of honorary grandmother to many of the younger servants in the castle.

But instead of her usual warm smile, now she stood before them, wringing her hands, deeply distressed.

Beside her was Gwyn, who mopped and swept the nursery. Gwyn was a fairly but not extraordinarily pretty young woman who looked as if she should be a nurse, nanny, or governess. In fact, she had taken the job of cleaning the nursery as the first thing that came along, and after a year or so of mopping up, not only after Amatus, but after any number of children of visiting lords and kings, she had come to dislike children intensely, and was secretly hoping, just once, to find a soldier who did not want to settle down and have twenty of them. She often had a slightly sour expression and rarely permitted herself to smile since she had been told it made her look motherly. The effect was dignified and adult beyond her years.

Now she stood, nervous, shy, and biting her lower lip in a rabbity way, looking down at the floor, as if many years had dropped off her.

The last of them was Trooper Roderick, and this was oddest of all. The soldier who had gone with the Twisted Man to witness the slaying of the hydra was one of Cedric's most trusted men, and now he looked uncharacteristically concerned, even anxious. He was a big, solid fellow, much brighter than he looked, for his phlegmatic temperament and his tendency to stare into space with his mouth hanging open gave many people the impression he was stupid. Eventually he gave up the army and became a distinguished playwright, specializing in long and bloody historical cycles, and it turned out that while staring into space he had in fact been composing whole scenes and acts.

At this time Cedric did not know his trooper was to be an important literary figure, but did know Roderick was much smarter than he seemed, and that he merely seemed uninvolved because it took a great deal to upset him. So to see Roderick alert, head up, glancing around nervously, was a bad sign indeed.

It took the King and his Prime Minister much less time to assess the situation than it takes to read about it, for of course they already knew these people and so understood at once that their behavior was uncharacteristic. "Well," Cedric said mildly, "this looks like something unusual and important."

"Come on in, sit down, and tell us what the matter is," Boniface said, in his kindest voice. "Anything that bothers three trusted servants so much is surely of concern to me."

They seemed no more comfortable seated on stools. With a glance around, Gwyn began it. "Majesty—er, you do know that today there was a Servants' Picnic? Well, that's how we all came to be talking to each other. Kind of between the sack race and the egg carry, you know. And there were things—well, each of us was bothered by something about these four new people you've hired, but none of us so much that we wanted to come to you with it . . . but when you put them all together, our three stories, I mean, well, you sort of . . ."

"You start to see something?" Cedric suggested. "Some pattern you don't like?"

Wyrna shook her head, her old dark gray hair swinging emphatically. "No, milord, we don't see any pattern at all. But what we do see is that there seems to be a place in all of it where there ought to be a pattern. If you see what I mean."

"Well," Boniface said mildly, "possibly the best thing would be if you could tell us what you saw or heard, Gwyn."

Gwyn nodded once, firmly, her jaw setting like a soldier's. It was at that moment that Roderick noticed her for the first time, and moreover she noticed him noticing her, and this gave her courage to proceed.

"Well, sir," she began, "it so happened that last night I was up in the Nursery Wing, scrubbing out gurry from the reticles in the wedgewood, when I overheard that new Prince's Personal Maid singing to the Prince. She has a lovely voice."

"She would," the King said, approvingly.

"And it was a pretty tune," Gwyn went on, seeming to gain confidence by the moment. "I don't remember what the words concerned—some old tale of a romance between the man who wielded the omnibus and the gandy dancer who loved him, I believe—except that the chorus ran:

> *And it's one for the morning glory,*
> *Two for the early dew,*
> *Three for a man who will stand his ground*
> *And four for the love of you.*

"You have rather a pleasant voice yourself," Cedric commented, "and the tune is indeed a merry one."

"Yes, sir, thank you, sir, but now I come to the difficult part. I went closer to the door to hear better, for I dearly love a good song, and then peeped through the door. By now the young Prince was sound asleep and I'm sure she was just finishing the song out because it's such a pity to leave a good song undone, and in case he should wake for just a moment before finally settling in.

"She was bent over his bed, and she was making . . . signs with her hands. Gestures, like, sir, but over and over, like . . ."

"As if she were weaving a spell?" Cedric asked with some alarm.

"I don't like to think that, sir," Gwyn said. "But my old grandma is a witch—nothing intended of her character, of course—and I recognized that one of the gestures Psyche was making was the Eighth Great Spell, the Octane."

"That's a spell of protection," the King commented, "and the melody and the words done with it sound to me as if they were part of a good destiny."

"But, sir," Gwyn pointed out, "if she can work the Octane, she is already far advanced as a witch in her own right. And a powerful one if she can remain young and beautiful while doing so. And why in the world would a powerful witch wish to work as—not to put too fine a face on it—a blower of royal noses and a singer of lullabies?"

"It is possible," the King said, smiling warmly, "that she likes children, and I assure you that if one really likes children, Amatus is about as likable a child as there can be."

Gwyn knew better than to argue with that. Besides, she had now discharged her duty, and she wanted to make sure her exit was graceful. "That may well be, sir . . . but working spells above the sleeping Prince—"

"Exactly," Boniface beamed at her. "You were quite right

to bring it to my attention. I'm happy that you did, and it speaks well of your devotion." He wanted her to go away happy, for he knew that it had taken considerable courage for her to come to him, and one can never tell when one might need loyalty and courage from even the humblest servant. Yet at the same time he trusted his feeling that great and good magics were at work here.

Wyrna spoke next. "If I may, Majesty, what I should like to tell you about was not much more serious. It was only that I had worked so often, cleaning and scrubbing in the Royal Alchemical Laboratory, that I know all the words of all the spells that go into the making of the Wine of the Gods, especially the ones they repeat over and over, and the words have gotten to be—oh, like a comfort to me, for they are now so familiar. And no one pays attention to an old scrubwoman, so they've always gone right through the words just as if I weren't there cleaning. So when I heard them add a little spell before each step . . . well."

"What did they add?" the King asked, and now his face showed just the faintest trace of concern. "I assure you there was nothing wrong with the Wine of the Gods they prepared."

"Well, somewhat, it was *how* they added it, too. The additional spell, I mean. That new Royal Alchemist, Golias, you might almost think he was laughing as he did it, as if he'd put a joke in, and that new Royal Witch, Mortis, seemed most offended by that, so as soon as he'd finished she'd repeat the same spell, but this time in that icy voice that sounded like a frozen branch snapped off a living tree in January. And what either of them would say was:

> '*Long after beginning,*
> *Long before time,*
> *Between eternity and perpetuity,*

45

Bracketed by love and magic,
Trapped between lucid and ludicrous
You are summoned to our aid.'

"And that just seems to me, sir . . . well, peculiar."

"It's a riddling spell," Cedric said, "something that they needed that wasn't right to hand, summoned by describing it to the spirit world in a riddle. Spirits, you know, love guessing games. But that's why the Wine of the Gods was unaffected—it was some ingredient or some propitious omen they were working into existence, rather than the Wine itself. If we can think what it was, then we can easily decide whether or not it was the sort of thing we might want them to be doing . . . let me think."

He thought for a long time, and then clapped his hands together with a delighted laugh. "Fetch the Royal Dictionary!" he bellowed, and Gwyn ran to get it from the library.

A moment later, he had turned to the Ls, and when he did, he began to laugh in earnest. "Well, well, well, now in their shoes, *that* is certainly what I would want. And it's no ill thing." He jabbed his finger at the page and showed it to them all, and there, between "lucid" and "ludicrous," was "luck."

A sigh of relief ran through four of them, but then Roderick spoke up and said, "Well, I wish the worries I've got were that mild, sir. But it's just this—that Twisted Man, he did a fine job with the hydra, no question, but when he had it down to just one head, he . . . well, I didn't think I'd ever say such a thing, sir, since that hydra had eaten two of my blood kin, my cousin Maizie Ann who was married to a cousin on another side of the family, Richard his name was . . . the hydra ate Richard too . . ."

The King nodded, not impatiently, understanding that every really important story has some minor characters in it.

"And, well, sir . . ." Roderick said, "all the same I felt sorry for the poor thing after he was done with it. He left the one head to keep it alive, and then he started to—hurt it. For fun. He'd give it a cut here and a whack there, nicked its ficus muscles right down to the apostrophe, again and again. You could see tears of pain running down its remaining cheeks, and it commenced to beg like a dog, wanting to be put out of its misery, but he kept right at it till, I suppose, he'd had enough fun playing with it. He's a fell fighter, sir, but cruel. Never saw a monster done for so neatly—but never felt sorry for one before, either."

He knew his speech was not the perfectly styled and mannered kind they had at Court, and this embarrassed him, especially because he could see that his embarrassment was causing Gwyn's heart to go out to him.

The King sighed. "So there's at least one dark omen."

"Not more than we'd expect, Majesty," Cedric commented. He was trying hard not to be influenced by the Twisted Man's making it possible for him to have exactly the job he wanted. He wasn't sure he was succeeding. "There is a conservation of omens, you know, and so many have been so favorable . . ."

"Indeed," King Boniface said, "but this bears watching all the same. And all of you were right indeed that something about it is redolent of a pattern which ought to be there but is not apparent. I presume, Cedric—"

"Not to me either, Majesty, but it is certainly early in the fairy tale. If it is to be one. I suppose all we can say is that we are grateful to all of you and we hope you will carry on in the way you have, and you will let us know if anything additional of note happens."

They all nodded, relieved, and when they went out Cedric closed the door and said, "Well, then, one ill omen to balance all the good ones. So there is little question that we are in a story, and no doubt we will know who the hero is soon enough."

Wyrna returned to her dungeon, and for years afterward

listened especially intently to the making of the Wine of the Gods, but all she got from it was the spell for luck she had learned the first day. She would often use that one, however, and it was noted by many people that things usually seemed to work out well for Wyrna. Roderick and Gwyn discovered that they both disliked children intensely, and began to see a great deal of each other. If any of the three of them ever noticed anything more about the four Companions, they never brought it to Cedric's attention, or so he said in the *Chronicle*, and if they told the King, the King did not mention it to Cedric.

Now the time whirled by like time in a story, as Amatus— or the right half of him—grew tall and strong. It was a good thing that Psyche's energy was inexhaustible, for the young Prince rocketed about all day long as if he would only exist for the next ten minutes and had to get all of life into it. One moment he would be climbing trees. The next, you would hear the clash of wooden escrees and he would be at it with the Twisted Man, whacking away with great ferocity in his early years, and later with increasing skill.

The minute you thought he had settled into that, you'd hear the clatter of his right foot on the roof tiles, and the shriek of Psyche as she swung out the window and climbed after him. On one occasion when he was twelve, he deliberately climbed a steep roof face that she could not manage in a long skirt. Boniface, watching from his own tower window, almost chuckled, until halfway up Amatus began to slip, and seemed to be headed for the stones of the courtyard below.

At that moment—hadn't the Twisted Man been right next to Boniface a moment ago?—the humped and distorted giant was rushing up the roof, catching the sliding Amatus by the triolet, and bearing him safely back inside by the collar.

That night, at dinner, Amatus was uncharacteristically quiet. Cedric asked him if fright had "settled him a little."

"You could say that," Amatus said. "I wasn't afraid of

falling—perhaps I should have been—but the Twisted Man said that if I ever gave everyone such a bad scare again, he would ask Father to let *him* punish me."

"What is that around your neck and hanging under your triolet?"

"The Twisted Man gave it to me." The boy pulled it out; it was a tiny silver whistle. "He said since I'm not making it easy, he would appreciate it if I would blow on this any time I am about to do something stupid—and that he expects it will more commonly be blown when I have already done something stupid."

But though Psyche and the Twisted Man were the favored Companions of his youngest and most physically active years, Amatus also spent much time up in the laboratory or down in the library, following Golias and Mortis around and generally being in the way. Alone among people in the castle, he never seemed to fear Mortis, despite her appearance. She seemed to pay him little attention, but things he needed—spells of protection and of power, spells for learning and discernment— were usually there for him when he needed them, even the powerful Trigonometric Spell, developed by Trigonometras himself; it was said that if you could survive that, nothing would ever seem difficult to learn again.

On the other hand, for those things he merely wanted, rather than needed, there always seemed to be something flawed about the spell; she gave him a spell so that he could know all his lessons the next day without studying, but he arose from his bed exhausted and feeling unwashed as if he had stayed up all night to learn them. He was invulnerable for about a week until he discovered that he could not taste his food, feel Psyche's hand on his cheek after she tucked him in, or feel the pressure of the wooden escree against his hand and know where the Twisted Man would strike next. Worse yet, he lost all pleasure in Golias's songs, and that was intolerable, so he finally went to Mortis and begged her to lift the spell—

only to learn that he would have to sweep out her chambers for a week, and clean the bat droppings from her rafters, and get all the gurry out of every reticle in the cracks of the wheatstone, before she would undo the spell.

Boniface watched, and saw how Amatus, or at least his remaining half, seemed to thrive in the care of the Companions, and like the wise King he was (for he had been shrewd for more than a decade before becoming jolly) he neither softened nor contradicted their tutelage of his son. Not when the Twisted Man gave the boy a great, heavy festoon for his thirteenth birthday and took him all the way to the Ironic Gap to stalk gazebo. Not when Psyche caught him tormenting a baby hydra and forced him to raise it as a pet and take care of it—and since he had gotten the poor thing up to more than thirty heads before she caught him, and each head demanded a separate bowl, the job became onerous indeed. Yet when the hydra died at the end of the summer—as they all must—he wept bitterly, and it was more than a week till he could bear to put the bowls away.

Not when Mortis would exact some high price to remove a foolishly requested spell, as we have seen.

Not even when Golias taught him more than three hundred verses of "The Codwalloper's Daughter."

4

The Beginning of Adventures

Golias was a fine alchemist, learned in at least a dozen sciences, and would happily discourse of any of them to Amatus, but though Amatus liked to learn and could learn to like most learning, he did not take to alchemy. Fortunately, like most good alchemists, Golias was a bit of everything, for since alchemy worked on the principle that whatever was, was like something else, and that ultimately the likeness was what it was, he had to know that not only were the plastrons of the human liver like the plasmids of the gazebo's horns and the strophes of common moulin's blossoms, but also that all three were far more like a sonnet than like a couplet, and much more like a lyre than like a bass drum.

So when it turned out that Amatus's interests—and perhaps even his talents—tended to music and poetry, that was what Golias gave him in great quantity. The young Prince read old stories of empires and gods, strange stories of airplanes and churches, and modern realistic stories about fighting dragons and rescuing princesses. He learned to recite great volumes of poetry, including the *Bonifaciad* that Golias was in the process of composing. He learned songs about spring and wine, women and wine, and spring and women.

Much of this he learned, not in laboratory, but out in the courtyards and even in the town square, for Golias was not officially any sort of tutor for Prince Amatus, but merely a natural teacher of the kind who will teach anything he or she knows to anyone who cares to listen, and so if a crowd collected the lessons became public rather than private. Golias was said to make learning so charming that after he left the square, truant children would try to sneak back into school.

There is hardly anything that will so interest anyone in practice as overexposure to theory, and in theory a prince was expected to develop some harmless vices and to fall under unsavory influences. Amatus extended the theory by becoming an unsavory influence himself. In extenuation, he led no one astray other than kitchen maids who, with an adolescent prince in the offing, had been carefully chosen by Cedric for their boundless tolerance and congenital sterility; various wastrel second sons of lords, who after all had nothing to do but to be led astray and otherwise might have made nuisances of themselves in the army; and dissolute children of wealthy commoners who might otherwise have spent their time angling for a peerage from someone likely to give it to them. Nonetheless, shortly older kitchen maids (the ones who actually did the work), conservative lords, and thrifty merchants were heard to warn the Prince's friends to avoid his company.

Now, one evening down near the deep, fast-flowing Long River, up which ships from everywhere came and where the Hektarian and Vulgarian immigrants to the Kingdom tended to concentrate, Amatus, who had developed a fondness for the wine and food of the Hektarian Quarter, was drinking a great deal of wine in the company of Golias, at the Gray Weasel, a little taboret at the corner of Wend and Byway. The wine was a good, rich, fruity red Gravamen, and the songs were good though familiar. Amatus liked to believe that no one knew who he was under his long cloak, and Golias quietly used discretionary funds to help most of the people there pretend not to notice that the young man with him had no left side.

Golias was playing now, on the nine-stringed palanquin, not terribly well—Amatus was already better at it—but lustily, lewdly, and loudly, for there was a lusty, lewd, and loud crowd gathered around them. Besides the red-faced, roaring Golias himself, there was Sir John Slitgizzard, third son of the Earl of the Iron Lake Marches and as dissipated a young man as one could hope to find, yet a deadly shot with the pismire and faster than lightning with the escree, said to have killed a dozen men in duels and rumored to have ridden with Deacon Dick Thunder and robbed a wealthy traveler or two in his time.

There was Pell Grant, a wench who had modeled for the illustration of "buxom" in the Royal Dictionary in her younger days, rumored to have taught the young Prince several of the arts of love. Next to her sat Duke Wassant, corpulent and with a pouty look to his red lips, yet known for speed and savagery with both his wit and his pongee, a man who had eviscerated thousands figuratively and just possibly a few literally.

Across from him, dressed in boy's clothing and armed to the teeth (and a bit beyond if one counted a small pongee concealed in the long tresses tucked under her hat) and looking far more the thug than any man present, sat Calliope, youngest daughter of one of the southern counts, with whom Wassant had had a brief and operatic affair when she was young enough to make it a matter for scandal. Not yet of marriageable age, if anyone had been so foolhardy, she was a focus of rumors far beyond unsavory, but Golias, who had carefully edited the Prince's social circle in general to surround him with people whose ways were worse than their hearts, had never done anything about her.

Those who were particularly honest had long ago conceded that Calliope had a streak of passionate generosity and kindness in her, leading her often to rush to the defense of the defenseless, and that many of her anonymous verses—most especially the erotic ones—had a tender beauty to them that could melt the heart. They would then, however, having bought credibility with the cheap coin of balance, regale everyone present with more interesting stories of violence inflicted on other young ladies, pranks and japes of a peculiarly sadistic nature on the better young men of the Court who sometimes tried to court her admitted beauty, and commoner lovers (or alternately married aristocratic lovers) in extraordinary profusion, some of whom were said to have killed themselves.

It was widely believed—and whispered as an open secret—that she and Amatus were lovers.

Of those present, it was known only to Amatus and Golias that she was not the daughter of that southern Count, but sole survivor of the royal line of the neighboring monarchy of Overhill, smuggled away as an infant by a faithful nurse when her family was massacred by Waldo the Usurper.

It was also known only to herself, Wassant, and Amatus (and perhaps to others who were perceptive enough) that despite her temper and language she was actually rather a prude. Amatus forgave her this on account of her crimson hair, and her poetry, and because when he had attempted to have his way with her, she had told him that he was a very rude young man and that he ought to learn to behave himself. Since no one had bothered to tell him that in some time, he was charmed by the novelty.

The song Golias was singing, thumping the triple bass string hard and plucking at the three doubled treble strings as if he were trying to tear his palanquin in half, was a roistering old thing called "Penna Pike," though no one knew anymore where or who Penna Pike was, despite many who had gone in quest for it down quaint and curious roads. The song was called Penna Pike because its chorus ran:

Penna Pike, Penna Pike, Penna Pike Pike Pike
Penna Pike, Penna Pike, Penna-Penna Pike
Penna Pike, Penna Pike, Penna Pike Pike Pike
Pen—na Pike!—Penna Pike Pike Pike!

The ballad itself told of a mortal woman stolen away by goblins and carried into the dark tunnels under the city, whose lover had come to claim her and had woefully returned to the surface, all too aware that a bigger soul than his would be needed to rescue her and to love her afterwards, and having realized his smallness of soul had taken up the trade of highway robber in order to die a nasty death upon the gallows and thus not have to face his own pettiness, only to discover that his skills far exceeded his integrity, and thus spent many years as a progressively more depraved brigand before he finally was burned in the place of a witch—or continued his career. The song ended less than clearly.

As Golias finished, "Cal" stretched a dirty boot up onto the table, picked something unpleasant off it with the point of "his" pongee, and said, "It does seem a pity that the poor girl ends up stuck down among the goblins. After all it was against her will."

"It's a law of magic," Pell said, smoothing her bodice to remind everyone present of which woman was currently supposed to be a woman.

Slitgizzard belched and grinned. "Laws are made to be broken."

"Magical laws are a different matter," Wassant said, waving to the owner for another plate of simile and protons, that dish at which Hektarians most excel. "Only poets and storytellers can break them, and then it must be done at the right moment. Her lover and the girl herself could not break them because they were inside the story."

"But we aren't," Calliope persisted, now too interested to remember to keep her voice deep and gruff.

"Near enough," Golias said. " 'Penna Pike' is a very old song—parts of it suggest a language that has long since passed from human knowledge—and knowing it to be so old, we must believe it to be peculiarly true, so true that if ever any part of it was not true, that part has since become so. That being the case, its laws of magic would be unusually strong. It would take a bold gang of adventurers to go down the dark tunnels to Goblin Country, still more so to carry her off in the teeth of the various ensorcellments . . . no, it's quite explicable why she has remained down there all these years."

"Well, then," Calliope said, "when do we start?"

Golias looked up and scratched his head. "You mean, start down the tunnels under the city? To rescue her? I suppose as soon as you like. It wouldn't take long if it worked, and preparation before going won't matter if it fails. Traditionally we ought to go at night when they are strongest."

"Wait a moment," Wassant said, not in the least pleased. "That's not at all what I'd have had in mind from you, Golias. Isn't it traditionally the job of the wise one in the party to give the dark warning?"

"I'm quite sure it is," Sir John Slitgizzard said, his face deeply troubled. "No reflection on your abilities, sir, but I have been on a few of these things, and when it comes to messing about with dark tunnels and vile things under the earth, we need a good hand for white magic with us, and one of the duties of that person is to tell us that we're getting into more than we're bargaining for."

Golias sighed, so deep a sigh that the candles nearly went out in front of him, and everyone there felt an icy hand pass up his or her back. "Know, then, since you are so determined, that such will be our course. We will pass for what will seem eons through dark caverns swarming with bats and corpseworms, in gunge composed of things it is not good to think about, our sole lights the lanterns we carry and the dim glow of corpseworms. At last at the border of Goblin Country—

always assuming they don't know we're coming and ambush us in the tunnels—there will be some fell monster, set there to keep watch, who will ask an unfathomable riddle; and should it be fathomed, we must then march boldly to the Goblin King, demand and obtain the girl, and finally, despite treachery (and with goblins you can always count on treachery!), carry the maiden forth without getting any of the steps wrong. And all of this will earn us a footnote in a moderately popular ballad, whereas if we don't, sooner or later some hero in need of a feat of prowess will come along and do it anyway. So the whole thing is pointless and extraordinarily dangerous. But did you not know that before?"

Pell Grant's arms extended farther around Sir John Slitgizzard, as if to protect him from going, and he seemed to lean back into her bosom, but whether from fear or because it was pleasant, who could say? The man's expression never changed.

Through all of this Amatus had sat silently, watching little pellets of cold sleet bounce in the street out where the light from the taboret spilled onto the cobbles, and sensing that whatever might be beginning, something was going to end tonight. The warm reds and ambers of the open hearth where the protons baked, the flickering of the fat candles, the soft hiss of the sleet outside and the rumbling of the big sleeping dog beneath his bench all seemed terribly precious to him, as if they would never be the same again, and part of him seemed to clutch madly at the last-departed notes from Golias's palanquin. The fragrance of the place—a compound of oak and tallow smoke, spilled Gravamen, steam from the piecemeal being boiled into simile, fierce margravine sauce, wet boots, and wet dogs—seemed to have an element he could not name, soon to be gone forever.

He took another swallow of Gravamen and noted that it gave him no more courage than he had had before, and finally said, "It seems we have an adventure to undertake. I have misgivings, I freely admit, and I would not have anyone come along who does not want to be there with all his heart . . . or hers," he added hastily (because Calliope, having again forgotten that she was supposed to be "Cal," was glaring at him), "so if we may delay by one bare hour, we can agree that any who are not here at the end of that hour need not come along, and that we will take no notice of comings and goings until that time."

One of Golias's low, dark brows shot far up onto his forehead at that point. No one ever really knew what Golias thought, for he generally seemed to be on all sides of all questions all the time, but the alchemist smiled a small, tight smile of utter satisfaction and grim purpose. "An eminently sensible plan. Let us then have our hour to sing, to eat, and to consider . . . and then we will go, assuming any of us are here."

The hour that followed seemed to fly by, and it must be said that Golias had never played the palanquin so well before, nor had so many of the old songs thundered forth so lustily.

Pell Grant went first, her fingers reluctantly slipping away from Sir John's broad shoulders, his hand clasping her little one before she went out the door of the Gray Weasel and down Byway to some other place.

Only a little later, Duke Wassant stood, bowed, smiled sadly, and said, "Sirs—I could avail myself of the sop to honor you've thrown out, but I do not spare myself my awareness of what I am doing. I am at your service whenever it is a matter of importance to the Kingdom, and in any point touching my real interests or yours. But it occurs to me that I have been along on many scrapes before this, and I detect in myself the first early traces of growing old, fat, and fond of comfort. I shall perhaps be sad in the morning that I decided to admit this, and a little wistful not to have been along when and if you return full of stories, but the fact is that a warm bed, and knowing that I shall rise from it to eat a good breakfast and have a day to use as I wish tomorrow, outweighs the thrill I feel. So I am away, and you may think it cowardice if you wish, but I trust you as my friends to understand it is merely a matter of not feeling a need for unnecessary danger."

"It is understood absolutely," Amatus said, rising and extending his hand. His own voice was unexpectedly deep and solid and from the corner of his eye he saw that eyebrow shoot up on Golias's face again, perhaps even accompanied by a trace of a nod.

Something in his manner must have touched Duke Wassant, as well, for instead of taking the hand and shaking it as might have been expected, with a low flourish he bowed and kissed the extended fingers. When he stood again, there was something of a salute in his manner, and under his cloak the Prince bowed, acknowledging it.

The room was distinctly colder, the fire glowed sad red rather than lively orange, and the spilled Gravamen smelled more sour after the Duke flung his long scarlet cloak about his shoulders, pulled the broad brim of his plumed hat low over his face, and strode out into the sleet. He was gone up Wend toward the Carpenter's Square in an instant.

"Time remains in the hour," Slitgizzard said, "and I prefer we keep all of it—but I will remain."

"And I," Calliope said.

Prince Amatus sat back down, carefully making sure that his cloak concealed the absence of his left side as much as anything could. What had come over him in that moment with the Duke? It had felt right and good, but now that it was gone, he felt tired and young.

"We will stay out the hour," he said softly. "And I would like to hear any song as long as it is of love and spring, and not spilled blood and night, and most especially as long as it is not 'Penna Pike.'"

Golias bent to his palanquin and plucked away at "The Codwalloper's Daughter," but though his voice was deep and true and the poetry as beautiful as the subject was bawdy, some of the color was gone from the Gray Weasel, and the sleet outside spattered harder in a nasty cold tattoo that mocked but never matched the tempo of the alchemist's strumming.

All the same, the Prince did not call for it to stop, but looked around as if drinking up all the sight and sound and smell he could while the last of the sand in the hourglass ran out, and even felt in his throat the words that would cry out for a few more minutes, or one more song, or one more glass . . . he fought them down, because he knew they would come in a boy's breaking voice, but it *was* a fight, and he knew, too, that he only won it because the boy inside him wanted to be fought down.

Just as the last strains of "The Codwalloper's Daughter" were bouncing around in the rafters, and Calliope pulled her boots off the table, and Sir John wetted his lips to speak, there was an all but unbearable moment when Amatus wanted more than ever to say, "One more dance of the shadows on the wall, one more merry tune, one more hoisted glass—"

And at that moment three figures, disguised, entered the taboret, and were recognized instantly, for even in long cloaks and many garments and veils, there was no mistaking the tall, thin woman whose skin was covered with scales and pale blue, or the huge, lumpy misshapenness of the man, and given that much, who else could the dark-haired, soft-faced youth in page's clothing beside him be but Psyche? The other three Companions had come, punctual at the time, and though Amatus could still feel the longing for this to be any other night, he knew now that it was time to go, and the dull ache of anticipated nostalgia no longer had any power over him. He rose silently, drawing his cloak tighter about him, and Sir John, Calliope, and Golias did as well, and then the seven of them were out in the icy, damp, windy streets, headed down toward the faint fishy foulness of the river.

If any saw them pass, it was only by peeking through the

slats of shutters, and no one would have had even one slat open if it could be helped, on such a night. They passed out of the Hektarian Quarter and on down Wend past the sweeping arches and pinnacles of the houses of the Vulgarians and among the little stupors where on pleasant summer days they had often stopped for tea. Following torches held aloft by Golias, Sir John, and the Twisted Man, at last they came to the place in the riverside walls where the city sewers poured into the Long River below them.

"It so happens," Golias said, "that I brought a rope along, although when I brought it I did not know what for."

The Twisted Man went first, handing his torch to Calliope and climbing down into the near-complete darkness, and Amatus was never sure afterward whether he had seen the Captain of the Guard descend, or whether he had merely caught moments when the twisting, bucking rope passed through blots of dim torchlight.

It would have been natural for someone else to go next, but before anyone had a chance Amatus had drawn on the heavy glove he carried with him for such occasions and was sliding down the line to the bottom. He had seen how the rope swayed under the Twisted Man, but nothing had prepared him for the wild way it whipped in and out of the darkness, sometimes swinging into the great sewer-mouth, and sometimes far out over the river, or for the heart-stopping slips every time his grip loosened. As he neared the bottom, the line began to steady, and with an almost-gentle bump his foot touched the slimy pavement.

"You might have steadied the line," he said to the Twisted Man.

"You did not need it. Those who follow will, so give me your hand here." Their three hands took up slack in the line.

"You're quite the bodyguard," Amatus said, not liking the whining tone he noticed in his own voice, and regretting it instantly.

"I'm not. I'm a mysterious Companion." The Twisted Man's voice rasped like a file screaming against a grindstone. "That's what the tale calls for. And if I were anything else, I would be the Captain of the Guard, and I would be carrying you home to your father and administering a sound spanking. Fortunately I have no taste for administrative duties and your father has a keen understanding of what goes into the making of princes."

"Enough chatter. The others are coming down. Slitgizzard will come last, so that he can help others onto the line," said Mortis's voice behind them.

Amatus knew better than to ask the Royal Witch how she had gotten there; possibly she had flown or just walked through some little fold in the world. So he nodded acknowledgment and braced his foot.

The first one down was Calliope, scrambling down and yanking the rope in all directions. Amatus helped catch her at the bottom, his open hand pressing upward to stop her, then letting her slide down into his arm, and enjoyed it a great deal. Psyche came quickly and lightly, barely moving the rope; Golias clambered after, more clumsily because he was stout. Finally Sir John Slitgizzard made his quick, neat descent, and they were ready for their journey into the dark wet spaces under the city.

5

Rational Beast and Rationalizing Royalty

*F*or a long time there was no need to speak, and so they only followed the torch that Golias held aloft, and glanced at each other now and then. Mortis was calm as ever, and now that they were belowground had thrown back the hood of her cloak so that her white hair and blue skin shone in the near darkness. Golias, John Slitgizzard, and the Twisted Man all seemed to be waiting calmly for something, and Amatus decided it must be because they were more experienced adventurers than he. He tried to act like them but all he could manage was a moment or so of it between his heart lurching at shadows and walking along as if he were trailing behind his father at some boring Court function.

Behind him, Calliope and Psyche walked; he didn't look back because he was afraid that either they would be cowering, and seeing them his own nerve would break, or that they would look more brave and unconcerned than he felt.

They had walked for a long time before they saw any signs of goblins. Since Boniface had given him the army, Cedric had been systematic and efficient about goblin control, and nowadays it was only a rare one who came to the surface, usually on a dare, and usually doing only slight harm, writing something scurrilous on a wall or dumping the milk sitting by someone's door. As they neared Goblin Country, they could see by-products of goblin control; skeletons of goblins and pieces of armor and escrees appeared around every bend. The skulls were the worst of it, for the torchlight flickered in the eye-holes so that for a moment a light would seem to dance in the skull's eyes, as if it were about to speak.

They were hideous, with jaws as prognathous as a bull-dog's, and bony ridges around the snoutlike noses. The skull seemed to slope straight back from the heavy brow ridges, and the bony crest down its middle was spiked and bumpy.

And those eye sockets—strange how your gaze kept returning to them—were round and deep as wells.

Amatus kept walking, deciding that if his courage was going to desert him, he would just have to go on without it.

Finally they came to a crumbling, rotten wood bridge across a deep crack in the tunnel floor. Before it there stood a wooden gate, and at the gate was a small, hairy goblin, unusually ugly, and with a glint of malice in his eyes that must have made even the other goblins nervous.

"Your business?"

Amatus remembered from Golias's lessons that you had to tell the truth in Goblin Country. So he said, "We are here to rescue a maid held here for many centuries."

"Oh, her. Sure, have a shot. Haven't had anybody except the occasional ambitious commoner in ages. Not even many of them. There are just seven of you?"

"Yes."

"And will there be seven coming out?"

At first he was going to answer "Yes," then "No, eight," then he realized, and said, "I have no way of knowing."

The goblin's eyes glinted with disappointment. "Very well, then. You might say you've passed a preliminary test. All right, advance through the gate, and then go across the bridge where the Riddling Beast will ask you your riddle."

The bridge swayed alarmingly and pieces occasionally broke off and tumbled far, far down into the black depths of the crevice. "This is the sort of bridge that someone might have to hold in a story," Amatus muttered to Golias.

"It is—whoops!" The bridge jumped sideways for a moment. "It is indeed. I rather assume it has been before and will be again. But not every prop is used in every story . . . surely you know that rule of magic as well. It may be here purely for atmosphere."

A bit of railing fell from under Calliope's hand and spiraled slowly downward until it was completely out of sight; two long breaths later, the sound of it whacking against stone reached their ears, and then a series of bangs and thuds as it made its way down into the depths.

"Enough!" Mortis shouted. They all jumped at the sound, and if the bridge had continued to sway it might have thrown one of them off, but abruptly it had become steady as stone and broad as the King's own highway. Moreover, the murk seemed to dispel, and they could see down into the depths far enough to perceive that the chasm was unpleasantly far to fall but by no means bottomless.

Mortis permitted herself a cold smile. "Golias provided the clue. This bridge was either important to the story or it was atmosphere. If the latter, it would be dispensed with as soon as there was enough of it. The word of power is the one that finishes a thing that wants to be true. I thought 'Enough' might be such a word of power in this case. One can count on nothing in this place, but some things that do not matter are easily dispelled."

They advanced across the wide, safe bridge and waited for the Riddling Beast. After a moment, there was a great rumble in the echoing cavern, and a furry head halfway in appearance between a bear's and a snake's, with jaws big enough to crush six men whole, poked around the rock on a long, dark-furred neck. On both sides of the huge rock, the leathery batwings could be seen spreading out. "What is it that goes on four legs in the morning, shaves the barber at noon, and crosses the road at evening, and what does it have in its pockets?"

"Myself and my own things," Amatus said at once.

"Your party may pass. Good job, by the way, most people need all three guesses. Best of luck up ahead."

"Do you suppose he'd have been so pleasant while eating us?" Calliope whispered to Amatus.

"Not at all," the Beast whispered, grinning. "Human tastes perfectly horrible. I have to force it down and it puts me out of sorts for weeks."

They proceeded up the road into Goblin Country. Now the corpseworms above and around them gave off a pale green light, and they were able to see more than enough. Goblin lords on litters raced by them, goblin merchants rode by with baskets full of goods, and in general there seemed to be goblins everywhere, though none took any notice of them.

After a long time, Calliope asked, "How did you know the answer to that riddle?"

"Practice and training," Amatus said. "Golias told me that whenever you are asked such a question, the answer is always yourself. The question about the pockets was the one that made me edgy."

"It was well answered in any case," John Slitgizzard said. "And it begins to give me hope that it went so well; plainly this is not the sort of quest I had feared it was, where loyal henchmen perish at every peril."

Amatus shuddered, for he knew there were such quests, and only then did he realize that this could have turned out to be one of them, and that Calliope and Slitgizzard had come along anyway. Even more than before he felt himself to be the coward of the party.

They had just begun to wonder if there was a turnoff they should have taken when they came to a sign: "To the Goblin Court."

"Odd that they use our language," Calliope said.

"It is the kind of creatures they are," Golias explained. "They make nothing. They only use that which others make."

The road to the Goblin Court was more trail than road, for it was little used. The goblins relished civil disorder too much to pay taxes to suppress it, and therefore the Goblin Court was less a seat of government than an expensive play-pen where prominent goblins sent their less capable offspring in hopes of accruing some political advantage. It was thus the home of every wastrel, ne'er-do-well, amiable idiot, effete malignant prankster, petty untalented sadist, dimwitted flirt, small-minded gossip, amoral boonmonger, and vicious sexual conquistador or conquistadora in Goblin Country, and wiser goblins stayed away from it as if it had been an asylum for the malodorous, which in a sense it was. Had the Terracottas, the royal line in the goblins, not been so erotically insatiable as to litter the goblin population with illegitimate children, they might well have died out long ago, for to be sane enough to rule they had to be capable of feeling what dreadful company they were forced to keep.

All of this Golias explained in a hasty whisper to Amatus, as they passed through the long row of gibbets from which hung the thoroughly gnawed skeletons—or scraps of skeletons—of men, goblins, and things that might never have been alive at all. The trail stank of charnel. Parts of corpses lay on the trail and they were forced to pick their way among them.

When Calliope accidentally touched a dead hand with the tip of her boot, it grabbed her toe and had to be kicked off into the mess at the roadside, and when Sir John slipped on a slimy patch and caught himself by stepping on a skeletal forearm, it turned and grasped at him with its few remaining phalanges as if he had stepped on a viper in the forest.

"Ha," Golias said at that. "I see the game now." From his cloak he drew a short stick of wood with a bit of cloth tied to the end, and a tiny vial which he poured over the end of the little stick. Instantly the stick and its bit of cloth grew into a broom, which stood upright in front of them for one moment, then began to advance up the trail, sweeping fiercely, clearing the path of the corpse pieces.

"One must be careful how one walks in Goblin Country," Golias explained. "Not so much to walk in any particular way as to avoid walking in a particular way; there's a pattern that sets it all off. In this case some sort of spell laid out in the bare spaces between the disgusting objects."

The broom, having cleared the trail for some distance in front of them, turned around and bumped up and down impatiently.

With a guilty laugh, Golias followed it. Amatus chuckled himself, knowing full well that the alchemist might have spent hours discoursing on the nature of pathways of malice and how they were laid out, and of the making and use of magic brooms.

In a short time, they rounded a bend to find themselves in a great, vaulted ci.... iber, obviously copied inexpertly from some building in the world up above. Their entrance caused a great hubbub, with goblin courtiers and ladies rushing everywhere to be seen to be in the right places.

The walk up the aisle was worse by far than the trail among the gibbets had been. The goblins at Court were for the most part mad, and entirely vicious, and being goblins they were an affront even to their own eyesight. Moreover the goblins at Court dressed in copies of the finery of the world above, cut and recut to reveal and emphasize whatever this particular goblin's distortion was. Here a cluster of vestigial arms in the middle of the chest had been set off with a décolletage as if the goblin lady were a human woman with a fine bosom; there a ruff graced the top of a hump on a courtier; everywhere, there were ever-flowing sores, the clothing cut away around them and sometimes sewn into the living flesh so that an open spot of raw flesh seemed to stick directly out of a rent.

Sir John swore softly under his breath, looked straight ahead as much as he could, and kept his left hand under his coat, near the swash that held three pismires and his pongee, and his right hand conspicuously upon the hilt of his escree. Psyche knelt a moment to adjust her boot, and steel glinted where she made sure the concealed throwing knives could be drawn in an instant. Amatus himself let his hand fall to the hilt of his own escree, and from the many motions he saw under the Twisted Man's cloak he suspected there was a census of armaments being taken.

The king and Queen—she was the real Terracotta, he a bastard upstart who had married her because she was his half sister—were not so deliberately or cruelly disgusting to look at, but the horrible mad stare of the Queen, with its mixture of will to hurt and stupid coquettishness, was bad enough.

"Why do you intrude upon our Court?" the King growled sternly at Golias.

"My master will speak of that," Golias said, "and you will listen, and then we will have what we seek."

The words sounded formal, and Amatus wished he had read more about diplomatic protocol, for they sounded more like the sort of thing one had to say in the Goblin Court than like a formal courtesy. But after all, to go anywhere with Golias was to wish one had read more, so Amatus plunged directly into the subject. "You hold among you a human maiden, a subject of the Kingdom, and her family having failed in her rescue, we seek her now."

"She is no maiden now, for we have raped her until she ceased to fight, then until she ceased to care, and finally till she lies and grunts for more of it like a sow," the Queen said.

"That is a singularly clumsy lie," Golias replied. "Being what you are, you obey laws more stringent than humans do, and you are not capable of so defiling her, however you may have heaped her with filth and forced her to live in foul confinement. Had your goblins attempted her rape, they would have died in the attempt, for a mockery of real flesh such as yourselves may not touch the real thing of power that is a maiden. This is written down in many books, some of them by me."

There was a long pause, and a great rumbling as the Queen clenched her shaking fists in fury and the ceiling began to tremble. Stone plunged in among the courtiers and ladies, and with a soft, squashy crunch, one goblin lady was knocked to the ground, her legs and lower back shattered by a boulder. She shrieked, then began to sob in agony; those around her began to point and laugh, except for a few who sat down next to her and wept, having a wonderful time with their sympathy, and a thin one who began to eat her hand. No one made the slightest move to help, until, with a grunt of disgust, Sir John Slitgizzard drew his pismire, cocked the chutney, set the lovelock, pointed it, and squeezed the trigger.

The pismire made a solid boom, and its heavy ball killed the goblin lady instantly. Amatus felt like coughing from the sulphurous smoke, but dignity forced him to draw breath slowly and carefully.

"It was bad enough she was suffering," said the Queen, "but now you have slain her." A greasy tear trickled down the Queen's cheek, matting the patches of hair. "I feel this strongly. We could almost be said to have suffered together, she and I, for I am a very tenderhearted queen and I do not like to see such hurts done."

The king sat up straight and thundered, "Who are you that you dare to slay the ladies of my Court before my eyes?"

Amatus noted that the ceiling failed to move for the King's wrath. If he had not known already, he would have been quite sure by now where real power rested.

"The stones fell from the Queen's anger," Golias said.

Now the Goblin Queen turned entirely white between the clumps of hair on her face, and her hands pounded the arms of her throne, and she shrieked, "I am not an angry person."

Rock and plaster fell like lightning into the crowd, but none fell among Amatus's friends or Companions, for they stood near the throne, and none fell upon the King or Queen. Everywhere ladies and courtiers scuttled for cover.

"You are upsetting the Queen!" the King declaimed.

"Give us the maiden and we will be gone," Amatus said.

The Queen's eyes narrowed. "You will obey all the conditions."

Golias's voice never rose in pitch or volume, but it was steady and sure. "We will never look behind us, never speak, never hold back or cringe, and never draw weapons unless and until one of our number is struck. We accept those conditions and choose to obey them voluntarily, knowing that you are a liar, knowing that you will cheat, because the life of the Prince's subject—aboveground and free—is more to him than the risk of your foul treachery. You but delay the inevitable. Give us the maiden."

"Turn your backs and she will follow."

"Show her to us, show her free to follow us, and then we will turn our backs."

The Queen curled upon her throne and wept that she did not know why she was not trusted, it was not fair, no one understood how hard it was to be Queen, and the King ineffectually patted her shoulders and shouted at them to leave her alone.

The Queen, sniffling, murmured that if they would all kiss her and say they were sorry, she would be willing to forgive them and to give them the maiden without conditions of any kind, but Golias pointed out that it was not in her power to release them from the conditions.

Finally, the Queen sat and sullenly stared at the floor, and the king commanded that the maiden be brought forth, but since all the courtiers and ladies had fled, and none was willing to venture back into the Court until they were sure the Queen would have no more outbursts (they could all be heard just outside the doors, hanging on to each other, weeping with fear, and assuring each other that nothing would happen), the king had to go and get her himself.

While he did, the Queen brightened up a great deal. "We so seldom get visitors here, and it's a shame because we're really nice people when you get to know us. Would you care for anything to eat or drink?"

"No," Amatus said, firmly. He was hungry and thirsty, but not for goblin food.

"We have galleries and galleries of paintings, and since we are so long-lived—that lady of my Court you murdered, poor thing, I can still see the look of pain on her face, but never mind that, we won't talk of what's unpleasant—since we are so long-lived, as I said, such a pity she died so young, centuries only, a child really, but we won't talk of that or of the sort of people you bring with you—since we are so long-lived, in those galleries there are no doubt pictures of your ancestors and your origins, really very interesting . . ."

"I am interested in looking at such things, but only on my own terms, and when it comes time I will come and take them and arrange them as I wish, burning the ones that never happened," Amatus said. He was beginning to itch, and he felt as if tiny apes were crawling over his body, smacking their microscopic lips at the drops of his cold sweat, trailing their miniscule dirty feet upon his skin, probing with little unclean teeth at his soft and vulnerable places as if waiting to bite down.

"As you wish. You always get what you want, I see. You make me very proud to have known you." She writhed around on the throne, brushing the fur of her face and straightening her gown, for all the world as if she were primping. "I don't see why you have to be so unpleasant when you're succeeding in everything you try."

The king returned with the maiden. She looked as if she had only been down there a day or so, and since time passes strangely in Goblin Country, that was probably all the time that had passed for her; it must have seemed a scant hour or so since her lover had come to rescue her and found himself wanting. She had probably not even slept since her kidnapping.

"Hello," she said, with a certain dignity. "You must be my rescuers."

Amatus moved forward to her, and there on the filthy floor of the Goblin Court, he threw back his cloak, revealing his half body, and knelt in the gunge, letting it stain his knee, knowing the gunge would wash off but the honor would not. He took her grime-spattered hand and kissed it, as if she were a grand lady of his own Court, and not at all as if she were what she was—a plump commoner girl, her face plain, teeth crooked, and nose splayed across her face. "Maiden," he said, "I honor you for what you have borne."

She blushed a deep red and said, "You can't go calling me 'maiden' all the way. My name is Sylvia."

"Isn't it remarkable what he's accomplished despite not having any left side?" the Queen commented. "And all for a fat girl of—well, let's just say her family is no doubt a challenge she overcame to get to where she is today. I do hope he won't do anything to dishonor her afterwards, though one could hardly blame him if he did, commoner girls really are practically pigs and they do whelp so easily, I'm sure I shouldn't have said that, you'll have to pardon me since I don't really know *what* I am saying half the time—"

"Shut up," Calliope said. When Psyche and Amatus turned to look at her, their eyes met across Calliope, and Amatus saw that Psyche, too, had been listening to the Goblin Queen more than she should. It was terribly difficult not to.

As if Calliope had broken some spell, Golias spoke up. "Sylvia, we honor your endurance, but there are conditions you must endure more. You must follow us, and we cannot look back at you. We cannot speak, even if you cry out for help, and the goblins will doubtless imitate your voice and cry out, even if you do not; you may dispute with them, but we will not be able to tell on which side your real voice comes. We must not cringe or hold back in our motion, so you must keep up with us, and it would be well if you did not cry out when you are frightened, lest one of us cringe because of it. Finally, we may not draw weapons until one of us is struck, so even should you see treachery, do not shout to warn us of it, for we might not be able to resist the temptation to draw rather than wait for the first blow to fall. Should they betray us, their first stroke or shot releases all conditions, and then you must run forward to join our group as quickly as possible.''

"I understand," she said.

"The conditions are awfully hard," the Queen added, "and I don't think you should even try until the rules are changed. I'm sure you can do it if you feel hope enough in your heart, but the conditions are so unfair that really—"

"Shut up," Amatus was able to say.

On the way out, the goblin king walked next to Amatus for a while, urging him to come back and patch matters up with the Queen, for surely they would be safer if they parted on good terms. The king himself was honorable, no question, and the Queen was too, once you got to know her you realized she didn't really lie at all, just told the truth her own way, but some of her courtiers might well misinterpret some remark of hers as a suggestion for something dishonorable, and if they did you would have to expect that they might do something . . .

It went on for a long time, during which Amatus longed to hear some other sound and was unable to tell the king to be quiet. The only sound besides the king's deep bass voice (which broke frequently into a kind of a whine) was the scuffing of the broom ahead of them as it cleared corpse parts from the trail. At last, they regained the main road, and with a cheerful "Well, you know, we get few visitors and we're glad you came—do visit again, and have a nice day, it must be close to daybreak up above," the king was gone.

Sylvia's voice screamed in terror and pain.

6

One for the Morning Glory

*A*matus made his step not hesitate. He kept walking, and after a moment he heard Sylvia say, "That was a goblin who is walking beside me—"

"Ouch! Ouch! He's hurting me!" the same voice said.

"And I expect he'll do it all the way up to the surface—"

"He's imitating my voice so you won't help me! Ouch! Ouch! Help! Help!"

The road was long, and this time the only goblins were in the dark behind them. Above their heads, odd shapes of stalactites stuck down into the light of Golias's torch, and though there was no wind in the airless dank, the flame danced and bobbed as if fighting back the dark, and shadows moved overhead in eerie shapes.

After a while the goblins tired of that game, and began instead to throw rocks far over the party's heads, clattering down on the road a long way in front of them. Every time they threw, they would shriek in Sylvia's voice "Look out!" or "Watch out!" or "Careful!"

The first few times it was unnerving, but then as it ceased to have much effect the goblins tried to make it work by doing more of it, for goblins have no aesthetic sense and so always think that if something worked once, surely more of it will work now. As a result, soon the great caverns echoed with a hideous cacophany of Sylvia shrieking behind them and rocks clattering to the roadway in front of them. The number of Sylvias shouting warnings was now so large that if the real one had done so, they would never have known, and after a while the implausibility of the situation began to affect Amatus.

Trying to fight down a giggle, he glanced sideways at Calliope, only to discover that she too was ready to laugh, and when he glanced away he caught John Slitgizzard's eye, and it was already straining with laughter, and so was Psyche's—and that was all, for all of them. They were not permitted to speak, not to look back, but nothing prohibited their laughing, and they did, good and loud and long.

The silence as they stopped laughing was astonishing. They continued to walk, and only the crunch of their boots told them that even they were alive in those huge spaces.

The bridge came into sight, and there was still no sign of anything or anyone. The Riddling Beast nodded in a friendly, businesslike way, not at all concerned with people going out, and as they walked by him even wagged his tail. They all scratched his head, especially around the ears (it took two of them to really scratch one ear well), and the beast was evidently delighted. Behind them they heard Sylvia scratch his head too, and heard him warn the goblins to stay well back. Presently she was behind them again, on the bridge, and the Riddling Beast called after them, "They have not touched her, and she is quite unhurt."

There was still no trouble.

On the other side of the bridge, as they passed the goblin who stood watch over the gateway, he said, "Please state your business and reason for leaving Goblin Country." He sounded bored.

Golias did not answer, but kept walking, for they had to reach daylight before they could speak. The others followed along behind him, also not speaking.

The goblin repeated the question, several times, shouting it the last couple of times, and they kept walking.

There was a bitter, icy hiss by Amatus's ear, and the heavy black shaft of a crossbow bolt protruded from the middle of Golias's back. With a great cry of despair, the alchemist fell forward, his hands reaching out to claw at the icy stone, the slick gunge smearing his face and beard. His torch landed in the gunge and went out; now there was only the light of the corpseworms.

Amatus whirled to see the keeper of the gate reloading his crossbow. "Sorry, rules are rules—" he began, with a poison-ous smile spreading across his face for just an instant before the Twisted Man's pongee buried itself in the goblin's left eye to the hilt.

Sylvia was racing forward to them, and behind her goblins in dozens and hundreds, armed to the fangs and roaring with glee, were pouring across the bridge. Unthinkingly, Amatus's hand reached under his cloak and found the first of his brace of three pismires, and he cocked the heavy bronze chutney, then set the lovelock with a soft click, as he drew the weapon.

"Steady, steady, use it when you're sure it will count," Sir John murmured beside him.

"Just like the target range," the Twisted Man's bass voice boomed on his other side. Next to him, he saw Calliope take up her place and draw her pismire as well.

And back behind it all, he could hear the gasping and the bubbling coughs of Golias as Psyche, Mortis, and Sylvia tried to ease his agony.

The goblins drew steadily nearer, their nostrils visibly twitching, tongues lapping out around their teeth, for though they liked anything that suffered as they ate it, they liked the taste of man-flesh best.

The goblins were ill-armed, with an assortment of rusty implements mostly stolen from the surface. There were many generals and field marshals, to judge by the uniforms, wielding everything from a crude omnibus at least two centuries old (harmless except as a club, for it was being held by the barrel) to a garden rake. These were the same sycophants who had previously distinguished themselves as nobility; most of them were in the rear rank, using their weapons to prod the "common soldiers" forward.

The first rush took a long time for the goblins to prepare. For a moment Amatus thought that perhaps they should take advantage of this to grab Golias and run for the surface, but next to him the Twisted Man, as if he had heard the Prince's thoughts, whispered, "With goblins, if you show them your back they'll have you sure. Now when they come at us"—he raised his voice just a bit so the others could hear— "aim for the hungry ones out front, those will be the ones they've kept in pens and starved, who are truly dangerous. And Sir John, if you could find me the three of their generals who seem most proficient at pressing them on—the ones who are doing the best job of frightening the middle rank—and shoot me those three—"

"Gladly," Slitgizzard said.

"Aim low," the Twisted Man added. "They're short, and besides that way if you miss or if the ball carries on through, something else may be struck."

Behind them, Sylvia and Psyche grunted and struggled to get Golias into a position where he could breathe. Beside them Mortis chanted the Septicemia, seventh of the Great Spells, said to be powerful against venom of all kinds. Every so often a little rough breath indicated that the alchemist was hanging on to life. After one such breath, the whole cavern seemed to become utterly still, except for the spat-spat-spat of a few stalactites dripping water onto the stone. Amatus heard the Twisted Man exhale, slowly.

The goblins lurched forward, propelled mostly by the clubs and blades behind them. The front rank ran straight at them, with no hint of cunning or tactics, only the passionate desire to sink teeth into flesh. Beside him, Amatus heard the Twisted Man's pismire boom, and bracing himself and taking careful aim, Amatus discharged his own into one onrushing goblin. Not pausing to see what the effect had been, he drew the second pismire from his swash, cocked its chutney, and fired again, striking down another goblin, and swift as thought used his final pismire, slaying a third. He had been aware that the Twisted Man and Calliope had also been firing quickly, and as he drew his escree, he had just time for a glance to see that there were other bodies lying dead, and that Sir John's shooting had opened up a hole in the goblin rear through which the middle rank had begun to flee.

Then they were rushing in on him. None of them were over four feet tall, and none of them did more with their weapons than swing them wildly, but there were so many that it was still dangerous. He was forced to do nothing but work as if in the simplest sorts of escree drill, striking out as swiftly as he could to stop each attacker. He had no idea how many he had wounded and how many had leapt back. He knew that many had already fled, but what were left now were the hunger-maddened ones.

It might have been minutes or days that went by in the dim light of the corpseworms. He slashed and thrust over and over, sucking in great breaths of dank, icy air and feeling the hot sweat pour down his arm, knowing his arm was too tired to continue and making it do so anyway.

Then the Twisted Man beside him gave a great shout, smashed down hard once with his escree butt, and dove and grabbed something from the ground. A moment later, when the giant stood, he had a goblin upside down in one hand, grasped by the ankles, his one huge fist audibly shattering the leg bones of the screaming, wriggling goblin.

"Unarmed! Cannot fight back! Arm is broken!" the Twisted Man shouted, waving the wailing, sobbing goblin around over his head by its heels as if he were an unusually cruel midwife for an unusually ugly baby. "Eat! Eat! Eat!"

He hurled the shrieking goblin, with an overhand motion that must have broken its ankles, right over the goblin mob and onto the stone behind it. The goblins whirled and converged on it at once, and its shrieks, sobs, and pleas for mercy echoed through the cavern, along with crunch of teeth on its bones and the wet tearing of its flesh.

Before Amatus could think what to do next, the Twisted Man had charged forward to the edge of the mob around the goblin who was being eaten, grabbed an unwary goblin from the back of the crowd, hammerlocked it, and forced it to drop its weapon. In another moment, he had broken its limbs and hurled another helpless goblin to its cannibal fellows, and both the screams and the chewing sounds grew louder.

He began to repeat the process; goblin hunger, after a long fast, is nearly bottomless, and so within the space of mere moments, the Twisted Man had fed all but one of them to each other. This last, bloated, helpless one managed a few tentative snaps at the Twisted Man's ankle before he kicked and rolled it to the edge of the precipice and flipped it over. It fell for a short way, though the illusion made it seem long, but far enough to burst into an undigested mess when it struck bottom.

They turned and hurried back to Golias. Psyche had drawn the bolt and stopped the bleeding, but it had been tipped with cold gunge from the floor itself, and the alchemist's face was turning a deep green.

"The wound is near the spine," John Slitgizzard said. "He may die if we move him."

"I will surely die if you do not," Golias said, his voice a soft bubbling. "And I think I shall die in any case. I would rather do it in sunlight if I can."

"Take him up," the Twisted Man said. "Gently—and with all care. Sir John and I will bring the bridge down, or hold it for a time if we cannot."

"The bridge stinks of spells," Mortis said. "I will have to remain with you. Amatus, most of the burden will be yours."

"I can bear it," he said, and bent to raise the alchemist onto his shoulder, heaving him up with the help of Calliope and Sylvia.

He could feel his friend's hot breath on his neck, and a warm, sticky place forming on his back.

"Let's go, then," he said.

He was surprised at how light Golias was. Amatus seemed almost able to walk normally while carrying the alchemist, and needed only occasional help from Calliope or Sylvia to keep the alchemist from sliding into an awkward position.

They walked swiftly. Psyche had lighted a torch and carried it in front of them. Calliope, with her own pismires and those of Amatus, guarded their rear. Sylvia fussed and clucked at Golias, trying to make him more comfortable, but the alchemist seemed to be unconscious again.

It seemed beyond belief to Amatus that they had entered the dark, wet, cold regions under the city scant hours ago, that the day before he had sat a whole afternoon in the sun with no smell of things long dead about him, or that the wet, warm spittle spraying on his neck and the slight weight on his shoulder were all there was of Golias.

His mind seemed to pass into his senses, the feel of Golias's trim beard against his collarbone, the slightly heavy roll of the alchemist's inert, hanging head. He remembered Golias's patience with him, how the first time he had read a hard book all the way through, Golias had merely smiled at him, clapped him on the shoulder, and given him a harder one as a reward; the long hours fingering the palanquin and having to be shown again and again what was right, even if difficult; the way that, when Amatus finished a fine flourish of rhetoric that failed to answer the point in an argument, Golias's mouth would twitch up at the corner, and he would say, "*Quid ergo, Amate?*"

But these were the sorts of thoughts one thinks about someone who has died, and that seemed like bad luck. Amatus pushed himself harder. The breath on his neck was weak, fast, and fluttery.

Psyche gave a little cry of joy. A moment later Amatus felt brick pavement under his feet.

They rushed on, and as they did Calliope whistled a soft warning that changed to another glad cry as Mortis, Slitgizzard, and the Twisted Man raced up to join them. "The bridge is down," Mortis said. "It will be a long time before it is raised again."

Sir John explained. "On my lady's advice, we allowed her to make one small hole in the magic around the bridge, and we cut through it there. It could never have been done at all but for the strength and fury of the Twisted Man, but we left the spells in place and brought it down by nothing except hard work—so now *only that* will bring it up again. It will be a long time before it is up again, if we may judge how the goblins feel about hard work."

The Twisted Man added, "And you should know also, Highness, that Mortis was able to alter the spell so that the Riddling Beast faces the other way, to keep goblins in rather than humans out."

"He was delighted with the change of purpose," Slitgizzard added. "Likes the taste of goblin better."

"But everyone knows the answer to his riddle," Amatus said. He was only half listening to them; the main thing was to get Golias into sunlight.

Mortis's voice was all but smug. "No goblin can easily answer a question whose answer is 'myself and the things that are mine.' So I would say it will be long years ere we hear of them again by that gate."

Golias's weight was growing lighter on his back, but Amatus noted with alarm that there was no breath—then just a tiny sigh—a gasp—and then again, no breath.

"I could carry him if you are tired," Sir John offered, but the Twisted Man said, "No, there is strength and perhaps healing in the touch of a prince, and no one else could carry him more swiftly." The deep voice boomed, for they were now fully into the tunnel through which the city's sewer ran. They could hear tinklings and tricklings as little pipes opened into the broad, deep trough to their left.

Psyche's torch dimmed for an instant as she went around a bend in front of them, and she gave a short cry of triumph. They rounded the corner and saw, down at the end of the great tunnel, the bursting of dancing, waving light reflecting from the river onto the tunnel ceiling—the sun was almost up and they were almost out.

In his ear, Golias sighed, "Not in the dark, *non in umbris sed in lucibus multis, Amate*—"

Amatus broke into a run, hurling himself forward. The alchemist now seemed to be able to take a little grip.

As they burst onto the broad stone platform, the sun leapt up from the river like a huge crimson ball, setting all the little waves aflame. Sir John spread his cloak in the sun, and gently Amatus lowered Golias onto it.

"Thank you most richly, Highness," the alchemist said. His voice was distant and weak. "In the light—remember—always in the light."

And then suddenly the weight, which had been airy and inconsequential against Amatus's back in that whole long carry through the foul dark, was so heavy against Amatus's supporting hand that the Prince was forced to gently lay Golias down. As if in a dream, he reached forward and closed the alchemist's eyes with the tips of his fingers.

As the others stood silently, there in the warming morning light, Amatus rose, looking down on his friend's dead face—

All of them cried out in surprise. Amatus stared at them. Calliope pointed, and Amatus looked down.

He still had no left side, nor any left leg, but there, standing on the ground beside him, right where it belonged, was what was unquestionably his left foot. It was even wearing a matching boot. He lifted it gingerly, found that he could move it, touched it to the floor and found he could feel his weight on it when he leaned.

As he looked around at the three survivors of his four Companions, he saw in their eyes that they understood and accepted, that this was what they had come for.

Then he wept, passionately and deeply, the way that men weep because they are men.

The sun continued to climb, on its way about the business of the world, and after a while all of them were also about various business, and if any of them ever spoke about that night again—except to Cedric, who interviewed them all—no record survives.

II

The Early Dew

I

The Prince in Black

O ne might have thought that Amatus would wear only somber black, not go out, and live in mourning for a long time. Boniface would have understood that, and insisted that others leave him alone until his grief began to heal.

Or one might have imagined that Amatus would instead throw himself into a more debauched and drunken life, trying desperately to forget what he had seen of death, lost in the wild parts of the city in sordid company, without the balancing hand of Golias to restrain him from the worst of it. Cedric would have understood that and protected him from his father's outrage.

One might even have imagined that Amatus would throw himself into his studies more deeply than ever before, and thus honor Golias's memory and work out his grief at the same time, perhaps threatening to become King Amatus the Scholar. Either Boniface or Cedric could have borne that.

What they could *not* bear was that he did all three. He dressed in black and drifted through the castle as if he had a murder to avenge, making Boniface nervous—especially since they had all grown accustomed to the sight of the youth with no left side, but to see him striding along accompanied by an otherwise unattached left boot was eerie.

Yet instead of sitting at windows with bitter ironic jests, or spurning the offered affection of Sir John and his other comrades, he barely seemed to notice anyone most days, walking about the corridors muttering, and then just when everyone was getting used to this, disappearing into the Royal Library. It was reported by Wyrna, who dusted those dark, candlesooted chambers, that he had been reading heavily in that dreaded work, *Highly Unpleasant Things It Is Sometimes Necessary to Know*, and that she was sure that under his elbow on the desk, unlocked, as if for reference, had been the blood-red leather-bound volume, *Things That Are Not Good to Know at All*.

And yet again, just when one might have expected him to have settled into a sensible obsession with the Black Arts, from which Mortis, as Royal Witch, might have been implored to rescue him, there would be tales of what else he had done—that late at night he would batter on Sir John Slitgizzard's door, or on Duke Wassant's, and that they would be off to drink and roister and roar the rips of the lower city.

Cedric had quietly put both young courtiers on his payroll, to report what the Prince spoke of and what he did, and when possible to get word to the Twisted Man so that he could follow them through the winding slimy-cobbled streets like a hideous shadow, making sure no harm came to the heir. And because Golias had been wise in his choices, and the two men, though bad enough in private matters, were true as steel to the Royal house, they reported all they saw, and it was such that Slitgizzard would shudder at the lewdness of the houses that Amatus now frequented, and Wassant would openly admit to being terrified at both the odds and the opponents Amatus found for duels.

At these accounts, Cedric would turn to the Twisted Man,

an eyebrow raised, and with a shrug under the folds of his cloak—a shrug that seemed to come from places you did not expect his shoulders to be—the Captain of the Guard would mutter, "Sir, I was in the shadows at the Prince's elbow, but truly, I had little fear for him, for he was a madman, and I myself would fear to face him now; I had more care to guard the Duke and Sir John."

Cedric would sigh, and Slitgizzard and Wassant would wish they had more words of comfort to speak to him, but they had none, and would return to their homes shaken with things they had seen the Prince do, and helped him to do, and wondering how much longer the rumors that there was a King Amatus the Wicked in the making could be kept down in the city. Often after one of those expeditions into the city night Sir John would give strict orders that his bed was to be ready an hour before sundown and that he was not to be woken until an hour after sunrise, so that he would see none of the night; just as often Duke Wassant would have his chambers dancing with the bright light of candles for the whole night afterwards, and would have his childhood nurse come in to sing and read to him.

If the Twisted Man felt anything from what was happening, he kept it to himself. Mortis, too, seemed to speak little of the matter, though Wyrna swore that the Royal Witch seemed sad, and would no longer go to the window to see the first rays of the morning sun, and often sat still in a way she had never done before.

Psyche sat in the sun, up in the Royal Solar, for many hours at a time, and sewed bright clothing for the Prince. She was the one, more than any seamstress, who had mastered the art of making clothing for his half-body. The cloaks she made were red as carnations, and the triolets as yellow as dandelions, and the breeches and hose alizarin, but as she finished each she sighed and put it into a cedar chest. The Royal Carpenter reported that he was making a new chest every three days, and the Chamberlain of the Royal Storage said that one new storeroom had filled with chests already.

It occurred to Cedric that perhaps Calliope could do some good; he went to her to ask for her help, but found she had already tried.

"He didn't hurt me," she said, as the two of them sat over tea on the High Terrace, overlooking the West Battue. "He had a haunted and ugly look, as if he'd been eating the wrong sort of things, and he glared at me. He—er, well, he stared at parts of me rudely, but it was, I think, the rudeness of some-one trying to drive me off, not any part of his nature. There was no hatred in him, and no lust, but he tried to put on both to get me to leave."

Cedric sighed. "The King worries about his son all day. Things run well enough, mind, because the Kingdom was in good order when this current problem started, but give it time, give it time, and surely it will deteriorate. May I ask— what sort of things—"

Calliope blushed, pushing her soft red hair back from her face, and Cedric abruptly remembered how young she was, but before he could stop her, she had looked up at him, blue eyes soft with hurt, and said, "Well, he—er, he stared hard at my . . . bosom, and told me that the worms ate the soft parts first."

A dark shadow fell across the table. They looked up to see the Prince standing over them.

"You are old, Cedric," he said, "and that is why a young girl blushes to mention her 'bosom' in front of you." (The sarcasm he applied to the word was the nastiest sound Cedric had heard, even with all his years receiving ambassadors and talking to government clerks). "But she trusts you with it all the same, because she is so young that she imagines that you, one foot in the grave as you are, have no more lurking lust in your flaccid old flesh. And she still fails to note that all flesh smells of the grave."

"You're ill," Cedric said quietly. "I am only glad that it is an illness that becomes a prince."

"Do you say I am mad?"

"*I* do," Calliope said, startling them both, and standing up. "I know your friend died. I know you didn't know it would happen and you'd never have gone down into the caverns if you knew it would.

"And I even know that you feel horrible because you got your foot back by his death and now you know that your other Companions will probably have to die—or maybe something even more horrible—before you can get back the rest of yourself, and you can't bear to lose your Companions. I feel terribly sorry for you, Amatus, and I can understand your being mad, but acting like a pig is not going to make it any better, and I don't see any reason to be around you while you act like a pig.

"If you want to come to my chamber and weep for six straight days, I'll listen to you and hold you as long as you allow me occasional food and sleep, or if you want me to go as your comrade on some impossible quest you may consider me packed, or if you want to go up in the mountains and howl at the moon for the next year I'll sit down here and wait for you to be better and never look at any other suitor, but I shall not take your abuse, no matter what is wrong with you."

She was out of the room before Cedric had even an instant to think. Part of the back of his mind elevated Calliope considerably as a possible Royal match; the Kingdom needed a good queen and he had just seen the makings of one.

He turned to Amatus and saw a half-face as hard as stone. "I am not the only mad person let loose in this castle," the Prince said quietly, "but I am the source of all the infections. I am sorry, Cedric. I am deeply sorry."

With that, the Prince turned and left. Cedric looked at the cold winter sunlight streaming in the windows, and quietly poured himself another cup of tea, and sat on the windowsill to drink it and to stare out over the city. He had been taking care of things for a long time, he realized, and as he looked at the bright multicolored roofs peeping through their snow-blankets, and the white buildings, many flying the Hand and Book flag, and the throngs running this errand and that, he felt a deep fear in him, for the health of the city was the health of the Kingdom, and the health of the Kingdom was the health of the Royal family—and he had just seen a great deal of its infection.

After a long time by himself, he left the room, and the winter sun sank, so that the shapes of the windows crept up the walls and ran across the ceiling and were gone, and the tea turned to a cold nastiness that the maid, the next morning, pitched from the window.

Meanwhile, Amatus made his way down the stairs, still feeling terribly sorry for himself, but also feeling that he had overdone this, and that like it or not it was time to begin to turn toward the air and the light.

First he stopped by the throne room and contritely—and briefly, because he was afraid he might lapse back into rude offensiveness—told his father that he was sorry for his recent behavior, and that he would be coming down to dinner tonight. King Boniface smiled at him, warmly at first, and then a slightly guarded expression passed over his face. By this, Amatus knew that he still did not look at all well.

Psyche was in the nursery, sitting quietly.

"I've come to apologize," Amatus said.

She smiled at him warmly. "You used to do that when you were little."

He had rarely been reminded that Psyche had been his nurse—he was used to thinking of her as a trusted servant of his own age—and now he came to her and sat at her feet, waving off her attempts to kneel. "How is it," he asked, "that you remain the same age? You are no different from what you were when I first saw you in the Throne Room, and now I'm grown—physically, anyway—half of me, anyway—and yet you don't look a day older."

She smiled at him, and there was mischief in it. "By the time you understand that, it will be the least important thing you understand. Promise you will think of me with love when you do understand."

He promised, and Psyche went to his closet and drew out a set of clothes she had hung there. "Royal purple, and deep blues, and some traces of red," she said. "Still sober as is proper, but not that dreadful black. You were not meant to be Prince Hamlet, my dear one."

She had not called him "my dear one" in many years, not since he was small, and at the sound of it he hugged her to him, and felt her arms around the right side of his waist again . . . and noted that his boots met her shoes, toe to toe, as they never had before.

They both looked down. "Do you miss him?" Amatus asked.

"No." She sniffled, and it *seemed* to belie her words, but he didn't *know* what she was weeping at. "Highness, you've never asked, so now I shall tell you: we don't all like each other. We share our duty to you, we know all the others do as well, we trust each other to do this, and we are content with this. I knew how much you needed Golias, my Prince, and would that you might have had more of him or more of the pleasure of him—but he and I were never friends. We could not be. It was not in the nature of things."

Amatus nodded, bowed, took up the new clothes she had made for him, and said, "Thank you for these. They are beautiful."

After he had dressed—not in his new clothes, which he saved for dinner, but in a simple blue costume that was somber without being grim, he went down to speak to the Twisted Man.

The Twisted Man, who was patrolling one of the parataxes on the castle's East Battue, nodded gravely, said, "Your apology is accepted," and added, "It would behoove you to go and speak with Mortis; she was wounded more deeply than either of us, because she liked Golias best. When you are done, I expect you to write brief notes of apology to others you have wronged—and then to be back up here *promptly*."

It was not a way to speak to a prince, but then Amatus had hardly behaved in a princely fashion lately, and he felt deep inside that whatever the Twisted Man had in mind it would be something that Amatus needed. "Thank you, Captain," he said, and trotted down to the lower reaches of the castle.

He found Mortis one level below her usual one, and a quick glance showed him she had gone so far as to move her furniture down into this lower apartment, away from all daylight.

There were lines in the witch's face where he hadn't remembered there being any before, and her eye were red-rimmed, with weeping, he thought. For a long time he sat next to her, not touching her, for he knew that her dignity could not bear that, but waiting for his offered communication to have effect. At last he said, "If need be, I will sit here for as many days as it takes, until you speak."

Her gaze held his, and he was reminded again that though she was able to maintain her beauty and fascination, she was indeed a witch and might have been millennia old, for the black eyes that stared at him had that memory of the beginnings of time that snakes do, and they were as cold.

When Mortis finally spoke, it seemed to come from deep within her. "My Prince, there is a secret which I should not tell you, for you must know it yourself."

"Then speak it, if you have decided to—"

She sighed, and as swiftly as it had come over her face, the reptile coldness and age was gone, and the Prince found himself thinking of the days when he had asked her why there were not magic cookie jars that never ran empty, or when she had quietly helped him through the forms of the Never-Voiced Declension when Golias had assigned him more than he could master. "My Prince, the reason I should not is close to the reason that you now have a foot. We will all pass from you at one time or another, but you will not necessarily gain by it if we do not follow the rules. Would you run the risk that it might be for nothing?"

He nodded. "Of course not. Then do not tell me. Did you want me only to know that there was such a secret?"

Again, her age rolled back from the old times of his boyhood to the old times before the youth of the world, and the cold face of the reptile stared at him . . . but then softened again. "My Prince," she said, finally, "my Prince, the sun will set soon, and you should be to dinner with your father."

"I've notes to write as well," he said, but made no effort to move. The dungeons were much darker and colder than the rest of the castle, but though Mortis's dress was of some thin stuff, she seemed not to be cold at all, while the Prince's winter clothes barely kept the clammy chill out of him. "You ought to come up to the sun and bask," he said, before realizing that the comparison might be unflattering.

She laughed—or did she strangle on a sob? "Time was the advice would have been good."

After they sat a long time longer she said, "You do need to go, my Prince, and I will not grow worse because you do. Truly I am grateful that you came down to see me."

As Amatus stood, he decided to broach the difficult subject. "The Twisted Man said that of the four of you, you liked Golias best."

She nodded, as if in dull shock. "That is true. Psyche could not really know or understand him at all, nor he her. And the Twisted Man was forever closed to the things that stood nearest Golias's heart, and Golias from those things the Twisted Man holds fealty to, because what was strength in one would be weakness in the other. So Psyche could not like what Golias did, and the Twisted Man could not understand what Golias was . . . but I, my Prince, I knew Golias for what he was, always, and though my love would not have been a good thing for him, though there was necessarily separation between us, yet I loved him in my way, and for the things we had in common."

"And . . . er, you survivors—"

Cold black ice stared in her eyes. "Our feelings for each other are none of your business." And then a little warm water seemed to well under it. "Yet I will say this much: that the Twisted Man sometimes suffers, just a little, because Psyche cannot feel what he wishes she could. Are you happier for knowing that there is that much more pain in the world?"

Amatus inclined his head. "I understand now, lady. I was wrong to have asked, and you were right to demonstrate to me the sort of thing I might learn by asking."

"You think, then, that I told you for your benefit?"

"I believe my Companions work to my good, yes."

She rose. "The sun will be down soon. Go."

He went. At his apartment he sat down at his desk and swiftly scrawled out letters of abject apology to Duke Wassant and Sir John Slitgizzard, begging that they forgive him for the things he had brought them to, asking them to aid in his repentance, and expressing the warm hope that some afternoon soon they might sit in the golden winter sunlight and sing the songs that Golias had taught them, songs of love and wine, in the snug warmth of his chambers in the castle.

With difficulty, he also wrote another letter—and there were many times as he wrote it when he could feel tears starting in his eyes, though the letter was a bare few lines:

My dear Pell,

It has been in my mind sometime past that I have treated you much like a plaything, and moreover like a disliked one that I wished to break. The Kingdom rests upon my behavior, finally, and this has been no behavior for a prince; I find I am forced to beg your silence of you, as you love your country, and yet I admit the wrongs I have done you have been such that you would be fully entitled to trumpet them from the rooftops. I appeal to your patriotism only; for my cruelties without number I offer whatever recompense will not endanger the state, and pledge to remove myself from your sight until such time as we shall both be healed of the things we have done together—if indeed we ever shall.

With warm regard—and nothing more—
Amatus.

That left the hard one; his note to Calliope was briefer, for between salutation and signature, he wrote only:

You are right, and I have been wrong. I shall always trust you to tell me the truth as you know it.

With a sigh, having settled all matters of any importance, he looked and saw that the sun was within a fingerbreadth of the horizon. If he had been there, he might have seen Cedric, at that moment, get up from the last of the cold tea back on the High Terrace. But since he did not, the scene passed unnoticed by him, and it was only years later, while interviewing Amatus for his *Chronicle*, that Cedric realized that as he had been sitting in despair for the Kingdom, the Prince had begun at last to take steps for it.

Amatus lifted the candle to the bottom of the strip of sealing wax, swiftly sealed the envelopes, and rang for the letter boy. He handed the letters to the boy with a whole golden flavin for a tip.

"Urgent dispatches, Highness?" the boy's voice cracked a little as he spoke.

"Urgent enough," Amatus said. "Apologies to my friends."

The boy goggled in a peculiarly foolish way. "I had thought—er, that is, Highness, I shall get them there as swift as thought."

Amatus smiled kindly. After so long, it felt unnatural. "You may descend the stair with me before you put on such swiftness. Had you thought that princes had no friends, or that princes never apologize?"

But he never found out which, for at that moment a ululating wail burst through the castle. Amatus clapped the boy on the shoulder and said, "Get the letters into town, and do watch yourself; this sounds like something I should look to," and had buckled his swash almost before the boy was out of the chamber.

2

Ill Omen and Ominous Illness

No," Amatus said, "I've no idea. It came from within the castle, of that I'm sure, and below my chamber, but for all my running up and down stairs I found no one who could direct me to its source."

"Exactly," the Twisted Man said.

Boniface looked from his son to his Captain of the Guard again, and then to Cedric, who also shook his head. "I was lost in thought, descending the long stairway from the High Terrace, Majesty. By the time I reached the bottom I found the castle in uproar, and met everyone and anyone running to and fro and hither and thither, but I learned nothing either. The cry came, and was gone. What sort of omen it was, I cannot say—except that it is hard to imagine it was not an evil one."

Boniface looked down at his plate and tore another piece off the baked haunch of gazebo with his fingers. The gazebo was young and tender, and normally his favorite dish, but tonight he had little appetite. Whatever signs of new health in Amatus were outweighed by the portents of that sourceless wail of pain. It had come from the castle, been heard clear across the city, all the way down to the Vulgarian Quarter near the river. The sunset's last light had shone upon the backs of practically every citizen of the town looking up at the castle and wondering how ill the omen might be.

"There is little we can do until the portent is repeated, or until other things begin to happen," Cedric reminded his King. "Let us not let what hangs over us ruin everything else while we wait for it to fall."

It took the King a moment to work through that last sentence, and then longer to decide that it was a mere pompous proverb and not a portent. While he thought this, absent-mindedly, he had taken a large bite of gazebo, and since it was good, it reminded him that however his heart might feel, his stomach had a good solid day of winter hunting to replenish. Though without much relish, he began to eat again, and this did make him feel better.

"I'll be going back into training tomorrow morning, early," Amatus said, "and I will do what I can in the afternoons to seek out the problem. A quest or a mission might be what I most need right now."

"Then you may have this one," Boniface said, and began to eat more heartily, for he knew well that something as important as this omen required a hero to resolve, and since his son had volunteered, there was an excellent chance that the earlier parts of the tale were being borne out and his son was thus a hero. Moreover, because that was the way things tended to work in the Kingdom, to have a hero undertake the job was to have it nearly accomplished.

No more was said about it that evening, and if the hall did not ring with joy, neither was it plunged in gloom. Cedric and King Boniface even managed to exchange tight, pleased smiles when Amatus got up early from the table, most of his second glass of wine untouched, and went to bed early. After he left, Cedric briefly informed the King of the young Prince's sincere apologies to his friends.

Boniface was deeply pleased at this as well, but he asked,

"And how does it chance that you know what happened where you were not present?"

"The letter boy, Majesty, is in my employ, as are a round dozen scribes; the letters were copied for my perusal before they were delivered. It would be a poor Prime Minister who did not get his nose into his sovereign's mail."

By then the candles had begun to gutter low, and the musicians and troupials were long since sent to bed, so the two of them finished off the bottle and went to bed without further ado; almost, they might have thought that matters were resolved, except that first, the night was filled with dark and hideous dreams that seemed to coil around their hearts like a snake of ice, and second, each had the same dreadful last thought just before falling into that evil, nightmare-haunted sleep: If the Prince's recovery of health was greeted with such a dark omen, could it be that it was not good news at all? And if it was not, what might that say about the character of the Prince himself?

Dark dreams had haunted Amatus's sleep as well, and his skin was pasty white, his lips an ill-looking purple, and his eyes ringed in dark circles as he looked in the mirror and threw handfuls of icy water into his face. The towel, even applied gently, seemed to scour his tender skin, and for a moment the thought crossed his mind that the major advantage in being decadent is that you are expected to sleep in. Still, he managed to bear splashing the cold water on his chest and back, and the harsh scrubbing of the cloth on his skin, and one more icy splash to take the harsh soap off before he toweled down again.

He might have had heated and scented bathwater, with soft, foamy soap, sent up to him at that hour, and the castle servants would have been glad enough to do it, but he had been well enough taught by his father and his Companions that to ask for such merely because he wished to be up and exercising was to make his whim others' work, and he was unwilling to do that.

Amatus dressed quickly—it was cold in his chamber, two hours before dawn—and noted that his half-belt and his trouser did not fit exactly as he thought they should. Well, this would be fixed, and soon enough.

The Twisted Man was waiting for him, looking grimmer than usual in the starlight, and after a preliminary bow, for the next half hour they fought with practice escrees, in dead silence, up and down the parataxis, its cobbles, slick with ice, untrustworthy under his boots, for the Twisted Man had always insisted that he practice in bad conditions, which had a way of turning up in real situations.

Even with the button on its tip, the escree left a set of dark black bruises on the Prince's chest, for he was not the fighter he had been before his months of confinement and darkness.

There was barely another pause, for a gulp of cold water, before they had pulled on packs filled with rocks and gone to run through the snowy streets of the city in the colorless light that was beginning to creep in over the river. Amatus fell more often than he ought to have, and accepted it as his just lot; each time the pavement, or the mix of snow and mud, or the brown puddle laced with gray slush, reached up and lashed across his front, he would push himself back up with freezing hand, bring his boots back under him, and be off after the Twisted Man, who never fell, though when he ran he looked like three dwarfs fighting in a blanket.

When the sun was full up, Amatus was shivering in soaked and filthy clothing, and they were down the hill from the castle, in the wood below the West Battue, practicing with the pismire. He forced himself to relax and aim carefully, and when this did not work he reached deep inside himself for calm and warmth to steady his hand, and when the pismire balls still tore off past the target to slaughter the snow-covered grass and knock loads of snow down from the laden pines, he surrendered himself to being a poor shot for the time being, and did his best.

He had hit the target a few times when the Twisted Man finally spoke. "Someone is coming up the trail behind us."

Prince Amatus lowered the pismire he had just discharged, and his hand went about the business of wiping out the barrel, brushing the burnt primer from the tip of the bronze chutney, and checking the lovelock. In a moment, a small boy, dressed in rags but reasonably well-fed, came around the bend in the trail.

"Yes?" the Prince said.

"Please, sir—my mother—Grandma says a prince's touch sometimes heals when the illness is an enig—enig—"

"When it's an enigma," Amatus said, pulling a thin triolet from his pack and sliding it on over his wet clothing. "Indeed, that's a very old saying, and so likely true; let me come with you at once."

The hut was comfortable enough, as commoner huts go, for King Boniface, and his father and grandsire before him, had been enlightened enough to make sure the commoners were comfortable if not stylish. There was at least a wooden floor up off the damp ground, and a fire in the hearth, and the hut smelled of breakfast bread and broth. But the woman who lay on the pallet, tended by her worried old mother, was pale and drawn, and her face looked older than it was.

The grandmother stared at the Twisted Man, but after all she knew a moment later who this must be, and suppressed her shudder at him. The Captain of the Guard bowed gravely to her, and Amatus threw back the quilted hood of his triolet and said, "Madam, I am sorry to be here on such an errand. Do you know anything other than that my touch will help? Is there some way in which I should touch?"

"The saying says nothing of that," the grandmother said. "She seems hurt to the heart and in the blood."

Amatus knelt beside her; he saw the woman's eyes grow wide as she realized who this half-youth must be, and reached out to calm her. Since her pallor looked like fever to him, he did without thinking what Psyche had done when he had been younger and ill, and put his hand on her forehead.

What he felt in his palm felt like a shock from scraping across the carpet; but it felt in his arm like a hard yank on his shoulder, and it felt in his stomach like the first surge that says that one has eaten something truly wrong, and in his heart it felt like cold rain on the day in November when you think of a lost love. He jerked back, feeling ill.

The woman sat up, breathing easily, obviously very tired and just as obviously recovered. Amatus staggered to his feet, barely managing to acknowledge the grandmother's low curtsy or the boy's deep, awed bow. He nodded to them, and with the little part of his mind that was not whirling, he realized that they would not expect him to be with them another moment, for after all a prince surely must have better things to be about than this. That meant that he could just say something and go.

"Be well," he said, his voice sounding like the croak of a dying toad in his own ears, and walked from the hut, trying to make sure that his detached left foot kept pace with, and stayed parallel to, his right.

The Twisted Man, at his heels, caught him as soon as they rounded the turn in the trail and were no longer visible. Prince Amatus had held himself together that long, but that had been almost worse than the original shock, for it seemed to drain his strength even more to pretend to be well. When the thick, strong arms of the Twisted Man wrapped around him, he slipped from consciousness for a few long moments before waking up being carried to the horses.

"You can set me down. I think I can walk."

"Are you sure?" The deep, cavernous rumble had as much concern in it as Amatus had ever heard.

"Let's try."

Once set upon his feet, he felt merely tired—and not much more so than might be accounted for by the morning's exercise thus far. "Let's see if I can do more shooting with the pismire, and after that perhaps I'll even feel up to some wrestling or some work with the trebleclef. I don't understand but whatever the sickness was, it seems to have passed through me quickly."

"If you are sure," the Twisted Man said. "But at the first sign of illness again, you are going home slung over the saddle. I will not throw away your life or health as a point of pride."

"Agreed. And neither will I. But I feel fine now."

An hour later, tired and sore, he had some of his old aim and precision with the pismire back, and they had fought several best-of-three bouts with the trebleclef on an icy log; Amatus had not won, but he at least felt that he had given the Twisted Man something to contend with.

As they rode back to the castle, and made the last turn onto the road up the hill, they came upon a group of commoners waiting patiently by the roadside. The Twisted Man looked at the Prince, and Amatus knew that it was in the Captain's mind that they should just ride on past, but he also knew that he was a prince, so he swung down out of his saddle and approached them. The Twisted Man dismounted and followed.

"Please, Highness," one of them said, "if you could—that is—" the man hesitated. "I'd not ask but that my wife has gotten so much worse in the past hour and seems unable to bear the daylight—"

"Do all of you have sick relatives?" Amatus asked. "All with the same illness I have seen already this morning?"

Silently, the crowd nodded as one.

"Well," Amatus said, sighing, and thinking of how ill he had felt after one healing.

The Twisted Man said, "If we are seeing ten sick here,

there must be a thousand—and some fresh corpses—in the city. You cannot heal everyone."

"I can do what I can," Amatus said, "though I am afraid you are right. I think we know now what that wail was about, though I have no idea what has brought this curse on us." He turned back to the little band of anxious commoners and saw that hope was dying on their faces, for they had not thought of what the Twisted Man was pointing out, and now they were ashamed to have asked. He made himself smile at them grimly. "There are . . . what, nine altogether? Then I shall do it, but you will have to make me a stretcher and bear me to each hut after the first, for I am weak and ill after I heal." He looked up again at the Twisted Man. "Go and get me soldiers from the castle to bring me home after this is done. I will be safe enough with these good people."

The Twisted Man managed, despite his distorted form, to bow in a way that at once told Prince Amatus that the Captain would obey, that the Prince's gesture was noble and worthy of him, and that all the same as his guard the Twisted Man wished to protest this. Then he mounted and left at a gallop.

It was worse than Amatus had imagined, for he had given them instructions that after the first touch he was to be carried to each of the victims and his hand placed on their foreheads, since he had no idea as yet whether it would work with him unconscious. This turned out to be a moot question, for each time his stomach, heart, and soul lurched at the sick shock coming up through his arm and shoulder, it brought him back to consciousness for a long, unpleasant moment, so that the next hour, for Amatus, was comprised mainly of waking to the brutal jolt, looking into the eyes of a man, woman, or child whose face was slipping quickly into peaceful, healthy sleep. Then the illness would wash over him and he would sink back into dark and bloody dreams, to awake again from another jolt with a foul taste in his mouth and a squeezing heave in his stomach.

He knew there had been more than nine, because they had asked him, and he had managed to rouse himself and tell them to keep him at it until the soldiers from the castle came, but it was not until he woke on a horse litter, on his way back to the castle, that he learned from Trooper Roderick, who was walking alongside, that he had healed twenty-seven of them.

"Highness, you can't continue in this way," Roderick said, and the Twisted Man growled in agreement. "Somehow the castle itself has thus far been spared, but there was word of a hundred cases in town just below the castle; no fresh cases since dawn, but no one who has it now looks to live till sunset."

"Is it all over the city?"

"No, not so far, Highness; it is a miracle that the castle is spared, for all the cases are close to it." Roderick's face tensed and then he visibly relaxed it as he looked away.

"Roderick," Amatus said softly, so that no one else would hear, "your house is just outside the castle wall. Is Gwyn taken ill?"

Reluctantly, Roderick nodded.

"Then I shall heal her," the Prince said, "even if my strength will not bear more. But I am feeling much better." He sat up carefully, and then brought his feet under him, and finally with a light bound he was on the road and walking beside them, as right as ever—except for not having a left side, but that was hardly unusual anymore.

"You recovered almost instantly from just one . . . and it took you less than an hour to recover from twenty-eight healings," the Twisted Man pointed out. "Perhaps I spoke in haste—if you wish to try it, you could probably heal the remaining hundred cases or so."

"Then I will do it," Amatus said. "But while I feel healthy and strong, will you race me on foot to the castle? We have the morning's exercises to finish."

He had said it—and then done it—because he knew it

would buck up the morale of Roderick and the other troopers, but the moment that he found himself pelting up the road, the Twisted Man beside him, cold damp air searing into his lungs, and sun beginning to break through the gray lid of snow clouds setting the colors of the evergreens and the red-berried holly off around him, Amatus realized he loved this, felt how acutely he enjoyed it. It seemed as if his heart was swelling against the walls of his chest, as if he were saying good-bye to all of this, just this moment, and only just now seeing it for the first time.

As they thundered, side by side, through the main gate in the East Battue, he found himself almost laughing.

The hundred cases—one hundred four, according to Cedric's *Chronicle*—of the plague, whatever it might be, took him a good part of the morning, and then he slept through most of the afternoon in dark and terrible dreams of being pursued by he-knew-not-what in the twisting and crooked alleys of he-knew-not-where.

3

The Plague Worsens and a Promise Is Made

*H*e had awoken feeling fine in the afternoon, and in the
evening he and Cedric had spent a long couple of hours
looking through the ancient chronicles of the Kingdom without finding anything much like the current plague in it. Indeed, the main thing they discovered was that the chronicles
were in a sorry state, which Cedric quietly vowed to put right
if he ever got the time, "though it may have to await my retirement."

When Amatus went to bed, a small part of his heart hoped
against all reason that the plague would turn out to be a matter
of a single day, that the plague itself might turn out to be the
omen rather than the disaster. No one was dead—yet—and he
had managed to get to every afflicted person as far as he knew.

But the next morning, after the running, and the practice
with escrees and pismires, just as before, there was a long line
of supplicants, and the morning passed in the endless sick,
horrible jolts as he was carried from one sickbed to the next.
Psyche went along with him this time, but there was little
she could do for him; Mortis had sent brief word up from
the dungeons that although she had no idea what might cure
the plague, that parts of her lore indicated that above all else

the Prince, though now more than old enough for it, would have to avoid the Wine of the Gods. This was unfortunate, for it had only just occurred to him that something that made him feel warmer and happier might well be the very stuff needed to speed his recovery after the cures were effected.

As Cedric noted, the pattern this time was more pronounced and obvious. The plague did not venture back into any house where the Prince had worked a cure, and thus on the whole the visited houses this time were a trifle farther away from the castle—which was again spared completely.

Cedric did not like the way that people were already beginning to mutter about the evident focus of the infection; it was as if a great finger had descended from the sky pointed directly at the castle.

In the afternoon, the exhausted Prince slept in his chambers, and Cedric privately visited with Sir John Slitgizzard and Duke Wassant, finding both, as always, helpful and loyal, and more than ready to go out as escort for the Prince on the following day. "There were one hundred thirty-two cases, twenty-eight in the village and one hundred four in the city, yesterday," Cedric said. "Today there were one hundred seventy-eight total, fourteen in the village and one hundred sixty-four in the city. If we are correct that it does not return to a house where a cure has happened, then there should be no more than two cases in the village tomorrow, but there will be many more in the city."

Sir John, who was not good at mathematics, nodded slowly, just as if he had been paying attention, and asked, "And there are many thousands of houses in the city—so we cannot hope that things will work out as they have in the village?"

"Very little hope of that," Cedric said. "We shall just have to find a cure, or a way to ride it out, or anything that does not involve the heir to the throne becoming dreadfully ill for longer and longer parts of each day. But what I have summoned you for is a slightly different matter. I want to know what is being said in the city—and though I have a dozen sources for what the aristocrats are saying, and a dozen more for the burghers, and yet a dozen more for the ordinary working folk, and even some sources among the Hektarians and the Vulgarians, what I do not have is anyone who can tell me what the city as a whole sounds like, for few people roam it from top to bottom . . . except you gentlemen, and the Lady Calliope, but she has shut herself in—rumor has it she has decided that Amatus has broken her heart—and so I cannot ask her. Will you go out in the city, tonight, and learn what is said everywhere, and come back with what you learn? For it is truly not the plague I dread so much as the way that people are taking it and the way the fingers are pointing."

Sir John Slitgizzard leaned back in his chair and nodded grimly. "I can tell you a bit right now, for I was about last night. It is what you have been dreading, I'm afraid—many people, noticing that our Prince has only recently begun to reform from a harsh and bitter existence and from hideous dissipations, believe he has brought a curse down upon the Royal house and that this is how it is being visited upon them."

Wassant looked up from where he had been cleaning his fingernails with his pongee, pursed his thick lips, and added, "And I have heard much the same. Two loud-talking rebels—who seem to be in league with some foreign power, and at a guess I should say with Waldo the Usurper—were busily spreading just such ideas for a good part of last evening, until they met with dreadful accidents in alleys."

"My thanks," Cedric said, and quietly passed a bag of gold flavins to the Duke. "And I can assume—"

"As always, the accident seems to have been a violent quarrel between the two of them, with both fatally stabbed," the Duke said, sheathing his pongee. "But it is easy enough to control those who talk in that way because they are in the pay of a foreign power. Far more difficult—and not at all desir-able—to shut up those who are loyal but merely worried.''

Cedric thought for a long time, and his hand began to stroke his beard, which he felt a certain residual longing to chew. He was on the brink of saying something when the noise from the courtyard brought him up short.

It was a great deal more than a mere low rumble, but not as much as a clamor; it was mostly voices. Cedric and the two nobles rushed into the corridor and from there to one of the galleries overlooking the public courtyard.

The scene below was confused, for such devices as ban-ners and picket signs were as yet unknown, so the sides had not marked themselves out, and besides, one side had not ar-rived for this purpose—it was only that the vegetable sellers, codwallopers, and cheesemakers who were allowed to use the courtyard in front of the clerihew, having inherited that right from generations of vendors, were as deeply loyal a gang of royalists as might be found anywhere, and so when the loose mob of malcontents had arrived, they had immediately as-sailed them.

Nor were the malcontents any better organized. There was one faction of them which had been stirred up by Waldo's agents. There was another which was made up of various peo-ple who sincerely wanted to ask the Prince or King for help, not being sure whether or not the Royal family had concerned itself in the process yet. There were some drunkards and ruffi-ans who joined any passing crowd, mainly in hopes of picking pockets or that matters might turn into a celebration that would allow everyone's bill to be footed.

Somewhere in the middle there were five passionate republicans, none of whom agreed with each other about any-thing except that it was the monarchy's fault.

By the time Cedric arrived on the balcony, those with complaints had gotten thoroughly intermingled with the stall-holders, hangers-on, and shoppers; an occasional punch was being thrown; many more people were busy trying to make peace between their immediate neighbors; and everyone was convinced that everyone else needed an immediate explanation. The situation was not exactly a meelee, nor yet quite a riot, but it was well beyond a hubbub and rapidly moving toward being an uproar.

King Boniface was out of the castle, fortunately, having gone fishing for the day at Cedric's strong urging, for he knew full well that things like this were apt to happen and that the King's nerves were on edge, so that he had wanted to get him out of the way before any trouble might begin. Amatus, naturally, was sleeping off the effect of the morning's healing, and the first thought in Cedric's mind was that *this assemblage of louts might wake him.*

He was not the only person with that thought, for opposite where he stood, from the clerihew doors, Psyche and the Twisted Man burst forth. It appeared that their plan was that Psyche would ask for quiet and calm, and the Twisted Man would make sure that she got it. But the confusion was far too great for most of the crowd to notice them, and the Twisted Man—thank the gods—was refraining from real violence.

Cedric cleared his throat and attempted to address the crowd, but, farther away than Psyche or the Twisted Man, he had even less success. Sir John Slitgizzard quietly drew a pismire and gestured to Cedric, indicating that he could discharge it into the air to get their attention; reluctantly, Cedric indicated he should put it away, for some of the crowd might be armed, and the shot might lead to bloodshed.

The mob rumbled and stirred like a jellyfish pulling back from a splinter. They all turned to face the gallery directly under Cedric. Someone was descending from the gallery; from the way the Twisted Man, Psyche at his heels, rushed toward that side of the courtyard, Cedric judged that it could only be Amatus.

He descended the stairs and stood in an open space in the

silenced crowd. The Twisted Man and Psyche flanked him, and a moment later Roderick and a dozen burly troopers had lined up behind them, creating an appearance of public order—as Cedric well knew, the beginning of actually restoring it.

Prince Amatus stepped forward. Though he had just risen from his bed, and apparently thrown on his formal clothing on his way down the stairs, his appearance was immaculate from the sparkling gold and gems of his half-crown to the polished tips of his boots. His smile was warm, and yet not familiar; at once you felt that he liked you, and wanted to speak to you particularly, and yet that this was a matter of business. "Thank you all for coming," he said, and in an instant the crowd—excepting only Waldo's agents and the five republicans—felt as if they had come here to bring weighty matters to the Prince's attention, and had forgotten the anger or fear of the moment before.

What a king he will make, Cedric thought. Next to him, Sir John Slitgizzard was thinking, *There's a courage and a presence to him.* Duke Wassant did not think in words at all, but instead felt in his bowels that he would be the Prince's man until he died.

The Prince went on. "I know of your fear of the plague, and your thanks for the healing that I have been able to work—though that has been little enough, I fear, and we cannot say whether at some future time my strength may be exceeded." He looked around at them. "And so you come to ask what else may be done. I promise you—we will find the cause of this. As you all know, it began with a dark omen whose meaning and source we have yet to find, and that omen was within the castle. Such things are often buried crimes or buried sorrows.

"I pledge you this. We will find out what it is, and we will do justice, no matter who or what the cause turns out to be.

And though I will pledge no more than that, my promise is absolute."

Everyone in the crowd murmured or whispered to everyone else. Some spoke softly to their neighbors because they were satisfied, and after all hadn't everyone said that the Prince was a reasonable, perceptive young man who was bound to do the right thing?

Others, with more perception, realized he had just given binding word without knowing the facts of the case, or what might be turned up, and strongly wished that he had not done so, because they had read or heard enough stories to know how badly such things often turned out.

In any case, the wind was thoroughly out of the sails of any sort of uprising. The drunkards wandered off, knowing that there would be little chance of cadging free drinks; the ruffians followed, having collected a few purses and wallets and slit a few pockets; and Waldo's agents followed. The rest of the crowd talked with each other politely for few moments, agreeing that it had been a productive gathering but they *must* all get back to their work and their families, and drifted off amiably enough. Last to go were the five republicans, split among the two who felt that Amatus's sincere response to a public outcry was a demonstration of how well self-government could work in practice (and favored carrying out the transition by electing him), the two who felt that all this was a royalist sham to discredit the movement, and the one who just wanted to point out to everyone that although things had turned out rather well this time the business of government was far too important to leave hanging upon the accident of having a capable person inherit the throne.

"You need not spend any time canvassing that particular sentiment," Cedric said to Sir John and the Duke.

"We wouldn't dream of it, sir," Slitgizzard said.

4

Things Needless to Say, Things Neglected, and a Puzzling Conversation

*I*t was needless to say that the Prince was as good as his word. In fact the only reason Cedric ever wrote such a thing in his *Chronicle*—or the King in his never-finished notes toward his autobiography, or Sir John in letters to his son many years later, for they all did write "The Prince was as good as his word"—was because it seemed de rigueur in a fairy tale. It spared a long description of the Prince going forth in his litter to work healings every morning, and studying in the Royal Library and Royal Alchemical Laboratory far into every night, eliminating one cause after another, following up little threads of history and every stray observation made by every shrewd commoner. Besides, it furnished a way to get into the next part of the tale.

So the Prince was as good as his word, and though his youth and strength bore him up, all the same he grew tireder every day. The plague seemed to settle to about two hundred fresh cases every morning, and by now every house near the castle had been visited—just once. The plague continued to spread away from the castle in a widening ring, like a ripple in a pond, never taking more than its two hundred or so, but never fewer, and slowly and deliberately moving outwards.

Now, Prince Amatus, because of his grief after Golias's death and his horrible misbehavior after, had many fences to mend and little time to mend them, so he necessarily neglected things and at the same time felt badly about the neglect. As a result, he seemed to be everywhere at once. He would be pawing through some dusty record in the library, then you would see him hand it off to some apprentice scribe with strict instructions to report anything that seemed even remotely relevant, and race down the twisted spiral of stone steps to the Royal Alchemical Laboratory, where he would be conducting some experiment on the blood or urine of a sufferer (only to find out that all that could be said was that the sufferers generally had less blood than, and about as much urine as, they ought to), and then he would be down in the Royal Witch's workshop to talk to Mortis, because he would realize it had been a full day since he had even said hello.

"This dungeon is too deep and dark for you," he told her. "Let us move you back up into the light and air, where you can breathe freely and see for a long way."

She shook her head decisively, and he noticed that she did not seem entirely well. "Have you suffered from the plague?" he asked her.

"Not directly." She sat heavily upon her chair. "Prince, I have no suggestions for you."

"What do you mean by 'not directly'?"

"We are all affected, Prince."

He sat down next to her. Her once purely white hair was showing little traces of yellow and gray; the sky blue of her skin was becoming more of a slate color; and her new scales were coming in larger and more irregular, so that her skin was losing its iridescence and becoming coarse and messy. There was a distinctly yellow tinge on her once-white fangs.

"We all age in some way or other, Highness," she said, and he realized that she had been reading his thoughts.

"I had not realized that," Amatus said. "Just the other

day, it seems, Psyche was telling me the opposite. Or rather—I had asked her why she did not age—"

"Oh, but she does. Faster than the rest of us, in fact. But not in her appearance. The last day you ever see her, she will look much the same as ever. The Twisted Man, too, is not what he was when we first came here; that might, perhaps, show, if you were ever to see any more of him than his hands, eyelids, or jaw."

Amatus waited a long time, but at last he broke the silence. "There is much I don't understand."

"That will never change," Mortis said decisively. "Except that *what* you don't understand will change." She sighed. "The sun is almost down. You should not be down in this part of the castle after dark, Prince."

"Why not?"

"That's one of those things you will understand eventually."

As the Prince stood, he saw that in the half hour of their conversation, Mortis had grown visibly older.

"It draws quickly now, Highness. Things are moving. You want your plague ended, do you not?" Her expression had always been cold, but now the line of her mouth was perfectly flat. She seemed to have no feelings about what she was saying. "I will tell you what I can. Do not be here after dark; this is no longer a good place for you."

"Because of what may happen, or because of what I may do?"

"Because of what you may see and what you may become. Three questions, then, Highness—Are you sure that all your friends are your friends? Is it possible that you were helped to drink the Wine of the Gods when you were young, but that the help was not to your benefit? And—listen closely to this question—what does it all seem like, whatever you may be told it is?"

The Prince nodded, committing the questions to his memory quickly, for he knew that these were the sorts of things of which portents are made, particularly when one is speaking to a witch. The first one seemed clear enough but was the sort of thing he did not wish to think about; the second seemed to be deliberately ambiguous, so he assumed it was; and the third was the kind of question that normally showed up only in riddles. He therefore decided to postpone any consideration of any of them. Events would propel him back to them soon enough. But even many years later, when he wrote his *Memoirs* and recorded the questions, he still had little idea what she had meant.

The Royal Witch stood up quickly, and swayed. "The sun is almost down, Prince. Get up to your tower. Go now."

There might have been urgency, or fear, or desire in her voice, but the strain was unmistakable, and so Amatus raced up the stairs before he had thought about it. As he went he could feel ice around his heart and a desire to sit down and weep forever; his feet stumbled and slammed on the slippery stones, and he continued directly up into the tower, bursting out onto the High Terrace just as the last rays of sunlight touched it. He stretched his hand into the sun, and what he felt then was like the shock when he took the plague from a sufferer—but in reverse. It was as if something huge, cold, gray, slimy, and ill had burst out through his arm, leaving his body. Feeling better than he had in days, he stayed to see the first star come out.

5

What It Was

*T*he next day, when the Prince went forth in his litter to heal the sick, he gave Duke Wassant, who was to head his escort that day, strict orders that after each healing, if the sun was out, he was to be carried out into the broad daylight. The Duke swept a low bow, his heavy body surprisingly graceful (or it was a surprise to anyone who had not seen him use his pongee), and asked no questions.

This alarmed Prince Amatus, for he had always relied on the Duke and Sir John to question that which they did not understand and that which seemed senseless, and thus keep him from a great deal of nonsense.

"Have you no questions, no thoughts about this?" he asked.

"Highness, I know you have spent long hours in the Royal Library and I merely believe that you have some reason for this. It does seem that since the illness leaves one cold inside and pale, that the sun, which makes people warmer and darker, might be able to drive it from you more quickly. But the major reason why I asked no question is because you gave the command with such dread, as if you feared what it might lead you to."

Prince Amatus was about to deny this when he noticed that there was a sick, grim feeling in his belly, that his breath was coming in tight gasps, and that his face was constricted in a ghastly grin, which—if there had been another half available to *not* grin with—would have been a ghastly half-grin. He was terrified, and he had not noticed it, and he certainly did not know why.

When he spoke, it was soft and almost shy. "You are right, of course. There is something I dread to know or dread to do. I do not know what it is, either. Perhaps the time has come to delve into *Things It Is Not Good to Know at All*. It might be in there by mistake. Many things are. But first we must deal with the plague; it is halfway down to the river now, and we might perhaps hope that when it runs out of city it will run out entirely, but I don't think we can depend on that. I'll ride the first stage; just bring the litter along."

The first one that day was a very young girl, her hair still uncut and her teeth still new and white in her terribly pale gums; when Amatus touched her the shock was deep and terrible, and he had only a moment to think it was worse than usual before he fell back onto the litter. They carried him out into the sunlight, and in his half-consciousness he was barely aware of the Duke explaining that this must now be done between each cure but that everyone would receive the healing touch just as always.

The sunlight had the expected effect and more; something foul and icy, like slush that floats on an open cesspool, burst out of his gut when the sun touched him, and he sat up, fully recovered. In short order, they had discovered it was quickest to carry him out into the sun, where he recovered instantly, and then let him walk back in for the next cure.

"Always, before, there was something of the sickness left in me when I recovered," Amatus explained to the Duke as they rode back. "The sun on my skin drives it out entirely, and though it feels as if I were dying *at* that moment, it is all over *in* that moment."

"Pity it's winter, Highness; we can't count on sunlight nearly often enough. Do you really feel well?"

"Better than at any time since Golias died." The Prince sucked in a great gasp of cold, clear air, sweet as dandelion wine and clear as springwater, and looked around at the streets before them, winding between the snug houses. Children in dirty—but not ragged—clothing played in the streets amid the puddles of water running off the snowcapped houses, and everywhere there was the smell of cooking. "The Kingdom, for all of it, is a good place," he said.

"Have you ever doubted that?"

Amatus turned his single eye on the Duke, and long after the Duke remembered that expression and eventually told Cedric about it. When Cedric wrote it down in his *Chronicle*, however, he could not remember what the Duke had said, and since the Prince could hardly be expected to know how he had looked, there was no way of recalling it for certain. Amatus remembered only having thought long and hard about the question, so perhaps that was what the Duke saw.

"Wassant, you are loyal to the bottom of your blessed soul, and so decent that you cannot conceive that a place might be utterly spoiled and poisoned. But I am to reign here, and so it is a question I must consider. Be glad you don't have to answer such questions." Then he was silent again, looking deep into the Duke, for the seriousness of the answer had surprised even Amatus a great deal. After that long moment of gazing at each other, the Prince laughed and began a merry song, an old ballad of how a gallant woodman crossing a bridge in the fog had lost his way, thought he faced a great giant, boldly drawn his trebleclef, and fought with the terrible being on the narrow bridge, only to discover that the bridge was the highway, the giant a windmill, and he himself only the dream of a butterfly who had been unable to imagine a Chinese philosopher.

The tune was jolly, so Wassant joined in after a moment, and then all the men took it up, singing in a rough four-part harmony that was traditional among entourages of fighting men in the Kingdom, who needed only a dashing officer singing lead as an excuse to burst into song.

When the song was done, the Duke was grinning and all the dark thoughts of the morning were fled for the time being. "Calliope loves that song," he said, "it's a pity she wasn't here."

Prince Amatus had a sudden thought. "In fact we haven't seen her since before the plague began. I had written asking her forgiveness and had never heard back from her. It is not at all like Calliope to sulk or not to forgive; I will have to call on her, today, to make sure that nothing is wrong."

"You could do that now, if you wished," the Duke said. "I would be happy to accompany you, or if you wish to meet her by yourself—"

"Why, Wassant, you're blushing."

The Duke looked down at the wet gritty pavement over which his horse was clopping and said, "Highness, I meant only to spare you any shame. I should have known better; as well spare the winter being cold."

Amatus laughed at that, a warm, clear laugh that made women look up from their washing and workmen from their tools, and though he did not notice it, the tone of his laugh, so free and warm, put heart in them and started rumors racing through the city that the Prince would shortly have found the cure for the plague and that good times would come around again before Winter Festival.

"Duke Wassant, what I love best about you is that your loyal heart has no governance over your rough tongue. Yes, we will visit Calliope immediately; send the men back to the castle to report, and let us go to her home right away."

In moments they were tying up their horses in the small, sunlit square where Calliope's house fronted.

Prince Amatus knocked on the door with some enthusiasm, for he had missed Calliope without realizing that she was who he missed or how much he had missed her, and so he was more eager than he might have thought he would be. She might still be furious with him, but he now at least had a good excuse for his neglect of the past few weeks, and he was sure that he could apologize more than adequately.

And making up with Calliope was always delightful; she had a knack for being petulant exactly long enough to make it a pleasure when the forgiveness shone through, without carrying it on so long as to allow one to think that she might be enjoying the situation.

He knocked again; it had been some moments, now, as they stood on the wet doorstep in the bright sun that seemed to pick out every crevice between every brick and shingle in the courtyard.

The door opened a crack, and the face behind it would not quite look out enough for Amatus to see anything other than that it was not Calliope.

"My lady Calliope is not in, or rather she is inside, but she is not in to you, or rather she is not in to anyone," the voice said, repeating verbatim the sort of thing that Calliope must have said.

The door thudded shut.

"I think she's particularly annoyed with you," the Duke commented.

"We might well infer that," Amatus said. "I had imagined that she didn't want to speak to me until I'd apologized, but I'd never thought that she wouldn't want me to speak to her until I had apologized. Well, I suppose there's nothing for it but some foolish heroics."

The Duke clapped him on the shoulder. "Now I know that you are healthy again."

Less than an hour later, after due reconnoitering (and a certain small amount of embarrassment while they established that they both knew the location of Calliope's bedchamber within the house, but despite both their best efforts had never been inside it), Amatus was looking dubiously at a curious iron device in the Duke's hand. "It's called a grig, and it's used by the daring herders of mountain leghorns in the high, rocky parts of my duchy, when they climb the stony escharots to bring down the strays. One says Secundine over it, then one tosses it onto any firm surface where it will cling, and then we climb the line attached to it. I'm quite sure we can get it all the way onto the Lady Calliope's roof without trouble, and after that it's merely a matter of climbing the line."

"Have you ever used a grig?" the Prince asked.

"I've climbed several escharots, and there was a time in my life when I used the grig daily," Wassant said. "Nothing to it."

In fact he had climbed the escharots when he was young, by the expedient of hanging on to the back of the harness of one of his father's leghorn herders, and he had used the grig as a paperweight while he was at school, but he saw no particular reason to alarm Prince Amatus since after all there was nothing to it.

To Amatus's surprise and Wassant's relief, the grig landed and held silently, with the line running directly by Calliope's balcony. There were no sounds from inside, so Amatus's guess that the thump of the grig would be audible only in the unvisited attic was probably true. He wondered for a moment, if the attic were truly unvisited, whether the grig had made a noise at all.

There was a moment of confusion between the two friends, for the Duke thought that he should go up first because it was his duty to scout for danger ahead of the Prince (and secretly also wanted to make sure that the grig was work-ing properly before he trusted the heir to the throne to it). The Prince, figuring himself for the hero of the story—and also knowing that the worst danger at the top of the line was likely to be Calliope—insisted on going first. Finally, to avoid the humiliation of having rank pulled, the Duke gave in.

Amatus went up the line quickly and gracefully as a mon-key, if one could imagine a monkey with one arm and a de-tached foot that followed him. In very little time, he had stepped onto Calliope's bedchamber balcony and signaled for Wassant to come up.

But as the Duke reached for the line, the grig let go of the roof, and fell to the ground. The rope coiled neatly at the Duke's feet and the grig thumped to the center of the coil, for though the Duke did not know it, Secundine had to be re-peated over the grig three times if the line was to be used for more than a single climbing. Once the Prince had let go of the line, the grig had been waiting only for a short tug to return to its master.

Amatus knew even less than the Duke, and was as furious as the Duke was embarrassed. But since the Prince dared not make noise, he was forced to communicate his anger to Was-sant entirely by gesture, and since the poor Duke was so ashamed that he was hanging his head and could not see the Prince above him, this was completely unsatisfactory.

After a few more angry gestures at the back of the Duke's head, Amatus gave up in disgust and turned to the problem of getting into Calliope's bedchamber. The doors onto the bal-cony were locked, but there was no bolt as far as he could tell, for there was no point in one three stories up; the latch was only there to keep the door closed.

The blade of his escree was not quite thin enough to lift the latch, but with some digging to make a hole, the point of his pongee was. The whole time, as he worked at it, he expected Calliope to shout from within, or someone to notice him, but nothing happened as he continued to pry away in the warm winter sunlight. He looked down to see that the Duke was now looking up, made an angry gesture, saw Wassant blush and look down, and felt simultaneously relieve and guilty. He knew he would forgive his friend shortly.

At last he had damaged enough of Calliope's woodwork to get at the latch, and pried it up. The doors to her bedchamber swung open in front of him, and he stepped softly inside.

Calliope was lying in the bed. She looked as if she were dead. He crept forward. A stench like a just-opened grave made him rear back for a moment, and as a light breeze blew the curtain, light washed over her. Her features were terribly pale and from the cast of her face he knew at once that she had had the plague since the first day, and he realized that because she had not wanted to go out, she had remained here, ill, until she was unable to call for help, and then continued to get worse. He mentally cursed her servants for fools.

As he stepped closer, he saw that her skin was as pale and white as paper, except for two unnaturally bright red patches, one on each cheek. Her lips were a bruised shade of blue, and the skin around her eyes was drawn and dark, leaving her cheekbones terribly prominent. She had lost much weight, and she had always been a slender girl.

Closer still, and now his heart hammered, for it seemed that anyone who looked so ill could not possibly still be alive. He knew how much plague must be in her.

He did not hesitate; he placed his hand on her forehead.

Though every time before had made the Prince feel as sick as if he had drunk drakeseed, though each time had felt like an arm-breaking shock and a giant's hand tearing his bowels from his living body, all that was as nothing to this. Always before he had fainted from the pain and sickness penetrating him, but this time the illness seemed to lock into his arm and pour straight into his brain and heart with such horrifying force that it was impossible for him to fall into the comforting darkness.

Her hand whipped up and grasped his wrist; her fingers were gnarled and long, as if they were barely more than bones, and they gripped with great force. The skin on her hand was completely blue.

Her other hand grabbed his wrist from the other side; it too was blue, and now he saw that the nails were long and ragged and dirty. With her right hand she fought to shove his hand from her forehead, but with her left she pulled his hand harder against her, so that between them his wrist was being slowly crushed. He could not imagine that anyone so obviously weak and ill could possess such tremendous strength, or understand the fierce battle she seemed to be waging with herself.

She began to kick and thrash, nearly pulling him off his feet, and gave a dreadful, keening wail, and her eyes flew open.

They were cold, indifferent, and remote as a viper's. Her whole body arched and kicked, arched and kicked again, then her lips pulled back to reveal that her canine teeth had grown into long, dirty fangs. Her breath stank like maggoty meat and burned like wet fire on his arm as she bent her force to breaking his touch on her forehead and bringing his wrist to her mouth.

He breathed the word as he looked into those feral frozen eyes. "A vampire. You're a vampire."

It might have been common sense then to slip her grip and turn and flee into the daylight, to return later with rosewood and garlic. But without thought or evidence he knew that though she was well on her way she was not yet truly undead, and so he let her keep her mad grip on his arm and with all the force and strength of his half-body, the Prince stood straight up, lifting her out of the bed with his single arm. Her toenails,

long as fingers and coated with filth, slashed at his leg, but he
kept his arm from her mouth and backed up swiftly.

She was so intent on biting him that he was almost to the
doors to the balcony before she realized. She finally gave up
trying to bite and tried to break away, but now he twined his
hand in her hair—the long soft red hair he had adored since
they had been children together, now coarse as a wild horse's
hide and filthy as a leper's loincloth—and dragged her by
main force, tears streaking down his cheek as he did so, until
at last he could again enfold her in his arm and place his hand
over her face, ignoring the sharp gnashing fangs shredding his
palm. He extended his detached left foot into the sunlight—

And the foul illness poured in great lumps of cold slime
down his arm, into his body, and somehow out through his
detached foot to where the sun burned it from both of them.
His belly convulsed, his chest and muscles surged with agony,
and his eye felt as if it were on fire, but he let it continue, and
he stared deep into the void of her eyes.

There was a tiny spark there, something that seemed to be
Calliope, and he let himself continue to stare into the vampire's eyes, willingly bearing the risk of being compelled by
her. The part that was Calliope grew bigger.

She ceased to bite. With a terrible effort, she brought her
forehead willingly against his palm, and now the sickness
surged from her in a thick slurry, invisible to the eye, that he
nevertheless felt passing through him like half-frozen diar-
rhea. In a moment her eyes were clear and bright, and though
deathly pale, she merely looked tired. The fangs receded and
she smelled of the sickroom, but not of the charnel house. He
knelt and lifted her up with his arm to carry her into the balcony's sunlight—

The bedchamber door burst in with a great clap, falling flat
to the floor, and over it Calliope's servants rushed in, all with
weapons, all deadly pale—every one a vampire.

Amatus swung the balcony doors open wider so that sunlight spilled into the room and they fell hissing back. He bore Calliope in his arm to the balcony; her breath, cold and rank but healthy, blew lightly against his neck.

He had not realized how long he had been struggling with her, and winter days are short. The sun would be gone soon, and there was no other way down. With a groan he yanked the doors closed, put Calliope down behind him, and stood with his escree at ready.

He pulled the silver whistle that the Twisted Man had always insisted he carry from its chain around his neck, and blew it long and hard, but he seemed to attract no attention. As long as the sunlight continued to spill onto the balcony, they would be safe enough, but this could not last more than an hour or so longer. He looked down, but there was no path along which he would have dared to climb even by himself, and a glance at Calliope showed that though she had been freed from her dreadful condition, she was weak and feeble. However they got out, he would have to carry her, using his single arm, and that made it utterly impossible.

Amatus had been quietly moving around the balcony as he looked for a way down from each corner and side, making as little noise as possible, and now he was close to the double doors. Abruptly, he wheeled and kicked them open.

Scenting the living, the vampires had been gathered near the doors; as the doors swung open, the sun, low in the sky, stabbed far into the room, and there were horrid screeches as the light hit them. But only two fell dead in the beams; the rest, shrieking and moaning, staggered out of the light. Clearly most of them, like Calliope, were not undead yet.

Amatus yanked the doors closed again. He sat down next to Calliope, and she slumped against him. Gently, he brushed her hair—still filthy but already seeming softer—back from her cheek. "Are you awake? Can I do anything to make you more comfortable?"

"You can give me your cloak. You hauled me out here in my nightgown, Highness, and though I'm grateful, I'm cold. How is your hand?"

"Not as well as it could be. You had sharp fangs." He took his cloak off and wrapped it around her; she tore a strip from her nightgown and bound his hand, carefully and neatly. "Have you ever done this before?" he asked.

"Tied up a wound, or been a vampire? The former was one of the things that my guardian thought a king's daughter should know." She snuggled against him. "I'm cold. You know, I remember all of it, and I surely wish I didn't."

Amatus glanced around, reflexively concerned that Calliope not speak of her true parentage where she might be overheard.

She had fallen asleep against his shoulder for a while, but as the sun sank, she stirred and woke. He blew his whistle again; this time he thought he heard distant shouting and crashing.

"This is not the way these tales end," Calliope said firmly.

"This is not the way that things end when they get to be tales," Amatus said, "but since ours is not yet told, we cannot count on it. There were a hundred dead princes on the thorns outside Sleeping Beauty's castle, and I'm sure many of them were splendid fellows."

There was a nearer, louder burst of crashing and banging inside, and Amatus noted that the broad yard below was now falling into shadow; the shadow of the building behind was now reaching toward the wall of Calliope's house, and in a little while would begin to climb the wall toward them—and then, in a few swift moments, they would be in darkness, and just as the first stars appeared the vampires within would burst out onto the balcony.

He put his arm around Calliope. "They're getting lively in there," he said. "Hunger, I suppose. It never occurred to me that this could be an attack of vampires, because no one ever died—but once a person was cured in the house (or even once a cured person was carried into it) the place had acquired a little of the white magic from the cure, and the vampire could not return to it. But how could it be that the vampire never killed anyone at the first feeding?" Belatedly, he realized that Calliope had said that she remembered everything. "You know who it is, then. Who?"

Calliope sighed and leaned against him. "Prince Amatus—Highness—if we die here, the answer would cause you great pain to no purpose. If we survive—then there will be time. I will tell you this much, however; there is only one, and because it detests its own nature and being, and would not wish its fate on anyone else, it has tried not to feed on more people each night than you are able to cure. If you had been summoned here the first day, my servants and I might have been safe, but before anyone knew it was already too late. You must understand that—"

There was a series of grinding crashes and thuds from within, and the sound of heavy things falling down stairs; then a rhythmic hacking noise that went on, growing louder and louder, and then more thumping and yelling.

"I wish Wassant had stuck around, and I suppose Cedric will be hard on the poor fellow," Amatus said. "Not his fault at all, though." He was not sure he believed this, but he did not want to die with a grudge against any friend.

The shadows were now reaching up the side of the building; the Prince checked all three of his pismires and laid them out carefully, chutneys already cocked. "I have heard it said that being shot will knock them down, and make holes in them, though doing little other harm. And perhaps I shall be lucky enough to hit ones who are still living and they will not rise till the following sunset, so I may win us some time. Besides, white magic was worked in the threshold, and that too may slow or harm them. Just the same, I'm afraid it will be settled with the blade—and those doors are wide enough for three of them to come through. It will not be long."

"Highness," Calliope said, "may I have one of the pismires?"

"If you wish. I suppose it frees my hand for the escree."

She shook her head. "No, Highness. I cannot choose for you, but I can for myself. I have been a vampire, or as near one as I could be and still return—the last feeding tonight would have finished me, and I would have been feeding in the city myself shortly after. I will not be made a vampire; the pismire is for me, if you fall."

Amatus looked into her eyes—a most remarkable shade of sea gray—and he saw nothing there but courage and firmness. "I trust your judgment," he said. "Take this pismire, and, if it comes to that, use it. I shall try to do the same for myself."

The shadow was now just below the balcony and creeping up toward them even as they watched. The sunlight still on them carried no warmth and now Amatus wished his cloak thicker and larger for Calliope, for she was shuddering with the cold.

"Soon," he whispered.

"Thank you for rescuing me."

"But I have not . . ."

"You rescued me from the worst of it."

There were many crashes, and wild yells—then many furious voices on just the other side of the door. Amatus set his escree where he could seize it the instant he dropped the pismire, and lifted the pismire to where its ball would go straight through the chest of a normal man coming through the door.

As the last rays of the sun fell on it, the door flew open.

There stood Duke Wassant, bloody and powder burned, but grinning from ear to ear, big and wide as life. "For the sake of all the gods, Highness, don't pull that trigger or they'll be writing ballads about us both forever."

Carefully, Amatus pointed his weapon at the sky, and gently released the chutney back to the safe position. "Wassant—then all that noise—"

"Was myself and some of my men. And naturally the Twisted Man knew you were in danger and turned up in the process, and good old Slitgizzard came with him; Sir John just chased the last half dozen of them up into the attic, Highness. We took as many alive as we could, and opened as many windows as possible so that the undead would die and the rest would retreat from us; there are several that we will need you to heal, though that had best wait until tomorrow morning when you've got the sun to restore you."

"You've done well," Amatus said. "I may yet forgive you that bit with the grig." The Duke flushed till red shone through his small black beard, and both of them laughed.

After a moment the Duke said, "You both must be freezing. It's plainly been days since there's been a fire in this house. I'll have someone get to it at once. Welcome back to your house, Lady Calliope, and I'm sorry for the condition we've put it in."

"All's forgiven if you can find a way for a lady to have a hot, private bath, Duke," she said. "And I do hope that among the servants—"

"There were deaths, lady, but few of them, and I can only beg your forgiveness, for we had little time—"

She inclined her head gravely to him, and he fell silent. Then she said, "I did not question your judgment, my dear old friend; I only wanted to ask that you make the living as comfortable as possible in their bonds until morning comes and our Prince can cure them. But as you must have guessed, this house is the first place that the vampire stops every night, and it will be here within a couple of hours, and you must be ready—and I would like a bath, and a meal, before then."

She swept past him into the house with more dignity than one might imagine a young woman in a torn nightgown and a borrowed half-cloak could muster. Amatus followed, and shortly all were gathered around a fire in Calliope's main dining room. Duke Wassant's cook—a talented fellow who everyone said was the main reason for the Duke's figure—had come over in haste, along with some hastily grabbed supplies, and improvised some astonishingly good food in a time so short that it was ready almost before Calliope came down from her steaming tub and hasty dressing.

It had made a considerable difference. Her face was still pale, but there was a pink sheen from scrubbing. Her teeth were white again, and when Amatus kissed her cheek, her breath was sweet and her hair—not yet fully restored, but clean and combed—smelled of flowers.

For a long time they did nothing but eat and sigh with relief. Sir John had joined them, having secured the attic, and though the Twisted Man ate little, he consented to sit at the table with them and take a little soup, bread, and wine. It was as good an evening as there had been in a long time.

But Amatus ate little, for he knew that there would be dark doings later that night, and Calliope had warned him on the balcony that it would bring him unhappiness. He looked from friend to friend and wanted to throw himself at each of them and be comforted; he thought of the balcony from which he and Calliope had been released, where she said the vampire landed each night.

"Borrow no trouble, Highness," Sir John said, beside him. "I took the liberty of sending a messenger for something, and if you will not eat, then you can be our entertainment."

He handed Amatus an instrument case—his own nine-string palanquin, the Prince realized. He took it out, tuned it, found it satisfactory, and idly strummed a few chords.

"We have some time until the vampire arrives," Calliope said. "If I may request—"

"Yes?"

"Would you play 'Penna Pike'?"

The fire crackled and burst, and the candles in the room seemed to waver just as if a cold breeze had blown through. Everyone in the room—even, perhaps, the Twisted Man, just a little—seemed to hold breath.

They are wondering if I am not yet over Golias's death, Amatus realized, *and much as they loved him too, they are hoping that I am, for we cannot mourn forever. And more than that, it is time.*

He had stayed in touch, roughly, with what was happening to ballads, and so he knew about the new ending of "Penna Pike," which gave an account of his doings, and of Golias's death, although he privately thought it was not an adequate version, for it omitted the other Companions, and Calliope and Sir John. Well, perhaps he could improvise a verse that included each of them—he had always been good at such things.

He strummed, and the palanquin felt as if it had come alive in his hand. He began to sing, and for no reason he knew—songs are that way—"Penna Pike" took him. He added the verses it needed, changed a few things that had always annoyed him, and in all made it his.

It seemed, as he played, that he felt Golias standing at his shoulder, and that somewhere in the middle, he remembered the one time as a child he had lost his temper and shouted that he was never going to learn anything—only to find that the next day he spent copying, one thousand times, *Superabo ob conabor*—"I will conquer because I will try"—in perfect lettering, on parchment, before the Royal Alchemist would speak to him again. Somewhere inside, a door opened, a wound closed, a note rang true. When he had finished, he saw faces wet with tears.

"What you sang of me is too much," Sir John Slitgizzard protested.

"And of me, Highness," Calliope said. "I was little more than a passenger on that voyage."

Duke Wassant heaved a deep sigh and said, "I hope this afternoon may pay for it to some extent, but I know now I shall always regret not having gone along."

Amatus bowed his head slightly, as Golias had taught him, for "if you have made a good thing, it should be honored, even if you do not yourself feel worthy of the honor."

He played for a while longer, rather well, he thought, but not with the magic that had enlivened "Penna Pike." It was no matter; magic could come when it wanted to.

For right now, he was with his friends, safe and warm, and the plague could be ended soon enough. Amatus had been wracking his brain for people who had died in ways that might make a vampire, but he had no idea. He was only grateful it was not Golias, for that would have been unbearable.

6

The Early Dew

*T*he palanquin was long since put away in its case, the fire banked, and the candles extinguished, and the sliver of moon that had pursued the sun through the day was about to set over the roofs in front of them as they sat in Calliope's bedroom, the doors open to the winter chill, waiting for the vampire. Beside the doors stood Sir John Slitgizzard and the Twisted Man, each with garden trellises laced with garlic, ready to bar the vampire's way back out. Calliope, wearing a garland of dried garlic blossoms, lay in her bed, seemingly asleep, for they wanted nothing to seem unusual until the vampire was well inside.

Grim and silent as death itself, Duke Wassant stood by with a hooded lantern, a supply of rosewood stakes, and a sharp ax.

And crouched in a little alcove, ready to step between the vampire and the bed, Amatus waited with stake and mallet.

The moment the way back out was barred, the Twisted Man and Sir John Slitgizzard would seize the vampire and wrestle it down. Then Amatus would stake it, and the Duke would strike its head off, and after they burned the rest of the corpse in the fireplace, they would fill the mouth with garlic, and bury the head at the nearest crossroads. It was the way vampires had been disposed of in the Kingdom since anyone could remember, and children had learned the procedure just as they learned what words were said at weddings, how to carry on their parents' trade, and not to allow anyone too young to drink of the Wine of the Gods.

As Amatus sat on his heels, his back against the wall, he kept turning over the last conversation they had had with Calliope. Just before putting out the candles, she had refused their requests, again, that she tell them who the vampire was.

"I will say this, for I have been down that road. It is repulsive and disgusting to the vampire itself—in some ways that is the very worst of it. It will long for release—"

"Can we not at least say he or she?" Duke Wassant had demanded.

Calliope shook her head, and the red silk of her hair flashed in the candlelight, but the swirl of color was as out of place as real red silk would have been at a funeral. "There will be a moment of deep shock when you see who it is. You must rehearse in your own minds that you will nevertheless do what needs to be done. You may trust me absolutely that no life remains in this vampire—it is absolutely undead—and that it is in the deepest pain and longs only to be properly released. It may well thank you at the moment you stake it, and bless you with the last bloody foam from its mouth."

"Are we lost, then, if we begin to talk to it? Does it have power to ensorcel us?" Sir John asked.

"Not according to the books, Sir John," Amatus had said. "They can fascinate the unwary in the way that a snake can fascinate a rabbit—which is to say, sometimes but not always, and it cannot possibly fascinate all of us at once. It might make one of us freeze for a moment, but it will not make any of us act on its behalf."

"Just the same," Calliope said, "and knowing you probably won't take this advice, I would suggest that we not talk to it. Even if it sincerely begs for the mercy of a killing, the urge to continue undead may overcome it and it may try some trick for which we are not prepared.''

Now Amatus sat, shifting his weight now and then between his attached right and detached left foot, and wondered. He knew he had had more than enough clues, for he had run through the list of people it might be many times, and the name had seemed to hang upon his tongue without his being able to speak it. This must mean that he knew but would not let himself know.

There was no one he hoped it was and there were many he hoped it was not.

Vampires, according to the old books, could be made in many ways. Suicide sometimes would do it, or a father's curse, if the stars were wrong, the motive evil, and the person already bent that way. Sometimes it might be something as simple as an improper burial. Occasionally a thoroughly evil person, rotten to the bone, desiring only to live forever and not caring who was harmed, might actually wish to become one, and this was almost always enough in and of itself.

And there was the long list at the back of the book: things that had been known, now and again, to make a vampire: thwarted lust and longing for vengeance; murder in the course of incest; dying in childbirth in the Temple of the Dead; an all-consuming passion for one who had died, leading to pining to death in close proximity to the grave; seduction by promises of pleasure followed by debauch and murder; an unconsummatable love affair with a ghost; many other things, some so odd that it was hard to imagine they could ever happen twice.

For the many-thousandth time Amatus ran over the list. At least it could not be his father, or Cedric, or Roderick, for all of them waited one floor below, with a reserve force of guards. If they did not catch and destroy the vampire, they would at least see who it was.

Something dark and flapping shot across the moon, at first like a bird. Vampires had no wings—how they flew was only one of the many open questions about them—but they were partial to flowing clothing, which hid the distortions in their bodies. It moved across again, and now he could see it was a human figure, standing upright, clutching a cape or cloak about itself.

Another swing across the moon—it was much larger now—and then it was visible. It did not flap or fly, nor did it appear to walk on air; it stood upright and moved, wrapped in its dark cloth, straight in at the window, growing larger and larger. The Twisted Man and Sir John stepped to the side and picked up their trellises.

The last moments before it lighted were the worst, for now he could see the bare, horny feet protruding from the heavy cloak, and how they were twisted into terrible claws. The single hand that stuck from the cloak was much too big, twice the size of the creature's face, and like the claw of some poisoned and distorted sea creature.

There was no sound as it came in through the window; the cloak fluttered but did not flap. There was the whiff of an old, wet tomb, and the vampire swept in to stand in the puddle of moonlight.

Sir John and the Twisted Man brought the garlic-laced trellises together behind the vampire with a sharp, silent motion. At the blotting of the moonlight, it whirled, but now it was too late; a single step showed it could not approach the trellises.

With a squeak and a clank, the Duke unhooded the lantern. The light was all but blinding, after so long in the deep moonlight.

"So," the wrapped figure said. "At last. This." The voice was cold and wet and barely a whisper.

Sir John and the Twisted Man jumped as one, jerking the figure's arms outward, forcing it backwards, seizing an ankle each, as it beat and struggled against them. Calliope rolled off her bed and backed away as they approached, then lunged forward, holding her garlic necklace out, so that the vampire could go no farther. Duke Wassant had closed in from another side, and they managed to force it down upon its back on the bed.

The fight seemed to go out of the monster all at once, and now it was pinned upon the bed, legs held by the Twisted Man and an arm each by the Duke and Sir John. Its swaddled head fell back, as if resigning itself to what must follow.

Gingerly, Slitgizzard snatched back the heavy hood it wore.

It was Mortis.

There was no question that she was a vampire, now, and quietly, in the back of his mind, Amatus realized how evident it had been in the last week or so. His feet seemed to pick themselves up and move him slowly toward her, the stake and mallet clutched in his hand. Calliope moved around beside him, took the stake, and set it upon the center of Mortis's chest. One quick, hard stroke would do it.

Her eyes had always been dark, but something had lived in them, and now they were empty.

He raised the mallet.

"How?" he asked.

"The scream you thought an ill omen was my dying of grief, Highness." He had never heard real warmth in her voice, but there had been something there—perhaps merely interest?—and now that was gone as well. The lamp flared and flickered, and the shadows of their clouds of breath danced wildly on the wall.

"Grief for Golias?"

"Grief."

He drew a long, deep breath.

The Twisted Man spoke. "Finish it."

Amatus raised the mallet. "I am sorry."

The vampire spoke. "If I could drink your apologies, I would drain you drier still. Either finish me or release me to feed. The choice is yours."

"I would heal you if I could."

"I am dead. Your touch works only on those who have not died yet. Either put my blood on your hands or put your blood in my mouth."

With a single, clean stroke, straight from the shoulder and swung with all his force, Amatus drove the stake through her and the mattress below, affixing her to the bed.

Her mouth opened wide in a dreadful shriek. Her tongue, long and black, flew out and was pierced and impaled by her fangs as her mouth snapped closed. The stench in the room was what one might expect from the piercing of a rotted, bloated corpse pulled from the river.

Most horrible of all, perhaps, was that for one instant, as her body returned to its proper form, her hand came up and reached for the stake, almost caressing it, as if trying to gently pluck it from herself, and her other hand reached for Amatus, as if wishing to hold his hand.

He reached for it without thinking, and Calliope slapped his hand away. Shock and pain made him look up, straight into the girl's eyes—and they were wide with fear. "You mustn't. Your hand is wounded. She could draw blood and continue . . ."

Mortis expired. There was no expression of peace, as the old ballads mentioned; there was hatred, bitterness, and above all self-pity.

Something stirred in Amatus; the world was different from what it had ever been before.

For a long time none of the others spoke a word. "Highness," Calliope said.

"What is it?" Amatus asked. He had expected some part

of him to come back, and he certainly felt different physically, but as he looked up and down his body he could see nothing—and yet it was different.

Calliope stepped close to him, resting her hand lightly on his arm, and leaned forward to whisper in his ear. "Your eye, Highness. You have your eye back."

Amatus looked up and around the room; time enough to look in a mirror later and see what he looked like—he had a feeling the effect was even more strange than the foot that seemed to walk of its own accord beside him wherever he went. For right now there was only the astonishment of discovering that the world had depth and a sort of reality to it that he had not seen in the time he could remember. "I . . . you all look so different," he said, looking around the room. "And so beautiful."

And then—perhaps from his own grief, or from the beauty of it all—he found that he did indeed have his left eye, for he could feel tears welling in both eyes and the force of blinking them back made the room dark.

The Twisted Man walked quickly to Mortis and put a cloth over her face. "Highness, you *must* go now—all of you must go—and send the King and the Prime Minister up to me."

His voice—in which fear or even concern had never been heard—was so urgent that they all obeyed at once, and in a short time found themselves on the street. "Stay as guests of the castle tonight," Amatus urged his friends. "We will sit in the tower room, with a bright fire."

To his great relief they all agreed. Of Amatus, it remains only to say that they spent the night gathered around the fire in conversations in which laughter and tears flowed freely, and went to bed late, all of them, and got up late for breakfast together. The next day Amatus healed Calliope's remaining servants, and they all helped Calliope to get her house back into order.

But Cedric, in his *Chronicle*, tells us of other things, which he swears Amatus never learned of. That may be true, for it is in Cedric's will also that his books be sealed unread for a century after his death, and Amatus tended to be careful and systematic about carrying out such wishes. So as to whether Amatus himself ever knew of what happened next, there is no one who can tell us.

When Cedric and Boniface came into the chamber, the Twisted Man had moved the lantern around better to illuminate Mortis's face, but left the covering over it. From the garments and from the blue skin they knew who it was, and they had both sighed, for fearsome as Mortis had been, she had been a superb Royal Witch, and they could not be sure how Amatus would take the loss of another Companion so soon after Golias.

The Twisted Man spoke. "I saw her begin to shift and change under the light before, and covered her face to stop that before he could see. What I show you now must remain between us forever."

In any other circumstance, Boniface would have objected, at least implicitly, to such an assertion of power over the royal person, but this time it seemed only in keeping. Cedric turned to the lamp and adjusted the oil valve a crack, so that the lamp was as bright as it could be, and drawing a candle from his pocket, he lighted it, and used it to light the candles in their sconces around the room.

The Twisted Man drew the cloth back, and said, "Now watch, Majesty and my lord."

Mortis's face was still beautiful, and in the bright light one could now see a sneer of contempt had settled onto it, except for a softness around the glittering reptile eyes.

But as they watched, the scales of her skin faded into it as if they had never been. The blue lightened to white, and then turned a soft pink. And the fangs which had been long and yellow as an old dog's when she was undead, now white and even pretty as they had been before, receded gently. Her features continued to change, the cheekbones coming down and sinking in, the chin broadening—

And the King cried out in deep horror and anguish; a moment later, Cedric gave a low, ill moan beside him.

The dead woman on the bed was now the very image of Boniface's Queen, who had died bearing Amatus.

"What can this mean?" Boniface whispered as he groped for a chair.

"As you have always thought might be the case, a story has come into the Kingdom, as they have so often before, and we are in the middle of it," the Twisted Man said. "I myself have seen . . . more than one story, shall I say, if you will permit me to leave it at that? And this may either be the sort of thing that *has meaning in* a story, or the sort of thing that is *merely in* a story. As for how she came into it—know this, Majesty. We came to be your son's Companions, and we traveled together, but we did not all come from the same places at the same time."

"But I buried her!" Boniface cried. "Cedric saw her into her tomb—"

"Who can say what you would find if you opened it now? And therefore better not to open it," the Twisted Man said. "And who can say, more than that, how it happened that your son was able to taste the Wine of the Gods, which should have been impossible? If there is nothing without a point in a story like this, then most surely there was a point to that, and what is it that makes you think that it is for your benefit, or for his, or for anyone's?

"In time to come, when the magic is draining so far out of the world that a vampire can be banished by crossed sticks and a sprinkle of water, when all that we do and say here will be spoken of in the brightest daylight or the darkest, wildest night without fear of bringing anything to pass, wise men will debate why there is any pain or suffering at all, and will say many foolish things and a few wise ones about it, but is it not enough for us to say 'pain has come this way,' and let it be? We do not yet belong to the gray, dull generations, or to times without meaning, or to times when meaning drains even from stories.

"We came from different places, and to be Companions, but not all of us are Companions for the same purpose. Do not ask me mine, for I do not know; or Psyche's, for it would break my heart to tell you; or Golias's or Mortis's, for now whatever it was is accomplished. But understand that they are not necessarily what you would wish them to be, and that they are not for anyone's benefit, though they may be, or they may work to someone's benefit.

"Let us strike off her head, fill her mouth with garlic, and dispose of her properly, for whoever she really is, and whether Mortis merely wore the shape of your dead Queen, or was she come back, or whether both of them were two faces of the same thing—she died as a vampire and we must see for the sake of the Kingdom that she does not rise again."

"You are solicitous of Amatus's welfare, for one who will not say that he came for his benefit," Cedric observed, as he moved to help the Twisted Man. King Boniface went to the balcony doors, opened one slightly, and stared out at the starry sky, and they did not trouble him for his help.

"I cannot say that I did not, either. I have duties to fulfill. But you know that when he was young he was often frightened of me, and I have heard you yourself mutter when I have tormented some monster or some enemy before killing it that you hope Amatus will never learn such things."

Cedric raised Mortis's—or the Queen's—head by the hair and carefully stretched out the neck for the Twisted Man's stroke. "I did not know you had heard that. I hope I have not hurt your feelings."

"I have none that can be hurt by any such comment." He pulled out his huge ax; Cedric pulled the head back by the hair, so that the neck was fully extended, and shrugged his traveling cloak around himself, for he expected a spray of blood.

There was none. The ax whistled, there was an odd tug against his arms and then a release, and her head was hanging by the hair in his hands. He turned to get the garlic—

They all, even the Twisted Man, shouted, for the body on the bed, which had brought forth no blood at all except for what had already welled up and dried around the stake, was folding and collapsing like an apple in the sun, but many times faster, so that shortly there was a bare husk there. The Prime Minister gaped as the head he held by the hair rapidly aged, dried, decayed, and crumbled to dust at his feet, leaving him holding a hank of hair.

"Well," said the Twisted Man, after a long pause, "I suppose we should fold up the sheet with what's left in it, sweep the rest off the floor, and then burn it all. We will have to apologize to Lady Calliope for burning the sheet."

They did, without talking further. As the last bits went blazing up the chimney, the Twisted Man stood and silently took King Boniface by the arm, and the two of them walked out the door.

Cedric did not follow, but the next day his discreet inquiries revealed that many people working late at night or early in the morning—dairymen, vegetable sellers, harlots, drunkards, poets, and the like—had seen the King and the Captain of the Guard walking through the darkened city, deep in conversation with each other, sometimes close together and the King laughing as if they were the best of old friends, at other times turned away and talking from the corners of their mouths as if they could barely bear to be near each other. No one had overheard a word of it.

So what they talked of, or why they returned to the castle only as sunlight first touched its top, must remain outside the story.

III

A Man Who Will
Stand His Ground

I

Years and Gossip Pass in an Ordinary Way, Until a Grim Conversation on a Beautiful Day

*W*hether or not anyone knew exactly how the "curse" on the Prince worked—and there were many who thought they did, and would loudly explain it to anyone willing to part with coin in a taboret or a stupor and to keep listening to the explanation—there was no feeling that it was an ill thing for the Kingdom. If anything, they rather liked it; those who had had a chance to hear the Prince speak, before guilds, civic groups, fraternal societies, and the occasional cult, delighted in trying to describe how there was just half of him there, except that two parts of the half that wasn't, his left boot and left eye, were there, but with nothing in between.

It was hard to picture it in the mind, and thus the description was never like the actual effect, and no two descriptions ever quite alike, so it made for an endless subject of discussion as long as there were people about who had never seen him. Moreover, when they did—for he did not keep himself particularly secret—they always disagreed with the descriptions they had heard to date, and rushed back to their friends to argue, and that too made for long discussions in the little corners of the city, as the seasons turned and everything grew older.

Prince Amatus—the right side of him, anyway—lost some of the look of a boy, and learned to do administrative work and bother about taxes, armories, roads, and bridges, to avoid saying anything that might upset anyone pious and to always look solemn in the presence of the Hand and Book flag. King Boniface grew grayer, but seemed to become more shrewd and more jolly each year, so that there were arguments about whether, in the chronicles, he ought to be called the Merry, the Cunning, or (the most popular) the Good.

In summers the Vulgarians sat at their ease at the tables outside their stupors, having one cupola after another of the dark brown tea they brewed in silver sampans, and squabbled loudly about the Prince's missing left side.

In autumn the hunters came down from the northern and western hills, freshly killed and dressed gazebo upon their shoulders. The air was fragrant with the roasting and curing of the meat, and as the hunters ate dripping slabs of roast haunch, and drank the foaming autumn Pilaster, they talked of how the good Prince could be a whole man any time he wanted, but he must lose his Companions to gain back each part of himself and he was too decent a fellow to shorten Psyche's or the Twisted Man's days.

Winter blanketed the town with snow and made all the many colors of the bricks and cobbles shine wet in its bright light, and in every little taboret in the Hektarian Quarter, they drank the deep red Gravamen that cheered their hearts, and sang the version of "Penna Pike" which had at last been finished by the Prince, and told stories of dark nights and bright courage about him, though in truth he had done nothing more dangerous or exciting than could be found on the practice field or in the hunt for a long time.

And when spring came and the gypsies, layabouts, and troupials returned to the city and set up their trestle stages in every square, many of the little plays and stories referred to the Royal house and the connections between it and the Wine of the Gods.

Because Cedric was still Prime Minister, as well as General of All the Armies, and as efficient and vigorous as ever, his many agents saw to it that there was much untruth mixed in what was said, and no one knew the whole truth of anything in the city. So when Waldo the Usurper, who every year grew more bitter and evil as he sucked the neighboring Kingdom of Overhill dry, sent forth spies to come and listen in the city, they went back bearing tales of the sort of peace and prosperity that Waldo longed to end, but they also told tales of magical protections and mighty invisible powers. When they described a people given over to the business of living and enjoying, they mentioned hideous curses and pacts with dark beings, made by the Royal family in times long gone for the protection of the Kingdom.

Most importantly, when the spies discussed the succession, they talked of many princesses turned back by the Prince, of his refusal to go courting, and of his fondness for the Lady Calliope obstructing a sensible political marriage and thus working to Waldo's advantage—and the rumors that Calliope herself might be of royal blood, when they came to Waldo's attention, were no more believable than any other rumors which came to the cold citadel at Oppidum Optimum, which stank from abuse and lack of cleaning, where the bones of Calliope's family continued to dry in the upper chambers. It seemed most likely to Waldo that Calliope was what she appeared to be, the rather attractive daughter of minor nobility with whom the Prince had become infatuated. After all, her name was a common one.

Then too, though Waldo had fearsome force at his command, perhaps he hesitated because he knew the Kingdom was wide and strong and rich and thus could afford a considerable army, and that Cedric, by dint of stretching and wise use of resources, had managed to make the Kingdom get much more army than it paid for.

Waldo may even have hesitated knowing that the giant, swaddled, distorted shadow that seemed always to be there at the least hint of danger to the Prince had come to the Prince as one of his Companions, and thus as some bit of personal magic. But if he feared the Twisted Man, we can hardly say whether it was because of his great strength, or his obscure origins, or because four times, when Waldo had sent assassins forth, they had not come back, nor had his spies been able to learn what had happened to them, for the spies had been found in various of the back ways of the city, some punctured by the pongee of Duke Wassant, some pockholed by a precisely placed pismire ball that spoke of Sir John Slitgizzard, and a few with their heads turned backward—which could only be the work of the Twisted Man himself.

Nor did Waldo have much hope of treason. Though Amatus was generous and saw to it that his friends grew rich in his service, and he grew more indebted to them for their hunting down the perils of the city night, the deep mutual obligation was not permitted to weigh down their friendship. The Prince remained on the best of terms with them, just as if they were old friends with nothing but friendship between them.

Thus they sat out one bright spring day, over the ruins of lunch, sipping warm Gravamen that was a gift from the proprietor of the Gray Weasel, on the High Terrace, facing the west, so that there was a fine view out over the city—and beyond it to the hills, which eventually rose to mountains, beyond which, to the west and south, lay the lands usurped by Waldo.

Duke Wassant was there, stouter than ever but still strong and quick, with his wits all the keener. Sir John sat at his ease, his boots up on the broad, low wall that enclosed the balcony,

letting the warm rays of the sun bake out a slightly sore shoulder and ankle, brought on by his vigor in his pursuit of spies
and gazebo. Had he been a reflective man, he might have been
reflecting that a life as active as his was the sort that informed
one, well before anyone more sedentary might notice, that age
was creeping up.

Next to Amatus, and leaning against him, her eyes dreaming of other things, sat Calliope, just at the fullness of her
beauty. And with all of them, sunning himself and letting his
old bones enjoy the feel of peace and safety, was Cedric, his
bushy beard and hair all gone quite white now, who had
found it unusually hard to talk to Boniface that morning
about threats to the Kingdom's security and so had come up
here just in case anyone might wish to spoil a fine afternoon
by discussing danger and fear.

"Does it not seem strange, in the sort of tale our lives are
becoming, to have evil come out of the West?" the Duke
asked idly, for like Amatus, he had acquired a passion for
learning, and particularly for learning the old tales, since in
the Kingdom there was a pronounced tendency for what
would be to be like what had been.

Cedric stirred slightly, without opening his eyes, like an
old dog dreaming of a rabbit, and Sir John, with a wink and a
smile, pointed to this.

But Amatus's answer was serious. "It is true that in many
tales the East is wicked, but they are tales of Kingdoms other
than this one. One reason the tales are so obscure to us is that
we are near the beginning. Time enough for geography to sort
itself out into oceans and continents, but that is not what we
are about."

There was much more that might have been asked then,
but no one to do the asking. For Cedric history and geography
were merely guides to where the forts ought to be, for Duke
Wassant geography was a matter of property and family lines,

and for Sir John Slitgizzard, as long as he knew who his friends and enemies were, and how to deal with each, there was no point at all in knowing anything else.

Calliope might have asked, had there been anything she wanted to know and did not know already, but she knew geography as well as Amatus did, and history rather better, and thus was not disposed to. And besides, the day was extraordinarily fine.

After a long pause, during which they did almost nothing but sip the Gravamen and look out at the sunlit landscape, Cedric decided to broach the subject further. "Since we have privacy here to discuss it, you do understand, all of you, that whatever clash there is to be with Waldo must come fairly soon?"

Amatus stretched, enjoying the sun and the breeze, and said, "I've had that in my mind for a year or so, and I know several of the reasons why it should be so, but none that wholly convince me."

Duke Wassant grunted. "He is sending a better sort, smarter and tougher, as his spies, and he sends them in greater number. Our spies tell me, also, that his army grows stronger and more ready, though his land grows poorer and bleaker. If he does not move soon he may never be able to, for an army like that cannot be borne on the back of commoners like those for long."

"I have felt that way, now and again—not what Wassant says, but just that war will come some year soon—for some time," Sir John said.

Calliope was silent, but she moved to the wall, resting her hands upon it, and stared into the distance. Cedric and Amatus, who knew, realized she was thinking of the family of whom she had no memory, of the bones of two older sisters, three brothers, and her parents, who all lay, decayed and dry, in the stone corridors of the citadel of Oppidum Optimum. Travelers who had bribed guards to show them said the skeletons were untouched: her father and oldest brother lay on the stairway where they had fought to keep Waldo's men back. Her oldest sister had been slain at the door. Another brother had been beheaded in the nursery, his dead mother's arms still around him. And below the blood-drenched family tapestry, tracing the Kingdom of Overhill from its foundation a thousand years before to the reign of Calliope's father, lay the crumbled and broken bones of the year-old twins, boy and girl, whom Waldo himself had swung by the heels against that wall until they came apart.

But Sir John and the Duke had no idea of this, and so to them it seemed that she looked out toward where the Winding River met the Long River near the horizon, and that her thoughts must be going up the road from there to the fort that Boniface had erected in the Isought Gap just after Waldo's first invasion had been thrown back at Bell Tower Beach, the year after Amatus had been born, and thinking of the number of young men who would die to hold it, who would perish so that the Kingdom might not be sucked dry as Overhill had been. Though they were wrong in the particular, in general they were right, for whenever Calliope thought of Waldo her blood surged and she thought of war.

She had never for a moment doubted that some day Amatus and an army would burst through the Isought Gap, or sneak through Ironic Gap in the north, retake the citadel, and hang Waldo from the famous Spirit Spire. So as she thought of her murdered family, she naturally also thought of the roar of culverts and the rattle of omnibuses and festoons.

Yet today, because it was warm . . . or the air smelled of spring . . . or perhaps she had had too much Gravamen . . . she found herself wishing, sadly, that no one had to die.

Except Waldo. She could hardly help wanting that.

It had been a long pause, for the conversation before had been pleasant and it was clear that the one to follow would not be.

At last Amatus said, "Will we be ready for the war, then, if it comes this spring?"

Cedric sighed. "More than we were last spring, less than we shall be if he holds off a year, and I am sure he knows this as well, which makes me think he will be coming soon, Highness."

"But will we be ready?"

"One never knows that for sure until it happens. Then either we win, in which case we were ready enough, though we probably could have been readier; or we lose, in which case we were not ready enough. We are as ready as I can get us. I think we will prevail, and I have done my utmost to make sure we will, but I can promise nothing, Highness. If war comes, matters are in the hands of the gods—and as you know, we know little of the gods."

"What remains that we could do?"

"Most of it is done. Our best scout, old Euripides, skied through the pass some weeks ago; he should be back long before their army can move, and if they are preparing they cannot conceal it from him. As for the rest, well, we have suitable arms for every man we can put in the field, and powder and shot enough to fight all summer. We've food enough if we don't have to stand a siege, and if we can keep the road open to the eastern provinces until midsummer, the early crops there will fill up the city's larder for a year. The army could do with more wagons, but if the wheelwrights step up their pace, it will be noticed by Waldo's spies—"

"Have them step up the pace. And had you not planned to sweep for his spies?"

"That was my suggestion. But no sweep is perfect, Highness, and though we have many of his spies left in place, and long lists of their suspected accomplices, we do not have all of them, I am sure, and some of them are bound to evade us and make their way west. And even if the wheelwrights' activity, or that of the forges or the powder mills, does not alert them, then I think you may fairly assume that the slaughter of all their other spies will."

The Prince nodded. "Suppose, though, that they are coming—then we gain time and preparation. Suppose they are not—then they lose many spies and we gain much in provision, so they will have to put it off longer. So long as we don't yet take men from their work to make them soldiers, the longer Waldo puts war off the stronger we are."

Cedric nodded. "We will do so, then."

Without turning from where she had been standing, Calliope asked, "Tell me again, Cedric: by what right does Waldo claim Overhill? Is it not part of the Kingdom?"

"It was once," Cedric said, for though he knew that Calliope knew everything he was going to say, and did not need to hear it, she had reasons for wanting Sir John and the Duke to hear it—she wanted to make sure the war would not end with sending Waldo's army back into Overhill.

So did Cedric. And if the Prince's friends, loyal tools of Cedric they had so often been, could not be convinced of the necessity of destroying Waldo rather than merely beating him, it would tell Cedric much about the politicking yet to be conducted.

Thus Cedric was carefully neutral in his explanation, as if Calliope were merely a bright, interested student of history: "Lady, some sixty kings ago, King Baldric the Easily Persuaded was King in the city, and he had a younger brother, Pannier by name. Pannier was a difficult sort, more so even than most younger brothers, and it became increasingly desirable to get him out of town and away from the capital, where he caused endless trouble. To this end, King Baldric created the title of Deputy Sub King in Charge of the New Lands, and since Overhill had just been settled, and Oppidum Optimum founded, he gave his brother the title and a seat, which put him many days' journey away.

"This should have sufficed, but Pannier was much more

than merely unruly, as it turned out. At first the courtiers around him learned to shorten his title down to Sub King, and then to drop the Sub, and at last he was in most ways the King of Overhill, until he went so far as to have a crown made, and then finally to place it on the brow of his son, Farthingale.

"Now at such a pass, heaven knows, many kings would have gladly fought against encroachment, but Baldric was fond of his brother, and fond of his troops, and saw that there was little to be gained from war and much to be gained from friendship, and so he ceded Overhill to the line of Farthingale, until such time as the line should become extinct, and Farthingale, being just as ambitious but not nearly so proud as his father, acquiesced in this by providing that if his line were to fail the succession would pass back here. Thus no war was fought and friendly relations were established.

"The ambition of the Kingdom was always to reunite the two kingdoms by marriage, so that one child might be born heir to both thrones, and princes and princesses from here often went courting in Overhill. Just as diligently, the Farthingalian dynasty of Overhill married carefully, avoiding anyone of our Royal lineage. And there matters stood—until Waldo seized power there."

Wassant nodded. "But it would follow, from what you say, that since he has slain their whole royal family . . ."

"That he is now occupying a province of the Kingdom, over which Boniface has jurisdiction. Yes. It would follow."

"But then . . ." Sir John was silent, for he was never entirely sure of himself when called upon to reason in words, and liked to chew things over a long time before reaching a conclusion. "It would seem that King Boniface and Waldo ought to be at war . . ."

Cedric shrugged. "Waldo is virtually at war with the human race. He has come close to war with Hektaria and Vulgaria more times than I can count. As for King Boniface, in the days just after Waldo's invasion, other things intervened;

Boniface's father had left the Kingdom a mess, his Queen—forgive my saying this, Amatus—though he loved her, had brought him misery, his armies were in the worst sort of disarray. Had we invaded Overhill we should have lost. As it was we barely beat Waldo at Bell Tower Beach. There was much painful effort put into getting ourselves to our present readiness, and I think that now we will be able to deal with him—sufficiently, so that we will only need to deal with him *once.*"

"Well, if Overhill is ours, we ought to take it back, if we can," Sir John said, privately rejoicing because he now knew everything he needed to know, and could leave harder questions to others.

There was another long interval, for the Duke had arrived at that conclusion well before Sir John had, but had been trying to find a way to undo it. To defend both the Isought and the Ironic gaps, with enough reserves to throw Waldo back if a pass fell, would be difficult but not impossible; to that extent Wassant thought they could win the war. But to carry the fight through one of them, and down to Oppidum Optimum, and then to take the city that Waldo had been fortifying for more than twenty years—this was going to be something else altogether.

Not that they could not win, but it would be difficult at the least and just possibly they might lose. In any case many fine young men, who normally should only have to trifle about what their sweethearts wore to the fair and what their rivals might scheme in the way of clandestine meetings, were going to be torn, sliced, or blown to pieces.

And though after all everyone must die, and keeping Waldo out of the Kingdom and ending his threat forever was about as good a thing to die for as was apt to come along, it was surely a good thing not to die right away. In the service of his Prince, Wassant had probably killed forty-five or fifty men, almost all of them at close range, and he had seen them die, often been the only comfort they had (how odd, he thought, that he had held a dying man's hand and whispered that his mother would be there soon if he wanted her, and he had done this a dozen times, always for men whose lifeblood he had just let out with his pongee). Wassant knew how dying was done, at least in principle, and he knew that whether you did it screaming and weeping like a coward, or merely bowed your breast and succumbed with the soft sigh of a stoic, you ended up dead.

He thought that Calliope, who must be thinking the same thing, was also sad for the slaughter of young men. He certainly knew that she liked young men. But her real thoughts were of the tradition of her family, of never permitting Overhill to be reabsorbed, and how because she had not grown up among them she could feel none of the power of that tradition.

She was wondering if her butchered family would approve of what was going to happen, for she could think of no one save Amatus that she would want to marry, and that would be the end of Overhill as a separate kingdom. The common people of Oppidum Optimum, whom she had never seen—who had no idea that she had ever existed, for what had saved her life had been the laxity in record keeping at the time Waldo had seized the castle, so that her nurse had been able to flee with her by pretending to be a vegetable seller—would doubtless rejoice at anything that put an end to Waldo. And the people of the Kingdom, who had gotten proud of their good King, and his princely son with the interesting affliction, would undoubtedly be happy to make patriotic speeches and otherwise rejoice at the readdition of lands, especially since the slaughters Waldo had wreaked upon Overhill meant that much good land stood idle and unclaimed there.

But in all truth, could she claim to be upholding anything of her family's tradition, other than its bloodline? She had read both books in the Royal Library about Overhill custom, tradition, and court etiquette, but for all her knowledge, she would never feel it deep in her bones, as a proper queen should. As well, then, to let it all fade . . . but if it were as well to let it all fade, then why not give up her notion of being royalty, which could only endanger her life, and merely hope Amatus would marry her out of a foolish and unpolitical whim? And would she not—if she admitted the truth to herself—rather be married because he liked her than because the political situation demanded it?

Which brought her to that dark question itself, and just as she was thinking it, she felt Amatus's warm arm slide around her waist.

"Well, then," Amatus said, "it seems that what must be, will be. Cedric, I can ask you only one question that truly matters—in your judgment, best of counselors and judges, are we going to win?"

Now, where there had been no debate at all in Sir John, and only some regret in the Duke, and a full-fledged argument within Calliope, there was a virtual panel discussion within Cedric. As General of All the Armies, he knew that one is never ready enough and that anything one is doing today will bring its fruits later than expected, and so he wanted to say they were utterly unready. Yet in that same role as General of All the Armies, he knew just as well that his forces were in as fine and ready a condition as they had ever been, and that the odds, matching only troops against troops, were all in his favor.

And yet again, as General, he did not like to see his troops die—he had lavished too much care and attention on them to see that calmly.

And then as Prime Minister, a dozen more considerations of state intruded; and finally because he was sensitive as well as intelligent, Cedric was troubled personally by even more issues, questions, and things not known to us at this late date.

So it was only slowly that he brought himself to say, after a long sip of Gravamen and a moment to savor the quiet safety of the day, "Highness, it depends on several things. If the roads dry on his side before they dry on ours, then he might take the forts in the passes, for we cannot adequately garrison and supply them against that. But dry springs are rare in Overhill . . . unless he has worked some powerful magic, in which case we must also fear that he will have found allies of the old and foul sort, perhaps the goblins to mention the obvious, but there are older and fouler things than goblins farther under the earth. And finally, he may have allies we know nothing of; new lands are still opening and new peoples coming into them. The Hektarians and Vulgarians to his north are friendly to us, and even might offer us alliance, but we cannot be sure he does not have some people of whom we have not yet heard ready to march with him to plunder us."

Amatus nodded calmly. "Many things may go wrong and many surprises may be in store. But can we win, as far as you know?"

"We can beat what we know him to have, Highness, thoroughly enough to permit us to march across the mountains and take Oppidum Optimum. But I cannot say whether his moves are afoot now because he has found a new source of strength, or because he has come to fear he will grow weaker with time. Either could be the case."

Amatus nodded gravely, and—knowing he was imitating his father and no longer embarrassed by the fact—he added that Cedric's advice was particularly good because it was given with particular caution. And then, because he was still young, and so were his friends, he added, "And is there anything we can do tonight?"

"Highness," Cedric said, "your job is the difficult one of pretending that nothing is going on, and of scheduling a busy social schedule with a number of rounds to a variety of embassies. You might take the Lady Calliope with you."

"He might indeed," she said, smiling. Now that evenings

had more light and warmth, she had been longing to be out and about.

"And what will it accomplish?" Amatus asked.

Cedric fought down his wish to say, "It might get us an unusually fine queen, one of these years," and instead replied, "It provides opportunities, Highness. You will force spies to move to follow you, and to communicate with each other, and this will expose them to the weapons of our friends here."

"So you will face danger while I attend parties? I won't hear of that—"

Sir John, to everyone's surprise, including his own, spoke first. "Highness, we will face those dangers because *we* must. *You* are the only bait that will draw them. The Duke and I could not lure four flies to a pile of manure. And though I trust it will not offend you, you are not the pismire shot I am, nor the Duke's equal with the pongee, nor do you truly match either of us with the escree. The work must be done, and my lord Cedric has been accurate about how and by whom."

Had it been as recent as a year ago, Cedric wondered, or had it been more like five, since he would have expected Prince Amatus to quarrel in defense of his honor? Now the Prince did no such thing, but nodded and spoke softly. "I shall try to be worthy of such service. And here, Duke Was-sant, take this silver whistle from me, just for tonight, and blow it if you or Sir John are in trouble; it summons help, as you may recall."

And then, just as if the whole conversation had not passed at all, they returned to drinking wine, singing, and gossiping about the new wave of ladies in waiting, some of whom were not waiting very long.

2

An Affair of an Evening

*T*he Hektarian Embassy, since time immemorial, had been noted for the quality of the tea given there; it was given late in the afternoon so that people would be all the hungrier, for the Hektarian Ambassadors wanted people to enjoy it, and Hektarian aesthetics are built around contrast.

The Hektarian Ambassador, who was unusually genial even among Hektarians, was particularly delighted today because Prince Amatus and the Lady Calliope, quite unexpectedly, turned up. Since the Hektarians serve tea as a buffet, so that people can converse and mingle more freely, there was no difficulty in handing them another plate, and it was with some delight that the Hektarian Ambassador also noted that Amatus, after accepting a plate of protons and simile and a glass of Gravamen, seemed to go out of his way to converse quietly with the Ambassador.

True, it was only pleasantries about the weather and family matters and so forth, but since one major aspect of the Hektarian foreign policy was to try to marry off one of their available princesses to Amatus, for the Ambassador to talk to the Prince about anything at all was desirable. And besides, he noted with some pleasure, one reason the conversation went on as long as it did was that one rather rude young man who seemed to be trying to work his way toward them—no doubt to petition for some favor or other—was intercepted by the Lady Calliope, who practically threw herself at the young fellow, standing very close to him and leaving him no courteous way to get closer to the Prince and the Ambassador. This was not the behavior of a woman who thought she was going to be Queen, and so some decision had plainly been made, which might account for the Prince's visit here.

If so the Prince was not rushing matters, whatever matters might be, for not long after he vanished from the party, collecting the Lady Calliope as he went.

As the two stepped through the archway, just out of hearing of the Hektarian guards, Calliope said, apparently to the air, "Young, blond, taller than Amatus, blue cloak and red boots, yellow star on the cloak, calls himself Miharry."

She said it softly, tenderly, as lovers do, and Amatus gently kissed her, so that even if the Hektarian guards had heard (and they did not) they would have thought the words they did not catch were endearments.

The two climbed into the Royal Coach and drove to the evening reception at the Vulgarian Embassy. The echoes of the clatter of their wheels were still sounding as Miharry himself strolled casually out through the gate.

He turned left, not in the direction the carriage had gone, and now he walked more quickly. As he did, he occasionally—at odd intervals—changed his gait, or turned around, but he saw nothing. If anyone had been looking back over his shoulder when Miharry was not, they might have seen a shadow that suggested a heavyset man, moving in a way that seemed improbable for one so fat, as gracefully and lightly as one of the girls who dance for flavins in the taborets.

Miharry stepped sideways into an alley. After a time he jumped out suddenly, looking wildly about him. There was nothing there. He stood in the dark street and sighed.

He was tilted backwards by the jaw. Something big was against his back. A blade as sharp as a razor lay on his throat.

"Where is your meeting?" a voice asked quietly.

Miharry did not speak.

"It does not greatly matter to me," the voice that went with the great bulk behind him added, softly. "You may struggle and die here, not struggle and be tortured until you speak, or speak. It is time to decide."

Miharry swallowed hard, and said, "I am sworn—"

"You are released from any oath at death," the Duke said, slicing Miharry's carotids and jugular and letting him fall forward, then wiping his blade on Miharry's triolet. He had always hated torture, and he hated to see honorable men break their word, and no doubt Miharry had some sort of honor. Spies usually did.

He made sure the spy was dead, and crept down the alley. Sure enough, he found a loose stone in a corner, behind which there was a piece of paper. He pocketed the paper and waited; from where Wassant sat, whoever moved that stone next would be silhouetted against the alley opening.

Then he drifted into the light sleep he had long practiced. Duke Wassant dozed pleasantly, his jaw tied lightly with a ribbon from his hat, because he knew that fat men often snore and even though he hadn't yet, he couldn't be sure when he might start. He woke without a start when there were footfalls in the alley.

The figure was muscular and well-built, and Duke Wassant knew it at once. He waited until the pismire was pointed off to the side, so as not to risk a snap shot, and said, "Sir John."

The figure did not move, except to let the pismire creep back toward the source of the sound. "Duke?"

"Yes."

"Give some sign."

Damn Sir John for his overcautiousness, anyway, Wassant thought, and then said, "No, *you* give sign. What birthmark does the Lady Calliope bear on her inner thigh?"

Sir John stood up straight. "I don't know *that!*"

"Then you are undoubtedly Sir John Slitgizzard. Anyone else would have made something up, being sure that you would know."

Chuckling, Sir John slid the pismire back into his swash— and then suddenly asked, "But we've only established that I'm me, Duke, what about you?"

"Who else would have asked you such a question?" The Duke came forward. "How was hunting?" he asked, putting his arm around Sir John's shoulder.

"Two of mine lying on top of your one. I'm ahead. I imagine mine were coming for a message from yours?"

"Very likely. Where did you pick them up?"

"The first at the Vulgarian Embassy, following the Prince out; the second joined him at a tavern. I left a man to watch at the tavern, a fellow named Hark. . . ."

"I remember him, a great deal of experience, and often there when things that matter a great deal happen." The Duke and his friend walked back up the alley, still alert, and the Duke said, "If you noticed the time—"

"A bit past the shank of the evening," Sir John said, "by the bell clock."

"Then we might go to the playhouse. The torchlight show should be beginning, and Amatus was planning to see it."

"Good, then," Sir John said. "Let us catch a carriage . . . we shall be less conspicuous and there will be fewer rumors flying about us that way than if we are seen walking the streets."

The Duke nodded, and at the next big corner they found an old carriage, much battered but clean enough inside, and told the driver to go to the Sign of the Rambunctious Gazebo.

"The Prince's own company is performing tonight, and several of his favorite troupials are in the principal parts," Sir John observed.

Duke Wassant had never much cared for the theatre, for it was a vulgar place, where like as not one might encounter a pickpocket or cutpurse. Besides, he loved good music, and theatrical orchestras were raucous; fine dancing, and theatre dance was anything but delicate; and truthfulness, and everyone in the theater was pretending to be someone they were not. Sir John, on the other hand, was passionate about theatre, and babbled on as they rode, of the fine troupials they were to see.

"It is really a surprise, I understand, to everyone except Cedric, that Roderick should turn out a playwright, but apparently he has been quietly pursuing it for years and they say that this is a remarkable piece of work," Sir John said. "It is called *The Masque of Murder*, and it is said to be about—"

"Please, Sir John, don't get yourself into a fret about it; what if we have to pursue someone before the show is over? You'll only be disappointed." The Duke shifted his bulk around, looking for a more comfortable spot on the bench seat of the carriage.

Sir John nodded. "Of course you are right. But it is hard not to, after what I have heard of this play—and to think that the artist was under our very noses—" But then Sir John sat bolt upright; in the dim light of the flaring candle sconces, reflecting from the oilpaper windows, he had a haunted, shadowed look.

"What is—"

Sir John gestured for silence and turned to raise the oilcloth shutter a crack. Keeping his head well back, he peeped through the opening, and whispered, as softly as he could above the din of the carriage wheels on the cobblestones, "We've just crossed Wend. Wherever he's taking us it's not to the Rambunctious Gazebo. I'm afraid that—"

The carriage lurched and stopped; Sir John leapt sideways, and there was a thud. Wassant saw the blade of the escree stuck through the oilpaper into the cushion where Slitgizzard had been, and was drawing his pismire before his mind said what had happened . . . *kidnapped.*

There was thumping on the carriage roof—the driver climbing back, or someone getting up there with a pismire to shoot them in the back if they burst out through the doors. With a slash of his escree, Sir John extinguished both sconces, and now it was darker inside the carriage than out.

In the pitch blackness there was nothing to see except the oval windows themselves shining through the oilcloth shutters, leaving a little square ring of light around themselves where the edge of the oilpaper was. There was no sound for a long moment, and then, very, very softly, the door lock began to turn.

Sir John cocked the chutney on his pismire, moved near the door whose lock was turning, and placed his hand upon the ceiling. He felt a little shift of weight, and now he knew where one of the foemen's feet was; pressed firmly along the ceiling, found the other by its resistance, and placed the pismire, muzzle against the ceiling, squarely between them. All this took far less time than it takes to tell, and during the bare quarter of a breath while it was happening, Duke Wassant had been cocking the chutney of his own pismire, and pressing his ear to the door to make sure that he knew from which side the unseen foe was turning the handle.

When he was sure, he placed his pismire close to the handle, in the spot where he knew the wrist must be, and watched the handle turn farther. It seemed to creep along, no faster than the minute hand upon a clock.

Wassant felt the soft tickle of a breath coming into his nose, and realized he was about to sneeze. He bit down on his lower lip as the door handle reached its full rotation.

So lightly as not to disturb him at all, and yet so firmly as to leave no mistake for its intention, Sir John's index finger touched upon the Duke's shoulder. With no jerk or tug to put the pismire the least off its mark, Wassant pulled the trigger, and both pismires bellowed like cannons in the enclosed space, their reports exactly overlapping.

The Duke kicked the door open, returned his pismire to his swash, and leapt through, drawing his escree in one smooth movement. He had footing on the cobbles and was whirling to check all sides before he realized that in the moonlight he had seen one man staring at the stump of his arm, and another slumped on the carriage roof, facedown, his hands jammed between his legs.

A dozen figures, all with escrees drawn, formed a semicircle around this side of the carriage.

A moment later Sir John was at his side. "Surrounded," Sir John breathed beside him. "All around the carriage. Wheels have been spoked—can't get it free and drive through."

Wassant nodded. Every one of the men facing them was hooded, and there were no torches to light them; they might have been statues.

They stood and waited, expecting the fight to begin at any moment, and when it did not, the Duke listened as the man who had lost his hand slipped into unconsciousness behind them, and then stopped breathing; listened longer as the ragged breaths of the man lying on his face faded away; listened and watched, and still the circle of silent swordsmen did not stir or speak.

His eyes had adjusted to the dark now, and he could see that their cloaks—gray-blue as all things were in the moonlight—were thick and hung with great weight on what seemed preternaturally slim bodies.

"What do you want with us?" Wassant demanded, when he began to fear that his attention might flag, yet did not want to begin the fight, for the numbers were so far against them that they would surely lose. "We are servants of the King and true liegemen to Prince Amatus. You have no right or power over us. Flee lest we slay you now.''

The circle of men—if they were men—about them did not move or make a sound. Many fast heartbeats went by, and then all of them stepped forward, as if in unison, with their left feet first, and took a single step forward and to the side, so that the circle constricted by half a pace and rotated a few degrees. The line of escrees pointed at them never dropped.

Sir John drew a pismire and said, softly and casually, just as if he were debating a minor point in politics, "Since you have had ample opportunity to shoot us, and you have not, your behavior seems to suggest to me, my friends, that you have been ordered to take us alive. Would any of you care to elucidate on that point? It is plain from the deaths of our coachmen that you have been ordered not to avenge any comrades, or perhaps it has even been made clear to you that our lives are more valuable than yours. Perhaps we can just find out to what extent this holds.''

Then he leveled his pismire at the figure most nearly facing him, cocked the chutney, took aim on a spot in the very middle of its body (for he had begun to wonder if it were anything human he faced), set the lovelock, and pulled the trigger.

The flash of the pismire's discharge seemed bright as day, and surely, Duke Wassant thought, this ought to bring help, and perhaps in any other part of the city it might—but this was the worst part, a place that few admitted was there, the section along Wend that was on no one's way to anywhere, where the houses had long since been abandoned because of fear of thieves and murderers, and whence the thieves and murderers had fled because things whose names they feared to speak had come to live in the houses, and gunge leaked up through the very pavement.

The figure before them bowled over backward, and lay still for an instant. Then it seemed to raise its head, and then to writhe peculiarly as if its neck were broken. It lay twitching upon the ground for longer than it seemed it should have been capable of twitching.

Another figure stepped out of the murk, over the body of the fallen one, and joined the circle. They all stepped forward and to the left again, once again closing the circle and revolving it.

Slitgizzard said something under his breath that the Duke found a little shocking. Indeed, even Sir John thought it was exceptionally profane, but the situation had utterly exhausted his vocabulary otherwise, and no lesser oath could possibly do.

While they waited, Wassant quietly reloaded all three pismires, and then—eyes never leaving the sinister figures—moved his own swash over onto Sir John's shoulders, retaining his escree and pongee, so that the better shot had all six of the pismires.

"You might try a few again," Wassant said, "and see if it slows them at all."

Fast as thought Slitgizzard drew, cocked, fired, and holstered four of the six pismires, so that Wend Street echoed with the booms and crashes, and the flashes seemed to stutter like a single great spark. Three of the foe fell, and then a fourth who was coming up to replace the first fallen one.

All four bodies began to twitch in just the same fashion as Sir John's other target had. Wassant watched this with the corner of his eye as he frantically reloaded.

"Even the one you shot first is still twitching," he breathed.

Slitgizzard nodded, a gesture that Wassant felt more than saw, for he had let the muzzle flashes blind a bit of his peripheral vision rather than put the great burning spots in the center of his sight. "If I could think of a way it could be possible, I would say that the heads are eating the bodies."

Then the ring of hooded figures took another step, and

then another, and another, now almost at the pace of a slow walk, always closing in.

"This will be the real business, then," Wassant said. "You might as well do what you can with these—here's the last of them reloaded."

The burst of six shots seemed to raise the dead, and the pismires tore out an arc of sixty degrees among the foe, so that there was a gap directly in front of them, but Sir John and the Duke had not run two steps toward that gap before it was closed up by reinforcements, and they were forced to step back to where they had been, back at the center of the circle. After a few more steps it was clear that the circle was herding them, and at first each thought that perhaps they would be forced to wherever they were to be taken prisoner, but then it became clear that for some reason they were being separated from the carriage, so that the circle around them could be truly perfectly formed.

"How can they care? They will have us anyway," the Duke muttered.

"Perhaps they are just so stupid that having been told to capture us in this way, they must do it in *exactly* this way," Sir John suggested. The two of them were back to back now, and the Duke had repeatedly sounded the Prince's silver whistle, but they knew no one from the castle guard or the city watch would dare to enter this part of town after dark, and so it gave them no sense of hope, only one of completion—they had truly tried everything.

The figures closed more tightly around them, and now they should have been able to see something in the dark hoods, but they could not. What they *could* see was that the hoods were not shaped like the heads of men.

Another two steps brought the hooded crowd shoulder to shoulder, at just the distance at which tips of escrees might touch if both opponents were fully extended. The two men could feel each other's breathing through their backs. There was no sound.

Very slowly, little hairy snouts began to poke into the light from the darkness thrown by the hoods; hairy snouts with yellow incisors. The heads themselves seemed to be collapsing and folding under the hoods.

"What—" the Duke muttered, and then he saw the red, tiny eyes flash, and the gray bodies leapt at them.

"*Rats!*" they shouted, to each other, and their escrees flashed through the foul night air, streaks of silver in the dimming moon, cleaving tiny bodies in the air.

Each of them knocked down half a dozen rats, cut into various sized pieces, in that first stroke, and many of the ones that landed did not land anywhere they could cling, so that they fell to the pavement and died under the stamping boots of the men. A few managed to get a grip and a bite before being flung off into the darkness, hurled against walls or over the rooftops to die far from the fight and plug the gutters or perhaps drop down an empty chimney.

They were not too many by themselves, but in fending them off, the men had gotten bitten, with all the threats of poison and sickness that that promised, and they had gotten pulled apart and thus did not guard each other quite so well when what had been under the cloaks rushed them, escrees pointing inward.

They were goblins, by their distortion and their mad eyes, but not as Sir John remembered them, for they were focused and disciplined, they sought to kill rather than to eat, and most of all, they plainly supported each other . . . when one was wounded, the others bore him out to safety and stepped into the breach, whereas in the old days a wounded goblin, like a wounded shark, was swiftly eaten by its fellows.

All of these thoughts crossed Sir John's mind in the little space he still had left in which to think in words. His left arm, roughly, was at Duke Wassant's left, so that they did not perfectly guard each other's backs, and they were so hard-pressed that they could not close up the difference.

The Duke fought just as desperately, and the odds were just as wretched, but his keen mind could not quite turn off. He noted that one slightly taller goblin seemed to move around the edge of the fray without ever quite closing into it, and seemed to carry his escree more as a precaution than with any sense of threat. Moreover, the escrees were not half-eaten by rust, as he would expect of anything that came out of a goblin trove, but rather were bright and seemed newly, if cheaply, forged. The goblins themselves were curiously well-dressed, and it was more odd that they were well-trained.

The only thing saving Slitgizzard and Wassant, the Duke thought grimly, was that whoever had trained the goblins had taught them only to obey orders, not to fight well. Indeed they often got in each other's way. When they did so sufficiently, Wassant or Sir John could lunge forward to pierce an eye or a throat, and even then the goblins pressing inward did not relent, so that their dead comrade would remain upright for some time because there was nowhere for him to fall.

Yet if they fought no better, only as if well controlled—Duke Wassant almost had a thought about that, but it was gone in the instant that moonlight glinted off a low-thrusting escree, which the Duke slipped to the outside before striking its holder dead with a blow direct to the heart.

It was at about the moment he received his third small wound—apart from the rat bites—that made Sir John realize that they might well not win. He'd never had a thought like that before.

The thought did not slow his arm—there was little in the world that could do that—but he found himself striking more fiercely and his heart sinking further at the same time, for he was the sort who would die well by instinct.

The Duke, who was the sort who would die well on principle, had reached the same conclusion some time before, and thus he struck and slashed with abandon as well; all around them the goblins were gathered in ranks six and ten deep, far too many of them to dream of bursting through. As the more subtle of the two, he knew how desperately important it was for Cedric to know what had become of them, and to know that goblins were involved and more capable than ever before, and so he fought just a bit harder, because he needed that split second he might gain in which he might—if he but had an idea—leave evidence behind.

Four long clouds, black as coal underneath and silvered with moonlight on top, like long low ships on some other errand, were headed for the moon. The two men and dozens of goblins locked in battle in the forgotten part of Wend Street were far too busy to look up.

But if the goblin leader saw it his heart must have been rejoicing, for goblin eyes are keen in the dark, and goblins are used to it and fight more fiercely when they have its cover. It must have seemed to him—and would have to anyone else who watched—that when the first dark cloud sailed across the moon, the end would come in a flurry of clashing steel (which would sound much like pots and pans being thrown down the stairs), the thuds of bodies on pavement (which would sound like bags of corn being dropped), the oozing of blood (which would make no sound), and the high mad cacophonous uproar of goblins cheering with their mouths full (which would sound like something best left unimagined). So as the rooftops that had glowed silver under the moon began to wink out, the cloud-shadows crawling toward them in a long single file, perhaps the goblin leader allowed his heart to surge upward, and even to imagine those sounds already in his ears.

He surely never heard the Twisted Man's omnibus, which tore off the goblin leader's head, sending him down to the gunge-wet cobbles, stone dead before he landed.

As the first foul finger of the black cloud stroked the clean white face of the moon, the Twisted Man fell upon the goblins from the rear with his great double-bladed ax, and laid into the press of goblins as if he were clearing weeds. Gallons of goblin blood, black in the blue moonlight, spurted from stumps of necks and limbs, welled in greasy pools onto the pavement, or spattered through the air in droplets blacker than coal. There were screams, but they were almost drowned out by the heavy thudding whacks of the Captain of the Guard's ax.

At first they stood to fight, almost as if they were men, but the death of their leader; or the sheer ferocity of the assault; or even the thought that was passing through Wassant and Slit-gizzard's heads at that moment, that whatever or whoever the Twisted Man might have been he was not human now; or all of these and things that only goblins know besides, drained their courage from them even faster than the blood drained from their dying fellows, so that they turned to run, slaying their fellows in their path.

And since the Twisted Man had begun to slash his way in a great arc around the two besieged men, this meant that the wave of panic ran in a spiral around the two men as well, the goblins in the innermost ring racing in a circle and slashing into the backs of the goblins in front of them, so that more goblins died by goblin hands than any other way, and the few survivors fled madly as a wooden horse thrown from an out-of-control merry-go-round.

Their repulsively reptilian bodies lay in heaps and piles, and the air was thick and sickly as a summer sickroom with the sulfur smell of their black blood. The two friends, hardly daring to believe their good fortune, wiped and sheathed their escrees and extended their arms in a courtly bow to the Twisted Man.

He returned their bow, and lifted their hands.

"How splendid of you," the Duke said at last, when he was feeling less overcome by his feelings. As he said it, the black mist pulled back from the moon, and the gunge on the slippery stones shone again, only slightly more appealing than the black voids the goblin blood made in the street.

"We owe you everything," Sir John Slitgizzard added.

The Twisted Man nodded. Perhaps he was not human enough to say that it was nothing, or perhaps he was too human. So he spoke only of business. "We must convey word of this to Cedric, King Boniface, and Prince Amatus. Goblins, well organized and armed—and out of their dark holes at all—this speaks of intervention, and not by any power we find friendly, nor necessarily by any that I know aught of. But first we must tend to your wounds—things this foul often fight with tainted weapons. You are both of such immense value to the Prince that I cannot allow you to become ill through anyone's negligence, least of all your own."

The three walked together, then, through that dark and abandoned part of the city and said little or nothing, but the two nobles felt as safe in the Twisted Man's company as they might have in the castle itself. After a long while Wend became a street that was merely dangerous, and they walked more easily; then one that was shady and slovenly, and their concerns lightened still further; and at last it was again the old familiar major thoroughfare, still crowded with people even at this hour because it was a fine spring night with a beautiful moon. It was as if they were only going down to the Gray Weasel.

The noise of the crowds on Wend had swelled enough to permit free conversation with little danger of being overheard, and so Sir John chose to ask, "Do you like us, Captain?"

The Twisted Man's hand went under his cloak, to a point just below his grayed and rusty mask which must have been his chin, and after stroking there for a moment, he said, "I remember 'liking' from long ago, and I suppose that I could safely say that I like you as much as I like anyone. I do not like to lie, I know, and I am comfortable in saying that much."

Duke Wassant, clever man that he was, saw some of what Sir John was getting at, and attempted to extend the question. "Could you say, then, that we matter to you?"

Was the Twisted Man's voice grim or bitter? Neither man ever recorded that crucial bit of evidence, but both wrote down his words in letters to friends: "All men matter to me. Too much. Far too much. This is part of what it is to have a curse."

The Duke nodded, though, not being cursed, he did not understand. "You feel all our suffering?"

"Feel it, feel how each of you feels his pain more than his fellow's, feel how all of you want someone to touch you compassionately and how none of you ever find that someone, feel the pain that all this causes . . . and . . . and . . ." Here the Twisted Man's voice fell to a dark whisper, like a soft breeze that was just enough to make corpses sway on a gibbet. "Feel the pain in you all, and enjoy it. And feel what it is that I am that I enjoy it."

There was a long silence, and then, so shyly and cautiously that afterwards both men wrote that their memories might have been altered by a dream, the Twisted Man said, "Still, I was not glad that you were in danger, and I was glad that it was to you that I could be of service. That is all I know of friendship nowadays. I hope it may meet your approval."

"It does," they said, quietly, together, and the three walked close to each other for a long walk more, but what errands they ran on, though dark and bloody and in the service of Amatus, were much of a piece with what has gone before. By dawn the city, if there had been some carrion bird that could smell the difference, stank of spies' blood and goblins' guts. And Duke Wassant and Sir John slept late the next day, for Cedric ordered that they not be disturbed.

It might be thought odd that they slept without dreams, or woke smiling to the bright afternoon sunlight, but the ways of the human heart are peculiar.

3

A Lengthy Interruption in a Council of War

*I*t was some weeks later, and word was down from the mountains that the snow had begun to melt in the Isought Gap. In that time the spy hunts had been fierce, and Waldo's agents had been killed or captured in great numbers, so that the city was already a battleground of sorts. Moreover, there had been two goblin uprisings, both serious, and Amatus himself had finally taken a punitive raid down into their tunnels to slaughter goblins, destroy their dwellings, and scatter white magics about.

There were more of them and they were better organized than ever before, but they fought less well and died more easily. When captured and tortured, all they would reveal now was that there was a new goblin king, and he was different.

"He must be, to keep them obedient so far away from himself," the King said grimly to Cedric, as the two of them climbed the winding back stairs to the Throne Room. "They have never before been able to follow orders once separated from their army—indeed they've barely had enough concentration to obey while they were still in their ranks. This is bad news, indeed, and would be even if Waldo were not on the move, or not in league with them—and I'm *sure* that he is both."

They swept by a long, graceful tapestry, woven by Psyche, depicting the history of the Kingdom since Boniface had assumed the throne. She filled in a new section every year, showing some event of the year, almost always including Boniface, so that as Boniface walked by the tapestry, Cedric noticed that his face became more and more like the one on the tapestry, until finally the resemblance was perfect.

"I have always found it odd that this castle is so snug and warm," Cedric said, the thought springing from who knew whence. "It seems untypical and not at all like a story."

"I am glad you did not say that it wasn't real," the King said, "for the whole power and strength of the Kingdom rests in its questionable reality. But there is wisdom in your question. Now, in most stories, there is a wicked usurper, which is why the castle is cold and drafty—for atmosphere, as it were. After he is overthrown—"

"Yes, I see," the Prime Minister said, "it is always said then that the castle rings with joy and warmth and love, and that they live happily ever after. But that is not this castle either—great sorrow has been known here."

"But never great sorrow without a point," the King said, "for if that were ever to be, the Kingdom would be merely real, and vanish to where your lap goes when you stand up."

There was now but one flight of stairs remaining for Cedric to ascend with his King, and he knew that he was being given hints of secrets that normally were only known to the Royal family, so with his mind on his diary for that night, he asked, "And how do kings come by this knowledge?"

"We read," Boniface said, and they were at the door of the Throne Room.

Most of the Council of War was already there waiting for them, milling around and chatting nervously under the War

Flag, the giant Hand and Book that hung in the Throne Room in time of national danger. Boniface elected to get a glass of wine and a little cheese, and to greet some nobles from outlying areas, before plunging into business, so after the burst of chatter when the King, Prime Minister, and General of All the Armies (counting Cedric in both roles) had entered, no one settled into seats.

Many of the nobility were there, especially those of the country south of Iron Lake, where the invasion would first thrust if it carried through the Isought Gap, but from all over the Kingdom as well. The old Count who had pretended for so many years to be Calliope's father was there as well, a brooding sadness about him which made Cedric wonder if he would carry out his part. Others wandered about, some trying to be effete and decadent and talk only of art and gardens, some trying to be bluff and hale and talk only of the hunt and the theatre, and a few quiet sad ones watching it all, thinking mainly of lives to be lost and lands burned, and wishing only to be themselves.

Duke Wassant and Sir John Slitgizzard were there, naturally, for they were widely known to be the Prince's men, and it was expected that whenever Amatus became King they would hold high offices, do his bidding, and help to keep his throne steady. They were so well suited to the job that there was little envy extended toward them, and much relief that the wild comrades of the Prince's younger days were now the steel-true friends of his maturity. They sat next to each other, the Duke polishing off a fine pastry he had been unable to resist, and Sir John sipping a strong brown tea of a kind that had only recently come in across the Great Desert to the east.

"I wonder whence this comes into our story," Sir John said, "for it seems to me such stories must be older than tea."

" 'Anything really old—not just in years—can have any number of times within it,' " the Duke quoted, licking the cream from his fingers surreptitiously, and wishing he did not desperately crave another pastry. "Golias always used to say that. I've no idea what it meant, but it seems to answer your question."

Sir John nodded. In his experience the best answers were that way.

Psyche and the Twisted Man came in together, a few moments later. The arrival of the Prince's Companions seemed to cheer everyone.

The Prince's arrival did not. Amatus and Calliope entered together, Amatus dressed properly for the occasion in half-triolet, trouser, and low court slippers, but seemingly in haste. Calliope was disheveled in a way that nearly shouted that she had just come from a bed. All eyes went to them, and widened.

The old Count strode to Calliope and slapped his purported daughter across the face with a sound like a belt hitting a drumhead. Tears welled in Calliope's eyes, but she stood upright and glared at him, her chin never dipping. The Count turned to the Prince.

"Highness, I have served under your grandfather, and under your father. It would seem my daughter has now chosen to serve under you. For the damage done my body in battle, I have only gratitude to give your grandfather. For the damage done my treasury in preparation for this war, I have only gratitude to give your father . . .

"And for what you have done to my honor, *Highness*, and that of my family, I give you such loyalty as a subject must. And no more. The friendship between our houses, though I have more to lose than you, is severed, and it will not grow together again. You may have this strumpet sprung from my loins, and use her as you like—she is your plaything to coddle like a poodle or butcher like a pig for your pleasure. I shall not stay to join your counsels."

Then the old Count lifted the medal given him after Bell Tower Beach, of solid gold, of which there were but eight in the Kingdom, from his neck, dandled it by its silk ribbon a moment so that the room fell silent with dread at what they were about to see, spat on it, flung it at Amatus's feet, turned with a great flash of his scarlet cape, and was gone. The heavy oak door thudded shut behind him.

The room went into an uproar, in the midst of which more than one door quietly opened and closed in the Throne Room.

Cedric shouted for order, and bellowed contradictory commands. Calliope burst into tears and collapsed against Amatus. Holding her up with his single arm, he guided her gently out. King Boniface began to echo things Cedric was shouting, especially the contradictory parts. More doors opened and closed.

Standing guard in the corner, as he was apt to be whenever anything important happened, Roderick wept openly with his men, ashamed also because a part of his mind could hardly refrain from imagining this as Act I, scene ii, of *The Tragical Death of Boniface the Good*.

Among the first to slip out had been Sir John Slitgizzard, and sure enough, as he waited behind the arras in the private room behind the Throne, the door opened again and a beautifully dressed figure stepped quietly out and went up the stairs. Sir John followed him silently to a storage room in the tower.

Then Slitgazzard drew his escree and shoved the door open.

The lord still held his quill in his hand, and the little bits of string used to tie up the message were stuck to his triolet, but it was clear that the pigeon had already flown—its cage was empty. Sir John lunged, putting his escree through the shocked lord's throat. The traitor crumpled to the floor.

Drawing a pismire from his swash, he stepped over the corpse, leaned far out the window, and peered upward. A lone pigeon was still circling its way upward, as they will when they look for altitude and have a long way to go. It was barely more than a speck, and no one knew the limitations of a pismire better than Slitgizzard, but nonetheless he tested the lovelock, cocked the chutney, rested one wrist upon the other, held his breath, and squeezed the trigger very gently. The pismire spat fire.

There was time for a long breath, and then great burst of feathers burst from the bird. Something broken and dead dropped down toward the courtyard. Looking down at one junior lackey who stood staring open-mouthed at it, Sir John shouted, "A gold flavin if you get me that bird!"

The pigeon hit the parataxis and bounced onto the low tiled roof of the clerihew, where it lay still. The boy scrambled up the gutter after it, and Sir John raced down the tower stairs to meet him.

The note on the pigeon's leg described the Kingdom as "on the brink of open revolt," which was not accurate, but it also contained a map and a list of force dispositions, which were. Sir John dug into his purse and tossed the junior lackey a gold flavin.

"They say you're the best shot in the Kingdom," the boy said. "They say that's why the Prince keeps you by him."

"Oh? Eh?" Slitgizzard said, for though normally he was the sort of courteous man who pays attention to children, he had been engrossed in realizing how much had been on this map and in this note. "Oh." He looked into the boy's shining eyes and smiled, for he himself as a boy had worshipped a soldier or two. "Er. That is, this was undoubtedly the best shot I ever made, or am ever likely to make, considering how much of it must be called pure luck. And even if it is not, certainly the most important. I am afraid I must go have a chat with our Prime Minister." He smiled at the boy, who seemed to have grown an inch just by standing near him, and turned to go.

"Sir?" the junior lackey asked.

Sir John turned.

"How . . . how would I make a shot like that?"

Sir John said, gravely, "There are only three things you would have to do: practice daily for twenty years, desperately need to make the shot, and be *very* lucky."

The boy smiled slightly. "I have been practicing daily for three years, since my father let me start," he said.

Slitgizzard favored the boy with a grin that he was to remember for many years—we know, for we have a letter the junior lackey wrote when he was old, in which that smile is described—and then, squeezing the boy on the shoulder, said, "Oh, well, then, just seventeen to go."

The northern baron and his two servants had gone out together, heads bowed, walking close to one another, as if deeply concerned or embarrassed, but they no sooner rounded the corner than they were racing full tilt for the Guest Stables. Within moments they were saddling their horses.

"Excuse me, gentlemen, may I help you?" said a chubby, well-dressed groom, approaching them.

The first servant said, "Er, well, yes, I suppose—I'm afraid I'm not very good at this—"

"Oh, shut up, Rufus, I'll get it for you in a moment," the second said. "Sorry, we are in a hurry, and if we're not supposed to saddle our own mounts I hope you won't be in trouble for it but—"

"No trouble at all," said the groom, as he drew nearer. Oddly for a groom, he seemed to be paying a good deal of attention to where he stepped. "But see, this here is important—" He reached for the saddle.

"Oh, well, certainly you can help if you—" The servant died then, his throat suddenly opened by a pongee that seemed to appear from nowhere in the groom's hand. Rufus died an instant later, a kidney torn open with the next stroke, and before the baron quite knew what was happening, the homicidal groom had him backed against a wall, pongee point at the baron's larynx, and the horses were screaming at the scent of blood.

"My lord," said Duke Wassant (for of course it was he) to the baron, "I do apologize for having slain your servants, for I suspect that they were not bad men, but merely fell into your company and became so. You may console yourself that they died quickly, not at all like what is going to happen to you if the tools now glowing red in the dungeon are used with any skill. You will keep your hands where I can see them, and you will come with me."

As the old Count passed through the gateway, a voice whispered, "A man who has been wronged may seek to avenge it."

"He may." The Count's tone was noncommittal, but he stopped walking.

"Where a master does ill the servant may seek another."

"He may do that as well."

The archway was in the oldest part of the castle, so old that no one quite had a name for it anymore, though a few very old people sometimes imagined they had heard people name it when they were small. The stones were encrusted with dead moss of a type no longer known, on which grew live moss of a type now rare. In the vaguely damp and musty odor, there seemed to have been no breath of air for a century, and the Count heard no sound but the stranger's voice.

"Were you to receive a visitor at your manor—"

"I am hospitable to visitors."

"I see. Then you can expect—" There was a low grunt, followed shortly by the sort of scream one might be able to make if a preternaturally strong being had its entire fist in one's mouth . . . followed by many short screams, and cracking noises that suggested finger bones.

"I will take him from here," said the voice of the Twisted Man.

"Could you not ask him questions first?" the Count said. "He might talk . . . without . . ."

There was a wrenching sound like a wing being torn off a chicken, another smothered shriek, and throttled sobbing.

"I was promised I might play with him until he talks," said the Twisted Man. "I shall take him down to the dungeon for just that purpose . . . and then he will have his chance to talk. It may be he will talk and spoil my fun at that time . . . or it may be that I will have the chance to play more. So I shall play with him on my way down there, to help him think about whether he wants it to stop when we get there . . . or to be only beginning."

There was the sound of dragging, scuffling feet, and a flurry of shrieks, still being forced through the huge fist.

The Count continued on his way to where his horse was saddled. He had no love for traitors. He had been more than willing to accept the scandal when Calliope had approached him about it, so that the traitors among the nobles might be sniffed out.

But he felt just a little sorry he had been part of this.

The next day, after the hangings, the Council of War convened in earnest. Despite the success of his plans thus far, Cedric remained deeply worried, for he knew from a diligent study of stories and tales that tyrants, conquerors, and such generally did fairly well before being overthrown, and sometimes did well for a long time, so merely being well-prepared and having right on their side was going to be far from enough. Indeed, he was also aware of the tendency, noted in all books of lore, for the good side to win out by some lucky chance at the last moment, and for the bad side to have all the luck till then. He was not sure it was even possible to prepare against a side which might well have all the luck, but consoled himself with the thought that he was only called upon to try—success was a matter for the gods to decide.

The others in the room were as grim and as bleak as Cedric, for they well understood that the slaughter of Waldo's agents was as likely to provoke Waldo as anything else, and the sheer numbers of spies and traitors had made Waldo seem more frightening. Moreover, word was from the western shore of Iron Lake that streams were breaking free early this year, so it might well be that the attack from Overhill would move soon.

The meeting began in the dull way that meetings usually do, with Boniface and Cedric running over the lists of who was to do what, how soon it was to be done, and so forth— things on the order of "Check this armory in the East, remove all the good escree blades and bring them to the city, send all the bad ones into the village to be reforged. Send word ahead so that the city may release that many blades to go up the Long and Winding Road to the frontier where they are needed," and "Find a hundred big farm boys—preferably with no ambition for glory—train them, and set them to guard that granary."

For all the color of the swirl of cloaks around the table, and the sunlight dancing upon it from the window, the room was cold, and people seemed to huddle together, and to speak as little as possible.

This meant an uncharacteristically quick meeting. They had almost reached the end of the business—the matter of training recruits part-time so that spring planting might go forward was just being discussed in a very reasonable way by some very reasonable minor nobles—when there was a commotion outside. Cedric's heart sank, for he had spent the better part of the winter reading old tales whenever he could, to assist in his getting ready, and he knew this to be the worst sort of omen in this sort of tale.

A moment later the doors opened, and a man came in. He had been tall once, but now he was stooped with age; handsome once, but sun and wind had played on his skin a long

time. He was dressed from head to toe in the soft hide of zwieback and gazebo, and a bushy beard fell almost to his waist.
His blue eyes seemed locked in a permanent squint.

There was a great rattle as he came in, for on his chest he
wore crossed swashes of pismires, and on his back he carried a
festoon and a great double-bladed ax. There was an answering
rattle from the corner, for at the sight of so much armament
headed directly for the throne, the Twisted Man had stood up
and flung back part of his cloak, exposing many weapons—
and something more fearsome, for those who saw quickly
looked away and never told anyone what they had seen of his
body.

The man dressed in hides bounded up the aisle and knelt,
and it was only then that they saw the many stains of blood on
his zwieback leggings and gazebo shirt.

Cedric rose and said, "Majesty and Highness, permit me
to present Euripides—our chief of scouts."

The scout bowed low, and then drew a deep breath, and
then said, "All my news is bad. I was a month escaping from
Overhill, with all of them hunting me, and carved the skis on
which I came myself, and have found a high pass I have named
in my own honor. And what I saw there was a mighty army by
day, and mightier by night for it is more than half goblins—
and things worse than goblins—for those men of Overhill
who would not fight for Waldo and could not flee him are
dead, but they stand in his ranks, and men who once stood
against him return from their graves as his minions."

The room seemed to shudder. Those who had fought vampires or goblins felt their hearts sink, for they knew that
though a man was more than a match for one, numbers would
tell. Moreover, those who had been in battle knew too well
what it would mean to face an army strong by day and
stronger by night.

"The news is grave, indeed, and yet I am bound to thank
you for it," Cedric said, and took out one of the medals that

he always carried for such occasions, to bestow it upon the scout.

But old Euripides remained kneeling, and now he sighed with a heartbreak so deep that there were those who claimed afterwards that the Twisted Man had shuddered. "My lord, that was prologue, for while I fought to find my way forth, the melt came early this year on the other side of the mountains, and they moved swiftly; often indeed I was in danger of being pinned between Waldo's scouts and the advance of his army. They have been on the move, my lord, for at least three weeks, and they are well-armed and ready."

Cedric grew pale, and nodded to Sir John Slitgizzard, who raced to the roof to sound the Invasion Bell, to let the city know that it would be war, this spring, in earnest, and to get every muster out. Then he turned back and reached to place the medal about Euripides's neck.

"My lord," Euripides said. "Do not. What I have told you thus far, I have told you only so that you will believe what I must say now."

The room held its breath.

"The fort in the Isought Gap is fallen, its armory there in Waldo's hands, and all the men made undead and brought into the Usurper's ranks. They are but scant days from here by easy marches, now. My warning has reached you too late, and I have failed you."

4

The Storm and What It Blew Before It

*B*efore the early spring sun had quite set that evening, the quickest-moving of the refugees were already coming into the city. And because the goblins would have taken a fearful toll of crowds waiting outside the city for the dawn, King Boniface gave orders that the gates that faced west be kept open in the night, and a dozen reliable witches and two hundred guards got no sleep as they examined each traveler coming in.

About every ninth one burned and died at the touch of rosewood and garlic. Sometimes the enemy had been particularly clever, finding some family too shocked to notice, making a beloved grandmother or a small boy undead, and leaving the rest untouched. There were fights in the lines at the gates, and by dawn there were several seasoned soldiers sobbing in the infirmary. This one had cut down innocent people who had panicked at shadows behind them on the brink of safety, that one had pried the remains of an undead infant from its living mother's charred arms, all had found some hideous prank in the train of refugees.

Roderick himself, most reliable of troopers, had felt his gorge rise when he had discovered twin undead girls, not more than two years in age, clinging to the bottom of a tumulus, their hands and feet wedged into cracks on either side of the single axle. They had flown straight at him; he had barely struck them with the white-magicked wand in time, and as he had done so he had looked up to see the shocked eyes of the parents who had buried them by the roadside only hours before.

Gwyn told her granddaughter, who told a later chronicler of the Kingdom, that Roderick did not sleep until late on the following afternoon, though he was off duty at sunrise. According to the chronicle we have, he did not move or stir, and told her nothing of what he had seen, but sat in his accustomed chair, tears trailing down his nose, while Gwyn rubbed his neck and sang things she had heard Psyche singing to Amatus.

There is a claim that he finally rose from the chair, undressed, and went to bed after she thought to sing "One for the Morning Glory," the song that Psyche never sang until Amatus was already asleep, which Gwyn thought must be some good charm. The better scholars of the Kingdom always doubted it, for you can sing it yourself and you will see that it makes no difference.

As the sun rose, the refugees grew more numerous and more desperate. Now that witches need not be employed, it went faster, for guards need only insist that everything be opened or turned over in the sunlight, but there were so many of them that the wait still grew longer and longer, and the great horde of refugees waiting outside the town all looked fearfully over their shoulders at the horizon, for they feared to be caught outside the gates of the city.

The fear became more real with each passing hour, for although Waldo's main force was encamped while daylight prevented the great bulk of his troops from moving, his living human foragers were moving on as broad a front as they could, driving everyone before them. Isolated lords in their castles took in as many as they could, and awaited the night with dread, but most of the ordinary farmers, merchants, and workmen of the Kingdom preferred to take their chances in the city, behind Cedric's army.

Toward late afternoon, things changed drastically again, for now the numbers were almost beyond counting, but no one had saved any possessions. Thus almost no inspection was required, and the crowd began to flow swiftly into the city.

The delay had even done some good, for it had allowed at least some temporary shelter and some kitchens to be set up. The Hektarian Ambassador, daring Waldo to make anything of it, opened his gates and took in hundreds; not to be outdone, the Vulgarian Ambassador followed suit. Calliope quietly moved to an apartment in the palace and ordered her servants to take in as many as they could; inspired by her example, many of the city's nobility followed suit, so that the castle quickly came to resemble a gigantic dormitory for the nobility.

That, and the efforts of the city to take everyone in, allowed the population to spend a few hours not thinking about what was approaching, and the hard work helped to make everyone cheerful and pleasant, so that Cedric made a mental note (there was no time for a diary entry) to write about how well they had all borne up, and Roderick, returning to guard, witnessed several moments of warm friendliness between people who ordinarily would not have gotten along, and thought that he must include them in *The Third Part of Prince Amatus*.

They struggled to make the city accommodate twice its usual population, and they succeeded. They worked endlessly in those last hours to get in enough food from the East to feed everyone for a long siege. Every man who knew anything of smithing, and many who did not, labored at the forges, shaping iron for the battle to come, and wagons of powder rumbled through the streets endlessly.

And still they knew that none of this might be enough. The fort in the Isought Gap should have held Waldo for some weeks, allowing the army to come up; it had fallen in less than a day, and no one knew how or why—or no one in the city did, anyway. Militia and the lords around the south shore of Iron Lake should have been able to make a stand where the glacier sloped down to Bell Tower Beach and the passage was narrow, but no word came from there, and whether the Second Battle of Bell Tower Beach had been fought and lost, or they had died to a man in their beds before they even knew of Waldo's attack, was unknown.

"It's the lack of knowledge that brings the fear," the Duke said, pacing on the West Battue with Sir John Slitgizzard and the Prime Minister. "If Waldo is behind it, it is some trick, because he is treacherous and crafty, and some simple trick, because he is stingy and cheap. If we knew the trick . . ."

"Then we would only know what he used before," Cedric said, impatiently. "He is not so stupid as to use it repeatedly."

"But he would not seem quite so fearsome. And if the trick were low and evil enough—and perhaps if it were the sort of thing one would kick oneself for succumbing to—" The Duke persisted more than usual, for he felt useless in the city and longed to be about doing something.

"That would be some gain," Cedric said. "I will grant that. But truth to tell, Duke Wassant, I have a mission for you here that is vital—and only you and Sir John are to know of this." He sat down upon the parataxis, drew a deep breath, and said, "It is an old law that one may not contemplate the death of a living king; it is a foolish law for the King himself is forced to break it from time to time. King Boniface, may he live a century more, says he will not be driven from the city; which is to say, he will conquer here, or he will die in the blazing wreckage. Now, if the former should happen, there is no problem, but in the event of the latter, we must secure the lineage.

Therefore . . . lean in close, for I do not wish to speak such things aloud . . .''

The two men bent inward until they bumped heads in front of Cedric, and after a moment's adjustment, the Prime Minister barely breathed, "We must secure the lives of Amatus and of the Lady Calliope. Don't start at me, this is not the sort of tale in which a minor character marries a prince, and she is much more than she seems to be. It is possible that the Kingdom might be retaken by the raising of a rebellion, but only if the Prince or the Lady are available for the purpose . . . unless you would prefer to try to get someone to follow one of our republicans?

"Now, your Prince has a fierce and loyal heart, and he will want to stay and fight. Duke Wassant, you must keep the battle going to prevent his being trapped. You know as well as I what that might mean as a practical matter."

"If Boniface dies—"

"You will take over the defense here, for you will be my second-in-command. If Boniface dies it is unlikely I shall survive him. Fight on until your army is gone—or perhaps until you win, if fate should be kinder to you than to the Royal house."

"Sir John, your duty is simpler, and smaller, and there are those who will not approve of it. You must take the Prince and the Lady—by force if need be—and conduct them to the Far North. There you will meet Deacon Dick Thunder—no, no, honestly, you fellows jump every time I mention anything I am not supposed to know. I know your youth was wild and bad, Sir John, and should anyone ever step forward to mention that he knew you when you went by the name of Escree Jack and rode with Thunder and his men, there is a pardon waiting for you in my strongbox. You'd never have been a suitably bad friend for the Prince if you hadn't done a few such things, eh?"

"Er, the last I knew, though, sir, the Deacon was no great friend to the Royal house—"

"Ah, but he's less a friend to Waldo, and being a practical man of affairs he's no republican either. And besides, there are two caches of gold along your way, so that you can probably buy the services of himself and his men—"

"If he doesn't just take the money."

"Just take the money when someone is tickling his vanity? Just take the money when there is a Robin Hood motif in the air? Surely you recall his aesthetic sense—"

"You're right," Sir John admitted. "Silly of me."

Cedric was to remember that last conversation for a long time, and in his mind it grew more important as years went on, for he had grown terribly fond of the two friends of the Prince, and come to rely on them as his most energetic agents.

In this, he had violated his own precepts, for many, many times he had told Amatus not to grow too fond of any man he might have to send to his death, to learn to command men's loyalty while seeing them only as tools to be thrown away, for just such betrayal is the essence of statecraft. Yet, here he was, wishing that it might be someone else he would ask to do these hard things.

Sir John was not a reflective man, and so he did not perceive any of it; and since Duke Wassant was not to write any memoirs, we have only Cedric's word that the Duke saw something in his eyes.

As if reluctant to part company just yet, the three of them walked down the stairs together, remembering this, talking about that. They had almost reached the foot of the staircase before the shouts came, and they had to run all the way back up.

As they looked to the west, they saw the Long River and the Winding River join; beyond them lay fields of wheat and flan, and little villages, fading into green. In the distance a great black wave spread across the whole plain.

"They cannot be undead," the Duke breathed. "They are out in the daylight."

"Nor can they be all living men; Waldo could not feed so many," Cedric rejoined. "There is some silly secret behind this. I feel that in my bones. If we but knew what we had to do, one little deed would be enough."

King Boniface joined them then, Amatus directly behind him. "So," he said, "it comes now. I've read your orders, Cedric, and I agree with all of them in light of the circumstances; is there anything more in the way of preparation we can do?"

"Only what is already under way. We will be as ready as we can."

"It will be enough," Boniface said firmly, looking at the three men firmly, first at Sir John Slitgizzard, who drew himself up taller with pride, then to Duke Wassant, who inclined his head slightly in obedience, and finally to Amatus, who merely looked back.

Cedric realized the old King was trying to rally their spirits with a confidence that he might not—or might?—feel. And he also realized that he was the only person alive who knew King Boniface well enough to see that. It made him feel sad to have lived so long; he must justify it by service to the King, one more time, before this was all over.

There was great fear in the town, naturally, and more once the sun was fully down, for whatever the secret that allowed Waldo to travel with an army of such size, it also seemed to allow his goblins and undead to catch up with his forces just after dusk. "They may just take us by front assault," Boniface said sadly to Amatus.

"Father," Amatus said, "I am glad we have had so many years together."

As for whether that was premonition, or just something

important for Amatus to say, no chronicler ventures an opinion. All do say, however, that Boniface threw his arms around his son and Amatus threw his arm around his father.

Just what the invaders were could not be told, for as they drew near a black lid of cloud had swept over the city, and it was so dark that every man on the walls was constantly, nervously checking to make sure that those at his side were his comrades, and dreading what must happen if he were to turn and find that they were not.

By sound alone they knew that Waldo's army flowed around the city as the tide flows around a sand castle whose careful constructor has delayed the inevitable by putting it on a hummock. First came the swift rushes of cavalry in the growing darkness, and the alarming realization for everyone in the city that they were riding as fast as, or faster than, ordinary horsemen might ride in broad daylight on level ground—so these could be neither ordinary horses nor ordinary horsemen.

The night resounded with the hollow booming of hooves, and with miserable shrieks of despair as whatever-they-were caught the last stragglers outside the city. The worst of it, by far, was that sometimes the shrieks would be followed by sobbing or pleading.

After the horsemen came the tramp of Waldo's infantry. It was not perfectly rhythmic, and there were stumbles and occasional crashes in it, but much of it was curiously voiceless, and many thought to themselves, *It is an army of the undead*, and shuddered deeply, and the rare occasion when a crash or a scraping sound from Waldo's side was followed by swearing or bickering almost raised their hearts, for it made the foe sound like living men.

And after the tramping came the squeak and boom of the little tumuluses, looted from thousands of farms or from refugees on the road, carrying supplies to the surrounding army. Still it remained dark, despite the best efforts of the dozen brilliant witches in the center of the castle courtyard; nothing, seemingly, could raise the blackness. The noises outside the walls might have been the making of camp, or the forming up of lines—it was impossible to say.

The sound that made hearts sink everywhere in the city was the groaning of big timber axles, and the squeak and scream of awkward, hastily made wheels, and the cries of mules and oxen as they were whipped bloody and forced to drag the great weights on. "They are bringing up siege engines," Cedric murmured, speaking everyone's thought. "Many hundreds of them, and heavy ones, from the sound of it. Cannon perhaps, or great trebuchets. They do not mean to besiege us long."

Runners continued to return to the castle with each new piece of news, and every runner was dirty with having fallen in the crowded streets, for they could see almost nothing in the darkness, and every so often one would arrive much later than the others, having gotten lost outright. They were boys, almost all of them, and from the lower parts of the city, bright lads who had been given a chance through some beneficence here or there, and in the candlelight of the King's chamber they showed their raggedness more than usual. The dark places where they had fallen and scraped themselves were black with blood. Yet each composed himself and spoke the brief message from the different captains of the wall, and the message was always the same—that the horsemen, the infantry, the supply tumuluses, and finally the siege engines had passed that way, heard but not seen.

Last of the runners was a young man taller than the rest, and ill-fed looking, with his bony ankles and wrists sticking from his livery. He had buck teeth, and his ears protruded. He drew himself up and gave a sharp salute, and then spoke the news. "Majesty, the watchers on the East Battue of the castle beg to report that the two siege trains were heard to join up below their walls."

Cedric nodded gravely, and again spoke what everyone was thinking. "Then they are in place all around us. I do not think they will be long in coming." He clapped the messenger on the shoulder. "Back to your watchers, then, with our compliments, and tell them to carry on, and that the King's eyes are on every man tonight."

The youth bowed and raced from the chamber.

"Well," King Boniface said, putting the last of the tiny wooden counters that marked the positions of Waldo's forces into place on the great map of the city, "the King's eyes would be on them if the King could see two feet outside this chamber. Are there horses for us saddled outside, Duke Wassant?"

"There are, Majesty," the Duke said. "Without delay, we can be wherever the battle is joined."

"We will go down to the horses, then," the King said, "and Cedric, you will come with us that far. There is nothing to be learned now from the map, except that we are surrounded and outnumbered and that the enemy would be a fool not to attack now, while his strength is greatest and we still know nothing of him. And I think many ill things of Waldo, but not that he is a fool."

Amatus and Calliope stood to follow the King, but he turned to them and said, "One task remains before we join the battle. If we can just raise the blackness, even for one instant, the heart might go back into our army, and then who knows what they might not do, with their backs to each other and everything at stake? Amatus, you have some gifts, and you are yourself in part magical; as for what magics your Companions carry, none of us know. Will you, and Psyche, and the Twisted Man, be so good as to join the witches in the courtyard and see what might happen? Sir John, I give you to help guard them, and Calliope, since I know I cannot forbid that you go along, I permit you to follow."

This was not entirely to Amatus's liking, for he knew that the assault might come from several quarters, and he had passed the point of false modesty, so that he knew that his presence might be needed to rally forces where the King could not be. But it was an order, and this was war. With a light clutch of forearms, he took leave of his father and headed for the courtyard, Psyche, the Twisted Man, Sir John, and Calliope following.

As the door closed behind him, King Boniface said softly to Cedric, "I wish this parting had not had a falsehood in it," and Cedric bowed his head, feeling a bit of shame at what he had brought his King to, though he saw no other choice. Perhaps because of the shame, he did not record the incident himself, but the indispensable Roderick, patiently standing by as guard, witnessed it, and put it without change into *King Boniface*, where many have said it is his finest scene.

Then a runner burst in, gasping, and said, "Majesty, the gate of the Bridge of a Thousand Faces—the watch at the gate—reports that many hundreds . . . many hundreds—" and fell dead, a red stain spreading on the back of his triolet.

In an instant the Duke, the King, and Cedric, were down the stairs, and in one more they were mounted, and, surrounded by Roderick and his men as escorts, clattering through the city toward the gate, fearing it was already fallen, but going in all the greater haste because of it.

5

Fall, Fire, and Flight

A matus and those with him just reached the witches at the moment that the other party set out for the Bridge of a Thousand Faces. Without a word Amatus stepped into their circle, concentrating on offering up whatever strength might be concealed in him to lifting the dark. His insides tingled, his eyes felt sore and old, and there was a half-sob born in his chest, but nothing happened. Beside him, he felt Calliope and Psyche join, and a moment later the Twisted Man and Sir John. He could feel the new strength surging into the circle, but nothing changed. For a long time they stood, giving all their strength to the witches, growing tired and old but making no gain. Though they did not move, they ached with effort. Then the Twisted Man seemed to glow with a blue fire like lightning, and something surged through them all with a wild, fierce cry in it, an icy fury that looked and saw and judged without pity or compassion, that ripped through the dark to look on Waldo as he was—

There was a deep groan in unison, and a flash of lightning crackled through the dark lid of cloud above the city, tearing a widening rent in the black clouds. Starlight suddenly shone down, and in a moment the bold, silver light of the moon was reaching across the city.

All around them lay every witch, on her back, stone dead. Their eyes were wide open. What they had seen had killed them.

Amatus turned to the Twisted Man and asked, "What have you done?"

"What we were ordered, Prince. No more than that. To lift the dark, one must see; and no good witch could see such things and live. If it will make you easier, you may believe that if they were truly good witches they would have chosen to die in the service of their King in any case. And if they only pretended to be good, we are well rid of them."

The Twisted Man's tone was flat and bland, as it often was, and yet Amatus felt deep in his bones that there was a streak of cruel pleasure there. It disgusted him, he realized, and as he looked around at the poor broken bodies of the witches he said, "It will be long before there is this much magic in the Kingdom again."

"Would you rather have hoarded it so that Waldo might have use of all of it?" The Twisted Man's voice was bleak and bitter. "The shouting, Highness, announces that battle is joined at the Bridge of a Thousand Faces. Let us go there to fight, and if the world, as it is, is too much for you to bear, then you can depart it there, I am sure."

Sir John and Calliope winced, for this was no way to speak to a prince, but Amatus merely nodded, and turned to close the eyes of the dead witch nearest him. In a moment all of them, except the Twisted Man, were also closing witches' eyes, and composing the sprawled corpses.

Sir John looked at the livid blotchy skin, greasy gray hair, yellow teeth, and stare of horror on the witch's face before him, and saw too that her hands were still bent in the warding sign that had prevented Waldo's evil from entering the circle. He placed his fingers on the dry, rough skin of the eyelids, and pressed them down. "Let me make so good a show when my time comes," he whispered to the hideous corpse.

A cold damp wind was blowing now, and as they stood the wind whipped the cloak of the Twisted Man close to his body, and everyone except Psyche shuddered. She took the Twisted Man's arm, and said, "If I may, I shall ride behind you."

But to ride through the city was no quicker than to walk. At the sounds of the attack, citizens had poured into the streets, some snatching up arms to fight, some possessions to flee, some merely to try to see. Then the clouds had torn, and there had been glad cries that the King's forces must be winning, and that the King himself had ridden by, and they had begun to surge toward the gate, but now that the moon was fully out, black smoke and flames could be seen from the direction of the gate, and those near it had turned away again, only to tangle with those still pressing toward it. No one knew anything, but they all shouted what they did not know to each other at the tops of their lungs.

The little party was often unable to move because of the number of citizens in an alley or street. Some of them cried "Hurrah!" and saluted Amatus, and others turned to spread rumors that the King must be dead already and the Prince riding to take his place, and a few jeered at his half-body because they thought that anything unusual must have had something to do with bringing the catastrophe on them. Children, forgotten by their parents, or perhaps having run out into the street and lost their way, wailed everywhere, and the air was full of anxious cries as people tried to find each other.

"We cannot get through in time to be any use to anyone," Sir John said. Amatus nodded, but they kept trying to find a way through.

When the King, Duke Wassant, Cedric, and their guard had ridden through, not long before, the streets had not yet filled with citizens, and they had gone through swiftly, so that they reached the gate while the fighting still raged there.

There was no grace or finesse to Waldo's attack. The first wave had died in a hail of omnibus balls without ever setting foot on the bridge; the second wave had perished on the bridge; the third had been cut down with steel and pismire.

But none of this mattered, for there was a fourth wave, and a fifth, and approximately the seventh wave was now coming over the wall. Men who stood and fought as bravely as ever still saw that there was no end of the enemy, but they themselves were dwindling, and much as they might force their hearts to go on, and their arms to keep striving, still they saw what must happen, and their blood turned to lead in their veins, and the icicles of fear swelled and bored into their hearts, and they fell despairing, struggling on but no longer believing it was for anything. The torch flames showed only the dark shadows under the helmets of Waldo's men, not enough to say even whether they were living or undead, but they caught the faces of the loyal soldiers of the Kingdom fully, and no hope shone forth there, but only the determination to die well, however little it might mean.

This came to Cedric in a glance, and he had but begun to draw a breath to give some word of advice to his King, but Boniface had already seen enough and took action. He drew his long sword—a ceremonial relic—raised it above his head, reared his great gray war horse, and cried to the mob in the streets and the disorganized soldiers around him, "Once more into the breach—"

Roderick felt the power that was in it, and drew the top pismire from his swash and spurred forward, following his King against the foe, his troop following his motion as one man. A part of his mind tried to remember the speech the King was making, for future use, and as he realized he was thinking of the future, he knew that hope had been born again in him, and this made him stand and lean forward in the stirrups and ride full tilt for a little group of Waldo's minions who were just now breaking from the press. The pismire roared in his fist, and the leader of the invaders went down; around Roderick other pismires barked and rang.

Cedric had rallied the men on foot, and now they began to press the foe back; more of the enemy poured over the wall and through the breaches, but it did not matter, for they were swiftly pressed back and slaughtered against the walls. No quarter was given or asked on either side, and the stones under their feet grew slippery with thick blood, black in the torchlight.

Then a great streak of lightning ripped through the dark, and the clouds peeled back like a torn blanket in a high wind. A mighty shout went up from the King and his men, and Roderick, guessing what had happened, shouted, "Amatus! The Prince has broken their darkness!"

"Amatus!" the men roared, and in moments they had carried the fight back to the wall, and the bodies of Waldo's henchmen were hurled before them, dead or dying. An unnamed vassal raced forward and planted the Hand and Book again on the gate tower, and soldiers swarmed around to defend it.

Duke Wassant, his escree slick with blood, had just the pleasant moment to think that they might yet succeed, when King Boniface staggered and fell.

Cedric was at his side in an instant, lifting Boniface up, and Duke Wassant and Roderick were there a moment later, but there was nothing to be done. A great, ragged hole had been torn in the King's chest, and his white beard was soaked with the blood that spurted from his mouth. He opened his eyes for just a moment, and they thought he might say something—a final charge for them to carry out, words of pride, even just a cry against the injustice of it all—but he did not speak again before, with a long, rasping, bubbling sigh, he died there among his men, the pale moonlight revealing the moment when his face went slack and his chest ceased to move.

The same despair that had fallen on the men before now seized them in earnest, and though they fought on and even advanced, something went out of them. Roderick stood then, not sure of what had taken hold of him, and cried out in bitter rage; the fury seemed to leap from him to catch the hearts of the men, and as the Duke shouted to get them formed up and fighting in good order, they began to lay into the foe with a fury beyond hope or despair, seeking only to slay until nothing remained.

Tears streaming down his face, Wassant gestured for Cedric and two of the soldiers to carry the King's body back toward the castle, then turned again to pull the infantry into formation and pour a red rage of volleys across the bridge and into Waldo's packed troops. He bellowed again and again, order after order, and men worked the culverts and fired the omnibuses until their hands stung and burned and their shoulders drooped, and continued to load and fire long after they felt like falling to the ground, their aim unspoiled by the tears that wrote white tracks through the black sulphurous ash on their faces.

Waldo's first assault fell back, and citizen volunteers could be spared to fight the flames in the houses near the gate. The clouds above split farther to reveal the cold indifferent stars. To see them at all was victory of a kind.

The Duke strode among the men now, touching one on a shoulder, calling encouragement to another, rallying them to keep firing. He hoped desperately that reinforcements might arrive soon, for if he could strike across the bridge now, before Waldo's forces were well prepared, he might even break through and stand some prospect of raising the siege. A thousand factors and matters for his attention whirled through his brain, but still he moved among the men, encouraging and guiding. For a generation afterward, every man who had been at the Bridge of a Thousand Faces on that dark night could remember something the Duke had said to him, or what he had helped the Duke to do, or just the sight of Wassant's heavy, soft body rushing from one place to another. Perhaps more remarkable, almost all of the memories were true.

Out in the darkness great shapes reared up; some later said they looked like whales coming up out of the earth, some that they heaved up like demon's heads peering over a wall. Duke Wassant saw clearly enough what they were, and he spoke a word, flat and foul, to which his name would always be linked in stories afterwards.

Beside him, Roderick spat. "Those are not aimed at us who fight," he said bitterly.

"Waldo had no business being here in the first place," Duke Wassant said softly, as if it were merely a pleasant debating point over a quiet game of dice in the Gray Weasel. "When he wars on us so unjustly, should we be surprised that he is a wanton brute?"

Roderick nodded, but the main thought that crossed his mind was the hope that Gwyn was watching from the window of their house near the castle, for he knew if she saw what was about to happen she would use the common sense he had married her for and get down into the cellar. He wondered whether he would live through this to look for her.

The first of the great engines belched fire and smoke; there was some enchantment upon it, for what came out of its mouth was not the bright streak of light they had expected, a ball or shell intended to set fire to the city. Rather, a great, glowing ball of something that writhed like worms swelled slowly up into the sky and drifted, slow as a summer cloud, over the city. It floated over the heads of the Duke's men at the gate, and on for some half of a furuncle before with a soft sigh, it resolved itself, and rained down as a mass of corpses, their arms and legs seen in the fire of its dissolution.

The Duke opened his mouth to order the citizen brigades,

with their weapons against the undead, to advance to destroy the fresh invasion, but before he could speak he saw that the rotting, decayed figures were standing up, covered with flames, and what they touched burned. In an instant a dozen houses were on fire, and though the undead fell swiftly enough to garlic and to rosewood darts, the fire they had set was more than men and women could fight.

Above them, countless more balls of swirling corpses drifted lazily onto the city, and the Duke saw in the moonlight that the engines that surrounded the city—there must have been a hundred in all—were all belching flame and smoke. "We cannot stop this," he said to Roderick. "The city will burn. We will have to fall back in the best order we can."

Even as he spoke, fires were bursting all over the slopes of the city above them.

When the balls of blazing corpses began to rise above the city, Amatus, his two Companions, and his two friends were hopelessly trapped in a mob that was unsure whether it wanted to flee madly in all directions, rush down to the bridge to join the fight, or loot the shops around it. Amatus had brandished his escree and compelled a certain limited public order nearby, but twenty feet away might as well have been in Hektaria for all the good his authority did. The smell of panic was thick in the air around them, and there was no clear thing they ought to do.

A ball of corpses fell nearby, and though the militia pounced on it—to have a clear task to do was such a relief from anxiety that everywhere the citizens were charging eagerly into battle against the undead invaders—it did not matter, for before they were put back to rest the corpses had set many fires, and it was not possible to put all of them out.

The struggle against the fire did, however, finally pull enough people from around Amatus and his friends to allow them to make a little progress, once they were sure fire fighting was going forward. They advanced almost a dozen houses before they were again penned in by a crowd.

As they tried to advance farther, Psyche gave a glad cry. A moment later she had jumped from the back of the Twisted Man's horse and was embracing someone in the crowd.

Amatus and Sir John exchanged baffled glances, but the Twisted Man seemed to regard it as perfectly normal, and merely brought his huge warhorse over to Psyche's side to ward off any trouble.

Unable to move in any other direction, Amatus, Calliope, and Sir John followed along.

The person whom Psyche had seen, and greeted with such a cry of joy, was Sylvia, whom they had rescued from Goblin Country years before. A few moments' conference settled that Sylvia, for some reason, must come with them; Sir John grumbled, and Amatus seemed disposed to argue, but something about the way the Twisted Man accepted it as natural told them that something unnatural—and therefore important—was about to happen.

In a short time, Sylvia was mounted behind the Twisted Man, and Psyche had climbed up behind Amatus.

"I don't understand anything," Amatus complained, as they worked their way forward again, at a snail's pace. Everywhere the city was going up in flames, but so little movement was possible that it seemed best to just move in whatever direction they could find. "We're nowhere near the fighting, our breaking the spell on the sky seems to have made no difference, and most of all I don't see what Sylvia has to do with anything. There's no reason for her to turn up like this, and even if it's merely coincidence, you're acting as if it were some great stroke of luck, and the Twisted Man seems to agree with you."

"Well," Psyche said, and he could feel mischief in her smile through the back of his neck, "you have to remember that you are a hero, and that this is the Kingdom. Things don't happen without meaning here. And since that's the case, it's a good sign to have someone from so long ago turn up. That speaks of a coming closure, and if the closure should be soon, then, no matter what must be endured along the way, by the nature of things Waldo's days are numbered."

Afterwards, Amatus was fairly sure that he had some question on the tip of his tongue at that moment, but it was never spoken and he never could remember what it had been. Instead there was a great roar from a house across the square from them, and people ran out of it screaming. Without knowing what was happening yet, Amatus and Sir John turned toward the uproar, and the Twisted Man swung with them.

Before they could even hear the panicked shrieks of "Goblins! Goblins! They're eating the children!" the goblins themselves were bursting out of the windows and doors of the big house. At the first sight of them, the few militiamen in the crowd who were carrying their omnibuses and pismires began to shoot, and the gunfire frightened the crowd almost as much as the goblins. In no time at all the square was a screaming melee, with Amatus and his little band trying to get across it to get into the fight with the goblins.

The militia fell in—there seemed to be a sergeant or two to hand—and began to give some account of itself, but then the walls of the house fell outward, and they were forced to back up. As the dust and rubble settled, hundreds of goblins surged forth.

The militia did their best to form a hollow square and keep firing, but it was a poor best, for few of them had drilled together or indeed ever seen each other until that moment. When the crowd at last cleared from in front of him, Sir John rode forward and took command, and got their fire coming in solid volleys, which began to tell on the foul things pouring from the great hole where the house had been, but too little and too late. The militia were forced to fall back, in good order, a few steps at a time.

At that moment, one of the houses behind them went up as well, and dozens of goblins began to leap out of the public well in the square. "They must have undermined the whole city!" Sir John shouted.

They brought the militia about and backed toward the one side of the square that as yet held no goblins, hoping to make their escape that way, but as they neared the entrance to the alley there, with a great roar, both houses came down, and a great, shaggy head, with teeth as long as a tall man's body, heaved up out of the ground.

Cedric's luck had been good enough, for he had little trouble in getting the King's body back through the streets to the castle. He had gone up the street that had the clearest view of the gate, and sure enough, few people had chosen to be in it. For an honor guard he had only two horse soldiers, and the King's body traveled in a simple tumulus they had grabbed from behind a vegetable-seller's stall.

When the first balls of corpses swept in over the city, he was already most of the way to the castle, and was getting some time to think. Any ruler like Waldo had an all but endless supply of corpses, and that explained the undead component of his army—and for that matter the goblin component, for goblins love man's flesh above all other, and though they prefer to eat it live and suffering, once it is dead they do not much care whether it is fresh. But where had Waldo found so many living warriors, and why, for that matter, were they so nearly faceless for the most part? There had to be some explanation for this . . .

For that matter, they had been fierce and dangerous opponents at first, but not long after the tide of battle had turned, it had seemed that they became slower and weaker. Of course, in the service of anyone like Waldo, it might be that an army that wasn't about to win and get its hands on loot and women was always on the brink of desertion.

He wished mightily that he could still be talking about all this with Boniface. It had not occurred to him until now that entirely aside from his being a fine monarch for whom Cedric had been delighted to be Prime Minister, the King had been Cedric's best friend. He knew he would need time to weep, and soon, but for the moment there was so much to get done that he could not.

He still found he was choking, and then realized that it was on his beard, for he had begun to chew it, a thing he had not done in many years. It tasted no better than it ever had before; he dragged it out of his mouth and wiped frantically with his sleeve. He knew that when King Boniface had been younger, he had found it disgusting that his dignified, efficient Prime Minister had such a habit, and often reprimanded him about the condition of his beard and sleeves. "Majesty," Cedric whispered to the bundle on the tumulus before him, "you cannot know how much I wish you were scolding me right now." And then, time for it or not, he wept, the sobs filling his chest completely and tears gushing down his face.

The tumulus rolled through the big castle gates, and all the ladies of the court were there. They gasped to see the King dead; Cedric did not even wipe his face, but commanded them sternly to "dress his body and build a pyre here in the court-yard, for he must be burned lest his bones fall into foul hands."

The women scurried to obey him, and he strode on into the tower. The barest shreds of a defense were available. Most of the guards who had been left on duty on the West Battue, which faced the city, were the too old or the too young. The East Battue, which joined the city wall and towered above it, was so strong that they had nearly stripped it of defenders, so though the men who held it were good enough, they were few in number. Still snuffling and feeling alone, the old Prime Minister, occasionally bellowing for messengers, climbed up the tower to the High Terrace where not long ago he had sat and drunk tea with Amatus and Calliope. From here he could see the parataxes of both battues, as well as most of the city. It would do as a command post, and perhaps the Duke would be able to fall back here with enough forces to make a stand.

As he looked out, he could see the city given to the flames. The streets began to fill with people trying to flee to anywhere that was not burning, and new fires erupted every moment. The smoke was getting dense, and bitter on the tongue, even up here. Even if miraculously they won tonight, the city would never again be what it had been.

Down below him in the courtyard, the women gestured upward; he gave them a sweeping motion of his arm, indicating that they were to light the pyre. There was great power in the body of a king, and Waldo had shown himself to be a skilled resurrectionist. King Boniface's body must not be turned to such an end.

The pyre flared; the Prime Minister whispered "Good-bye, Majesty," and the women of the Court keened, the sound rising to him. Such was all the funeral that could be accorded to Boniface the Good.

The castle went unattached for a long while; Cedric ordered that anyone who could reach it be granted refuge, for supplies and weapons there were far in excess of what he and his tiny forces could use, but few enough came through the gate. He saw houses fall and goblins boil up from below, so Cedric set women to guard the drains and wells with pikes and halberds, but no goblins came through. Apparently the castle rested on tougher rock than the rest of the city.

After a long while, there was a stir in the streets below, and with a slightly lightened heart, Cedric saw that it was Duke Wassant and a sizable body of troops. They thundered in over the drawbridge, and the Duke bellowed at once for it to be raised behind them. In no time at all the parataxes of each battue were fully manned, and now, bleak and bitter as the situation might be, at least they were in a place designed to stand a siege.

Beside him, the Duke gasped out, "We were nearly cut off. The city is now in such panic with goblins boiling out of every well and cellar that nothing can move in the streets, and citizens are being eaten where they stand, or changed to undead en masse. The city is dying, sir, it will never be the same."

Cedric sighed. The flames of the King's pyre now roared and danced high, in what might almost have been defiance. "I had surmised as much. Nothing is moving in the streets near the castle as yet, so I would suppose they either have something special waiting for us, or they are waiting to clear the streets so that they can bring up forces in an organized way. I've issued swashes, with three pismires each, to all the women; most of them will be able to take two of the foe with them if they choose, and still reserve a ball for themselves."

Wassant shuddered involuntarily. He knew the sort of thing that would happen to women taken alive. "There is one marvelous thing that I should tell you," he said, "and we saw only one bit of it, but when that huge monster took off down in the press of the fighting—"

But he did not tell Cedric just then, for at that moment the great flock of vampires swept in out of the night. The battle was hard and furious on both battues, and the omnibuses with their charmed slugs wrought havoc among the oncoming vampires, but even so there were far too many of them. In very little time there was the clash of escrees and the roar of pismires on the parataxes, for they had not been able to keep the vampires off, and then, with a rumbling groan, the drawbridge fell open, as a few vampires seized the works tower. Waldo's army poured up the dark streets toward the opening gates.

Cedric and Duke Wassant tried to be everywhere at once,

but all they managed to do was to keep finding places where more men were dying, slaying three and four for every life they gave up, but losing because they faced twenty or thirty times their own number. As Waldo's army poured in it seemed to lose force—to grow weaker, as if some ailment had struck all of them—but still it came on, and if they grew weaker, they grew in numbers more quickly.

A moment came when the Duke and the Prime Minister crouched, with Roderick, in the Royal Library. They had been driven steadily back and it had been their only route of retreat. For the time being the enemy had lost track of them, and they were in a place they all knew well, and so did not need candles or lights. "There is a back way from here," Cedric breathed, "but I am loath to take it while our people fight on."

Most of the shots being fired now were by the ladies of the court, to be sure; above, they would hear two quick bangs, and a third one slightly delayed; some other lady had taken her two shots at the foe before she cocked the chutney, placed her lips over the muzzle of the pismire, and took the lesser evil. Women had locked and barricaded themselves in, wherever they could, dying alone or in groups, always fighting. No doubt many more were hiding in places not yet found, and unquestionably sooner or later some of them would manage an escape. It was not much consolation, but anything that could be kept from Waldo's hands, now, was as much victory as they dared to hope for; and while the fight went on, even in that small way, and even though they could do nothing to assist it, the old Prime Minister and the Duke could not bear to flee.

"We may wish to escape," Wassant said, keeping his voice low in case something might be listening, "not to save our own hides, but to join the Prince. What I had wanted to tell you was that—"

The door burst in. More of Waldo's odd soldiers poured

in. In the dim light it seemed even more to Cedric that they did not have faces of their own, that if you threw back the helmets you might see eyes and noses and mouths but it would not add up to a face. They all seemed curiously alike— except for two taller ones in the rear—

The three men's pismires boomed again and again in the dim library, always finding a mark, but all that happened was that more of the faceless men came in to replace the ones who had fallen. Then Roderick and Duke Wassant drew their escrees, but there was only room for one in the narrow passage, so the Duke stepped forward to hold it.

Waldo's men attacked as if they had never been trained, or had no minds of their own. But there were many of them, and the Duke was tired, and his own bulk was in his way in the narrow passage.

And, this time, when one of the foe fell, the rest seemed to acquire more courage and energy almost at once, as if it had crossed over to them from their dead comrade.

A thought struck Cedric, who was still frantically ramming home the balls in his pismires, and without knowing why, he cocked the chutney of one, raised it, and carefully shot past the Duke into the face of one of the two foe who were not faceless.

The man fell, and suddenly, all of the faceless ones sagged. At once the Duke cut two of them down, but he took a cut under his triolet as he did so. Cedric aimed and fired again, and the other man who was different collapsed.

The faceless ones seemed to lose all heart and nerve, weapons dropping from their limp grasps, and the Duke slashed into them fiercely, carrying to the end of the aisle, slaughtering as he went, opening up a space so that Roderick could lunge in as well. In a moment, the three were the only living ones left in the library.

But the Duke's cut was deep and grievous, and even in the dim light it was clear that it was heart's-blood staining his triolet. He sat down, gasping, and spoke softly, "Now, at once, Cedric, you must know. The Prince lives, and so do the Lady Calliope and Sir John, outside the city. I do not know if Sir John will be able to convey them where you wished, but you can . . ."

Bloody coughing interrupted him. "Tell Amatus . . ." but whatever it was that he wanted to communicate to the Prince, at that moment Duke Wassant died.

Gently, Roderick lowered their fallen comrade to the floor, and slipped a wreath of garlic and roses that he had worn under his own triolet around the Duke's neck. "If it takes them any time at all to find him, he'll be spoiled for their use. My lord, do you believe him?"

Cedric spoke softly. "I do. And what I have just learned may be enough to take the Kingdom back, if we use it well. What will you do now?"

"Well, my lord, if there's not some good reason to stay with you . . . er, that is—"

Cedric nodded. "Of course, Roderick. You have a wife to look after, and you will want to look for her. Come with me through the passage, and then go your own way for a while. You will know when the time comes to fight again."

"And I will be glad to do so, sir. Er—if I don't find Gwyn—"

"Then I suggest you load a moneybag with a great number of rocks, and a few small, jingly coins, and hang that on your belt, and ride north along the Long River Road to where it forks. Take the fork to the right, away from the Great North Woods and Iron Lake, and continue for a day up into the mountains to where the road curves back toward the source of the river. And if you should by any chance meet with robbers, I suggest you mention that you are an old friend of Es-cree Jack."

Roderick repeated the directions, and then asked, "And my lord, what will you—"

"You might mention, if they seem about to torture you, that when last you saw me I was walking south, toward the Bitter River. There is now work to be done everywhere."

As they had been speaking to each other, Cedric had carefully slid back one bookcase, and now he waited a moment by the door this had revealed. "We cannot be sure what will be at the end of this passage, so we must go through it silently, and be prepared to fight without sound at the far end. Poor Wassant—besides himself we will miss his pongee."

The passage was dry, but cool and utterly dark. When at last Cedric cautiously opened the door, there was no one there; they were alone on the rocky hillside. Behind them, bright as full dawn, the city blazed, and the smoke of its burning reached like a great hand to blot out the stars and turn the moon as red as an infected wound.

"Remember," Cedric whispered to Roderick, though there was hardly a man alive who remembered more things more completely than Roderick.

Moments later, they had parted, Roderick heading back toward the city, and Cedric setting off to the south, until he was sure that Roderick would not see him double back and head north on the Long River Road. There was much to grieve for tonight, but if he did not reach the Prince with what he knew, there would be more.

It seemed strange that the fate of the Kingdom should come down to one old man with too many memories and slightly sore feet. But at least the Kingdom still had a fate, or a possibility of a fate, and at least there was one person still bearing it. He kept his pace moderate and cautious, but he kept it up, and dawn found him many furuncles to the north, along the banks of the Long River.

6

A Man Who Will Stand His Ground

*W*hen the monster's head reared up from the underground, Amatus felt the story moving away from him, and his heart sank inside him for he knew that this must presage some great shift in the tale, and likely someone dear to him was to die. Nevertheless he pulled his omnibus to his shoulder and took aim at one of the monstrous eyes.

But just as his thumb turned to cock the chutney, Psyche shoved the barrel up into the air, and shouted, "Don't!"

Amatus lowered the omnibus for just an instant, and saw Sylvia running straight for the monster. He shouted at her to come back, but she paid no heed. He sighted the omnibus again, but the Twisted Man beside him said, "Psyche is right. Sylvia has come back into our tale for a reason. Since she told you not to, do not, Highness."

It was a strikingly mild thing for the Twisted Man to say, and that was why Amatus lowered his omnibus for the second time, inwardly groaning with the hope that all this would eventually make some sense. Sylvia ran on, through the scattering and screaming crowd, to the very point where the stones of the crumbling walls were rattling on the pavement, and shouted something up at the creature.

With a gesture that looked like a bird who was not sure whether to eat an object or not—and like a cat who had just discovered its tail to be inexplicably wet—the beast sat back on its enormous haunches and stared at Sylvia. Then it gave a whimper that all but deafened them, and then—eagerly, happily, it bobbed its head from side to side, climbed farther from its hole, and arced its neck downward so that Sylvia could scratch its enormous nose.

"It's the Riddling Beast!" Calliope exclaimed.

Not knowing anything of the riddling beast life cycle, it was hard to say that it had grown *remarkably* in the last ten years, but it had most definitely grown. Sylvia beckoned and it followed her into the square, as joyfully as a lost puppy finding its owner.

As it came all the way up, they all gasped in wonder, for it had tremendous wings; a house might have sat on either of them with room for a modest garden in back and perhaps a fountain in front. Now that it drew closer, it seemed to recognize all of them, and it shivered all over.

"It's like a big dog," Sir John said, awe in his voice.

"I *beg* your pardon," the Riddling Beast said. "Would *you* care to be described as 'like a big monkey'?"

The Twisted Man shouted and they turned to see a mob of goblins rushing them. Pismires banged and escrees slashed, destroying the few in the lead—

And suddenly the night was pitch dark; an instant later it was moonlit again, and the Riddling Beast, who had flown just over their heads, had landed among the goblins, crushing dozens on impact, squeezing more between its powerful claws, and sweeping with its head to gobble down many of them whole and alive before biting the last one in half. The rest fled screaming.

"We were the first ever to speak kindly to him," Sylvia said, "and to scratch his nose, and when Mortis reversed his spell he got to eat goblin, which he likes much better than human. So he likes us, and when the spells were broken, down below, by Waldo's warlocks, he came up here to find us."

The beast had mopped up the remaining goblins, not so much in the way a mop does water or soldiers do opposition as in the way that a hungry man does gravy, and as he turned to them he was still chewing, faint shrieks and groans emerging from between his champing teeth.

"Well, we surely have use for him," Amatus observed, "but I think we had best fall back to the castle before—"

"Highness, even with this beast on our side, the city is lost," the Twisted Man said.

"This is despair!" the Prince said, turning to him, his hand moving as if he might strike his guardian down.

"This is truth." The Twisted Man flung his words with the same abandon with which he might fire bullets into a mob of goblins. "You may look in any direction and see many hundreds more burning corpses raining down. You can hear the groan and thunder as the earth yawns open over and over again to vomit up more goblins. There is no—"

And he groaned and pointed to the moon. A dark cloud with many holes seemed to move across it—

Calliope swore, under her breath. "Vampires! A great flock of them!"

Psyche spoke to Amatus gently. "My dear one, were you only yourself, you might choose to stand and die anywhere, and none would argue with you about it. But you are a prince and you matter, and if you die then there is no restoration of the Kingdom, and if there is no restoration then no one's death will mean anything. This is a debt which you owe to us all."

"What do you propose?" the Prince said, and his eyes flashed with dark anger. "I shall stay and fight, with my father and the others," he added, for he had no way of knowing that Boniface was already dead, his pyre already blazing.

Sylvia softly said, "We might all ride on the beast's back to somewhere far away. And a fight may be started again while you live; if you do not, it cannot."

Then the Prince stepped back and looked from one of his Companions to the other, and said, "I no longer know whether you are here to help me, or to harm me, or whether perhaps you are just here. I have a duty, and I know it well enough."

The light from the flare of a collapsing, burning building flashed on his face, and his mouth was set in cold determination. "I owe the Kingdom my life. I do not owe it my honor. Brave men are dying everywhere and the city falls while we stand and argue. I cannot—"

And at that moment he felt his outspread hand, with which he had been pleading for their understanding, seized and snapped behind his back. He turned to see Sir John Slitgizzard holding his single wrist with two of his, and then, deftly, the Twisted Man tied Amatus's hand together behind his back.

"Can he escape?" Sir John asked, as they struggled.

"Had he two hands, he might," the Twisted Man said, "but since he has only one, it is tied twice as much together."

Amatus fought as well as he could, but there were four hands to his one, and in very little time he found himself being thrown onto the back of the Riddling Beast—who had sat watching the whole thing with a sort of amused detachment. There was room enough up there for everyone, and for twenty more besides, and the rest climbed on around him while Amatus continued to kick and struggle.

"Can you move him somewhere where he doesn't thump right on my spine?" the Riddling Beast asked. Calliope and Psyche dragged Amatus to the side. He had tried shouting, but the fur of the beast was long and thick and all he could succeed in doing was getting that into his mouth. He managed to roll himself over and sit up, but found he could not stand with his hand tied behind him.

Sir John and Sylvia were up by the beast's neck, talking to him, and Sir John was saying something about the Lake of Winter; the Twisted Man was sitting grim and silent beside Amatus, and Psyche and Calliope were tying saddlebags and weapons onto the beast's fur. A band of goblins burst into the square, and the Twisted Man jumped down to dispatch them—or rather, since he had the time, to wound them all mortally so that they could lie about screaming to amuse him.

The beast, still listening to Sir John Slitgizzard, nodded twice, and its rumbling voice said, "That sounds best to me. We will go there at once. I'm sure I've room enough to get into the air from here."

Amatus looked around him, knowing he might be seeing the city for the last time. The Twisted Man was right; there was no way of getting free of his bonds. All around him he could see the rain of balls of corpses, and though there were still many cries of pain and horror, the battle yells, the shots, the clash of steel were beginning to fade—and this could only mean that resistance was slackening. Flame and dark smoke twisted up in broad braids from all over the city.

The fight had gone out of him, at least for the time being. He realized that they needed him if they were to carry the fight on . . . and yet . . . and yet . . . countless friends were doubtless dying or suffering out there.

Cavalry galloped at full speed into the square, Duke Wassant at its head. There was a moment in which the horses reared, and then Wassant saw Sir John and the others; Sir John and the Duke waved in salute, and then the troopers galloped on through and continued on their way.

Amatus wept, for in that wave he understood all of Cedric's plan, and knew that he had seen the Duke for the last time—and with his hand tied together he could not wave good-bye.

A moment later the Twisted Man had scrambled back aboard, and seated himself next to the Prince. "If it will ease you, Highness, you owe this to the Duke; his sacrifice will mean nothing if you do not flee."

"You may untie me," Amatus said, "I give my word I will go with you. As you say, it is owed."

The bonds were undone in an instant. By now the crash of falling buildings was everywhere. The goblins had been thorough; many houses were undermined with tunnels whose timbers were now ablaze. Though it had been a cool spring night, it was now as hot as summer day, and the smoke was growing thick and foul.

"We must go now," Sir John said, and with a nod the beast raced forward and leapt into the air. One instant it felt like being a mouse in a box on the back of a galloping horse; the next, as if the whole great hairy back had shoved up against them and batted them into the air.

The great currents of hot, rising air, which poured upward from every quarter of the city, caught the Riddling Beast's wings, and he rose on them, climbing high above the burning city. Below, they could see the great fires and the fallen-in places, and the citizens being herded together and driven like cattle out onto the plain, captives to whatever might be Waldo's whim.

The city was dying—these were just its last thrashings—and whatever might grow there again, the old city of Wend Street, of the Hektarian and Vulgarian quarters, the city in which Amatus had grown up, was gone now forever. He thought that he ought to weep, but did not; instead, he felt cold steel in his voice as he said, "This will be paid for."

Sir John, Sylvia, and Calliope sat straighter and seemed to take heart. The Twisted Man nodded, once, very deeply, almost a bow. Psyche stretched out on the beast's broad back as if to go to sleep, though she kept a light grip on its fur.

The beast made a great, wide turn, having gained all the height it could from the hot air over the city, and swept north. The encampments of Waldo's army fell away beneath them, and then the blazing cottages and fields in the nearer villages, and finally a couple of burning castles on nearby hills. Then the countryside below began to look quiet and untouched, but it grew wilder and wilder, and fewer and fewer little roads joined the Long River Road.

The night rolled on under the broad wings of the beast, and every so often he would chat with them about what was below. He said that he was not yet tired, but he was not sure he would be able to ascend into the northern mountains while carrying them. "I'll take you as far as I can, but, you know, even though there's a great deal of it, I am only flesh and I do feel your weight. The great question for me is, after I set you down, what's to become of me? I'm sure you won't take offense if I mention that I really don't want anyone going on a quest to slay me . . ."

"Of course no one will! What a horrible idea!" Calliope said, indignantly.

"Nobles are great idiots for hunting," Sylvia said, "but I don't know that they are such great idiots as *that*."

"Somebody of Waldo's might," Sir John pointed out. "It would, of course, give us all great pleasure to see such people eaten for their pains. But I'm afraid our friend is right. People have a way of either forgetting or of becoming too familiar; somewhere is needed for the beast to go where three or four generations hence—while he will still be a young beast—some local village youths won't go trying for heroics, nor will he be constantly asked to come down and push the swings for the county fair."

"Exactly," the beast said. "There's also the matter of food

supply. I trust it will not offend for me to mention that human smells and tastes dreadful; goblin, on the other hand, has a pleasant, rich, chewy quality—"

"There are goblins everywhere, if you know where to look for them and have a good nose," the Twisted Man said. "They are abundant in the mountains north of Iron Lake—after you drop us off, just fly half a day or so to the west."

"Splendid," the Riddling Beast said. "And perhaps, once these irregularities are taken care of, and the King is back on his throne, some system of friendly questing—something that caused favorable but reasonably fearsome tales to be borne back to the city—might be instituted?"

"Of course," Amatus said. "We will send forth our brighter young courtiers to ask your advice about—oh, whatever odd things come to hand, as long as they aren't riddles."

"That would be marvelous," the beast said. "And it can be riddles as long as *I* don't have to ask them. One of the deep frustrations of my former position was that I am much better at riddles than most of the people who came to me were. It seemed silly for me to always be asking and them to always be guessing."

"Done, then," Amatus said. "The quest for the answer from the Riddling Beast shall be the highest honor in the Kingdom, going only to our most magnificent young courtiers."

"I don't much care about magnificence, but do try to send bright ones," the beast said. "If I am only to have one conversation or so per year, it would be dreadful to draw a dullard."

"Absolutely," Amatus assured him. "But are those the Northern Mountains looming on the horizon?"

"They are indeed, and just in time," Sir John said. "The sun will be up soon, and whatever we may feel, we must all have rest, and I should prefer, given that we will be pursued by the undead and by goblins, to sleep outside in the bright sun."

Now the rest of the journey was almost too swift, for the sun rose as they descended, leaving the Great North Woods behind to their left and moving in among the mountains north of them whence the Long River flowed. The mountain peaks burned a brilliant white against the sky, the slopes below rolling from pale greens to almost blue-black, and they found themselves in the middle of the sky in as fine a dawn as ever happened in the mountains that towered around them. The beast flew straight on into the rising valley, looking for the highest point along the Long River at which he might set them down safely, for it was still a long journey to the Lake of Winter, where Sir John had been told to guide the Prince.

The beast ended up doubling back, for the last few miles were unfortunately thickly forested and there was no good place to set down between the cliffs; though they were sorry for his extra trouble, they were glad for the chance to fly more, for now that they were used to it and had come to trust the beast, they were fascinated with flying and loved the look of the land from up here, and they knew that this was, in all probability, the last time they would do it.

At last, with a soft *flump* of his leathery wings, the beast settled onto a mountain meadow, and they climbed down. Each of them, even the Twisted Man, scratched the beast thoroughly on the nose and rubbed his ears, and the beast himself seemed a little sorry to lose their company. He made the Prince promise especially that when the Kingdom was restored, there would be questers coming to talk to him, and he also offered any other help that they found he could provide later—"though since I shall be far up in the mountains I am afraid you would be a long time in summoning me." Then with a last nod of farewell, he leapt into the air again, and they waved until he was merely a dark dot in the sky.

"And now, like it or not, we all must sleep through a good part of the day," Sir John said. He had seen enough signs of exhaustion in Amatus, Sylvia, Calliope, and himself to be sure it was necessary.

"I will stand guard, then," the Twisted Man said.

"First guard," Sir John corrected. "We all must rest."

"I will not grow tired."

Sir John might have argued, but the figure of the Twisted Man, swaddled as always in a dozen wraps, capes, and cloaks, clanking with weaponry, standing there in the bright, clear air of a mountain morning, caused the words to die in his throat. "Very well," Slitgizzard said, "I rely on you to tell us what you must do to remain fit to fight, and to do it."

"Thank you," the Twisted Man said. And he sat down on the grass of the little rise above them, as comfortably as if he might be planning to watch birds and butterflies all day. Psyche quietly sat beside him, and though Amatus thought he ought to protest, and Calliope and Sylvia wanted to volunteer for another shift, Sir John hushed them as if they had been three children, and watched them fall asleep before he stretched out himself. He had just a moment to glance up at the hill and see Psyche leaning against the Twisted Man's shoulder before he fell into a sound sleep.

When he woke, it was midafternoon, and the Twisted Man still sat up there, still as a statue, just as if he had not moved in all that time—except that there was a garland of dandelions around his neck. Slitgizzard swallowed a smile and looked to see Psyche gathering more dandelions nearby; he sat up and saw the butterflies that filled the meadow. The warm sun struck his back where the grass had made it damp, and he sighed, a little wave of contentment washing over him, before he recalled that the King was almost surely dead, and the Duke and Cedric with him, and that everything that remained of the Kingdom was within the scope of his eyes, for he had no doubt the isolated garrisons, if they had not already fallen, would fall as soon as Waldo's attention turned their way.

He rose to his feet. A silent groan in his lower back and legs reminded him that, though strong and fast as ever, he was no longer quite the young adventurer he had been.

Psyche waved to him merrily. The Twisted Man stood,

and came down the hill to them. "It has been quiet," the Twisted Man said, "peaceful and pleasant. If you think there has been rest enough, it would be wise to be moving."

Psyche looped a garland of dandelions over Sir John's neck, and smiled at him. "You feel it, too, then. This meadow is a good place."

"It is," Sir John said, "but not the place where we ought to stop. We cannot hope that our flight was completely un-detected by hostile eyes, and even if it were, we must assume that a column of troops will be headed up the Long River Road to take possession of these territories. By then we must be beyond the narrow passages above us—preferably beyond several of them, and all the way to the Lake of Winter."

The Twisted Man nodded; he seemed even more quiet than usual. Psyche dropped another garland over the Twisted Man's head, and beamed at him. "Just twenty or thirty more, sir, and you might pass for a gentleman."

The Twisted Man spoke softly. "I appreciate your words, most of all because I know they are not true."

Sir John Slitgizzard was not subtle, nor clever, and know-ing this he was about to ask what that particular riddle meant, when Amatus, Calliope, and Sylvia sat up. This meant that the whole conversation about the beauty of the meadow and the need nevertheless to get moving had to be repeated again with six people instead of three, and so it took even longer.

At the end of it, Sir John had another thought, for his own stomach was beginning to rumble. "I brought along some bis-cuit and dried meat in the wallet of my triolet; it's enough for everyone to have a bite before we start—"

"I did the same," Amatus said, "so we've two meals, though scant ones—"

"Well," Psyche said, "while you were sleeping, I found a few large bushes of berries, and some arrowroot and Queen Anne's lace, so we can stretch that food a bit—"

The Twisted Man nodded. "And as it happened, I had a

bag of spare rations on my saddle, which I brought with me, so we've plenty. You are right, Sir John, we might as well eat—though we ought to do it quickly, for there is ground to cover and pursuit to evade."

They gobbled down handfuls of berries from the bushes Psyche showed them, and made that the better part of a meal, with a few biscuits and the roots that she had found for them to fill it out. It took little time, but still the sun was farther down when they set out upstream along the Long River, now not much more than a deep, fast mountain brook. The road here was nothing you would want to take a tumulus over, and they had to watch their footing, but still it was not dreadfully hard, and they made reasonable progress as the road bent down into the dark green gloom of the mountain forest. Emerging from that small valley, the road took them up and up, through the last thick parts of the broad-leaved forest and on into the heavy pines and firs. Now the air smelled sweeter and the heavy scent made them all move a bit quicker, for in it there was the damp and cold that promised night soon.

"The gloom here is appalling," Sir John commented, "and from the look of things we have much uphill in front of us. I wish that we had at least gone through the first of the narrow passes by now."

Amatus grunted. "I wish that wishes were indeed horses, and that therefore, being beggars, we could ride."

The road dwindled to barely a track, with crushed needles lying thick in its ruts, and still they went on. The soft decaying needles at first felt good under their tired and sore feet, but they slipped and gave way, and thus their legs had to work the harder for it, so that after a while they were tired and sore from climbing the slippery slope. Meanwhile the sun continued to sink in the west, and though the occasional tree that stuck up into the sunlight shone with fierce color, the shadows in which they toiled became almost as dark as night itself, so that they saw each other only in silhouettes against the bril-

liant amber light. They were beginning to stumble with tired-
ness, and Sir John ordered a halt so that everyone might eat a
little more biscuit and a strip of dried gazebo, but this helped
only a little and it was an effort to get started again.

Luckily the moon was waxing, so they would have a bit
more of it tonight and it would rise earlier, but still there was
the danger that they might find themselves groping along the
road by only the light of the first bright stars . . . and if the
enemy indeed knew where they were, they might be set upon
by vampires or other things that flew—

Up ahead, Sylvia gave a glad cry and rushed ahead. They
all hurried to follow.

The road bent down again, at last, and into a narrow,
steep-walled defile filled with trees. It was the first of the
passes, and just at the point where it bent out of sight, a rick-
ety wooden bridge spanned the roaring gorge. The last of the
evening sunlight was just bouncing off the far wall.

"Let's hurry—I know this place well," Sir John Slitgizzard
said, "and once we are across the bridge, we will find a fine
place to camp for the night, with clean water and very likely
something we can do for food."

They all rushed down the road at a great clip, not quite
running, but savoring the pleasure of being able to see far into
the distance again, and Sir John pointed out some of the more
prominent peaks and peaked promontories. It might almost
have been a picnic that they were going to, now.

Then Calliope happened to look back, and gave a shout,
for a band of men was bursting from the forest from which
they had come, all armed, and plainly not friendly. They all
ran as hard as they could, and matters did not seem hopeless,
for even one man might easily hold the bridge, or Sir John
keep them back with his deadly pismire—

They flung themselves around the last bend, and Psyche,
Calliope, and Sylvia shot across the bridge, hair streaming behind them, like three mad spirits in a story. Close behind,

Amatus and Slitgizzard pounded over the swaying structure, leapt to the side as soon as they were over, and drew pismires.

Before their eyes, the bridge collapsed, fell into the gorge, and was swept away.

They looked up in shock to see that the Twisted Man had taken it down with two strokes of his double-bladed ax, and now awaited the foe, his omnibus on his shoulder.

"Run, fools!" he bellowed to them. "Run or I die for nothing!"

For a long second they stared; the band of men coming from the forest, now, was not two dozen as it had appeared, but at least twice that number. Moreover, as the sun began to sink there were squeals and chatters that suggested goblins were eagerly waiting for the dark.

"He is right," Sir John Slitgizzard whispered, though he felt his stomach sink within him.

"May you find whatever it is you have sought," Amatus shouted to the Twisted Man, who raised his right arm in salute, then turned to face the foe.

Amatus and Sir John Slitgizzard ran, and behind them they heard the bark of the Twisted Man's omnibus, as the first of the enemy fell before it.

Now, as for what happened next, it is purely conjecture, but it is the conjecture of several of the fine woods trackers that were in Deacon Dick Thunder's band, and so though we cannot be absolutely sure it is true, we can be sure it is not absolutely false. This is what must have happened, and if not this, then something like this:

The Twisted Man had always been a deadly shot, and since he had his omnibus and two braces of pismires, the seven shots Sir John heard would account for the seven of the foe who were found shot. Then the Twisted Man must have drawn his escree with his right hand, and his double-edged ax with his left, and then fought on like that. He had slain seven men in their first rush, all with balls planted neatly between their eyes, so they would have advanced cautiously. Besides they were supposed to take the fugitives alive.

Two or three of the boldest were knocked from the road, skittering down the steep gravel bank into the gorge, where they were swept down to the opening of the defile, if they survived, and farther still, if they did not.

After that first, brief rush, then, as Sir John urged Amatus and the women onward, ten of the forty foemen were fallen, without any injury to the Twisted Man. Whether his heart lightened with hope, or whether he just continued to fight as he always did, could not be known even if a living witness had been found, but he had not given an inch, and the Prince and his party had gained a great deal of valuable time.

The next rush met with only slightly better results; the Twisted Man had no time to reload, and so they fell only to the blades of his whirling weapons, but the road was narrow there—barely enough for a single horse—and thus they could close with him only in ones and twos. He struck them down, and—in his usual way—when he could, left them wounded rather than dead, forcing the other troops to care for them.

But he must have been at least a little puzzled by these strangely identical soldiers who advanced upon him, for they were not demoralized in the least by the screams of the wounded; they did not even seem to notice them.

Still, at the end of the second rush he had accounted for another five who were dead, and two grievously wounded, and the puddled blood made the pathway more slippery and dangerous for the next rush.

This was by the time that the sun was going down quickly, because all of Thunder's best trackers agree that it was during the second, bloody rush that the Twisted Man seemed to have taken two soldiers prisoner. He hamstrung one with his escree and broke the other's knee with the flat of his ax, then dragged them in behind him while the others were too confused to mount another rush. A few quick strokes with the pongee to slash through their flesh and destroy their tendons, and now they could neither stand nor grip anything; they lay, crying and begging for death, behind him.

Whatever might be said of Waldo, and of men who would voluntarily serve him, they had some loyalty to each other, for the next rushes upon the Twisted Man were wilder than before, with men apparently scrambling to get at him and save their fellows. They met with no better success. He killed a few more, though he was now too hard-pressed to choose to wound them, and their bodies, too, tumbled down into the raging stream below.

And the sun, which had been creeping away, touched the horizon, and the sky began to darken, indigo invading blue.

He fought on, though he may well have guessed what was to come. One man was too badly wounded to retreat, but the Twisted Man was too hard-pressed to drag him over to his other prisoners, and so the man lay bloody and dying between them, crying out for water or mercy. He received neither; nor could he have imagined what would happen next.

When darkness had just fallen, the rocks resounded with horns and with howling, for the mountains had always had more than their share of goblins, and now they were bursting forth to their ally's aid. Thankfully none came from the little stretch of rock behind him, but still his situation was now desperate, for goblins can climb and scramble many places a man cannot, and thus they could come at him from up and down the slope. Moreover, though they were still little skilled, these goblins too seemed to have mastered disciplined fighting, and they advanced in tight, orderly ranks.

He took his first wound in the calf as he rushed forward to seize the wounded man. In and of itself the wound was not serious, but it slowed him considerably afterwards.

For the time being, however, he had grabbed the broken, gasping man and lifted him over his head. The man may have seen what was to come, and screamed for help or mercy, or perhaps even begged the Twisted Man. If so, the Twisted Man no doubt enjoyed it. More likely the man was unconscious.

The Twisted Man shouted, "Man's flesh! Man's flesh to eat!" and hurled the man into the back ranks of the goblins.

The new "discipline" of the goblins was a relative matter; they still fought together only about as well as a mob of human farm boys without training might do in a pinch. At the prospect of man's flesh, they broke ranks at once and set upon the hapless man, and even their officers broke discipline to join them. Waldo's men were forced to draw blades and pismires and to fight their way into the goblins, killing many of them and receiving many wounds in return, and the battle that raged there on the road was nearly as dangerous as the one against the Twisted Man. At the end, besides the man who had been eaten, there were a dozen goblins dead and one more man sorely wounded.

"Why do men make alliance with goblins?" the Twisted Man taunted them.

They gave no answer. Now that their allies were back in ranks, they prepared for the final attack—stopping only to knife any goblins who appeared to be pulling things from concealment and chewing on them.

The rush this time was organized tightly and came in three prongs. Two big men came up the road with escrees drawn to engage the Twisted Man. Above him on the rocky cliff, a small band of goblins attempted to descend behind him, and below, creeping for toe- and fingerholds on the steep, loose bank between the road and the rushing river, another three goblins crept inward.

The Twisted Man took the men first, as most dangerous, and struck with a ferocity that must have appalled one of them, for there was a clear mark of his heel turning; Dick Thunder's woodsmen were so skilled they could read a track upon a track upon ten tracks, but this one cut so deeply that they thought he must not have been struck at all, but turned and fled when the man beside him was struck dead at the first blow. This had happened faster than the enemy had planned upon, and the goblins were not yet in place; snatching up one of his reserve prisoners, the Twisted Man again screamed "Man's flesh!" and lifted the man up. The prisoner, having heard what had happened before, shrieked, begged, and wept—or wept anyway, for three teardrops were found in one of the marks of the Twisted Man's boots—but to no avail. He might have cried to his mother, or to whatever dark gods Waldo served, but it did not matter at all. The Twisted Man hurled him forward into the press of goblins.

Again, ranks broke and chaos ensued, though not so much as before, and indeed his comrades managed to drag the wounded prisoner from the clutches of the goblins before he was entirely dead, though the marks on the ground show he died shortly after, large parts of him gnawed away before the goblins could be stopped. This time there were two dead men and nineteen dead goblins, and in the meantime by hurling stones the Twisted Man had been able to bring down the goblins crawling above him.

When the single-minded little party of goblins tried to leap onto the trail behind him he had more than time and attention enough to bring his double-bladed ax about and split all three of their skulls at a stroke, leaving their brain pans leaking open as he kicked their twitching bodies into the river.

But somewhere in the process—perhaps from one goblin dart that had found a mark, or even from the escree of the last man he had killed—he had taken a wound in the shoulder, where the blood runs close to the surface and where the muscles he would need with which to fight were attached, and now, too, he was slower from the wound he had taken earlier.

Moreover, the men, having seen two of their number fed

to the goblins, were of no mind to give respite. They drove the goblins together upon the road—killing a couple more of them in the process—and then pushed them forward from behind, slaughtering the laggards without compunction. Driven by fear, the goblins rushed upon the Twisted Man in a wild fury, and though he butchered them as they came, here and there one would land a blow or a bite before dying, so that he grew battered and he bled from a dozen places, and his breath came in great heaving gasps.

It was fully dark, now, and the moon did not penetrate to this side of the steep-walled gorge, so that they fought on as dim shapes to each other. The men were at some risk of running out of goblins before the fight was over, but they pressed on, prodding at the laggards with their escrees and turning their pismires on any who tried to climb up or down from the road. The black shadows occasionally flashed with a pale glimpse of steel, and when one of the men shot a deserting goblin, there would be a great orange flash upon the rocks, but for the most part it happened as a clash of steel in the dark.

At last the Twisted Man stepped back and placed his back to the rocky cliff. Even now he did not surrender; he did it only to sow confusion in the enemy ranks, for the first rank of goblins charged forward and threw themselves upon the helpless prisoner he had retained, and the Twisted Man would let no more pass, so that the men behind them were eventually forced to cut every last one of the goblins down to rescue their screaming comrade.

That finally brought the last seven men face to face with the Twisted Man, and now, they, like he, were far past the point of fighting for any reason at all except to kill and to hurt; they had seen bloody things done and their minds were filled with longing for more, and that was all. They closed in and struck with a fury as blind and deep as his, and it was the opinion of Thunder's senior woodsman that they had often struck each other, for in that dark storm of clashing blades and spraying gore, the Twisted Man died, but all seven of his opponents did as well, and at last all lay there to be gnawed by the few hungry goblins who returned later.

Far away, by now, high up on the road and well beyond any sound of the battle, Amatus felt something different, and looked down to see that he now had, besides his left foot and left eye, a left arm. He flexed it once, then spoke to the others. "He has died."

They did not ask how he knew, but they turned to see what part was regained. He raised the arm, quietly.

"I never knew him well," Amatus said, "for all that I saw of him."

"He preferred it be that way," Psyche said.

They walked on until dawn came up, and they had just found a comfortable meadow to stretch out in—for there was now no sign of pursuit and they were tired—when they heard hoofbeats behind them.

At once, Amatus and Sir John Slitgizzard drew their weapons, and stood waiting for what might come around the bend of the road.

The first thought was that it was not Waldo's men; it was a grizzled old fellow, his face battered raw by wind and rain, brown eyes and gray hair bleached by the sun, clad in ragged gazebo hides, an omnibus slung on his shoulder and an escree dangling at his side, on a great red stallion, and behind him there was a band of equally tough and seasoned—and equally ragged-looking—men on horseback.

There was a long pause. "Escree Jack," the old man said.

"Deacon Dick Thunder," Sir John replied, keeping his voice just as level and neutral as the old man's had been.

"Richard?" Sylvia exclaimed.

Deacon Dick Thunder looked at her, and something inside him seemed to collapse. The old man dropped from his saddle and ran toward her; neither the bandits nor the Prince nor any of his company seemed to know what to do.

Deacon Dick Thunder, terror of the mountains for decades uncounted, knelt before the plump commoner girl and whispered, "I must ask your forgiveness."

IV

The Love of You

I

Old Friends and Unexpected Meetings

*W*ith everyone in the small party exhausted (except, perhaps, for Psyche), the wisest thing to do seemed to be for everyone to sleep before matters were sorted out; yet the excitement was such that this was impossible. In a short while, it had all tumbled out, while everyone claimed that they were just going to bed and would talk in the morning: about Waldo's invasion, and the slaughter of the city; about how Amatus had gained an arm; the ride on the Riddling Beast, and, at her decision, even Calliope's real identity, "for," as she said, "if I am to be a rallying point, I must be known to be one, and if we fail, Waldo will kill me about as dead no matter what."

Yet even that news was overshadowed by the great shock of discovering that Deacon Dick Thunder was the husband who had been unable to muster the courage to rescue Sylvia from Goblin Country, as had been told in "Penna Pike" for all these years.

"But I thought 'Penna Pike' was centuries old," Calliope protested.

"The older a song is, the truer," Psyche explained, "and 'Penna Pike' was so old that it had to be constantly true."

Perhaps because she had always been a little suspicious of Psyche, Calliope let that pass.

"Well, to tell you the truth, it was turning coward that turned me to a life of crime," Thunder was admitting to Sylvia. "I had always dreamed, you know, of heroic deeds and that kind of thing, and here with a genuine chance to do one, and a song ready to go if I managed to pull it off—and not even that difficult a task at that, you know—well, I just turned tail and ran. Didn't have the stuff of which heros were made and that was all there was to it. So I drifted north, and you might know how it is, when you already think you're a deplorable fellow, you get to thinking that you might as well do deplorable deeds. I started out shoplifting, you know, and then got into purse-snatching, then stealing chickens, which led to sheep and then cattle and horses, and pretty soon I was a fair all-around thief, but you know a thief gets no respect, there's no advancement, and sure enough, that meant if I wanted to get anywhere I should have to turn either robber or pirate, and you know how little the sea agrees with me, Sylvia, it was robber or nothing.

"I was dreadfully worried about it at first because, you know, I didn't think I had an ounce of courage, but I found I was an adequate shot with a pismire, and could swing an escree about reasonably well, and most of the time when you're robbing you're dealing with unarmed people, or ones you have the drop on, anyway. So I nerved myself up to learn to use a weapon or two, and got steadily better at it, and well, here you see me. Leading robber in the Kingdom. But it's all compensation, really—our counselor, here, with the band, has stressed that to me repeatedly. I need to learn to accept my successes in one set of ballads and not worry about my failures, you know, over in that one other ballad.

"Oh, and everyone else—my real name, by the way, is Brown. Plain old Richard Brown. It was just no sort of name for a robber chief, you know, so I called myself Dick Thunder, and then when I instituted, as simple public relations, a practice of not robbing the poor, and of tithing some of our take to the widows and orphans and so forth, which cost us little financially but got commoners to lie about having seen us and not to cooperate with the police—well, this quite meaningless little publicity stunt seemed to earn me the name of the Deacon.

"And there was a certain resonance and social advantage to the way things turned out, you'd have to admit. 'Deacon Dick Thunder's Men' just sounded a lot more grand than 'Richard Brown's Purse-Snatchers and Chicken Thieves.' "

A muttering of agreement ran through the men.

Naturally it took much less time for Sylvia to tell what had become of her—after all, her time in Goblin Country had passed like one long dream, and after that she had taken a job as a waitress in a small taboret for a time, before she found that tips were always better among the Vulgarians and moved into that part of the city to work in a stupor.

Finally, with everyone's tale told, so late in the day, Thunder—it seemed impossible to think of him as Brown and besides his men would not hear of it—suggested that they might ride to one of his secret camps in the woods, eat something, go to bed early, get up late, and in general get themselves into better shape for the days ahead. The idea was so sensible that Amatus muttered to Sir John, "I can well see how he came to be leader of the band."

"That's it exactly," Sir John whispered back, "but for all the gods' sake don't go mentioning it. He won't hear of the idea that he got to be leader for his administrative skills and common sense. *He* still wants it to be because he was the boldest, baddest robber from the Lake of Winter to the Bitter River. Don't hurt his feelings—he's terribly sensitive."

As they neared the camp, they were greeted by tens of children and a dozen women, all of whom seemed excited and each of whom seemed to have a husband or father among the band. In very little time, they seemed to be the center of a considerable parade. Because of his strange appearance, the children avoided Amatus, but they mobbed Calliope and Sir John, never having seen a real Princess or a real knight before.

Dick Thunder dropped back to talk with Amatus. "I hope we can keep the war from coming up into the northern frontier, here. These camps have gotten to be more towns than anything else, over the years; many of the men only rob part-time now, and mainly work as farmers, and quite a few of them have nice houses they would hate to lose."

Amatus smiled. "It would seem that portions of the Kingdom marked 'unsettled' on the maps are very well settled."

"Well, there are no claims or deeds—"

"These things can be made good. *If* there's a Kingdom anymore, instead of a—what would you call it, anyway? a Usurperage? or a Usurpy, like a duchy or a county?—but I digress. I see you have many bold men among you, and quite a considerable force here, and that they all certainly have things to fight for."

"Part of what makes them formidable," Thunder said, with a nod. "Bachelor robbers are no use at all. In the first place, they've no respect for wenches, and that gets the men among the robbees upset, and before you know it some silly fool has pulled out a weapon and then almost anything can happen. And what's more, when a bachelor robber happens into a lot of swag, do you suppose he's going to keep working? Oh, no, he heads into town to spend it, where he's like as not to get caught and make us all risk our necks in a rescue, and very likely he'll end up betraying secrets. But a married robber—especially in a *band* of married robbers—now *there's* a robber. He won't bother a wench at all, because he knows the other fellows will talk to their wives and sooner or later it will get back to his. And as for spending it in town—well, fat chance. There's savings to be thought of, and new shoes for the children, and perhaps some new thatch for the cottage,

and if the swag is big enough it starts to look like a down payment on something.

"And it's no bad deal for the robber himself, you know. A
bachelor robber doesn't take care of himself, out climbing
trellises to ladies' windows all night long, or drinking and
roaring if he's not, runs foolish risks just to impress women,
can't cook to save his life so he ends up eating the same three
greasy stews at the same three greasy inns over and over, so
he's sick half the time and hates to go back out on the road
. . . but a married robber, after a few days out shooting and
stabbing and sleeping on cold ground, he comes home to a
decent meal and a clean home, gets a good bath and some
sleep and spends some time with his children, and he's up and
ready in a week for whatever you want."

Amatus was not sure of what to say, but he ventured to
Thunder that he must know more about running a band of
robbers than almost anyone else.

"Oh, I suppose so. Still, it's what you do when steel's
drawn and some fool is thinking of keeping his well-got gains
for himself that makes you a real robber; always been careful
to stay on top of that. In addition to the administrative work,
which I just hate, but to tell you the truth there's no one else
here to do it . . ."

He was still talking about it as they at last came into the
"camp." It was plain at once that it was better developed and
laid out than most of the King's Settlements out to the east.
The low rise of ground was topped by a solid stockade, and
the buildings themselves were substantial and prosperous, for
all of being painted in blotchy browns and greens. There was a
big mess hall inside the stockade, but only about half the men
were going to eat there tonight. "Some of them have family
here, as you saw," Thunder explained, "and many of the rest
have been invited to dinner. We try to encourage that sort of
friendliness among the families in the camps."

They rode on into the stockade, and there they found a

splendid meal, comfortable quarters, and in short everything that they could hope for. It was not home, and the city and perhaps the Kingdom were still lost, but all the same it was something to gladden the heart.

2

The Lake of Winter

A week later, Amatus stood by the Lake of Winter, with Sir John Slitgizzard, Calliope, and Psyche at his side, as Deacon Dick Thunder pointed out the sights. "Over there is where the White Mountain glacier comes down almost to the water's edge—a bit like Bell Tower Beach down on Iron Lake, but because it's colder up here, the river flows from the glacier only in the summer months, briefly and ferociously. There are good harbors on the eastern side, and many places that would make cherry and apple orchards, but you know Royal authority never quite ran all the way up here, and I'm afraid that sort of development is beyond my means right now. There are some loggers, potato farmers, and gazebo hunters in little camps on the other side. What we have on this side is some little towns of fishermen (they haven't paid their taxes to you or their protection money to me in decades, and heaven knows neither of us is like to have the heart to collect it), a few farms, and your 'castle' if you want to call it that. The garrison there—well, you'll see."

They rounded the high, rocky point together, and before them a low peninsula spread out. At its tip there was a small, crudely built castle, really not more than a simple rock battue surrounding a keep with a crude log clerihew.

"Such a place could be held, but not against a real army," Sir John muttered.

"Still, it is possibly the last castle in loyal hands," Amatus said.

"That's a matter for interpretation," Thunder said, and they rode down the winding trail, around the little bay and out toward the castle. Halfway down the land again hid it from them, so that when they next came upon it, it was from below, and though it was still obviously small, it looked much more forbidding.

"Palaestrio! Oh, Captain Palaestrio!" Thunder shouted. "Come out and amuse us!"

There was scurrying and noise inside the castle, and finally a helmeted head poked up. "You just go on your way, Dick Thunder, it's ten whole days till our next payment is due."

"Ah, but I want something different from you this time," Thunder said, a broad grin cracking his face. "Something it will cost you nothing to give—"

"I will give you nothing! I am the King's agent in these parts—"

"If you don't, you can forget about going out berrying or on picnics all summer," Thunder said sternly, bellowing it so that the Captain could hear. "Now be a reasonable fellow and come down and talk!"

"That's completely counter to all our agreements!"

"Circumstances have changed. Now, don't be a whiny captain. Just come down here and have a talk. It's not as bad as you think. I promise."

"Oh, all right. I'll be down in a moment." Even at their distance, almost a furuncle out of omnibus-shot, they could see that he was stamping away petulantly.

"How on earth did—" Amatus began.

"Well, your father and his ministers made a habit of sending men they had their doubts about to the more remote posts," Thunder reminded him. "And do be kind to Captain Palaestrio, Highness, he's not really a bad fellow and he didn't have much choice but to pay us tribute. If it were just him, he might have stood up to us, but you know many of his troopers have been in this country twenty years, most of them are from around here, and they sort of grew up afraid of us, and he's too tenderhearted to ask them to risk their lives—"

Amatus felt a little confused as to just what he should do.

He noticed that Slitgizzard was fighting a smile, Calliope grinning openly, and Psyche had a quirk around the corner of her mouth, a smile about to break loose. "Oh, all right," he said, "I will not do anything terrible to him, or even frighten him particularly. But I still want to know what's been going on here."

The wooden gate of the castle opened, and two men came out on foot. The Captain wore something that approximated appropriate dress for a royal officer—though his triolet was threadbare—but the man who walked beside him looked like a more ragged version of one of Thunder's men.

The two of them drew up sullenly in front of Thunder, but before they could speak Amatus drew back his cloak, revealing how much of his body was missing. The two soldiers stared for a long moment, and then Captain Palaestrio went to his knees. "Highness," he gasped, and, dimly grasping the situation, the man beside him imitated the Captain's actions.

"Rise, Captain. I suppose that I should demand to know why the Royal Treasury has been paying tribute to a robber—"

"But it hasn't, sir, not a penny. All the tribute came out of the boat business, the restaurant, the general store, things like that."

Amatus's eyebrow shot up; it was impossible to tell

whether he was quizzical or surprised, since he only had one brow, but since he was blinking with both eyes it was probably surprise. "The boat business?"

Dick Thunder explained. "Captain Palaestrio—well, actually, Sceledrus here, with a cut for the fort, the Captain, and me—operates a ferry service around the lake. It's the only access to the outside world for a few hundred gazebo hunters, loggers, and potato farmers," Dick Thunder explained. "As for the restaurant, well, the Captain has been accepting tax payments in fish, game, and vegetables for a long time, and you would hardly have wanted that shipped down to the city, now would you? So four days a week there's a fine little restaurant here with a view of the lake; today is one of the days, I believe—"

"Yes, it is," Captain Palaestrio said. He seemed to be recovering a little confidence, for with a slight smile he added, "Even if it weren't a restaurant day, after all, we have a firm policy that whenever royalty visits we open the restaurant."

"I didn't know that was a policy," Sceledrus said.

"That's why I write policies and you run the boats," Palaestrio explained smoothly. "I remember things like that."

Sceledrus nodded, satisfied.

Amatus was beginning to see some of the logic in all this. "And I imagine you have a general store because—"

"Well, we're the only place that a trade caravan wants to put in, and we are at the end of the road, and not everyone can come here as soon as the traders get here, and the traders seldom want to stay long," Palaestrio explained. "Besides, we need a way to keep putting money back into circulation. Because of the other businesses, all the flavins in the Far North would end up in our coffers if we didn't keep pumping them back by buying things. And somehow or other prices always go up considerably just when a caravan gets here, so . . ."

Amatus looked from Deacon Dick Thunder to Captain

Palaestrio and back, and the first thought that crossed his mind was that these were two men Cedric would be happy to have in any capacity. That made him think of Cedric, and of the city, and that Waldo's men would be coming in force sometime soon, and he said, "I think what I would like, if it is possible, is to gather as many of the people from around the lake and the forests around it at a meeting, here, in, oh, one week's time. If you could consider extending credit to your employer, Captain, I should like to give them all a good meal—"

"Done," the Captain said.

"Going to be expensive," Sceledrus said.

"Shut up," the Captain added.

The castle turned out to be pleasant and snug inside, if not much as a fortification; "I suppose we could have taken it at any time," Thunder said, "but where would we go to buy ammunition and get blades reforged? And besides, it's a clean, safe place for my bachelor men to go to blow off a little steam and meet nice village girls." His faded brown eyes twinkled. "In fact, a few times when things weren't going so well, we loaned Captain Palaestrio some of his tribute money back."

Sir John scratched his head. "A royal outpost accepting loans from robbers?"

"We gave him very favorable terms, and he was quite punctual about paying it back."

That night they slept in the guest rooms in the clerihew, and though the sheets were rough-woven wool and the floors bare wood, everything was clean and neat, and they woke up greatly refreshed.

Dick Thunder, as Cedric had predicted, had turned out to be enthusiastic in his support; the robber who comes to the aid of the True King, after all, was a highly respected part of a thousand old songs, and one could hardly become leader of a great company of robbers without deep sensitivity to such matters. It was his suggestion that they divide up for a few days to travel around the mountain country and stir up interest in the meeting.

Since Sir John Slitgizzard was well known as Escree Jack, it made most sense for him to travel about from robber camp to robber camp, and since Calliope's status as a princess seemed to work well in winning the loyalty of the robbers, she agreed to travel with Slitgizzard. "It's just the natural reaction of men who've never seen real royalty," Dick Thunder explained, embarrassed by some of the displays of enthusiasm. "And as a sole survivor of a legitimate line, you win their hearts immediately—I mean, someone like you is *supposed* to get help from robbers."

That left Amatus the job of touring the lake on Sceledrus's ferry, a job slightly complicated by the fact that Sceledrus seemed to be in awe of Amatus. This was not just a matter of Amatus being a prince, or being minus most of his left side; Sceledrus had always accepted what Captain Palaestrio told him so uncritically that it had never occurred to him to wonder whether or not any of it might be true, and the thought that it might be left him awestruck.

Psyche came along with Amatus, and no one seemed to argue about that; the greater surprise was that Sylvia was going to go out with Thunder to cover the other little settlements to the south of the lake, high in the mountains.

"All I need do is talk to them about what happened to the city," she said. "It will be no problem; these people have worked hard for everything they have, and when they hear that someone might come and take all of it and spoil the rest— well, they've lived with robbers all these years because it's an exceptionally well-managed crew of robbers that never takes too much. That's not at all the same thing. They'll come right around, you'll see. Besides"—and here she leaned in toward Calliope, with a grin spreading across her face—"it so happens that this provides me an excuse to travel a few days with Richard."

"Are you—er—"

"Of course I am. He was a perfectly fine lover, and would have made a good husband. He didn't happen to be a hero, and it's obvious that he felt just terrible about that. But how often, in the average marriage, does a need for heroics come up? It will just take him a little time to get used to the idea again."

When they parted, it was still fairly early in the morning. Sceledrus and his crew refused any offer of help from Amatus and Psyche, so they sat on top of the little cabin, waving a farewell to Calliope and Slitgizzard, who turned to ride off west, and to Dick Thunder and Sylvia, who turned southward.

That first day they made a quick run across to a lumber camp on the southeastern shore. Amatus had plenty of time to rehearse his speech on the little boat as it raced over the sun-bright waves, and he used almost all that time to become nervous.

Yet when he stood in front of loggers' cookhouse, the ground before him green with moss in the golden sun, surrounded by the tall, blue pines, he felt at home. He glanced briefly at Psyche, received a warm smile, and turned back to the crowd to speak.

He explained first that they lived in the Kingdom only because there was a king, and felt foolish as he said it, though he noticed that this seemed to come as a surprise to Sceledrus. Then he told them of places they had never seen and might never see, Overhill, and the city, and the country south of Iron Lake, Bell Tower Beach and the marshy lands below the Bitter River, the great sweep of the deserts to the east, the Great North Woods that stretched between the Long River Road and Iron Lake, and made them feel what those lands had been before Waldo, and then told them that Waldo had them, and that all that was destroyed, or would be soon.

He went on to say that Waldo would most assuredly be coming this way, for it was not in the nature of a person like Waldo to allow anything to remain outside his grasp, or unspoiled once it lay within it. He promised them nothing but blood, iron, and fire, and offered them only the choice of going to find it or of waiting for it to find them at home.

And quietly, at the end, the loggers—every one of them taller than Amatus, each with muscles like granite—came forward, and one after another promised him they would be at the meeting, and that they were ready to do whatever had to be done.

He shared their evening meal, and they were painfully shy around him, but he made a point of speaking to each of them.

The next stop required a long run across the lake, taking advantage of a night wind, and because it was a calm night most of the crew slept. Before bedding down, Amatus and Psyche sat up on the cabin, looking at the stars and moon and watching the dark shadow of the boat crawl across the reflection of the heavens.

After a long while, Amatus said, "Only you are left."

"True."

"I would gladly have remained half a man to have kept all of you, even Mortis, whom I feared, and the Twisted Man, who sometimes disgusted me."

"It is not a matter for you to choose, Prince Amatus. None of us would choose to be whole if we fully knew the cost, but we are not free to be anything else. You know that with my passing, you will be whole—"

"Physically. I miss Golias even now, as if it were a wound, and the others—"

"And you will miss me. There are things that must be."

The breeze was steady but not strong, and the boat cut through the pellucid surface of the Lake of Winter with only the slightest splash or slap now and then. All around them, the towering peaks slid by, and far to the north, in front of the bow, the great mountains that were part of what shut out the wider world reared above them. The stars were clear and close, and for a long time Amatus enjoyed their light without thinking, and watched the moon setting over the western mountains. Finally he said, "Do any of you know of the way of your passing?"

"It is in keeping with us, Highness. That is all. Golias died in the light, having explored in the dark. Mortis died like the thing of secrets she was."

"And the Twisted Man?"

"In spite and hatred." Her voice was flat and toneless.

Amatus sat a long time, listening to the little noises the water and wind made, smelling the cold wet air that flowed over the mountain lake, down from the glaciers and onward into the valley of the Long River. It was cold enough to make his face just a little raw.

"Dick Thunder's men say they found him with the garland you wove for him around his neck. I do believe he loved you, or something like it."

"Something like it," she said grudgingly. "We are not all your friends, Amatus; you learned that Mortis was not, and perhaps you know that Golias was and I am. As for the Twisted Man . . . he was neither friend nor foe. He was just something that had to be."

Amatus sighed. He felt compelled to ask again. "Can you tell me of your passing?"

"I have been at your side for many years, Highness. When I am not, you will be whole." She rose and went below; a moment later he followed, and after a long time, he fell asleep. Tomorrow he had to speak at three camps; the day after at four; and then he would be back to Palaestrio's castle.

At every camp, his reception was much the same; people seemed ready to offer love and loyalty. If he had not held the image of the city in flames, of the mighty army Cedric had spent twenty years building destroyed in a night, his heart might have begun to rise with hope.

Almost too soon, Sceledrus and the crew were racing the craft back to the castle on the shore, and as they neared it they saw that the castle flew the Hand and Book banner. "This is strange," Amatus said. "That banner should fly only over the current residence of the King. I suppose it is likely that my father is dead, and that I am King, and that is why they have done that, but they ought not to have until they were sure."

"Watch and wait, Highness," Psyche said, gently.

He did not have to wait long, for as they drew nearer he saw that Calliope and Sir John Slitgizzard had already returned and were waiting for them, and Deacon Dick Thunder and Sylvia were there as well, with Captain Palaestrio—and someone else.

Amatus was disembarking before he saw that, beneath the powder burns and the raggedly trimmed beard, it was Cedric; and when Cedric greeted him with "Majesty," he knew then, and thus it came into the stories, because it was true, that the first time that he ever heard that he was King, he wept.

3

Tales Are Told, Things Are Learned, and Plans Are Made

*T*hey were the better part of the day in hearing each others' tales, but the story of Amatus's journey is already told. Cedric's journey involved nothing so much as continuing to put one foot in front of another, for so many fields and houses were abandoned that he had plenty of food and slept in beds most days, so there is little reason to recount his adventures here.

Indeed, Cedric himself gave only a sketchy account at that time. "It is certainly interesting for a man my age to take up burglary and trespass," he said, "but it is not of great interest in the telling. I walked; I looked after myself; I gradually accumulated a pack that would keep me going when the houses ran out; and I came here because here was where Sir John was to bring you." So if you wish to read of his journey, you will have to look in the chronicles of the Kingdom for yourself, and be warned that most scholars generally skip over that passage, pausing only to infer what they can of the social conditions and economic statistics of that age.

Cedric seemed sadder than the rest of them at the death of the Twisted Man, for while the Twisted Man had repelled most of them with his grim bloodlust, to Cedric that had been a most desirable quality in a Captain of the Guard, and so he had paid it as little attention as he did the warrior's physical deformity. They were deeply grieved to hear of the death of Duke Wassant, most especially Calliope, for he had been her first love; and all were saddened at the passing of the King, but Amatus, having lost his father, spent a long half day on the tower staring out at the Lake of Winter, and no one cared to go up to talk with him about it.

But when everything was accounted for, there remained Cedric's news. From the Royal Library, he had brought *Highly Unpleasant Things It Is Sometimes Necessary to Know* and *Things It Is Not Good to Know at All,* and more importantly he had brought his observations.

"I didn't care to travel in daylight," he explained. "It's true that there are many more of them at night, but the undead and the goblins are not so disciplined as to be able to conduct much of a search. And they did not seem to know that they were looking for me, either; one disadvantage of taking a city so quickly is that in the random destruction it becomes hard to see just what you do or don't have. So I had the days, when I wasn't sleeping, to lie back in a bed or sit in a chair and *think.* And the thing of greatest importance is just what I realized back in the Royal Library—when you kill the identical ones, the remainder become stronger; when you kill the nonidentical ones, the remainder become weaker.

"Now, it so happens that in *Highly Unpleasant* there's a discussion of soul-sharing as an evil thing done by various wicked wizards over the ages. Bodies are made, and two or three soldiers share out their souls to a company. If one of the made men is killed, all the rest have more soul—and so get stronger. But if one of the real men who supply the souls is killed—"

Amatus nodded then, gesturing for Cedric to get on with it. "I see. They are all weaker, even the other soldiers with souls of their own, because the company of soldiers is sharing fewer souls. And if you were to kill all of the real men—"

"I saw it happen. The made men stagger limply; they are alive, but only in the way that a muscle may still twitch on the butcher's block." Cedric sighed. "Moreover, I had the dubious pleasure of looking up the procedure in the source itself, *Things It Is Not Good to Know at All*, and there I learned that like all such dark magics, this one has a price higher than any sane person would think it was worth. To have the power to do this, Waldo has had to give up his heart, and leave it somewhere. If we find that and destroy it, his power will be gone like dew on summer grass."

"I have never understood the name of that book," Sir John said, "for surely we have benefited from the things in it, and we have kept it in the library."

"These are things it is not good to do," Amatus said, "and to know about them is possibly to be able to do them—and that being the case, once you know them you are never out of danger. Notice, for example, what the knowledge has done to Waldo. Then can Waldo even be killed at all by ordinary means? And if we did find a way to kill him, what would become of his army?"

"Oh, I would say that if you cut his head off, or stabbed through his eye into his brain, or perhaps even slipped a pongee into his kidney, it would be the end of Waldo. It would be surer and more swift to find that heart and throw it into a fire, cut it in half, something of the kind. As for his army—well, he'd lose the power to move souls about. The made men would be nothing more than twitching flesh, and I would suspect that his few real men would be greatly disabled from the shock. That would be more than a third of the enemy at that moment—and as for the rest, for all his taste for massacre, Waldo has had to leave the bulk of the Kingdom's subjects alive (someone has to produce the wealth) and there is bitter hatred for him everywhere. We have had plagues of the un-dead and goblin invasions before. I should guess that with-out his army there in daylight to guard the undead's resting places and the entry holes to Goblin Country, your common-ers would make a brief and satisfactory slaughter of them, even if they had only farm tools and rocks for the job."

Amatus nodded. "And did you get a sense of the country as you passed through it? Is there any fighting spirit left?"

"Plenty, if they but saw a way to win."

"Well, then, they must see some victories."

Dick Thunder coughed softly. "You have seen their homes and camps, King Amatus and Sir John; what do you suppose our northern people will be as fighters?"

"Silent and systematic, I should suppose," Amatus said. "They often eat by the omnibus and the festoon, so I imagine they must be more than fair shots. But they've no reason to know the escree—I speak here of the fishers, hunters, and log-gers, Dick, I know your robbers know their trade—"

"Begging your pardon, High—er, that is, Majesty," Sir John said, "I think you've badly understated the case. I earned my name of Escree Jack by knowing how to do anything at all with the escree other than use it to roast potatoes and chicken legs. But on the other hand, they are astonishingly good shots—hunters learn not to waste balls, Majesty. I would say they would be no good at all against real troops in close, but if they can keep a distance they could shoot any army ever formed into the ground."

"Just so," Dick Thunder said. "So if we might imagine what would happen if we were to fight Waldo's army in the daylight, somewhere with a lot of bushes and rocks to hide behind and plenty of room to run—"

"Shoot the real men until the made men are staggering and helpless, and then turn loose the lumbermen with their axes and the fishermen with their voltage spikes," Cedric said. "I think it's a splendid thought. Can we arm and provision an army out of this country?"

"It's late spring now," Captain Palaestrio answered. "It hardly matters, for this is the time of the year when we must buy food from the south anyway. There's nothing there right now but whatever is in the cellars from last year, still too much snow for a man to think of going up after the gazebo and not much meat on them if he should, and the big runs of fish are not due until the streams clear, in a month or more. If the Kingdom has been ruined, then we might as well be under siege no matter what, for if we fight and do not win we will starve, and if we do not fight we will starve. Only if we fight and win is there hope."

As discussion wore on it became clear that they could put perhaps as many as a thousand men under arms.

"That's nothing to the hundred thousand or so that rampaged through the city," Cedric pointed out. "But two thirds of those cannot come out in the daylight. And that leaves us perhaps thirty-five thousand at worst to face—and what I have counted on the trail, when patrols passed me, was that there were no more than one real soldier to fifty made ones."

A cracked, old voice spoke above them. "That's for the horse patrols. For foot it's nearer one to a hundred now, since many of his men—his *real* men—are falling from a soul-sickness of some kind." They had all looked straight up, into the broad boughs of the big fir tree under which they sat, and to their surprise, there was old Euripides, finest of the Kingdom's scouts.

"It took you long enough to get here," Cedric said, smiling. "What kind of a scout do you call yourself?"

"An almighty poor one if the truth be told," Euripides said, climbing down, "for had I but seen these things in Overhill a few months ago, we might all be speaking of them over a warm dark Gravamen at home. But, late is better than never, most of the time, anyway. Now, as I was saying, it looks a great deal as if their actual numbers are about a hundred of these bags of meat to one real man, and what that does to the real man is dreadful to think about." He sighed and scratched. "A fellow might ask for a bit of biscuit—"

"And he might get a full meal if he did," Dick Thunder said, grinning. "How in all the names of all the gods did you find your way through my sentries?"

"Tight, I found it. Very tight. Nigh to impossible," Euripides said. They all followed Thunder as he wandered over to where Sylvia was at work on the day's soup; partway there the robber chief turned and whispered to Amatus and Calliope, "She always made the most extraordinary soup. Never thought I'd ever taste it again. If only . . . oh, well."

At Calliope's insistent nod and gesture, Amatus said, "Well, you know, Dick, it's always just possible she's been carrying . . . oh, you know, they don't have torches down in Goblin Country, but up in the city they do, and . . . well, you know the custom. I would bet she carried a torch everywhere she went and that's why no one asked. But I've not seen her with a torch here, now, have you?"

Hope flared in Thunder's eyes. Amatus clapped Thunder on the shoulder.

The soup was indeed good, and as more of it got into Euripides they got more and more of his account, and their hearts brightened. Further, the account of the outrages in the countryside filled them with fury, and more so because each of them knew that—as anything connected with Waldo tended to—it all rested on a low, shabby, dirty trick.

"Well, then," Cedric said, in his second mug of the dark Pilaster that a Vulgarian trader had let Captain Palaestrio have on credit, "there is merely the question of what is to be done and how we are to do it. By daylight, I do believe the Army of the North—which has a certain splendid ring to it, and in these sorts of tales a splendid ring is a promising thing to have—can very likely massacre the human part of Waldo's army, and once that is done we will have ourselves quite a successful revolution under way, with a great slaughter of goblins and undead. The question then, given that we win such a battle—do you think we should fight it, say, somewhere below the rapids of the Long River?"

Dick Thunder, King Amatus, and Captain Palaestrio, who all knew something about fighting wars, nodded at the wisdom of the choice. Calliope and Sylvia nodded because they didn't know what Cedric was going to talk about next and wanted him to get on with it. Psyche was quietly staring into space, her thoughts far away, and Sir John Slitgizzard and Sceledrus nodded so as not to be left out.

"Well, then, if we win the battle there we may depend on revolution to rise quickly, but there is bound to be some delay on the way to the city, for every little village will want to hold a celebration, and there will be the stragglers to hunt down and that sort of thing. Of course with the countryside going up in a rush, most of his goblins and undead will never get back to the city, and the walls are long and hard to hold, especially with the damage recently done, so it will be weakly defended when we get there. But I'm afraid lowlands farmers won't be much as soldiers and we can't count on much of my old regular army finding out in time to rejoin us, let alone still having their arms with them. We should be lucky to reach the city with the Army of the North, plus an equal body of trained men (though not in their old units, more's the pity), and perhaps three times that number of men who are far better with a hoe than with an omnibus. That should get us through the city wall well enough, if we've had enough success—there will be few real men in the city, and they will all be desperately ill. But I don't think, even should we break through in a mad rush, that it is enough to carry the castle, and that worries me a great deal."

"Suppose we do not," Dick Thunder said. "Can we starve out Waldo?"

"In time, perhaps. But to have him merely cornered is like having a viper pinned under a stick—the snake is in trouble but you are still in danger. What he might do from there . . . well, he is altogether too clever to be given such a chance."

"Then no doubt you have something in mind?" Amatus said, his lone eyebrow rising. "I long ago noted that any wise minister does not raise a problem until he has some action he wishes his monarch to take to remedy it."

"Nothing is more gratifying than an apt pupil," Cedric said, his eyes twinkling a little as he fluffed out the sad remains of his beard. "Well, you're right, of course. It seems to me that this matter of his heart being apart from him must be in the story to some purpose, and that means that we ought to do our best to find it, for surely it would solve many problems if we did. So there needs to be a minor quest of sorts in all this, I should think—someone must try to find the heart and destroy it.

"Then, too, it seems to me we need one more thing done as well—and that is a diversion. If we could cause Waldo to leave the castle—better yet to leave the city altogether—then we might well take it without much of a fight at all. And if that should happen, then it would be a matter of tracking him down, with the possibility that at any moment someone might find his heart and burn it or cut it into pieces as well—for he would not be able to go near where it was. Once we have the city and castle again, and his foul army is dead or driven back into its holes, well, then his powers for malice are greatly reduced, and if we are then thorough and press our search, I have little doubt we can bring this tale to a happy enough ending."

He wished instantly he had not said that last, for it caused Amatus to wince with pain and look at Psyche. For a long time the only sound was old Euripides gulping and slobbering at his soup, for, spending as much time as he did away from hot food and other people, his table manners were as bad as his scouting was acute.

"Oh, well, then," Amatus said at last, "since it all sounds like common sense, I imagine you've a way of allocating us to those duties. I had at first thought that I ought to be on the quest, but questing is really a prince's game, and I am a king now, so I shall have to lead the army. Psyche travels with me, always, and I would not dream of leading the army without having along the two men who everyone in this north country is going to trust as my lieutenants—that is, Deacon Dick Thunder and Captain Palaestrio. So that leaves the rest of you for the other two purposes . . ."

"Ahem," Sir John coughed. "Er, I had a thought. Sort of a thought, you might say . . . er, well, you know, with one thing and another in the city, it happens that I never did a proper knight-candidate's quest. No one raised any, er, objections, because at first I was wild and bad and no one expected me to do anything expected of me, you know, and then after that I was in one adventure after another with my Prince, and so I think most folk thought I had, but . . ." his voice trailed off hopefully.

"Of course, Sir John!" Amatus said, clapping his hands together, and then lurching backward in surprise because it had never made a noise before. "That's exactly what you will do, then."

"Er, that wasn't the whole thought," Slitgizzard said, looking down and nearly blushing. They waited for him to go on. "It seems to me that, well, perhaps . . . well, you all know I am not very clever. That seems to be widely agreed upon. And looking for things requires some cleverness, rather than mere skill, which I have in abundance. So I thought rather than look for the heart directly, I might go seek out the Riddling Beast, and ask him where to look."

"You've no business saying you aren't clever," Calliope said, beaming at him. "That's a very sensible idea."

Sir John did blush, then, and they thought it was embarrassment at the compliment, but it was relief that he had not made a fool of himself. Perhaps Calliope sensed this, a little, for she hastened to change the subject. "Well, that leaves me, and Cedric, and Euripides, if you can spare him, Amatus, to make the diversion. And I've got a fine one in mind."

Amatus nodded. "I think up in this country we can rely on Dick Thunder's men to do our scouting without much danger. And much as I will miss Cedric's good advice, I think a wily and experienced old head put to the job of making trouble can probably make a great deal where we need it and when we need it."

"Who are you calling old?" Cedric said, but he beamed at the compliment, which reassured Amatus a great deal. He had not especially wanted to have Cedric looking over his shoulder during his first great battle as King, but he had not wanted him to realize that.

"Why, good old Calliope, of course," Amatus said, smiling in a way more innocent than any innocent person has ever achieved.

"Be that as it may," Calliope said, "here's the diversion I have in mind. To do what he did, I'm quite sure that Waldo stripped Overhill bare. And though the commoners there may be twenty years more borne down and worn out, they are also that much angrier. I think I might stir up a rebellion there—and perhaps if luck were with me, might free my family's citadel at Oppidum Optimum myself. That ought to make Waldo start moving—so he's likely to be most of the way to Iron Lake before he hears the city has fallen behind him."

"Promise you will be cautious," Amatus said.

"Yes, dearie," Calliope said, much too sweetly, and despite knowing that Amatus was King, the rest could hardly avoid laughing, so Amatus could not resist laughing either.

"Well, then, be reckless and do foolish things and endanger yourself needlessly, if you really must, but for all the gods' sake come back safe," Amatus said. "I think we have a strategy here, and had best get about carrying it through."

4

Quests and Diversions

O f Sir John Slitgizzard's hardships on his quest, perhaps we ought to say nothing, for he scorned to complain, and perhaps in deference to him no one wrote any record of it. But in fairness we must say that his courage and endurance must have been considerable.

We do know that he chose to go the quick rather than the easy way. The longer way round would have been arduous enough, for it would have meant descending the Long River, crossing where the bridge was down, descending through the foothills, taking the fork in the road to the Great North Woods, following that dark, little-traveled, and sorcery-ridden road three or four days through the Great North Woods until he came to Iron Lake, finding a boat or more likely walking around the lake some days more until he found the road that ran along the lake north from the Ironic Gap, and then finally hiking up into the mountains along the Iron River into the wild and dangerous country where the Irons themselves lived. They were an often inexplicable people, hard to see precisely, and though they were not always danger-ous, they were never entirely safe either.

Passing through Irony would eventually take him among the highest peaks, where nothing much lived—except various monsters, goblins, gazebo, and now the Riddling Beast.

But this was the easy way and it was *not* the way he went. Sir John knew that there was one high pass—so high that anywhere else in the lands known to the Kingdom it would have been counted as a mountain in its own right—between the Northern Mountains, which rose above the Lake of Winter, and the nameless mountains north of Iron Lake where the Riddling Beast had gone. In another month, there would be perhaps half a chance of finding that pass clear of snow, but there was no month to wait, so Sir John set forth, "and don't worry about it," he said to Amatus, before Sceledrus took him across the lake and up the little river to where his journey was to begin, "it's one thing to set a quest for some shavetail wet-behind-the-ears youngster who's never proven himself at anything, and quite another to set a quest for a man with some experience, eh? A quest is supposed to be a challenge."

Sceledrus reported that Sir John had seemed cheerful as he led off the two pack mules whom he had purchased from the area's wealthiest potato farmer. He had been offered them as a loan, and had refused to take it, "for I don't expect them to make the journey all the way, and if by some miracle one or other should survive, well, I can at least give him an honorable retirement."

The last Sceledrus had seen of him, Sir John Slitgizzard had been on his way, whistling "The Codwalloper's Daughter" off-key (and as loudly as possible, to compensate).

It was only the day after Sceledrus reported this that Calliope set forth. She would proceed down the Long River, then take the Great North Woods Road west to Iron Lake, and finally enter Overhill through the Ironic Gap.

Amatus was surprised at his concern for her. It was a dangerous journey, but not more dangerous than other things she had done. It was important, but not as important as either Sir John's mission or his own. Yet he felt sorrier than ever before to see her go.

He realized his feelings were entirely consonant with a happy ending, and for just a moment he had to find Psyche and make sure she was still there.

Calliope's journey through the Great North Woods with Cedric and Euripides was as uneventful as any riding vacation. The Great North Woods had been a royal preserve for ages untold, never touched by settler's ax or soldier's boot, and it was filled with things that might make other quests, or with things that in another sort of quest might have to be overcome, and there was hardly a clearing without a knight's grave, a hill without an ogre, or a dark copse without dark doings in its dark past. The Great North Woods Road was said to have been there before the Kingdom, and perhaps before the Great North Woods, but nothing was known of how it had been made, nor even of what kept it open. For though it saw little enough traffic, it was always in reasonable repair, ready for any traveler who needed it—though, since it ran without branching from a road through a wilderness to a great flat stone on an unpopulated shore, there were few who did.

And this time, despite all the adventures waiting for other travelers, nothing happened during the four days' journey along the road. Euripides was heard to mutter regularly that it was "too quiet," but almost always, shortly after he did, animals in the woods would begin to make noises, as if they wanted him to be more comfortable.

When they were not silent they argued about why there had never been any goblins in the Great North Woods. Euripides thought it was because goblins could only go where at least one goblin had been before, which Calliope thought rather begged the question, but her own hypothesis that whatever the Great North Woods was, was older and stronger than what the goblins were, was by her own admission no better. It gave them something to debate when they felt like talking, which was not often.

Now and then a view or vista opened up and they saw some ruin or mountain, old and encrusted with history, but more often they saw only the great arch of trees above the road.

Each night, just as they became tired, there was an opening adequate for them to camp on, with dead branches lying there for a fire. They ate from their packs, dining well enough on pan bread made from piecemeal, jerked gazebo, and other simple fare.

Finally, just before noon of the fourth day, they came to the Flat Rock, a piece of stone broad enough for a thousand men to stand on that stuck into Iron Lake at the very northwest corner of the Great North Woods for no particular reason except that it had to be somewhere. They ate a quick lunch on the Flat Rock.

Calliope never knew just what impelled her to walk to the end of the Flat Rock. But as she reached the point farthest out into the water, something glowed on the horizon.

As Cedric described it later, the glow became something you knew would be in the corner of your eye if you looked away. Then it grew, and Calliope stood as straight and still as if a million people were watching her.

A ship heaved above the horizon, her great brown sail painted with deep blue stripes, an indescribable flag flying at her mast, making for the Flat Rock with swift dignity. Cedric and Euripides ran forward to join Calliope, for Cedric's first thought was that Waldo must have built a navy, and Euripides's was of pirates.

So softly you would not have known she was there with your eyes closed, the ship slid up beside the Flat Rock in the bright sunlight, as solid as the Rock itself and yet strangely cut into the air around her, as if she were a trifle more real than anything else around her. She rocked gently there, not an arm span from the Rock (for the water was deep on that side). A gangplank swung down from the side of the ship to crash onto the Rock.

No hand rested on the tiller, no sheet or line had a hand upon it, no one raced across the deck to make anything happen; it all just happened, and now the ship rested there, as if waiting for them. "What do you suppose—?" Calliope whispered.

"I suppose as little as I can manage," Cedric replied, his voice low. "This is the sort of thing that every story assures us cannot be ignored. A ship like this is going to take us to somewhere we need to be, rest assured of that. The gangplank, there, looks uncommonly solid and stable; do you suppose we might see if we can lead the horses and mules up it?"

"We'll need fodder for 'em," Euripides pointed out.

"I doubt that. At the pace with which this ship sails, there is no doubt in my mind that she can be at any corner of Iron Lake in a matter of a few hours."

"How do we know she's for us?" Calliope whispered, again, gingerly placing a foot on the gangplank.

"She's for you," Euripides said, firmly.

"How do you know?"

"Because when you touched her just now, the flag at the mast, which had been indescribable, became the Raven and Rooster, the flag of your family," Euripides said, pointing upward. They looked and it was so.

A little later they led the last mule up the gangplank, and everything was off the Flat Rock. Calliope asked, "Now, do we raise the gangplank or—"

The gangplank slowly raised itself and knots formed in the lines to make it fast. There was a subtle shifting underfoot, and first the ship was drifting sideways, and then her sails caught a wind that had not been blowing an instant before, and they were racing across the water, far faster than a galloping horse ever goes, all in a deep silence.

Calliope was still trying to make sense of the ship's arrival. "You say it came to serve me, because it started to fly the Raven and Rooster, but I've been to Iron Lake, oh, dozens of times, and I've never seen this ship before."

Cedric grinned; little would discourage him now, for the arrival of ancient, unknown, and obviously beneficent magic must mean that Waldo had at last gone too far and was about to bear the consequences. "It was never time before. Things will draw on swiftly now. This is an excellent sign."

The ship had arrived at the Flat Rock just after they had finished their lunch, and they had spent perhaps the better part of an hour boarding her; but long before they had any thought of being hungry again, or of stretching out for a nap, the western shore of Iron Lake was drawing near, and there, among the scrub brush, they saw another rock, not unlike a smaller Flat Rock, with a ruined stone wall rising above it and a road winding up into the trees above.

"Where are we?" Cedric asked.

"I have seen this place," Euripides said, "as I have seen most places. The fishermen in these parts often call it the Old Port, so I have always assumed at one time it was such. That grassy road—which never outgrows, though there is no traffic on it, much like the Great North Woods Road—winds up to join the Royal Road not more than a double dozen furuncles above us in the hills, just where the Royal Road bends and heads up into the Ironic Gap. This ship has saved us some days' travel and danger."

Even as Euripides spoke, the ship brought herself, as delicately as a cat finds a favored spot on a pillow, to the side of the rock. The gangplank came down, and presently they had disembarked their horses and mules.

They had expected almost anything of the ship—that she

might then sink, or transform into something else, or perhaps sail back over the horizon—but it was only that as they looked at her, wondering what she would do, she ceased to be there. In a long breath more of the water flowed together where she had been.

Headed up into the mountains, they made splendid time. By late afternoon, they were encamped not far from the fort at the top of the pass. They built no fire, and lay well back from the road, everything made as silent as it might be, for the fort must be held by Waldo's soldiers, and they planned to rise well before the dawn to see if they might find a quiet way around it.

Long before dawn the next morning, as Calliope and Cedric yawned and gulped cold water from their bottles, old Euripides, making less noise than a shadow on dark moss, crept forth to see what he might find. As he went, Cedric and Calliope got matters in order, muffling the hooves of the horses and mules, whispering gently to the animals to keep them quiet, making sure more by feel than sight that nothing was left behind. When they finished they sat silently together on a log for a cold breakfast of jerked gazebo and piecemeal biscuit.

Euripides should have been back by now, and yet he was not. Undoubtedly he had encountered some difficulty and would be here soon.

Calliope whispered that he might as well nap, she would stand the short watch until Euripides returned, so Cedric spread his cloak on the ground and lay down. She could barely see him, and she was alone in the dark with her thoughts. She thought of Amatus, and of how Boniface had fallen and the Duke had died, and the passing of the first three Companions. It was strange how Psyche had at first seemed merely charming, and then had become a friend, but when Calliope had come to understand more of the nature of the

Companions, she had realized her friend was a force in the world like wind, truth, gravity, or levity.

Now the morning stars were beginning to fade, and there was only the Morning Star itself, bright and glorious, burning down through a hole in the fir boughs. Euripides was now hours late from a half-hour mission, and if he did not come immediately they would have to wait till the following night.

The gray false dawn came and went, and took the Morning Star with it, and still there was no sound, and no sign of Euripides. A low red sunrise, portending storms, came up, and then the gray clouds frothed over the blue of the sky, so that it was gloomy and gray and nearly as dark as it had been before sunrise, and still there was no trace of the scout. She thought of waking Cedric, but saw little benefit; if Euripides was captured, they must hope that he did not talk, for they could not move without detection until dark fell again that night.

Cedric woke when the hoofbeats came from the road, and then they both stood when they heard Euripides's voice call for them. They glanced at each other sharply, and Cedric stopped knocking leaves and dirt from his cloak and beard just long enough to whisper, "It might be a—"

But he did not say "trap" for at that moment Euripides came out of the brush, and with him were three men, who all knelt before Cedric. The old General and Prime Minister— still with a leaf or two sticking to him, and his thin hair an unkempt mess—had the courtier's gift of instant dignity, so he raised each of them with a gentle hand, and as he brought the last one up, he exclaimed, "Captain Pseudolus! Gods and more gods, I'd have thought the fort fallen and all of you dead!"

"Then there *was* a war," Pseudolus said. "We hear little up here in the Ironic Gap, and what we do hear is old. One absurd fellow did come up to tell us that someone named Waldo was now in charge of the Kingdom and to give us a set of ridiculous orders. Obviously a prank, or perhaps something garbled from that other Waldo, the one that lives in Overhill. So since what he said was not bad enough (and we thought not true enough) to hang him for, we beat the messenger till he could just manage to stand, and put him on the road in a nightshirt with a sign about his neck that said 'Fool.' I suppose if I see that little man again I owe him some sort of an apology."

"No very deep one," Cedric said. "I think perhaps we should begin with an inspection of the fort"—with that he winked at Calliope—"and then proceed from there."

A more astute man than Captain Pseudolus might have noted that the inspection of the kitchen was unusually thorough. But then a more astute man might have surrendered the fort, before.

Cedric determined the next morning that Pseudolus had about one hundred omnibusiers and escreesmen, in good order and well-drilled. "Well, then," he said, beaming with satisfaction, "I think we have the beginnings of your army, here, Highness."

Pseudolous appeared startled, but Cedric rode over whatever objection there might have been to say, "Your faithful preservation of the royal forces in this country will stand as an example of fidelity forever, and if you are married, Captain Pseudolus, you may tell your wife that you and your heirs will be nobility if I've any say in it—"

The poor Captain, who had known perfectly well that he was sent to the Ironic Gap because it was thought less important and he was thought less capable, could hardly contain himself, and babbled his thanks.

"Nonsense, nonsense, it's all well deserved," Cedric harumphed.

"And if the Kingdom should be so ungrateful as not to give you the title," Calliope added, "you have the word of the current Princess and future Queen of Overhill that you will hold title, power, and pelf there. Not that there's much pelf, the way Waldo's handled it. Is there some motto that runs in your family?"

"Well, my old man always said I had more loyalty than brains, ma'am. And his father said the same about him." He hesitated, then blurted out, "I'd no idea you were a queen, and I do hope I haven't done anything wrong—"

She beamed at him. "You've done everything perfectly. And I've only just decided to be a Queen. And we'll put your family motto into Latin and it will make a splendid impression on your crest. '*Quam stultus sed quam fidelior.*' But now I must ask of you, Cedric—as Prime Minister of the Kingdom, and General of All the Armies, can you extend a bit of military assistance to a neighboring Kingdom? I should like to borrow, er—"

"Well, I do believe we will have to call what we have here the Army of the West, and yes, the Kingdom will certainly loan it to you. Captain—you will immediately ready these forces to go with the Queen—we are riding into Overhill. Oh, and since I am of at least the rank of a Field Marshal, I suppose we will have to make you Acting General or something of the sort for a while. We can work out the implications for your pay later. How soon can we be ready to march?"

"This afternoon if you like, sir, I've kept 'em sharp."

"Tomorrow morning will be soon enough. You may want to go and tell your wife of your rise in the world."

As Captain Pseudolus went out, they heard him mutter, "Well, well, the old man always did say 'do what you're told and don't think too much,' and now I see he was right."

The next morning, as they rode over the pass and down, they made a brave display, and Calliope's heart was high. She had quietly promoted herself to Queen now that she was going home, and she noted that Cedric had accepted it without a murmur; indeed, Euripides seemed more comfortable having the clear title of "Majesty" to address her by. Moreover, the mountain country was beautiful at first, with its pine woods bending near the road, and clear shining cataracts pouring off many ledges, for with early summer the snow melt was now at its fullest. Eagles flew overhead, gazebo and the elusive little zwiebacks bounded in the brush, great fish leapt from the streams, and it might have been a splendid royal vacation for the first few hours.

But about the time they broke to eat the noon meal, the road was falling into the sort of disrepair that meant that not even highwaymen had bothered with it in years. This might have been tolerable to the eye if only the forest and mountains that had been reclaiming the road had been as beautiful as those of the Kingdom, but as they descended, there were fewer leaves or needles on the more and more distorted trees. The grass that had grown across the road was no longer thick and green and wet, but straggled like the hair of a drowned woman, its green mottled by blacks and browns, and with the scratchy dry roughness of the skin of a mummy. No gazebo were seen anywhere, and the two zwieback they saw were stunted and sickly. The brown and greasy trickles that rolled down the mountain side smelled fouler than Calliope would have thought possible.

It grew worse with time, and the poisoned-looking trees and grass gave way to dead ones, and then to sour dirt, and then the sour dirt became dry ash. The river beside them crept downward in a thick translucent ooze. When the air was not bitter and dry it was sour and damp; whatever life there might be watched from ledges and crevices invisibly.

"The nature of a ruler is the nature of a land," Cedric said. "You might think with Waldo gone—"

"It's better than it was last year," Euripides said.

Just before sunset they came to what they thought were the ruins of the first village. There was not a building with a wall standing altogether straight, or a door that did more than lean against its frame, or anything that moved in the dusty square. But as they passed, there were rustlings and scrapings. The villagers were coming out.

Though their faces were old, they were young, mostly, perhaps because their parents had starved to save them, perhaps because they were more immune to despair and so had not decided to die quite yet. They wore rags, and stared.

Calliope dismounted and approached the oldest of them, a man who might have been forty, and said, directly and firmly, "I am Calliope, Queen of Overhill, and I am here to take possession and to expel the Usurper and all his forces." Behind her, in the ashy breeze, the Raven and Rooster flag that one of Pseudolus's troopers had sewn for her fluttered and flapped a moment.

She had expected anything from great rejoicing to bitter railing, but not that the man would burst into tears and sink to the ground. Calliope bent to lift him, and said, "It's all right, it's all right, stand up, please . . ."

He stood and bowed, finally, and murmured, "I am one of the few in this country old enough to recall that flag, Majesty, or to even know what a queen is. But the others will learn."

That night they ate field rations again, plus dressed meat from gazebo shot earlier in the day, and though the troops might have thought it no better than middling for on the march, to the villagers it was a feast. Calliope moved among them, asking here, picking up a story there, coming to understand. Many in the village had traveled, to sell what little the mines yielded (mainly proscenium, and a few semiprecious stones, samnites and smithereens, chiefly) or to serve in Waldo's forced labor battalions. Overhill was all much like this, "bled down to nothing to build his army for the war on the Kingdom, and now thrown away as a husk," one woman said. "It's as if it's not enough to shake all the wealth of the world out of Overhill, he wants to make sure that no one will ever come here again."

In the morning, they found they had volunteers, most of whom did not seem fit to march a single furuncle, but they selected a few of the strongest. They could be armed only with staffs and clubs, but that did not seem to trouble them. They kept pace, and they were quiet on march, Cedric noted, and after a while he added to his notes that their faces were set in grimaces of hate, and then that every so often a smile—very different from the grimace—would creep across their faces, and finally at the last stop of the day he noted that they seemed to be getting taller and stronger with every furuncle they marched.

In the course of their first full day in the kingdom, the Army of the West passed through eleven more villages and towns along the road to Oppidum Optimum—Cedric's diary, and the notes Calliope began to keep with an eye toward putting Overhill back in order, both agree on that. They found fresh recruits at each one, and by the day's end their numbers, in addition to the eighty or so men Captain Pseudolus had supplied, were up to between 650 (Cedric's number) and 825 (Calliope's).

Late in the evening they captured a crumbled, rusting, and useless arsenal, from which they retrieved nothing of value except some escree blades, and took, without fighting, an army granary, guarded by one sickly sergeant and seven of the made men. They quietly beheaded the made men, and the sergeant seemed to recover, but later that night he died in a thrashing fit, his eyes wide with horror.

When they opened the bursting silos—filled by extortion from the starving farmers, years back when some corners of Overhill had still grown wheat, barley, or flan—much of it had rotted. Yet there was enough still good to replenish rations, and by late that night, when Cedric and Calliope at last laid down their pens and went to bed, heads full of plans and decisions and questions, it was clear that this diversion should get far enough to get Waldo's attention. Beyond that all hopes were wild—and abundant.

The following morning, they found that four thousand new would-be recruits for the Army of the West had arrived in the night.

5

Matters Begin to Reverse, and Favorable Endings Are Pointed To

*W*hen at last he wrote the brief *Memoirs* of which we have a fragment, Amatus passed over the battle on Long River Road with a few brief sentences. *Robber Baron: The Rise of the Thunder Family from Terror of the North to the Kingdom's Most Respected Barony*, which purports to be by Deacon Dick Thunder, contains a lengthy account, but its authorship is fraudulent, it is plain that parts of it were collected from people who were not eyewitnesses, and it contains outrageous lies.

So our best guide is probably Amatus's description, which agrees with the equally brief report filed by Captain (Acting General) Palaestrio, with such details as the purported Thunder biography can supply; but the reader must remember that he or she has been warned, and has only herself or himself to blame if she or he ends up believing in things which did not happen.

Amatus picked his ground fairly far up into the foothills. As the Army of the North prepared, from the way the new King stared into space with some frequency, others assumed he was working on strategy, but Psyche knew.

"Look here, Majesty, stop mooning about Calliope, who

will be just fine, and get down to working out your disposi-
tion of forces," she said, laying a hot plate of breakfast before
him.

He looked up and smiled so sadly that many were glad
they could only see half of it. "Was it so obvious? Well, then,
sit with me, take notes for me, and we'll get the battle plan set.
I confess I have neglected it, but truth to tell it is a simple
thing."

Without exactly asking, or not asking, she sent messengers
for Thunder and Palaestrio, and the Council of War was
under way. As Amatus said, it was a simple thing, now that
they knew the secret of the made men. The real men whose
souls were so divided up had only wit enough left to follow
orders, which Waldo himself would have to give.

Waldo was cunning, but his situation would be impossible. He could not let the Army of the North come down to
besiege him, so he must come up to fight it, and in these hills
he could only come up the Long River Road. And from the
Long River Road, a thousand of the best hands ever laid to an
omnibus or festoon were waiting to cut down his men. Thus
Amatus's plan amounted only to getting Waldo's army to
where the Army of the North could shoot the real men, and
staying under cover until Waldo's forces fell apart.

Once they did, Amatus's men carried improvised hand
weapons to use in butchering the made men—the lumbermen
their axes, the potato farmers sharpened spades, and the fishermen their voltage spikes.

Waldo's one hope had lain in forcing them to fight at
night, but again, they had the better of him, for he had to take
the offensive after a few days of Deacon Dick Thunder's raid-
ing. Thunder's men would ride up to some village, purchase
the houses and property with an IOU drawn on the Royal
Treasury, allow people to carry off whatever of their own
goods they wanted, carefully (so as not to endanger anyone)
burn the village, and then pay a few trusty souls to ride to

Waldo's nearest garrison and report the raid. This made it certain Waldo would ride north, for already songs were being sung that he had no power in the North, that his writ stopped at the Winding River, and in the Kingdom, even under a usurper, song today was true tomorrow. Everyone knew that, for it was in the oldest songs.

So Waldo had marched north with his full army, but during the day his men, real and made, were no longer adequate to guard his goblins and undead, and Thunder's men would crash into camp from one side or other, grigs whirling on ropes tied to saddles, to drag tenting off his helpless forces, slaying hundreds of goblins and undead at a stroke (and always costing Waldo a few more real men in the attendant shooting). The goblins began to desert down every hole they could find, and the undead, who could not desert, now waited to die more than they waited to feed. Thus, as Waldo neared the positions Amatus had prepared in the hills, since he thought he faced only Thunder and some two hundred riders, it seemed safer to the Usurper to press the attack and try to beat them once and for all, either by daylight or by keeping them engaged until the sun fell.

As simple things are wont to, Amatus's plan worked. Thunder's men, pursued by most of the horsemen of the foe, raced up the road, and as the outlaws passed the arranged marker, omnibuses barked and rang from every rock and tree above. The real men fell dead in droves, and the survivors, catching the load of so many made men upon their souls, plunged from their saddles. Behind them, the advancing army of foot shuddered and began to crumble, but the real men remaining, who had little left of their souls except their fear of Waldo, forced themselves to continue.

Behind Waldo's army, undetected because Waldo had no one fit to scout, grim-faced northern gazebo hunters climbed into the trees, and lumbermen and potato farmers crouched behind bushes and rocks, for though the land was too rugged to march an army through, these men were tougher than the land. At Sceledrus's signal, omnibus fire roared out of the hills behind and above Waldo's main body, and more real men fell. Sceledrus said later that it seemed that many of the real men deliberately stepped out of the press of their soldiers, holding their weapons well to the side and baring their chests to the shot, and died with smiles of relief. And it may well be true, for surely the burden of having their souls so sliced and parceled must have weighed down on them until they were glad to have it lifted by any means, and besides, it is not the sort of lie that Sceledrus was capable of inventing.

Waldo, naturally, rode away swiftly when he saw how it was going, and those of his real men who were not cut down as they fled had left so much of their souls behind in the made men that they could go only a little way before collapsing. The battle had begun halfway through the morning, and before noon Waldo was headed back to the city as swiftly as he could manage, the remnants of his army trailing after as best they could. Late in the day, Thunder's men rode in and set fire to the carts carrying the undead.

When the goblins had failed to appear in any counter-attack that night, it was clear Waldo had lost his ally.

In the next few days, the provinces declared for Amatus as fast as the news could spread. The tiny garrisons Waldo had left behind, counting on fear to control the populace, often had as few as five real men, and now that the secret of their nature was out, there would be a brief period of fierce fighting as some local lord, or mayor, or leader of any kind brought firearms to bear upon those, and then a swift slaughter and a burning of the undead. The goblin hunts were rapid and brutal, for there was much to avenge, and indeed goblins were not seen again in many parts of the Kingdom for decades after, because in their victory they had grown careless, allowing their holes to be noticed, so that when the tide turned the goblin holes were sealed forever.

But of what each individual did in the Battle of the Long River Road, all is lost, unless you are willing to believe the outrageous lies in *Robber Baron*. It seems likely that few of Amatus's men were even hurt, and it is not clear that even one was killed. As they neared the city, those who saw the grand array of Amatus, Psyche at his side, Deacon Dick Thunder and Captain Palaestrio flanking them, and the Hand and Book fluttering overhead, were so moved they spoke often of it all their lives afterward, so much so that no one was ever quite sure how long ago it had happened, since many who were born after had heard their elders tell it so often that they thought they themselves had seen it.

The arrival of Calliope into Oppidum Optimum was much like Amatus's march to the city in spirit, but meaner and poorer in flesh. After twenty years of Waldo, Overhill was a poisoned waste with people scattered across it, far less hospitable than it had been a thousand years before when settlers had come over to it.

But people dug out what little they had, and Captain Pseudolus's soldiers seized the granaries, so that for the first time in many years there would be grain to plant (if it could live in Overhill) and at least no immediate famine. Most people stayed only long enough to get the grain, salute their new Queen, and return home to get planting under way, but a few from every village stayed with the Army of the West.

So by the time they reached Oppidum Optimum, they had several thousands of people with them, and when they found themselves opposed only by six real men and about eighty made ones, the fight was brief and left pretty much to Pseudolus's forces. In an hour or so the real men were all picked off, and then the job of dealing with the rest was mere butchery.

They had not found an omnibus or festoon in all of Overhill, though it had once been renowned as hunting country, for eliminating those had been Waldo's first project, not from fear of what a rabble with a few of them might do, but merely from a feeling that the ability to defend themselves—however inadequate—was apt to invite a rabble to form.

As the bodies were dragged to the side for burning, Calliope asked, "Why do you suppose anyone ever followed Waldo? Apart from the made men, who hadn't souls of their own, or the goblins or undead, who were only looking for a meal, why would real men enlist? Look how thin and sick his real men were. What did they get from this?"

Cedric nodded. "Majesty, it seems to me that in a sufficiently wretched place, men can always be found who think it is 'realism' to believe that things, as they are, are the only way things can be, and then to look for the soft spot in things as they are. I suppose that accounts for a great part of them; and then there must have been some who cared little how much they were hurt so long as they got the chance to hurt others."

Euripides, beside them, sighed and shuddered. "It's not as if it were ever hard to find a man to do a bad thing."

The ceremonies were ragged, but done with great enthusiasm; the Raven and Rooster was hoisted from every mast in the citadel, except the one atop the Spirit Spire, for temporarily no one could find the door to it.

Three strong men climbed to the famous brass weathercock on its high pole before the gate of the citadel and oiled it and got it working, and in short order the five iron ravens once again circled the brass weathercock, who clutched an upraised spear in his wing so that he always seemed to be guarding against the wind. It was merely a large version of the sort of thing found in toy shops all over the Kingdom (at least before Waldo) but they all cheered madly to see it working.

Calliope made a brief speech formally taking possession, and everyone who was staying went off to see what they might do with the old houses and buildings of the town, for Oppidum Optimum was empty, and Calliope had said that any-one who would put a house back in decent order could have it, and leave it to his or her heirs.

They had reserved the afternoon for Calliope to go up to the room under the base of the Spirit Spire, where her family had been murdered and from which her nurse had smuggled her at the last moment. She was up there a long time. First she climbed the stairs to gently pick up and wrap the bones of her father and her oldest brother, who had been all of sixteen on the day he died. When they were cleared from the steps, she ascended and went through the burst door to the royal cham-bers.

There she found, first, her oldest sister, who lay, a dry husk of bone, skin, and hair, beside the door. The bones of her arm were shattered and broken, and it took Calliope a mo-ment to realize that the girl of twelve had thrust her own arm as a bar through the hasps of the door. She gathered her up and wrapped her in silk as well, talking softly to the remains.

The chopped bones of her mother and of the brother who had been six were next, and these too she wrapped for burial. The worst was the infant twins, only a year older than Cal-liope, whom Waldo, with his own hands, had battered to pieces against the wall. There were many pieces, and it was not at once obvious which went with which, but Calliope sorted them patiently, and wrapped them carefully. It was almost dark when she finished, and summoned the porters to carry down the sad packages, light as sticks and paper, into the fam-ily tomb.

When Sir John Slitgizzard came around the edge of the steep ledge—almost a trail, in that some long-ago traveler had left a cairn here and there to mark the way—he was surprised to see a bare stone valley, easy to walk through and sheltered from the wind. He had gone no more than a dozen paces before he saw the cave opening, and since it was this mountain from which he had seen the Riddling Beast fly, he was filled at once with hope.

The inside of the cave, however, dashed it immediately, for there was evidence of a great cooking fire, and there were many human bones scattered around. Plainly this was the cave of an ogre, and though Sir John would normally have stuck around to dispose of the creature (it was one of Cedric's most strictly enforced public health measures that any man-at-arms who found an ogre must slay it), he had a mission to fulfill. He was only surprised that the ogre had been able to survive on the mountain with the Riddling Beast, who seemed too good a sort to tolerate ogres.

He was about to go back out into the dry valley when he heard the terrible scraping noise coming in. At once he was crouched behind a rock, drawing and laying out his pismires and omnibus, wishing for his father's old heavy-barreled festoon, for ogres are thick of skull. A moment later something big moved in the doorway—and then Sir John gave a glad cry.

It was the Riddling Beast, who had obviously just finished disposing of the ogre, for one enormous three-clawed hand stuck out from between two of the beast's teeth. Sir John stepped out from the rock, and when the beast saw who it was, they romped about with each other, just as two dogs who have been friends and had forgotten about each other's existence will. Of course the romping had to be fairly careful, since the beast might have squashed Sir John under a single claw, but nonetheless they celebrated physically until both were panting.

"I'd just changed addresses," the beast said, proudly. "Wonderful cave here was being taken up by a scrawny underfed ogre; apparently there's some sort of story about a valley north of here where human beings live nearly forever, and travelers are often on their way up to it. But not enough travelers to really feed an ogre well, and the sort of traveler who wants to live forever tends to have been watching his diet, so there's not much meat on them."

"Are the stories true?"

"Of course. They're old and hopelessly distorted, so they must be true. If you like, when we've done whatever your mission is, perhaps you and I could go and have a look for it; it's the kind of place a human being might want to know the way to." The Riddling Beast sat down, breathing hard, laughing between roars. "I've had a month, now, of being out in the light and air as much as I like, and though it's a little lonely, a diet of fresh goblin and gazebo, plus plenty of exercise, has been working wonders. Your friend the witch was very kind to set a term on the spell so that if the Goblin Country acquired other gates, I should be free. Whatever became of her?"

"A bad end, I'm afraid," Sir John said.

"Well, she was still a splendid witch. I imagine you're here questing about something or other, Sir John, so I suppose you had better tell me what it is."

Slitgizzard nodded. "If you don't mind," he said, "I'll make a little fire first, and perhaps put on some water to boil—I need to make tea or soup or something—and we can talk then. It's apt to be a lengthy problem."

"Humph! Why didn't you say so? I've a few dressed-out gazebo hanging in the old digs, just for snacks now and then. I'll be back in moments, Sir John, and you can have steak or stew or whatever it is you make out of gazebo. Will one do?"

"Er, surely," Sir John said, "even hungry as I am I doubt I could eat more than a single haunch."

"As you like. I'll bring along a couple of spare gazebo, and if you don't mind roasting them, I've not had cooked flesh in ages and it's not bad for a novelty."

"By all means," Sir John said.

Fortunately the ogre had maintained a good stock of fire-wood, and Sir John was able to have a big, roaring fire going by the time the Riddling Beast came back. He had even had time to scour the spits thoroughly, so that he had some hope that all taint of man's-flesh was off them. The Riddling Beast had indeed done a fine job of skinning and gutting the gazebo (Sir John later learned that he used the tips of his sharp claws to peel them, rather like shrimp), and they had hung just long enough for full flavor, so Sir John shortly had roasting what he would have thought a splendid meal for fifty. In practice it was a splendid meal for Sir John and an appetizer for the beast. Neither spoke for a long time as they enjoyed it.

Finally Sir John said, "I really am neglecting duty, here, and should have told you my mission straight off. Somehow it seemed rude to proceed with it right away."

"A matter of timing," the Riddling Beast said. "In tales of the kind you seem to get caught in, Sir John Slitgizzard, timing is essential, and you'd not have made it so far without it. If you've delayed, there was some reason for the delay, you may be assured."

Slitgizzard nodded, and then explained what he had come for, recalling everything anyone knew about Waldo. "It seems that 'Where is the heart of Waldo?' is about as good a riddle as any to try your skill at."

The Riddling Beast sat down, and thought long and hard. Sir John occupied himself with all the little mending, fussing, checking, and fixing that one must do at the end of a long jour-ney. There was little sound as they sat comfortably by the fire, except for the occasional clicking of Sir John testing a love-lock by pressing back on a chutney, or the scratch of the beast's great hind leg upon his shoulder or ear.

The light had nearly died when the Riddling Beast sug-gested that they sleep upon the problem. Since the beast was warm-blooded, and a sound, still sleeper, it was no problem for Sir John to curl up against him and be asleep at once. *And surely*, he thought, *if there is a safer place to sleep in all the world, I do not know of it.*

He awakened in the middle of the night when the Riddling Beast whispered, "Sir John, I know the answer."

"Oh?" he yawned.

"I kept trying to think of the oldest saying that might apply, and I finally settled upon 'Home is where the heart is.' Then I thought that Waldo had no home—he came into Overhill as a beggar with his horrid old mother, as you recall; and then I realized that he'd have left the heart with her, and that most surely he'd have left her where no one would bother to go, and the place no one would bother to go, nowadays, is into Overhill. And I realized she must be guarding it, even now, in Oppidum Optimum—"

Sir John swore. "And Calliope and Cedric are headed there! Probably are there already!"

"Well," the Riddling Beast said, "if you're packed, I carry nothing. And given the number of goblins running about these days I expect I could get a meal or two on the way. Perhaps we should fly now, since the moon is up?"

In moments Sir John's pack was clipped to the fur on the beast's back, Sir John had a solid grip, and they were plunging into the sky. Had he not been terribly worried for Calliope and Cedric, because this was the sort of thing that could only mean a rescue, and rescues meant danger, he might very well have enjoyed the way in which the great muscles under him flexed, and the sight of the bright moonlight shining on the snow and ice below. Long before the sun came up, they were over the last northwest tip of the Great North Woods; the Flat Rock rolled below them, and the sun came up as they passed over the dark silvery sweep of Iron Lake.

6

Of Towers and What Was in Them

*A*fter the burial of her family, Calliope had no plans at all, really, other than to get Waldo's attention. She had thought that seizing his old capital would do that, surely, and had made all preparations to disperse her subjects against reprisals, and then to flee with her forces. Yet no word or message came down from the Isought Gap, and after a couple of days she dispatched Euripides and a few of the local men up the road to see what might be happening there.

In the meantime she was determined to add sting to the provocation. She had been filled with a fury deeper than words by what she had seen in the chamber where her family had died, by the condition of the citadel, and most of all by the condition of her people (how swiftly they had become hers!— and how unbearable it was becoming that she had spent safe comfortable years in the Kingdom while her people suffered under the boot and lash of Waldo). She knew Amatus's Army of the North was far better armed and equipped than her own hastily assembled force, and that Waldo would probably not get many furuncles toward the Isought Gap before the city fell behind him and he was forced to turn and fight Amatus in the open. Yet a part of her, privately, wanted to be the one to put an end to Waldo, for she felt that of all living persons, he had wronged her most.

She confided some of these feelings to Cedric, thinking that he ought to be given a chance to talk her out of them, but instead found him inclined to agree. "If magic has a law," Cedric said, "it is poetic justice, and to have the power of poetic justice on our side would be a great thing indeed. Moreover, I think that I know what would amplify the provocation sufficiently, if word got back to him. I noted that on your entry to your country, you quite properly took up the title of Queen. Still, you have not had a coronation—and that might be easily done, as you have the requisite foreign representative in the person of myself, and you have Captain Pseudolus, who you can make a baron or something, for nobility. That's two noble witnesses, one foreign, which is all you need. A dozen commoners should be no trouble to arrange."

"I suppose, now that we know that there is enough unspoiled grain to feed everyone and get the crop in," Calliope said, "we could manage some sort of feast for the occasion. We could make it a pot luck or something, since one thing I can't afford to do yet is establish a genuine royal household."

"Splendid!" Cedric said, stroking his beard. "If I may say, a people so recently rescued from starving is likely to take well to such an expression of the common touch."

"Oh, it's just practical," Calliope said, a bit crossly, for she was already realizing just how much politics were likely to get into her life from now on.

"One can hardly show a better common touch than by being practical," Cedric persisted.

"Then spare me any touch of nobility. I was wondering . . . I've at least a dozen women who've come by asking what they can do, and have not had much use for them—the men can always be put to pulling down rotten buildings and repairing things and so forth. Do you suppose it would be too much to ask a few of the women to clean the dreadful mess out of here, and maybe even clean the dust off the dishes, so that the citadel would be fit for the coronation?"

"I think you would find that they thought of it as a labor of love—and an honor so great that they will squabble with each other to help."

She smiled at that, but the old counselor was wise as always, for shortly she found herself having to adjudicate claims on the honor of cleaning, and in no time at all most of the citadel was becoming positively pleasant. She resolved that should she wind up married to Amatus, the kings and queens of the reunited Kingdom would have a tradition of coming here frequently. The light, graceful arches and open domes— the place had never really been built to stand a siege—large windows, and general airiness and spaciousness of the place seemed to bathe her in a soft white glow. Old garments found hanging in closets turned out to fit her after sprucing up by some of the washerwomen (it was a small miracle that they had been able to find the spruce to do it with). The gowns were not as fashionable as what she had once worn, Cedric thought, but they became a queen.

One mystery remained within the citadel. There was a door behind the Bloody Tapestry (as it had been dubbed, and though Calliope shuddered inwardly, she knew the importance of having it as a symbol, and that the name would stick to it as firmly as the dried blood now did). Most likely it was the unfound door to the Spirit Spire.

But there was no lock or knob upon the door, and since the hinges were on the other side it must swing that way, but even the pushing of four big soldiers did not budge it. Because almost anything could be behind that door, Captain Pseudolus posted a guard on it, and the guards tended to come back with stories of noises during the night, mainly thumping and whining.

"You know," Calliope said, as she pored over a map that Captain Pseudolus's best surveyor had made for her, "I would guess some secret of Waldo's is up there. But for tonight I have to get crowned, and we can worry about it after that."

"Well," Deacon Dick Thunder was saying, "it didn't work as a diversion, but it did liberate Overhill. And I'm glad the others are safe." They were seated at council of war inside Calliope's old house in the city, one of the few that had so stalwart a basement floor that no goblins could get into it, and had gone unburned by the invading army. Word had been everywhere in the city and Kingdom of a new Queen of Farthingale's lineage in Overhill, but still Waldo had done nothing but retreat into the castle with his remaining forces.

Everywhere in the city, the great hunt for goblins and undead was on, and the masons worked night and day sealing holes (after the citizens had first poured boiling pitch, or shoved piles of blazing wreckage, down them). No one bothered trying to enumerate how many goblins and undead had been slaughtered anymore.

They had recaptured so many arsenals and stocks of arms, and so much of the army had come back, that Waldo was now completely surrounded in the castle, ringed round with culverts and companies of omnibus and festoon men. No shot had come from the castle in two days

Dick Thunder's men had proved their great value as snipers, and Waldo's forces were dwindling steadily; an hour did not go by without a half dozen shots from around the castle— and every day some shots found a mark, even if it was only a made man. In more exposed parts of the West Battue, corpses of Waldo's men lay exposed for days because there was no time, day or night, when they could be retrieved.

Though there was now an army more than adequate to take the castle, Amatus still delayed the final attack. He hated the thought of losing men. "The time could be more propitious, and so could our plans," he explained to Thunder and Palaestrio that morning. "I don't doubt there will have to be a front assault, or that it can only be directed at the West Battue. I only want something else going on as well, not a diversion but another thing Waldo must fear, for it's clear he can no longer exert enough control over a complicated situation, and fewer good men will die if the Usurper is distracted by another genuine menace that he dare not ignore."

Then Psyche spoke softly. "Majesty, you recall that Cedric was aware of, and escaped through, a secret passage from the library. I believe I know the spell for opening the door from this side—I learned it from Golias long, long ago. No more than a few men might go through, however—the passage is winding, narrow, and dark, and the opening at the library small, so only one man, or at most two or three, could make the trip."

"One man might do much," Amatus said. He rose and tossed a log into the fire, using his left hand; this was partly because it was new enough so that he still consciously enjoyed the sensation of using it, and partly because he was trying to build up its strengths and skills, making it do all the training his right arm had done under the Twisted Man's tutelage. "And this is a tale that cries out for a single combat. If I go with Psyche, into the castle, to slay Waldo by surprise, can you all manage the front assault without me?"

"We would value you as our banner and ensign," Dick Thunder said. "The Army of the North—which, incidentally, has been calling itself the 'King's Own Omnibuses' lately, so if you don't like that you should try to nip it in the bud—likes to feel that they are especially yours. But they are staunch fighters and I think that even if you died in your sleep tonight they would happily take the castle to put Calliope on the throne."

"The Regular Army is in good order," Palaestrio said, "and would be more than happy to be in at the kill. Indeed, Majesty, either army by itself could easily take the castle now. Waldo's power has largely melted away like snow; if I were altogether certain he was an ordinary mortal, I would almost advocate walling him up in there and letting him starve, for he has no power to break our siege. But that is not the sort of thing that happens in these tales, and I believe our King going in for single combat could be an inspiration to all of us. We could allow you a sizable head start, Majesty, and then announce the fact to your forces just as we commenced the full assault."

After that it seemed to Amatus that time blurred and raced faster, until the next morning, when the gray light of just-before-dawn was breaking across the countryside. It had been thought a poor idea to call any attention to the King's whereabouts, let alone to the tunnel, until the last moment, so with only Roderick as guide and guard, Psyche and Amatus approached the hidden door. Roderick himself took a few moments to find it, and he had noted it carefully in his own mind for future use. "Best of luck, Majesty. And you too as well, miss, Gwyn sends her love."

"Love is always the best thing to send," Psyche said, "so I shall keep hers and send her mine. Tell her I think often of the days we both worked in the nursery."

Roderick nodded and bowed slightly, just as if he had received a vital royal command. Then Psyche turned, and pressed her face to the hidden door there in the dark grotto, and whispered something to it. It swung open easily.

Amatus pulled his cloak close about him, for well he could imagine what would happen if a half-man—well, slightly more than half—were spotted in the castle. Aside from the cloak, he had taken the precaution of putting on captured livery of the enemy, for an armed man in the right clothing running through a fortress under attack would be unlikely to be questioned, if it were not too obvious that large parts of his left side were missing.

"I shall follow you to the library door," Amatus said to Psyche. "Will there be a spell to open that as well?"

"I hope not, Majesty, for I don't know one."

"This might be a very brief bit of heroism, Roderick, so I should wait to see how it comes out before you begin drafting it into your plays."

Roderick, who had been listening closely just so as to get it right, flushed deeply, but fortunately it was too dark to see this, and no one would have known if he had not later told Gwyn.

"Well, then," Amatus went on, "assuming we can open the door at the other end, let me be first through. You may return safely down the tunnel if you choose—"

"I am always with you."

"I know," he said gently. "But if you could choose, I wish you would choose safety, for I go into harm's way. If you must come with me, then, stay close behind. I rely on your discretion as to whether or not you draw or fire a weapon, but I'm afraid we must not speak until they catch on to us. I shall go directly to the Throne Room, for by all accounts Waldo will be in there preening, or bellowing orders, depending on whether or not he knows he's being attacked. I shall try to shoot him as soon as I see him, for there is not much sense in being sporting about this with anyone like Waldo, and after all there is honor and glory enough merely in getting back out alive. Once Waldo is dead, I suppose I shall improvise."

Psyche nodded, and said, "I will be with you."

As he followed Psyche through the cool, damp darkness, Amatus had more than time enough to think, but what he thought of was written in a lost part of his *Memoirs*, or told to Cedric in such confidence that it did not even end up in that worthy counselor's diary, or perhaps he never told anyone.

He brushed past Psyche to open the door and stepped into the dark library. There was no one there, but the shouts and distant gunshots from above told him the attack was under way. Drawing escree with one hand, and pismire with another, he kicked the library door open and stepped onto the landing. There was still no one there, so he raced up the stairs, his intent now all on getting to the Throne Room. He silently thanked all of the gods that he had been an active boy and knew every small passage, or at least every one that small boys had been trusted with. In what seemed no time at all, he burst into the Throne Room, to discover no one there.

Waldo, say what else you might of him, had never been a coward, so most likely he had gone to the High Terrace to direct the battle from there. Amatus raced up the stairway.

He passed one slit window, turned the corner to another, and all but collided with a made man carrying a great armful or loaded omnibuses, probably to a sniper. The man stood erect, saluted, and handed Amatus all of the weapons, then marched on down the stairway.

Amatus set the omnibuses down, then glanced through the window. On the roof of the clerihew before him, he could see a dozen real men, directing the fight on the West Battue before them. He snatched up the first omnibus, cocked the chutney, and shot the rearmost real man through the back of the head, a clean shot that made him think of Sir John Slitgizzard, and of the Twisted Man, and that the Duke had died down below, in the very library Amatus had come in through. He snatched up another omnibus, and downed another real man; and another, and another . . .

He had killed half of them before they knew where the shots were coming from, and as they scrambled to escape, one fell from the roof of the clerihew to the pavement below. As he struck, the others staggered—the shock was at last too much—and the made men on the parataxes wavered. At once the tops of ladders began to poke above the West Battue, and a thousand grigs whistled over and found a grip. The Army of the North was coming over.

With a great roar, the lampoon placed against the Main Gate blew an opening. The Regular Army was coming through.

Amatus turned and ran up the stairs with renewed strength, looking for Waldo.

At the top of the stairs, the guard waved Amatus through. The cloak must be hiding enough of his appearance. He dashed down the corridor, past another guard, and found the High Terrace empty. He turned to the made man—could they even talk?—and asked, "Waldo?"

"The nursery," the guard said.

Amatus rushed down the stairs, seeing no one now, for all the ones who could still stand, made men and real men alike, were rushing frantically into the courtyard to fight the armies pouring in. When he reached the nursery door, it was barred, but he could hear someone—a man's voice, but a broken one—sobbing with fear inside. He threw his shoulder against the door, again and again, till he felt a great bruise forming on his shoulder and even his feet ached with scrabbling on the stone floor and trying to get one bit more purchase that might be turned into one bit more force against the door.

The voice inside went on sobbing and cursing; Amatus realized, as he battered the door again and again, that the judgment of everyone that Waldo was no coward had been premature. Before this, no one had ever seen him lose.

Early the morning after coronation—just as Amatus and Psyche were saying good bye to Roderick at the mouth of the secret passage—Calliope was up and bustling about the citadel of Oppidum Optimum. It was not yet light, but since her arrival Calliope had become industrious and disliked remaining in bed for any length of time. The kitchen knew this, and had the hot rolls she liked best waiting for her.

"It was a splendid coronation, Majesty," the cook said, pouring Calliope more chocolate. "Surely the finest *we've* seen, anyway. And all done legal and proper, too."

"Thank you," Calliope said. "I'm glad you enjoyed it. I hope the cleanup won't be too much of a strain."

"When I was coming in, the night crew had just finished. They said there wasn't much, Majesty, garbage and mess is mostly food, you know, and Overhill folk don't waste food by leaving it laying about. And people took their own pots home, and many stayed to help wash dishes."

Calliope was mortified. "If I'd known so many were working, I'd never have gone off to bed!"

"And they all knew that, Majesty, and that's why no one told you. You've got to let people love you, now and then, you know. It's not an easy thing, but there it is."

Calliope smiled. "Then perhaps I could get a spot more chocolate, and another roll? I seem to be bursting with ambition this morning, and I would as soon have the energy to carry some of it out, and not have to stop for lunch until I've something done."

After her breakfast was finished, Calliope made a quick, quiet round of the citadel, finding everything in perfect order. Last of all, she climbed the stairs toward the tower, but at the first landing she was met by a guard.

"Majesty," he gasped, "I've been sent as runner for Lord Cedric and yourself. The noises behind the door are louder than ever, and we are frightened."

"Run and bring Cedric, then; I'll join your comrades." Calliope turned and hurried up the stairs.

The noises were indeed loud, and Calliope was glad that three of Pseudolus's troopers remained on guard; the thumping was a deep, rhythmic double thud, over and over, and the wailing might have been an animal in pain, a woman in pleasure, or both at once, but it was piercing, whatever it was.

Calliope had had the tapestry taken down to be cleaned, for she was sure the stains would never come out, but she had no desire to have the tapestry crusty and smelly; she hoped someday to hang it in a hall she seldom went to, and to think of it never. In the now-exposed wall, the smooth, rounded door met the arched doorway without crevice or crack for even the edge of a knife blade.

She could see the men were afraid, and there ᵣre she must be bold and confident. She advanced to the doo just as if she had been a lifetime professional at ridding citadels of mysterious noises before dawn, nodded at the guards, and placed her hand on the door.

Afterwards, no one agreed on what had happened. Two guards said that Calliope pushed the door open and it gathered her in with itself. Another said she fell through the door. And Calliope herself just said that she touched the door and found herself standing on the other side of it.

It was obvious at once what had happened; she was now the rightful Queen, properly crowned, and thus some of the citadel's magic was working for her. She turned to go back through the door, and found that it would not budge; nor could the guards on the other side do aught about opening it again. Finally, as the thumping and wailing grew louder still, and were joined by occasional strange sucking noises, Cedric arrived. He and Calliope agreed, shouting through the door over the din above, that there was little to do but for her to see what was in the Spirit Spire—whatever it was, it was meant for her alone.

The stairway was icy and the steps were slick and wet; the only light was the beginnings of gray dawn, just now peeking through slit windows on one side. The stairs spiraled up with an alarming inward tilt to a banisterless central well, and all the angles got steeper as she climbed.

It had always been called the Spirit Spire, but so much tradition had been lost under Waldo that no one knew whether it was because it was thought to be haunted, or unusually spiritual, or what. At last, just when Calliope began to fear for her footing, and to imagine sliding down a step into the central shaft and falling all the way to the stone floor far below, she came to the top, opened the door, and found herself on the flat roof of the Spirit Spire.

The thumping was coming from what could only be Waldo's heart, sitting on a pedestal, enclosed in glass.

The wailing and sucking came from a naked woman so old, so wrinkled, and so distorted that at first Calliope thought she must be some giant reptile. She moaned and cried and rubbed her face on the glass; that made the wailing, and every so often she would kiss the glass, sucking it so hard as to produce audible smacking and slurping. Her skin, like the hide of an old hippopotamus, loose and thick and wrinkled, was a sort of gray blue, and her phlegm-gray hair hung like a heavy curtain soaked in grease around her face. Her hands were the worst, for the nails were long, broken, and dirty, and the black dirt made a fine tracery in the wrinkles on her blue-gray skin. Even from where she stood, Calliope could smell the woman—and it was not the foul body odor she might have expected, but like a wet and sentimental copy of roses, as if she had been drenched with some badly done scent to hide a still fouler odor inside.

She could only be that figure that had disappeared from the story a generation before, Waldo's mother.

She turned, saw Calliope, and flew straight at her in a screaming rage. The Queen had had no occasion to arm herself, but she was young and strong and used to fighting by now, and she punched the hag hard in the nose. As she did, she felt the leathery old toothless lips try to engulf her hand, and with a cry of disgust she shoved Waldo's mother backward.

But the foul creature was stronger than she looked, and she reached forward, closing her hands on Calliope's neck, squeezing with great force, her thumbnails crossing on the Queen's windpipe and her fingers meeting in the back, pressing Calliope downward. Even with the force of her thighs, and the floor at her back, Calliope could do no more than force

enough space for a few more breaths. She dug into her opponent's eyes with her fingers, but felt only dry dust, for her eyes
had dried up long ago; Waldo's mother saw nothing, thought
nothing, merely grinned and simpered and moaned for more
to cram into herself.

They tumbled and thrashed. All the things Calliope had
done would have freed her from any wrestler, but the grip on
her throat was still slowly tightening. The floor was slick with
gunge that soaked into her dress to join the icy sweat.

They had thrashed and rolled to the pedestal, and now
Calliope let the grip close on her throat, risked blacking out,
and reached up to pull down the heart itself in its glass case.
The edges of dark were creeping in on her, and in a moment or
two she knew she would be unconscious. She had some idea
of taking the heart as a hostage.

But the glass shattered as she touched it, and suddenly it
was Waldo's living heart she held in her hands. At once the
grip on Calliope's throat relaxed, and she sucked in cold dizzy-
ing air, foul with the odor of false roses. Her hips braced and
she kicked hard against her naked opponent's stomach, not
seeming to hurt her but flipping her over.

Now they were both on their feet, struggling, pulling
Waldo's heart between them as it pulsed and shook. The
Spirit Spire seemed to sway around Calliope, and she dragged
the heart and the hag back toward the edge.

Now Waldo's mother was whispering. "Give me, give me,
give me. Want it, want it, want it. Oooh, sweet, sweet, made it
just for me, all mine, sweet, sweet, want to eat."

Calliope dragged her another step. The Spirit Spire had
not just *seemed* to shake—it was beginning to wobble, and to
slowly precess with a great thumping and rumbling; the
Queen's footing on the gunge-slick pavement became less secure, but still she fought to be nearer the edge, far above the
courtyard. Waldo's mother was now licking at the heart, her
toothless gums not able to tear a piece from it.

A pismire roared somewhere close at hand, and the side of the hag's head exploded like a puffball. Her grip relaxed. With a convulsive heave, Calliope hurled the heart far over the edge, and then, the spire tilting under her, she slipped down the pavement, fingers scrabbling for a grip that was not there.

The hard stones of the courtyard opened beneath her, and she lost the last of her grip and fell.

She had just long enough to think that this was going to become a matter of legend—the Queen for less than a day who fell to her death—and to hope that Waldo's heart might land on something fatal to it.

Then a great, furry back was under her, and she landed on it with a *woof* like a kicked dog. She almost tumbled down the hairy back, but Sir John caught her by the collar, and she grabbed into the fur of the Riddling Beast, hanging on for dear life as the Riddling Beast spiraled up and away from the falling Spirit Spire, which crashed down into the empty courtyard.

Calliope, the Riddling Beast, and Sir John Slitgizzard all saw Waldo's heart impale itself upon the spear of the weathercock by the front gate, and burst like a balloon full of thin tar; a moment later, a piece of the spire knocked the weathercock from its perch and slammed it to the stones, taking the impaled heart with it. A moment after that, the whole Spirit Spire came to pieces and fell into the courtyard and across the wall, burying the nasty punctured and squashed mess that was all that remained of Waldo's heart.

They glanced at each other, and knew that the story must even now be ending. Calliope started to laugh, for it was good to be alive, good to be rid of things like Waldo and his mother—and then she vomited, for she remembered that Waldo's mother had wanted his heart to eat. She ended up apologizing profusely to the Riddling Beast, and washing his fur herself, but that was later.

7

The Love of You

*T*he sobbing suddenly ceased, and then there was a great shouting in the courtyard outside, for (as Amatus learned later) what remained of Waldo's army had fallen dead, as if so little of themselves was left that they perished with him; or perhaps, as one later writer noted, with Waldo's death the pieces of soul all returned to their owners, and the volume of evil done was greater than any one real man could bear. Whatever the cause, there in the bright morning sunlight, the real men fell screaming with expressions of horror, dying in fits. The made men just fell over dead.

But these were things Amatus was to learn later. For right now the young King was getting exhausted and frustrated, and just a bit cross, and he was wondering what sort of end of the story this could be, with Waldo still behind the door and himself standing here in utter futility, shoulder bruised, tired and sore, but having done the little he had done in the battle entirely as a sniper.

Thunder and Palaestrio came up behind him, shouting his name. "I am here," the King said, "and unhurt. Waldo is beyond this door but he's stopped making any sort of noise."

"Get a man with an ax," Palaestrio bellowed, and a great,

burly lumberjack came up the stairs. He stepped to the door, swung his ax twice lightly to get the distance, and then with five neat chops took out the hinges and bolt. The door fell inward.

Waldo lay dead upon the floor, his hand clutching his chest. "His heart," King Amatus said. "Sir John, or someone, must have destroyed his heart."

But he said it only because, unlikely as that was, what was before them was more astonishing. Waldo the Usurper, in exactly the way Amatus had once had no left side, was missing the whole right side of his body. "He always traveled heavily cloaked, and no decent person saw him face to face, or at least not and lived," Deacon Dick Thunder mused. "Now perhaps we know why. I suppose he too must have been given the Wine of the Gods—"

"Majesty!" Palaestrio cried. "Majesty, when did—where did—"

"Quiet!" Amatus snapped. He had just realized Psyche was not there. He shouted her name twice before Palaestrio could restrain himself no longer and cried out, "Majesty, Majesty, forgive me for being the one to tell you, but, sir, you are *whole!*"

Amatus looked down and it was so. He was as any other man, with his left side as complete as his right, beginning on the left and continuing all the way through until it was his right. It was all there, without hole or seam, and when he saw, he wept. Dick Thunder quietly conducted the King to a private chamber and left him alone to compose himself.

They never found Psyche's body; Amatus thought perhaps she had died early, and that was why his appearance had not alarmed any of the guards he encountered. Calliope, when she heard of it much later, found herself wondering if perhaps there might have been some link between Psyche and Waldo, and could never quite shake the thought, which troubled her deeply because she had loved Psyche too.

Much later, in his diary, Cedric speculated that although Psyche was gone and Amatus whole, that did not mean that Psyche had necessarily died. *Perhaps,* he wrote, *what was required was that she be here, and then be gone. We never do learn all the rules of anything important, after all.*

The Festival of Liberation, held on the first day of summer, was the biggest festival in the Kingdom for many centuries afterwards, and if the Kingdom could still be gotten to, and you did, you would find the Festival of Liberation celebrated in the good old way even now.

It was set forever upon the first day of summer, the day when Calliope destroyed Waldo's heart and Amatus's armies retook the castle, and it was always an occasion for oratory, fireworks, parades, pageants, and plays. The first year it was celebrated, it was a special day in any case, for it was the day that Calliope and Amatus were finally wed, and the Kingdom regained its province of Overhill.

The festival was merrier for that, but not so merry as perhaps it might have been, for so much was still being done, and it would be late in the reigns of Amatus the Great and Calliope the Brave before the city was at all what it had been, and before the summer capital at Oppidum Optimum was the fine place it was to become. Wreck and rubble, wrack and ruin, remained to be repaired, rebuilt, or razed, and almost all, from highest to lowest in the Kingdom, were just released from mourning.

Still, the rebuilding went forward swiftly now, even though the ever-dependable Cedric had resigned his posts and was hard at work on getting his *Chronicle* in order, as well as producing edited editions of many chronicles that had been rotting in the Royal Library for decades. Captain Palaestrio and Deacon Dick Thunder—now Count Palaestrio and Baron Thunder—had been put in charge of reconstruction, as General of All the Armies and Prime Minister respectively. Palaestrio was doing splendidly at it, for, as Cedric pointed out, Palaestrio's skills at maintaining an army on next to nothing were the very skills the Kingdom needed in a time when taxes must not be raised. As for Thunder, what better qualification could one have in diplomacy and statecraft than having run a large and celebrated gang of robbers?

Sir John Slitgizzard became Captain of the Guard, which gave Amatus and Calliope a marvelous excuse to have him to dinner as often as they wished, and to use him as baby-sitter and honorary uncle for all their many children. Once a year, in good weather, he would take a month off to ride north and visit with the Riddling Beast, and it was said that many years later he and the Riddling Beast flew off together to some remote valley, for they had become the best of friends. The beast was never lonely between Sir John's visits, for he turned out to be good at every sort of problem, and to enjoy most of them, so many people made the long trek to talk with him. Amatus offered him any number of nicer places than the mountain hold, but the beast wisely demurred, pointing out that where he was, only people who were serious about their questions would come and see him.

On the night of the wedding, and the first Festival of Liberation, the troupials—a hastily organized company dubbed Lord Pseudolus's Men—were to give the first play since Waldo's invasion. They were all in a high state of excitement, or so the word was from backstage, for most had been working as weavers, carpenters, joiners, tailors, and so forth to make ends meet, and were delighted to have professional work again. Roderick was impossibly nervous, for the King and Queen had requested that since the occasion was so joyous, a tragedy be given for the sake of balance, and Roderick had been afraid that he would be accused of spoiling everyone's enjoyment.

He need not have worried, for the production was a great success, and indeed *The Tragical Death of Boniface the Good* was performed every festival for centuries afterward. As the third act ended, Sir John Slitgizzard (on stage) and Duke Wassant (also on stage) were just parting to their separate duties in the collapsing city, and Sir John (again on stage) raised an arm to the departing Duke and shouted, "Farewell, farewell, old friend, die only if you must, live for your Prince!"

The troupials bowed for the act end, and the audience applauded wildly. Sir John, the real one up in the stands, said, "Now, I know I never said anything like that in my life. I've no such gift for words."

Calliope, radiant in her wedding gown, smiled at him and teased, "Are you sure that is not what you meant?"

"I'm not even sure what it means," Sir John confessed. "Anyone who knew poor old Wassant—oh, gods, how I miss him even now—would know that the man loved life, and would only die if he had to, or if honor required. I'd never have given him such silly advice and he'd have laughed at me if I did."

Calliope's hand squeezed Amatus's under the table, and they traded winks, as Amatus said, "Now, surely you don't begrudge Roderick taking something commonplace, which you might actually have said, and helping everyone to appreciate its significance?"

Sir John looked out upon the great swarm of people below, across the city itself, to where the sun was beginning to sink. At least on an outdoor stage this silliness could only go on until the sun was down. "Why, I've never said a significant thing in my life," he said.